Trouble of the Most Wonderful Kind

a novel

By Stephanie Pass

To The Women Who Dare To Dream Again,

This is for those whose hearts ached but whose spirits refused to break. You doubted your strength and whispered fears of being trapped forever in a loveless relationship.

But you took that first terrifying step, leaving behind what no longer served you. You are not defined by the past but by the strength you discovered within yourselves.

One day, you'll look back and see the incredible woman you've become. You are braver than you believe, stronger than you seem, and wiser than you know. And the love you craved? It's patiently waiting.

So embrace the adventures that await, and know this—You are worthy. You are loved. You will find your happily ever after, whatever it may be, sweeter than any you could have ever imagined.

With unwavering belief from one who's lived it,
Stephanie

* * *

TROUBLE OF THE MOST WONDERFUL KIND - PLAYLIST

"With Somebody" Public Library Commute
"i think about you all the time" The Maine
"Think I'm Gonna Make It" Emily James
"Damn I Miss You" Mokita, Nightly
"What if I Love You?" Gatlin
"Somebody Else" The 1975
"North" Fly By Midnight
"No Choice" Fly By Midnight
"I Think I Like You" The Band Camino
"Lovely Enough" Emily James
"Nervous" joan
"Youuu" Coin
"The movies" Nightly
"Like I do" Nightly
"About You" The 1975
"Avalanche" WALK THE MOON
"Saw You In a Dream" The Japanese House
"See You Later" The Band Camino
"Dangerous Hands" Austin Giorgio"
"Happy for Me" Emily James
"The feeling" Nightly"
"Past Tense" Emily James
"how to exit a room" The Maine
"Is It Over Now?" Taylor Swift
"Everyone Knows" Cafune
"radiohead" Nightly
"Someone Who's Trying" The Band Camino
"Meet Me at Our Spot" Willow, The Anxiety

"Funeral Home" Landon Conrath, Ber
"Say We'll Make It" Vacation Manor
"Bloom" Aiden Bissett

BOOKS BY STEPHANIE PASS

0.5 THE ALCHEMY OF US
Available Now

1 TROUBLE OF THE MOST
WONDERFUL KIND
Available Now

2 SOMETIME AROUND MIDNIGHT
June 2025

3 THE BEACH HOUSE
September 2025

Prologue - Edison

Seven years ago

"Hi! I'm so sorry!" she said as she skidded to his table, cheeks flushed.

Without waiting for him to reply, she slid into the opposite side of the booth with a bashful smile. A whiff of sunshine and something sweet drifted towards him. He pressed his lips together to stop a smile as she tried and mostly failed to contain her windswept curls with a headband.

"Sorry, I'm late. I am so glad you're still here."

He wasn't sure how to respond. He was about to order when this redhead sat down and started talking to him like she knew him. He certainly didn't know her, and he was positive he would remember a woman like the one currently sitting in front of him right now. That smile and those dark blue eyes, she seemed like someone you wouldn't forget, couldn't forget.

She was beautiful in that girl-next-door way. His attention returned to her hair, those vibrant ginger curls that seemed to defy gravity, going every which way. He needed to reach out and tuck an unruly one behind her ear.

He raised his eyebrows and gave a tiny head shake. "No worries." He wasn't sure what else to say. With a friendly smile and a quick glance at the menu, he added, "I was just about to order."

Was she meeting someone? Did she realize she had the wrong person? Should he ask? He wasn't going to ask. He didn't want to ask.

"Perfect! I'll have whatever you're having," she said, giving him a small smile and shrugging. From the moment she sat down, he had an undeniable need to get to know her. Who was she?

The waitress came over, and he kept glancing over the menu at this intriguing woman while ordering. Her freckled cheeks were still flushed, and she had this cute little wrinkle between her eyebrows as she searched the depths of her canvas bag. He couldn't help the corner of his mouth tugging up when he spied a dog-eared paperback of forbidden love peeking out. Her breath hitched when she pushed it back in.

He took a chance and asked, "Everything okay?"

Her gaze lifted to meet his in a sudden collision, and he felt a current whip through him, something he hadn't felt in a long time. It sent a flutter through his entire body and stirred something deep within him he couldn't quite identify.

She gave a little sigh and nodded, "Just feeling a little crazy. I forgot all about this. My head's been in the clouds with graduation coming. I was studying for my finals, and when I got the text from Rebecca asking how our date was going, I felt terrible for missing it. I ran as quickly as I could to get here." She held her hand next to her mouth and whispered, "Truth be told, it was probably more of a fast walk. I think only zombies could force me to run." One corner of her mouth pulled up, her eyes full of delight. "Or chocolate cake." Then, she chuckled. "Thank god I live just down the street. I hope you're not mad at me. I feel terrible."

A smile tugged at his lips. "It's really okay. Why would I be mad at you?" Even if he didn't know who she was or what she was talking about, whatever was happening between them was a breath of fresh air. She seemed so sweet and sincere, unlike any of the women he'd met on those ridiculous dating apps.

"I don't know many people who would wait around more than a few minutes and definitely not over an hour for their blind date to show up!" She shook her head while chuckling. "I don't think I would have," she said with a sheepish smile, emphasizing it by raising her eyebrows.

Clarity hit him like a wave as his smile faltered just briefly. He leaned back in the booth, his stomach doing a back flip.

She looked him over and narrowed her eyes. "Though Rebecca did say you had a beard, she said you would never shave it off."

A slow smile spread across his face as his eyes crinkled with delight. While the waitress set their order on the table—two mochas and two slices of blackout chocolate cake—he decided to play along. He gave a little chuckle and watched her while drinking his coffee. He debated telling her the truth, but he couldn't do it. She was so captivating, and he was already enjoying this. Her. Way too much. Somehow, his thoughts went right to how they would have a fantastic story to tell their children one day.

He shrugged as a flirty smile bloomed across his face, revealing his dimples. Internally, he winced at his bluff as he said, "Well, you know Rebecca. She told me that thing had to come off, or you'd never date me."

She arched an eyebrow, staring at him before bursting into contagious laughter. She tried and failed to hide it with a hand over her mouth, and he couldn't help when his own chuckle erupted.

Through her laughs, she nodded and said, "That sounds like Rebecca!"

She cleared her throat, held her hand over the table, and said, "I'm Claire with an I. Your blind date for this afternoon."

He took her hand and gently squeezed it. Without realizing it, his thumb caressed her knuckles. His need to touch her surprised him.

"Hello, 'Claire, with an I.' I'm Sonny, and I have a feeling I need to thank Rebecca for setting me up with you." Her cheeks turned red again.

As he released her hand, he could see her fingers tremble slightly from the same unexpected spark he'd just felt. She managed a subtle nod while picking up her coffee, but he saw the look of shock just briefly before she took another sip. Had they unwittingly walked into an Austen novel?

Sonny couldn't take his eyes off her. He desperately wanted to know her, to touch her again, even if it was just her hand. He wanted to lose himself in the sweet, unmistakable scent of her—it was completely intoxicating. He had a feeling, an inkling of awareness, that he was headed for some delightful trouble — trouble of the most wonderful kind, and he could not wait.

Two days later, having spent every moment together since they met Friday afternoon, they were saying goodbye in Sonny's truck. Her scent was all over him, and he savored it. But it was so much more than that. This weekend, it had been more than just a physical connection. It was as if she was his missing piece as if they seamlessly complemented each other right from the start—a lock and key fitting together so perfectly that it left Sonny in awe. The pull between them was more than magnetic. It was gravitational, an orbit made by the cosmos just for them.

Sonny gripped her hips, hauling her towards him across the bench seat of his truck. Their lips came together in a languid kiss, but she pulled him deeper into it. She wrapped herself around him, little moans escaping her.

"Claire," he murmured, his breath hot against her skin.

His fingers went to her hair. His desire to claim her, to lose himself in this moment, battled with his need to keep control. He didn't know what this was or how it happened, but he wanted it and clung to it like she was his drug. He wanted so much more—of this, of her.

Sonny pulled back as she slowly opened her glazed eyes, searching his face. He gave her a lazy half-smile as he adjusted himself and stepped out, reaching the other side to open Claire's door.

He held out his hand, and she took it, never dropping his gaze. He pulled her in close again when she stepped down from the truck. His hand went up to the red flower she still had in her hair from their picnic at the wildflower farm, pushing it against her ear. He wrapped his arms around her waist and gave her one more kiss.

When he pulled back, he held her gaze, his eyes almost pleading, before forcing himself to say, "Goodbye, Poppy," his voice raspy with unspoken desires.

Her breath hitched as she stepped back, her hand staying in Sonny's until she slowly let go, turning towards the building. He was rooted in place, watching her walk away. When she grinned at him over her shoulder, waving one last time, he couldn't help cracking a half smile in return, a dimple forming on his cheek. She stopped one last time at the door to her building, looking back, and he fought the urge to run after her, to feel the warmth of her hand in his again, to steal just one more kiss.

Sonny had never believed in love at first sight. But something happened between them this weekend. Was it love? He didn't know. Somehow, these three days had felt like forever, a lifetime with her.

He was counting the hours — minutes and seconds — until they could see each other again later this week. It couldn't come fast enough.

Chapter 1 - Claire

Present Day

I stepped out of the backseat of the rideshare, gave my curls a fluff, and tucked the wildest ones behind my ears. Why did my hair always look like I stuck my finger in a light socket?

Taking a shaky breath, I reached down and smoothed my skirt before looking up at the looming courthouse. This was the end of the seven-year ordeal known as "Pete." That idiot hadn't even hired an attorney, nor did he plan to show up today, a fitting conclusion to the loneliest time of my life. Today was the day I was finally taking back my freedom.

I turned to give the driver a quick wave, but he was already rolling up the windows and about to drive off. I looked through my bag to ensure I had everything, and that was when I realized my mistake. I had left my favorite book, _The Time Traveler's Wife_, in the back of the car.

Waving my arms, I yelled, "Hey! Wait!"

I tried to get his attention, running in my heels a short way, but I gave up as he turned the corner. Fuck.

Something fluttered in my peripheral vision across the street. Turning my head, I saw a woman who looked strangely familiar. Her hair cascaded down her back in waves of black so dark it almost looked blue. Her alabaster skin contrasted sharply with her crimson lips, and for a moment, I couldn't help but watch her and wonder if vampires were real. Her taffeta dress was adorned with lace overlays and puffy long sleeves. The neckline went clear up to her throat, and she had black lace-up boots I wished were mine. She looked out of place, maybe even out of time.

Was she watching me? I couldn't be sure, but she followed my rideshare with her eyes as it drove away before she turned towards me, smirking, a hint of amusement on her face, as she waved her fingers. I stumbled back, immediately feeling a sense of unease, before going up to the courthouse. Who was she? Was she just being friendly?

Frustration bubbled in my chest more about my book than that strange woman. How in the hell did I leave it in the car? The only reason I took that stupid rideshare in the first place was because everyone told me how confusing the parking was here. But I ended up trading my favorite book for a few minutes of convenience.

I thought back to the ride, trying to figure out how it happened. My bag had been upright the entire time. How did it slip out? I let out a frustrated growl, startling a woman drinking coffee nearby. She scowled at me, and my cheeks heated as I offered a friendly smile.

This was going to drive me mad. I left a lot of books around town, but this one I hadn't wanted to give up. Books had always been my happy place, even as a child. The need to read was like the need to breathe. It's why I became a librarian, even when my parents tried to convince me it was a dying profession.

I felt ridiculous admitting this, but that book had been my lifeline for the past few months. It gave me hope that somewhere and somehow, you could find your person, even separated by time.

I had been lonely in my marriage, but living alone felt ten times lonelier. The things that hit me were always surprising, reminding me of the loss of my marriage — couples grocery shopping together, families together at the park. It was hard, but I learned to keep myself busy. Otherwise, I'd spend my days in bed crying my eyes out. I took all kinds of classes, wandered through all sorts of stores, and my absolute favorite thing was to find dusty secondhand bookstores.

Months ago, while walking around the downtown square, a flyer perched on a light pole caught my attention. It advertised a bookstore just beyond the city in the quaint little town of Ponder. I snapped a photo of it and put the address in my phone when I got to the car.

Twenty minutes later, I was met with a sight I hadn't anticipated. There it was, just a couple miles on the outskirts of the town on the main road to Ponder. A majestic two-story Victorian home painted in a vibrant shade of pink with black spires that stretched towards the sky like some gothic Barbie dreamhouse. Beside it was a mammoth weeping willow tree, its branches gently caressing the ground. The gardens around the property were a sight to behold, blooming with every color of flower imaginable. There was even a koi pond along the pathway from the driveway to the front porch.

The whole thing felt surreal, out of a storybook. I half expected a unicorn or a satyr to wander by. Yet, the most peculiar sight awaited me as I drove into the small parking lot. Guarding the gated entrance of this strange pink house were two towering statues made from stacks of concrete books.

When I approached the front door, I wasn't sure if I should knock or walk in, but then I saw a weathered sign swinging in the breeze, proudly proclaiming the name: The Enchanted Attic. As I pushed open the creaky wooden door, the scent of old paper and ink enveloped me, so familiar and comforting. The shelves were lined with volumes of every size and genre, and each and every single book was wrapped in a plastic sleeve, as if someone lovingly cared for them all. I had stumbled upon a hidden gem and fell in love with it.

Every time I visited, a small bald man with dark brown skin and a kind smile sat in an overstuffed recliner at the check-out. He never spoke much, but he always had a different book in his hands. I never saw any other employees, nor did I ever see any other customers. Was this my very own magical bookstore?

The last time I was there, the man saw me walk in, immediately smiled, and said in a deep tone, "I have something for you."

I gave him a confused smile. "Me? Are you sure?"

He narrowed his eyes as he tilted his head, beckoning me to follow him before he abruptly turned and began to walk toward the back. We entered a dark room, and the lights came on with the snap of his fingers as if by magic. The room was covered, ceiling to floor, with boxes full of books. In the center of the room was a large wooden table that was hideously ornate and seemed ominous with the pentagram design inlaid on the top and legs carved as serpents.

He stared at the boxes and said, "Hang on a

moment," as he moved them around until he found the one he was looking for and brought it over to the table with a grunt. I was still standing by the door when he looked up and inclined his head for me to come to the table. I followed and stood opposite him.

He gave me a quick nod, "This is for you."

I looked at the box and then at him completely confused. "This isn't... I didn't order any-"

He interrupted, "It's yours. She wanted you to have these." The man puffed out his chest, pulling his shoulders back and putting his hands on his hips. He gave me a look like this was his final answer.

"She? But, who? Who wanted me to have these?" My eyes darted around the room before looking back at him. He turned his piercing gaze to me, and that's when I noticed his eyes were the lightest blue I'd ever seen, almost clear.

"You should go." He pushed the box towards me.

I put my hands up to stop the box from falling off the table. I stared back at him for a beat before shrugging and opening the flaps of the box, quickly skimming the spines of the books. It looked like they were paperback... romance novels?

"How much are they?"

He pulled his head back, as if I insulted him. "No cost! They're yours for the giving. Just take the books and go. But hurry!" He skirted around the table, heading towards the door not looking back. What was happening?

Something was telling me to be cautious, but the whisper "free box of books" sent a little thrill down my spine, like I was being about to go on an adventure. I let out a groan as I heaved the heavy box in my arms and walked to the front. He was back in the recliner, a novel in his hands, as if none of it had just happened.

I lifted the box up as I stood by the front door and said, "Thank you!" before I walked out. He smiled and winked before immediately going back to his book.

At home I set the heavy box on my coffee table and immediately dug in. I pulled out each book, setting them in two stacks next to the box. After removing the last book, I noticed a folded yellowed book page as if it had been ripped from one of them. There was something handwritten but faint that I couldn't quite make out, maybe a poem.

"Oh no." I whispered, setting it aside, worried it had fallen out of one of the books.

I carefully flipped through each book, looking for a torn edge that matched the page I found, but none of the books were missing pages. I went back to the page, realizing it was much older than any of these books.

I took the paper over to the lamp on the end table. With a delicate touch, I unfolded it, praying it wouldn't crumble to dust in my hands. Surprisingly, it was not as fragile as it initially looked, as if it had been infused with a newfound vitality. The once barely there ink had darkened, and the words now stood out with clarity as if they glowed. A breath caught in my throat as I began to reveal its secret.

I picked up the pen and notepad I kept on the end table and copied down what appeared to be a riddle:

> In these pages, tales unfold,
> Of lovers brave and hearts so bold.
>
> Seek a soulmate or twin flame,

For love can hide in their name.
With gentle strokes, trust is made,
Like ink on paper, feelings cascade.

Turn the pages, with a curious mind,
Let the story help you find,
The bond that binds, with a spark of mystique,
True love comes for those who seek.

"What in the world...?" I whispered, feeling something tingle in my chest as I opened one of the books and gingerly set the folded page inside. I bit the corner of my lip, wondering what I'd gotten myself into.

"I can't believe I'm even entertaining this as anything but complete nonsense, but... What is this?" I shook my head.

I tried to ignore the little voice in my head that desperately wanted to believe this was real, telling myself to stop. Just stop. This was ridiculous.

I chose one of the books, dumping the rest back inside, but my eyes continued to flick back to the words I had copied. Who in their right mind would believe a book could help them find true love? It was preposterous. Surely, this was some kind of joke. Carrying the box to my bedroom closet, I chuckled to myself.

But it didn't take long before odd things began to happen with the books, things I couldn't explain. The very next weekend I went back full of questions, but the pink house was completely empty. Just as suddenly as I had found it, it was gone. I tried to find more information about the store and the owner, but there was nothing. Eventually, I gave up, but even now I'd find myself driving by the big pink house, still empty, wondering what happened.

I came back to reality when I realized a woman behind me was speaking to me.

"Miss? Are you going inside?"

Confusion laced my eyes as I took in my surroundings, returning to reality and realizing I had been blocking one of the main doors to the courthouse.

"Oh... sorry."

I hurriedly opened the door for the woman, following in behind her, looking for my attorney.

After several long minutes of searching, I felt a sense of relief when I found her sitting on a bench outside the doors. She gave me a little wave, and I sat down beside her as the minutes stretched on while we waited. When the courtroom doors opened inviting us all in, I felt a sudden sense of uneasiness. I stopped abruptly before going through the door as a shiver ran down my body.

My attorney looked back at me. "You okay?"

I tried to tell myself it was just nerves, but cold dread coiled in my belly, a premonition poking at me with its claws. Somehow I just knew I hadn't just lost a book but something had been unleashed. That torn page with the riddle came to mind. Was this the start of it? Some delightful surprise? It felt more like a harbinger of chaos. Something was coming to completely upend my life.

My face stretched into a smile, a mask coming down in place, as I followed after her. I choked out, "Just forgot... something."

Her smile was kind and reassuring as she patted my shoulder. The warmth of her touch was like a lone ray of sunshine peeking through a churning storm. "It'll be over before you know it."

Single. Three simple questions and the scratch of the judge's pen were all it took. Anti-climatic? Yes.

And no. This divorce had been a battle I had fought alone on tear-stained pillowcases as I learned to live on my own. But now I could officially say it. I was a single woman. I could do what I wanted. I could be who I wanted to be.

On the way home, I couldn't decide whether to call my best friend, Darci, to paint the town red or stay in for a quiet night with a book. When Darci didn't pick up, my choice had been made.

My fingers flew across the phone screen, ordering enough pasta, bread, and dessert for a small nation. Cheesecake and cannoli for two? Why not? I deserved the whole damn restaurant.

I was certain a bottle of champagne was hiding in the depths of my fridge, perfect for my party of one. I went to the fridge to hunt it down, and when my fingers brushed the frosty contours of the bottle, I grabbed it, holding it up in silent victory before heading to my bedroom.

Sitting in the middle of my walk-in closet, I popped the champagne cork, not caring I was spilling a bit on the carpet. I pulled off my heels and took a swig straight from the bottle, relaxing against some boxes still not unpacked after months here, and I stretched my legs out.

I let out a heavy sigh, "What am I going to do with myself now?"

As if on cue the box of books shifted and nearly fell over. I awkwardly crawled over to it with the champagne bottle still in hand. I needed a new book after losing my favorite one today. I was craving something spicy, something I could read tucked in deep in my bed. This was my deep dark secret. As a librarian, my taste in books should be a little more high-brow. But I could lay in bed and read romance novels all day long. All those perfectly imperfect book boyfriends got me through some of the most terrible years of my marriage.

My fingers tiptoed along each of the cracked spines. Every one held a potential world I could get lost in. I dug out a book near the bottom of the box. It called to me like a siren. Just as I pulled it out of the box, I jolted from a knock at the door, and my stomach rumbled. Slipping the book under one arm, I carried the champagne bottle like a club, hoping my food had arrived.

A little while later I sank into my favorite chair at my tiny kitchen table with my book and a plate piled high with cheesy garlic bread and doma bianca tortellini. I peeked at the container with the cannoli, debating on whether this was a time to eat dessert first. There was a knock at the door.

"Claire? It's me! Open up!"

I opened the door with a big smile.

Darci's eyebrows were nearly at her hairline when she asked, "It's official? You've joined the single ladies club?"

"Yep!" I smiled, hugging her back as we danced through the living room. Darci had a way of bringing out the silliness in me. It was one of the things I loved about her. I nodded my head towards the kitchen. "Now get in here and eat some of this food with me."

She giggled. "That sounds wonderful because I'm starving!"

A few minutes later, we were both sitting down on the couch with plates of food piled high. I tossed my book on the coffee table and pulled my hair back into a poofy ponytail while Darci grabbed the remote and pulled up a true crime documentary. "So...I found this new true crime documentary that's supposed to be really dark and twisted. You up for it?"

"Aren't they always dark and twisted?" I asked, amusement dancing in my eyes.

"Well, yeah, but this one is like..." She started speaking in a monotone. "her arms were cut off, her legs were cut off, her head was missing..."

"Sounds like our kind of show." I chuckled before picking up the cannoli and taking a big bite.

"Perfect! Let's get this Crimebrarians party started!"

I took a swig straight from the champagne bottle and nearly choked on it. "What the hell is a Crimebrarian?"

"True Crime? Librarians? We're the Crimebrarians?" She shrugged, wiggling her eyebrows.

I rolled my eyes. "You know you're ridiculous, right?"

"Yeah, but you still love me." She smirked shoving half a slice of garlic bread in her mouth as she pressed the button on the remote.

When I started working at the library, Darci and I became fast friends and bonded almost immediately over true crime documentaries. After working together for months at the library, we bumped into each other at the mailbox at our apartment complex one afternoon, not realizing we lived in the same place. Pretty soon, we were having weekly "murder nights," ordering takeout, and watching true crime while she whipped up fancy cocktails. I don't know what I would have done without her during some of those lonely nights living on my own.

After I sent Darci home with some leftovers, I stumbled to the bathroom still in a champagne buzz. But even though sleep promised oblivion, I couldn't ignore the call of the book I chose earlier.

The books from that box were... special. They weren't just ordinary paperbacks, they were puzzles wrapped in worn-out spines. And it seemed like the heart of each one lived in its margins. Scribbled notes covered nearly all the blank spaces of all of them.

I picked it off my nightstand, cradling it close, feeling the familiar thrill of anticipation coursing through me. Those notes weren't just annotations — they were something else entirely. I wasn't quite sure what, but they seemed like fortunes or prophecies, maybe even whispers of love and loss. Tonight, as I sank down into the bed, lost in the pages, I was an explorer, chasing the secrets hidden between the lines of text until I couldn't keep my eyes open anymore.

Chapter 2 - Edison

"Can anyone escape their fate?" Edison asked his fantasy lit class. This was the question at the center of _The Night Circus_.

This was one of his favorite lectures because it always turned into a lively debate about free will versus determinism. Tonight, his students were so worked up that he let it take over the entire 90-minute class. While walking to his truck after classes, Edison grinned, hearing some of his students continuing the debate as they walked to their cars in the darkened parking lot.

It had been a few semesters since he'd taught a night class, and he both loved and hated them. Getting home after ten o'clock on these nights made the days suck, and his coffee intake was at an alarming level, but it was worth it. These courses were often filled with the bleary-eyed mothers juggling children and careers and the work-worn hands of people trying to find a better life. He saw their thirst for knowledge and dedication that he often didn't see in typical college kids.

Never in a million years did he think he'd be doing this—teaching. He had moved up here after grad school without much of a plan. But to his surprise, he found himself enjoying his job. It was only part-time, but that was a luxury he could afford with the secret he kept closely hidden.

What paid the bills and what no one knew because of his tight-lipped non-disclosure agreement was that he was the primary ghostwriter for Brendan Cross, the huge best-selling author for a couple dozen spy thrillers. He had never even gotten the chance to tell his parents before he lost them a fews back. Truthfully, he longed to tell someone, anyone, this big secret, especially when some of those novels were now movies.

"Professor!" Edison heard someone calling him across the parking lot. "Professor Wright! Wait up!" He looked up and immediately realized who it was: Holly, a student from his last class tonight. She waved at him enthusiastically, a broad smile lighting up her face as she hurried towards him in the parking lot.

Edison hesitated for a moment, aware of Holly's likely intentions. He feigned interest in his phone, but he noticed four other students from class watching them closely across the parking lot. He couldn't ignore her, so he offered a polite smile and waved.

As she approached, he asked, "Yes, Holly? What can I do for you?"

Her voice brimmed with excitement. "A group of us are going to Alchemy for coffee to keep the conversation going from tonight's class. We'd love it if you joined us." She wore a flirtatious smile and ran her hand up and down his arm when she reached him. He stiffened. She seemed to always find a way to touch him, even in class.

Edison paused, "I appreciate the invite, but I don't

think I'll be able to make it." He really would have enjoyed diving deeper into tonight's topic, but there were lines he wasn't willing to cross with students.

A look of disappointment washed over Holly's face as she nodded. "Oh... well, perhaps another time?"

He offered her a curt smile and said, "Probably not." She gave him a pout before turning back to the students waiting for her.

When he reached his old red truck, he got in and let out a pent-up breath, looking over his shoulder to see where Holly went before starting it up. He mentally worked through a checklist in his head realizing he needed to stop by the grocery store on the way home to pick up food for Bandit, his rescue Boxer dog.

Driving out of the parking lot, he thought about the kind of woman he wanted to date, remembering that unexpected blind date from years ago. She had infiltrated his dreams for years now. He fantasized way too much about running into her again. His heart raced when he thought about what he would do if he could get a second chance with her.

Glancing in the mirror, he saw himself as an average-looking guy, but he couldn't deny the attention he received. Often people chuckled and told him he looked like a Viking, and sure he had Nordic ancestry, but really? He was never sure how to respond.

At 6'1, Edison possessed a sturdy physique with broad shoulders and a narrow waist due to his athletic days in high school and college. His dark blond hair was closely cropped on the sides and slightly tousled on top, and the trimmed beard he sported for the past couple of years was a point of pride for him.

At 35 years old, the chiseled abs of his youth had slightly softened. He didn't mind indulging and enjoying life's pleasures, even if it made him softer. He hadn't had any complaints from the women he'd had casual encounters with over the years, and he still maintained an active lifestyle running daily with Bandit.

Edison was an introvert who liked to keep to himself, but something drew people to him. It didn't matter if it was the grocery store, school, or anywhere. He assumed he just had one of those friendly faces, but people often approached him when they got a good look at his eyes. He had heterochromia, a harmless condition where his eye color was three colors bleeding into one another, a mix of golden whiskey, emerald green and rimmed in a storm of blue. Both he and his sister had inherited their mother's eyes, and he didn't understand the allure. But it was always the first thing people mentioned to him.

Women, especially, were easily drawn to him, but Edison had never been a player. Ever since he had that chance encounter with that bubbly redhead with her unforgettable smile and those dark blue eyes, he struggled to find a lasting connection with anyone else. He chuckled to himself, remembering Claire. Somehow, she mistook him for her blind date, and he went along for the ride, never confessing he wasn't the guy. He never did things like that, but in that moment, he couldn't help himself. He had been instantly smitten.

Nearly from the get go, she had left an imprint on his heart. When she sat down in his booth, her smile hooked him immediately. There was something about her, and he was entranced from the moment their eyes met.

They spent an entire weekend together with

plans for more, but she canceled on him a few days later without explanation. She stopped responding to his calls and messages, leaving him confused and heartbroken. He had fallen fast and hard, and then she vanished. He thought they had both been falling, but in hindsight, he wondered if it had all been one-sided on his part.

The last morning they were together, it was a cool spring day, and he decided to take her to Fireflower Farms for a picnic on a whim. It was a wildflower sanctuary known for its breathtaking fields of vibrant blossoms, and she had never been.

He'd called up a friend at a local deli, and she gave him a bag packed with an amazing charcuterie board. He and Claire wandered through the colorful meadows, where the sweet scent of wildflowers permeated the air. Edison's heart raced as he led Claire to a shaded, secluded spot under the canopy of a huge live oak tree.

Despite being surrounded by such beauty, Edison only had eyes for her. Her smile lit him up from the inside. He remembered the way the breeze played with her curls and the way she looked at him. That secret smile she had, like it was only for him, sent a shiver through him, blooming up to his chest. He sucked in a sharp breath, like the world had suddenly stolen his air, all because her eyes lingered on his just a beat too long.

He plucked a crimson poppy in the surrounding meadow near their blanket. It was a perfect match for Claire's hair. Gently, he tucked the flower behind her ear, the colors blending seamlessly. She blushed, her eyes sparkling with affection.

"Poppy," Edison whispered softly before leaning in to kiss her gently along her jaw. He realized he had found the perfect nickname for this enchanting woman and was overwhelmed with emotion. He wanted so much more with her.

Occasionally, he'd go down another rabbit hole in search of her, but it was always a dead end. He'd get angry with himself for, once again, chasing the memory of a woman he'd most likely never see again. His mind swirled with questions. What happened? Where did she go? And most of all, why?

One night he'd hit one of his lowest points, consumed by heartache. He had tried to drink himself into oblivion, but instead he drunkenly stumbled out of a bar into the tattoo parlor next door, seeking something, a symbol that would forever be etched on his skin, to match what was branded on his soul. In that desperate moment fueled by liquid courage, he finally made the fateful decision he had been considering for years. He chose a poppy flower to be permanently inked on the inside of his left upper arm, those scarlet petals serving as a secret tribute. Through the years, on many quiet nights, he would find himself tracing his fingers over the intricate lines, finding comfort in the reminder of her as he drifted off to sleep.

Edison had been on plenty of dates, searching for someone who could measure up to Claire's memory. But repeatedly, he found himself disappointed, wishing to hear her laugh and see her smile again. No matter how beautiful or intriguing the woman he met, he never found that spark of magic he had felt with her.

Pulling into the parking lot, he felt a strange tingle along his tattoo. He scratched it absentmindedly, wondering if he'd been living in the shadow of that fateful weekend for too long. Edison was tired of longing for someone he might never find again. He wanted to move on. He wanted to finally stop living in the past.

Chapter 3 - Claire

When I was a little girl, I always wrote or doodled in my books, even my school books. I couldn't help the laugh that escaped as I thought about how much trouble I got into. Every year, my mom would make me use my allowance to pay the fines.

But I couldn't help it. Something told me to do it, something I didn't know how to explain back then. It was as if a whisper in the back of my mind told me to write in my books. Sometimes, I could ignore it, but other times, I just couldn't help myself. As I got older, that whisper changed. It wasn't just telling me to doodle; it talked back to the characters and sometimes even the author.

Since I got that box of books that whisper grew louder and harder to ignore, I found myself writing things I couldn't begin to explain, almost like clues or pieces of a puzzle. Other times, I'd find notes in my handwriting that I didn't even remember writing. But something even stranger started happening with the books.

Every time I finished one of them, I felt this gnawing deep in my belly, an intense desire to leave it somewhere very specific—a restaurant, a park bench, or somewhere else. It was like I was compelled to go to these places. The longer I waited, that gnawing feeling would spread until I was a ball of anxiety.

I never told anyone about this little "gift" of mine. It was a secret of my very own. I loved it because it wasn't just leaving a book, it was as if I was part of grand scheme for someone else—a chance encounter waiting to bloom, a secret pact with fate. Who knew what would happen? But after finding that riddle, I indulged in what ifs. The whole idea of it was so far fetched, but what if? What if I was helping someone find their true love? You never know, right? And that made me feel like I was some mischievous book fairy sprinkling pixie dust out in the world.

The first time it happened, I dreamed about a church I'd never been to. Then, I overheard someone talking about that same church at work. I kept seeing signs for it everywhere—mentions on social media, a flyer pinned to the bulletin board at work —always the same church. I realized something was telling me I needed to go to that church to leave the book. The need to go there was overwhelming.

I showed up Sunday morning for the service feeling nervous. When I walked in as the sunbeams slanted through the huge stained glass window above the doors, it felt like a spotlight was on me. There was a hushed quiet of whispers, and the floor creaked as I made my way to a pew. Sitting on the velvety blue cushion, instinct said I shouldn't be there. I wanted to leave as soon as possible. When I took the book out of my purse, I swore it felt lighter like it might fly out of my hands at any moment. I placed it behind me in the pew, partially hidden between the edges of the cushions.

Walking up the aisle to leave, I zeroed in on a dark figure that didn't belong. The seance dress was the first clue—black lace and velvet up to her neck amongst a sea of pastel colors. Her eyes went straight through my soul, and my breath hitched as fear twisted in my belly. Before I could get nearer, she was gone in a flash. Who was that woman, and what did she want... with me?

Just as I was about to exit the church, a young woman ran up to me, the book in her hands. She shouted, "Miss! Miss!"

I turned around and stopped halfway up the aisle. She smiled and tried handing me the book. "I'm so glad I caught you. You forgot this."

I hesitated a moment, feeling the flutter of guilt roll through my belly. I shook my head and gave her a friendly smile. "Oh no, that's not mine."

She looked puzzled and then looked past me for someone else. She muttered, "Oh, I could have sworn..."

I shrugged. "No, not me."

I watched her look around again before she turned away, opening the book and flipping the pages. She must have seen something she liked because a smile bloomed across her face before she closed the book, hugging it against her chest. I felt a ripple of hope that maybe she would find her true love with that book.

Just like that, I left books around the city. When I finished a book, my dreams would turn to a particular place, sometimes places I knew, sometimes not. People around me would talk about the place I had dreamed. It would happen at work, a coffee shop, standing in line at a movies. That strange, anxious desire would well up, and I'd know it was time to leave the book. But there were times it wasn't always like that.

A couple of times I accidentally left behind a book before I had finished reading it, forgotten on a table in a cafe, dropped somewhere on a rainy sidewalk. When I'd lose a book, I'd have dreams about where I lost the book, and something would reassure me. But when I lost _The Time Traveler's Wife_, my dreams weren't about where I lost it. They were different this time because they were about that guy, Sonny, I'd met on that blind date years ago. It made no sense.

Why was it different this time? Maybe because I was still reeling from leaving it behind. Maybe because it was my favorite. Whenever I thought about it, I'd feel something I could only describe as a premonition, like something big was about to happen. Good or bad, I had a feeling I'd soon find out.

Why was that book so special time? I'd read it at least half a dozen times. Each time, I'd leave more comments and doodles. I'd even been using the few blank spaces in it as a journal, writing little messages to myself in the margins and on the blank pages, phone messages, funny quotes, and even a grocery list or two. It had turned into a little history book of me this last year being on my own.

Thinking over my life, longing tugged at my heart. My marriage had never been like Clare and Henry's in the book. I'm not sure I was ever in love with my ex-husband. I chose Pete for security. But, like the book, I quickly learned what it felt like to be lonely and long for someone who was never there, even though he was there, right there in the next room. But it was like looking through a window when it came to Pete. He never let me in.

Yet, that wasn't our only problem. We were at different stages in our lives. When we married, I was just 21, just graduated from college, ready to start my life, and he was settling into the comfort of middle age in his mid thirties.

I should have seen the light when he was too tired to consummate our marriage on our wedding night. We didn't make love once during our honeymoon. Sure, we had laughter and what I thought was love, but he was always too tired for intimacy, too tired for me, like I was just too much.

But things changed just a year into our marriage. One summer day, Pete came in from mowing the yard, pale in a cold sweat. He laid down in a recliner, his strong body too weak to move. Within hours, his head pounded with unimaginable pain when he'd never had a migraine in his life. I rushed him to the emergency room, but the doctors couldn't figure out what was wrong. Nothing showed up on the tests.

Days turned into weeks and then months. He couldn't get out of bed, much less work. He was wasting away before my eyes. I would often find a quiet place to hide and cry my eyes out in fear of becoming a young widow. Months into his mystery illness, his doctor gave him heavy doses of IV antibiotics, and within 24 hours, he had made a near-complete recovery. It was nothing short of miraculous, but things were different after that.

That illness stole more than his vitality. Sure, he had been indifferent to me, but he became a stranger. The ridiculous lie about the water bill was the first clue. Then came the mortgage, the car insurance, the credit card bills. With each lie, the knot coiled around my gut pulled tighter, leaving me choked in a panic.

His flashing rage was, by far, the worst new development. He would erupt out of nowhere, and his anger focused more on me as the years wore on. I could never figure out what set him off or how to prevent it.

One night, hearing noises outside, I flung the

garage door open to find Pete silhouetted in the night, rage flowing through him as he hurled knives at the wall. My panic grew.

"Pete! What are you doing?"

Throwing another knife, he seethed, "Get out."

"Pete, I just want to help you. What's going on?"

He turned briefly before stalking towards the wall to grab the knives. "You! You ruined everything."

I tentatively widened the door, "What? What did I do?"

Facing away from me, he rolled his shoulders before lifting a knife, "Nothing. You don't do a goddamn thing."

"Pete, how can I help--"

Before I could finish, he turned to face me, the knife in his hand and his face filled with fury, "You can get the fuck out. Now!"

I wanted to fix this, to help us, but he refused counseling. It was only a matter of time before hurling knives at the wall wasn't enough. Soon, he moved to breaking my things and flinging them at me, like the heirloom jewelry box my aunt had given me. I was thankful it hadn't sliced my leg open, but in the sweltering Texas summer, I took to wearing jeans to hide the bruise across my thigh.

My mother had always told me that sex was the glue in a marriage, but after Pete's illness, the little intimacy we once had disappeared entirely. We were roommates, and our shared bed was a distant memory. He went on frequent business trips, moving his things to the guest room between trips. My suspicions arose, but any evidence that these were more than just business trips was hidden in his office at work.

As the years passed, the weight of my solitary

existence next to the man I had married grew heavier. I was slowly dying inside, crying myself to sleep alone in my bed most nights. I yearned for his touch, even a simple hug or holding my hand. My only physical contact was the fleeting touch of the grocery store checkout person handing me my change. Yet, I stayed, clinging to the illusion that there had to be others who lived celibate lives in their marriages and who lived happy lives.

Desperate to escape the loneliness that consumed me, sleep was my safe place, my happy place, and I began to have intimate dreams about that guy from college, Sonny. They felt so real. I would wake and instantly try to claw my way back to the dream, back to him. One time, I woke up suddenly, and for a moment, it was real. Laying there, I could still feel him on my skin, his scent on me, on my clothes. I shut my eyes, trying to find my way back, but it was hopeless. Instead, I went to my desk and wrote all I could remember from the dream, tears streaming down my face as the words poured out of me. Whenever things felt unbearable, I'd seek comfort in that story, creating a lifeline for me during that time.

One day, one of those dreams led me to a tattoo shop. I hesitated outside, my hand on the door trembling. I never had a tattoo or wanted one before, but I needed something, a tangible reminder of a happier time. And I chose Sonny.

I settled on a small sun design on my left hip with some elegant script around it, etching the words, "I wish I had known that the sun would never shine without you." One good thing about having a sexless marriage was I'd never have to explain it to Pete. He'd never see it.

Two years later, I finally reached the end of my rope. My mom came over and was frightened by the dead look in my eyes. She found me crying. She sat me down and told me I was scaring her, and that scared me. I realized I needed to leave Pete. I called a lawyer, and my mom helped me pack before Pete got home that day. We filled both our cars with my things, and she drove home. I would drive to her house after I told Pete.

When he got home, I met him at the door. "Pete," my voice was surprisingly steady, "We need to talk."

I braced for the anger, but he seemed almost dejected as he sat down in the living room, running his hand through his hair.

"Okay?"

My voice was a whisper, thick with emotion, "I can't do this anymore... with you."

He let out a soft sigh, "I know. I knew it was only a matter of time."

I blinked, the coil of anxiety loosened just a little in my belly. "You did?"

"Yeah." He stared at the floor before looking up at me, unshed tears in his eyes.

I had nothing left for him, so I said, "I've already called a lawyer," as I leaned down, grabbing my bag beside the couch. "I'm going to stay with my parents. I'll be back to get my things."

He pulled off his tie, tossing it on the side table as he let out a breath, nodding. "Okay."

Walking out to my car, it had been almost too easy, and I kicked myself for staying so long. Now, a year on my own and with the divorce final, I was ready to dip my toe in the dating pool again., though the mere thought sent a shiver of cold panic down my spine.

I tried to avoid thinking about how starved for affection I was. I couldn't remember the last time I'd been hugged, much less kissed. Humans were made for touching, kissing, fucking, and where was I? I was practically virginal at 28 years old, and I hated it.

Five years without sex will change a person. Don't get me wrong, I wanted to do it. Badly. But the fear of being intimate with someone after such a long time consumed me. Yet it was more than that. Would I even remember how to kiss after this long? Would someone be able to tell? Take advantage of me? Or worse, pity me?

Chapter 4 - Edison

Edison arrived at the grocery store less than an hour before closing time. The parking lot was nearly empty. He dug around in the center console for a quarter and headed over to the carts, pressing it in the slot and pulling the chain to release it. While the chain dropped, the cart wouldn't budge. It seemed to be stuck on something. He yanked harder, and the cart lurched backward, nearly knocking him on his ass, rolling over whatever it was stuck on.

He crouched down to see the problem and noticed a paperback book flapping back and forth in the breeze, the pages dirty and bent. He leaned between the carts still chained together, inching his fingers to reach under them as far as he could to pull the book towards him. Finally brushing it with his fingertips, he grabbed it and dragged it towards him before standing up.

It was a well-worn copy of _The Time Traveler's Wife_. He flipped through the pages and immediately noticed it was different and unusual. He'd never seen a book with so much marginalia. Nearly every margin had handwritten notes. He was mesmerized.

Edison had written his master's thesis on

marginalia and loved studying the hidden history of margin notes. There was something magical about reading other people's thoughts who had read a book before you. But it wasn't easy to find books with it. Secondhand bookstores usually refused to accept them, which meant they were often tossed in the trash or sometimes donated to places like thrift stores.

Paging through the book, something told him it had a secret he needed to discover. Edison stood there, deeply engrossed, turning page after page, getting lost in the notes, lists, and quotes before glancing at his watch and realizing he was running out of time to get inside before closing. He set the book on top of the child's seat in the cart and took off through the store. He grabbed dog food and all the groceries he needed for himself with 10 minutes to spare and headed to the checkout.

When he got to the front, only one lane was open. How were so many people in line when just a couple of cars were in the parking lot? It seemed everyone else in the city was checking out.

Glancing at the book, it called to him. He picked it up again and opened it, slowly flipping pages until he found a grocery list a few chapters in. He studied it for a bit and then paged through more, reading comments here and there. Something pulled him back to the grocery list, and he noticed it had brands only sold at this store. That was interesting.

Looking over the list, he noticed the words were becoming more challenging to read. The text looked lighter, and he was squinting to see it. Was it written in pencil? He didn't remember it being so light a moment ago.

He rubbed his eyes, glancing away before looking back at the page, realizing he could see just fine. Watching it fade into oblivion before his eyes, his breath hitched, and it was just gone. Completely. The spot was just blank. What was happening? His heart raced, and his hands shook, causing him to drop the book with a loud "Thwap!" on the floor. Most everyone in the line was startled and turned to look at him.

With a sheepish smile and bright red cheeks, he said a little too loudly, "Sorry!"

He picked up the book and set it in the cart again, trying to ignore its hold on him while he waited to check out. He felt a wave of anxiety every time he glanced at it. Had he imagined what had just happened? He couldn't stop the urge to open the book and check again.

He carefully opened the book, hoping he wasn't about to unleash something. He slowly turned the pages until he was sure he found the place where the grocery list had been.

His eyes widened when something completely different was now handwritten in its place.

Claire isn't looking for you, but she'll find you.

Claire? His tattoo prickled. The only Claire he knew was the one he had spent a weekend with years ago. He still had dreams about her, waking up with the taste of her on his tongue. Had that weekend been real, or did he dream her up? Sometimes, he wasn't sure.

He shut the book but then thought better of it. He flipped through again, and this was definitely the right page. He was sure of it. Not believing his eyes, he furiously flipped through the pages again and again, looking for that damn list. Each time, he just kept returning to that quote. What the hell kind of book was this? He let it fall closed again in the cart.

Edison felt a chill, but his heart beat wildly as a bead of sweat dripped down his temple. He peered around the line, wondering if he was ever getting out of this store. He ignored the book, his eyes darting everywhere else, pretending it wasn't taunting him, sitting in the cart begging him to open it.

His attention was caught when he heard a woman's laugh at the front of the line. Her voice was familiar. His head popped up, and he tried looking around the people in front of him. Shit, was that Holly? Did she follow him to the grocery store?

"Have a good night, ma'am." The clerk said.

A feminine voice replied, "Thanks! It's almost closing time." She chuckled, "I hope you get out of here soon."

That voice, that laugh, but it was impossible.

He murmured, "Claire?"

He had looked for her for years. But tonight, there she was, at a grocery store a few blocks from his house. His heart raced as he craned his neck to get a better look. The woman never turned around, so he couldn't see her profile. But... that fiery red hair was unmistakable. The same shade he remembered running his fingers through all those years ago. It was pulled up into a twist in a clip with curls piled on top of her head. She'd filled out a little more. Her curves hugged a long, flowing purple floral skirt, and a creamy strip of skin was bare under her fitted white T-shirt. Her hips swayed as she walked out the door, carrying two reusable grocery bags and a small brown leather backpack slung over one shoulder.

Before he could debate whether to go after her, his legs were already moving him toward the door, leaving his cart behind in the back of the line. His speed increased until he was jogging.

He stopped, turning in circles in the parking lot. Where did she go? A wave of disappointment flew through him. Had she already driven off? A flash of red hair caught his attention through the passenger window of a red Civic at the side of the store.

He slowly walked to the middle of the parking lot and stopped about 20 feet from her car. The last thing he wanted to do was freak her out. But he couldn't stop staring. His heart ached at seeing her again. She looked almost exactly how he remembered her.

She was in the driver's seat, messing with her phone. She did a double-take and looked over at him. Her eyes widened and then narrowed as she focused on him. Her gaze darted around the parking lot before they came back to him. She raised her palm in a small wave, giving him a polite smile, before looking away and quickly backing her car out to leave. His hand raised automatically, waving back. His face bloomed into a smile when he caught her eyes in the rearview mirror.

Watching her drive away, Edison was thunderstruck until a car honked at him to move out of the way. Snapping out of it, he ran back inside, grabbing his cart and checking out in record time just before the clerk closed the register.

After loading the groceries in the truck's bed, he tossed the book across the bench seat. He leaned forward, exhaling a long breath as he grabbed the steering wheel and closed his eyes. He'd seen her. All those years, and she was here. His pulse thrummed with anticipation and fear. Had he missed his chance again?

He glanced over and picked up the book again, paging slowly, searching for that quote about

Claire, convinced he'd probably find the grocery list again. But the quote was still there. Was he going crazy? Between the book and seeing her tonight, he still wasn't sure he could believe any of it. He tossed it across the seat, giving it a wary look, before heading home.

Chapter 5 - Claire

The grocery bags were heavy in my arms, adding to the exhaustion from a long day at the library. Hunger gnawed at me, and I couldn't wait to get home and settle in with some comfort food like mac n cheese or a deep dish and a good book.

When I got in the car, I plugged the aux cord into my phone when I felt a prickle of unease. That's when I saw her again. That strange woman who looked from another time was sitting in a beat-up sedan across the parking lot. The church, the courthouse, and now here? This was the third time I'd seen her. My breath hitched. She smirked at me each time, almost like she was challenging me, sending shivers down my spine.

Was she following me? Or was this some small-town joke where everyone knew everyone else? The coincidences seemed too perfect. But maybe I was making this a bigger deal than it was. Yet, I still felt the chill of unease.

She gave me that same creepy finger wave as she drove away. I watched her pull out of the parking lot, but I still felt like someone was watching me. Something in my peripheral vision caught my attention, and I turned my head to see a bear of a man staring intently at my car. He was big and blond with a beard, and frankly, if he hadn't been staring at me like he'd seen a ghost, he looked pretty damn hot. But his hands were empty--no grocery bags, no car keys, just standing there, staring... at me.

That coil of dread reared its head in my belly again. How dangerous could a guy wearing a lavender dress shirt be? His head was tilted like he was trying to figure something out.

What the? Was he... flexing his hands like some Viking Mr. Darcy? As soon as our eyes met, it startled him. He flinched, stepping back, but his gaze remained fixed on me. There was something about him, a lingering echo of something. Did I know him?

My heart beat wildly like it was a trapped bird trying to escape my chest. Was it fear? Attraction? Maybe a little of both. Maybe he was looking at something on my other side? I looked out the driver-side window, but there was nothing of significance. Facing forward, I took a deep breath and slowly slid my eyes his way again, taking one more peek, and immediately looked away when I caught his intense gaze.

He never moved, but I started the car, dreading that, at any second, he might walk over here. I was leaving before any of that happened. My quick wave was more of a question as I reversed. When I caught his eye in the rearview and gave him a hesitant smile, my breath caught in my throat when he returned both. His smile was more mischievous smirk than a grin, revealing dimples hiding in his beard. Something about that smile seemed... familiar. My pulse quickened as I drove away, not from fear but something I couldn't quite figure out.

Too many crime documentaries sent me straight

to Darci's apartment instead of mine. When I parked, I grabbed my grocery bags and ran to her door, knocking furiously as I looked behind me. I probably should have called. What if she wasn't home? I peered over the balcony, looking for any suspicious cars. Darci opened the door almost immediately with a confused look on her face. Her chestnut pixie hair was a total mess.

"What the...?" But before she could finish, I slammed the door shut and locked it as I checked the peephole.

"Are you okay?" Darci asked, pushing me out of the way to look through the peephole herself.

Handing her a grocery bag, I said, "Something weird happened. When I got in my car at the store, this guy was standing in the middle of the parking lot, and I think he was staring at me. And it did not help that he looked like he walked straight out of Valhalla."

Darci shot me an amused look. "Did you say hello?"

I shrugged, "I mean, I did wave at him."

"And then what happened?"

I set the bag down on her kitchen counter and huffed out a breath. "I had to grab some things at the store tonight. When I was getting ready to drive away, I felt like someone was watching me. First, I saw this weird lady who keeps showing up around town everywhere I go, but then I saw this, um, guy just standing in the middle of the parking lot staring right at me."

"Who was he?"

I raised my head to the ceiling and sighed. "He looked familiar, but I don't know." I sighed as I grabbed some frozen meals from the bag to put in her freezer.

Darci unloaded the refrigerated stuff from my other bag onto the table. "No clue who he was?"

I shrugged as I sat down at the table. "For a second, I had this flash of recognition when he smiled, but..." I shook my head. "I just don't know." I sighed.

Darci wrinkled her brow, "What did he look like?"

"Well, he was big and blond," I smiled, "His hair was that short, messy thing guys do that always looks so good, and he had a beard. Not like a scraggly one, but nicely trimmed. And I think he was wearing a light purple button-down shirt with rolled sleeves and... khakis?"

"A beard?" Darci's face lit up like the Cheshire cat.

I rolled my eyes. "Yes, a beard."

She wiggled her eyebrows. "Maybe he thought you were cute?"

"Is that part of meeting people now? Staring at someone in the parking lot?"

Darci shrugged as she grabbed the pint of cookie dough ice cream I had just bought and two spoons. She nodded as she sat at the table and handed me a spoon.

"When we made eye contact, it..." I swallowed, "I don't know, it seemed to surprise him. He flinched and stepped backward."

"Hmm, that doesn't sound like a serial killer stalking his next victim. Maybe he thought you were someone else?" Darci ate a bite of ice cream.

"Maybe..." I slowly nodded, "Yeah, he probably thought I was someone else."

"You're sure you didn't know him?"

I shrugged, "Like I said, I don't know!"

Then, it hit me. I knew exactly who he was. I stopped dead in my tracks and gasped, turning to

Darci with my mouth wide open.

Darci's eyes went wide as a slow grin spread on her face. "Oh god! You do know him?"

I raised my eyebrows and cocked my head to the side.

"What? Tell me!" Darci's eyebrows were about to shoot off her forehead. "Who is he?"

"There was that guy, Sonny, back when I was in college. He didn't have a beard back then."

She nodded thoughtfully, "Okay..." She snapped her fingers at me and said, "Oh wait, I think I remember this story. Blind date? Hot guy? Blond hair? You spent the best weekend ever with him? And what happened?"

"Yeah," I breathed out. "That was him... then Pete showed up and begged me to marry him. I canceled the next date with Sonny and ghosted him." I shook my head. "God, I should have never married Pete. What was I thinking?"

Darci stood up and hugged me, "Don't beat yourself up. You were young. He'd bought you a house, Claire. You wanted security and away from your mom." She shrugged.

"I know, but I so regret it. God, I was so stupid."

She raised an eyebrow, "But wouldn't this be such a strange coincidence?" She grabbed my hands, "Wait! Was he wearing a wedding ring?"

"Uh," I rolled my eyes, "I don't know. Probably. He was such a sweetheart. Someone's probably snatched him up by now."

"Or maybe he's still pining for you." She smirked as she sat back down and took another bite of ice cream.

"I doubt it." I sighed, "God, I still remember our last kiss. I swear he made my toes curl." I lowered my voice to a whisper, "I still have dreams about him." I stared up at the ceiling. "Why I gave all that up for Pete, god only knows."

"You have to find out if it was him. What if he's the one you were supposed to be with this whole time?"

"What, like soulmates? That's not a real thing."

But really, who was I kidding? How many years had the memories of him consumed my fantasies? I still remember how he could send a shiver of heat through me with just a glance. Even now, I thought about him way more than I should. I still regretted never giving him a real chance. He made me feel things in that one weekend that I never felt in my marriage.

"How do I even find him? I don't even remember his last name." I forced myself to stop pacing and sat back down, taking a huge spoonful of ice cream and sucking on it. We finished the pint, eating in silence, nothing but the sounds from a party downstairs.

A huge grin spread over Darci's face. She dropped her spoon in the empty carton, scooted her chair back, and stood up. "This could be your fairytale moment!" she exclaimed. She ran over to the couch to grab her laptop. "We're librarians, for fuck's sake! We can research anything. What can a private investigator do that I can't?"

I rolled my eyes at her.

A wave of heat went down my spine when an unexpected memory bubbled up of Sonny's body hovering over mine. What if we reconnected after all this time? Would he remember me? Would he want anything to do with me? He probably hated me for ghosting him. He was probably happily married with kids by now.

Scooting my chair around to see what Darci was finding, under my breath, I said, "Maybe there's a chance?"

Darci winked and grinned at me. "Watch out, I think you're drooling."

I felt my cheeks heat, and I breathed out a laugh. Maybe I had finally lost my mind.

A few moments later, in a sing-song voice, she said, "Well, well, well. Look what I found!" She pushed the laptop over to me with a smug grin.

Chapter 6 - Edison

When he got home, Bandit excitedly greeted Edison in the kitchen before putting his foot in his food bowl and flinging it toward Edison. He chuckled and set the bags down on the floor.

"Okay, buddy. I've got your food right here. Just give me a minute."

He opened the bag of dog food and filled the bowl, setting it down in front of Bandit. He wagged his tail as he devoured it. It was late, so it was time for bed. Bandit settled on the bed with Edison.

He took a deep breath, hesitant to open the book now that he was completely alone. He'd seen enough horror movies to know what magical things could do to a person. Eventually, his curiosity got the best of him, and he grabbed it off the nightstand for one more look.

A photo fluttered out between the pages, landing beside him on the bed. He was surprised there was something loose in the book since he'd dropped it so violently at the store. The photo had a group of people dressed casually with tote bags and backpacks, huddled in a doorway under the tiniest awning he had ever seen, sheltering from a rainstorm. Only one woman with very familiar wild red hair wasn't in sunglasses in the photo. She was unmistakable. His breath hitched. Was this *her* book?

The camera caught her mid-gesture, tucking an escaping curl behind a freckled ear, her hair a molten halo in the sunlight. Though she was barely visible beside the giant man beside her, she was all Edison could see, peering at the camera from the corner of her eye almost hesitantly, a playful half-smile on her lips as if she were keeping a secret. What was she thinking?

Seeing her in this photo, he yearned to find her and unravel the mystery of where she'd been hiding all this time. He peered closer at the picture, wishing for a magnifying glass to get a better look at her eyes and their mesmerizing shade of dark blue, tinged with hints of violet. His heart ached when he remembered how easy it had been to get lost in the swirling currents within those eyes. It sparked a fire, leaving him desperate for her touch, a desire he had tried to keep locked up for so long.

Logic suggested any one of the people pictured could be the book's owner, or maybe none of them, but as Edison studied the photo, he noticed something significant. Claire was holding this book. Only a bit of the corner and spine were visible, but it was the same blue color and had an identical dark smudge on the spine.

He tried to contain his hope and excitement, but his mind began creating what-if scenarios. Was it just a coincidence? Something more?

He set the photo down on his nightstand and sighed. How was he going to find her again? The things he remembered—her first name, sweet scent, the way she tasted, the sun-kissed freckles on her shoulders—wouldn't help him. How do you find someone whose soul had entwined with yours for just a fleeting moment?

He tossed the book aside, growling in frustration. He grabbed his laptop off the nightstand. He googled the best ways to find someone. The most common suggestion was to start on social media. He sighed in frustration, knowing he'd tried that years ago. He'd come back to it so many times, too many times, but it never panned out.

One idea he'd never tried intrigued him—a reverse image search with the photo. Maybe it would work, and this photo would lead him back to her. After snapping a picture of the photo with his phone, he held his breath. Several similar images popped up. His heart hammered through his chest as he scrolled through the long list of images, but minutes later, it felt hopeless, probably just another dead end.

The next page opened, and he saw a thumbnail of the same photo. It was on the local public library's online newsletter. With a shaky hand, he clicked through. The page opened to an old newsletter from months ago. Most of the images, including this one, were missing. But maybe this was a clue. Did she work at the library?

Click, click, click. He scanned the website with manic focus, every fiber of his being screaming for a hint, a name, another photo, anything related to her.

"Come on, show me something," he muttered, frustration gnawing at him with each dead end.

He glanced at the clock, and futility crashed through his desperation. It was two o'clock in the morning, and he was still no closer to finding her. He shut the laptop, the silence screaming louder than any click.

He placed the photo and book both back on the nightstand. Turning off the lamp, he lay down, staring at the picture, the glow of the streetlights illuminating her like a spotlight. Even with all the dead ends, a spark of hope burned inside him. This was further than he'd ever gotten before. Her face filled his dreams as he drifted off to sleep, whispering a sweet promise that they would cross paths again soon.

He was a bundle of energy the rest of the weekend, determined to find her. He tried several more suggestions online, but they were all dead ends. As a last resort, he decided to call his sister.

Edison and Mallory were nearly 10 years apart but very close. They both made a point to talk every week, but it hadn't always been that way. When Edison had gone off to college, they grew apart. Mallory was young, and Edison was living his own life at school. But when they lost their parents five years ago in a freak plane crash, they clung to each other, rekindling that close relationship they'd had as kids.

Edison harbored a lot of guilt for their deaths. They were on their way to see him when it happened. His dad had been a pilot for nearly 35 years and loved the sky, but halfway through the trip, a crazy storm came out of nowhere. The reports painted a harrowing picture of his father's desperate attempt to land in an open field, which ended in a head-on collision with a car on a two-lane road. His dad died on impact, but his mom, clinging to life, lingered in a coma. Edison and Mallory never left her side, but she passed a week later. They found solace in each other during that difficult time, navigating the loss together, which forged a stronger bond than ever.

Edison dialed his sister, knowing it was likely

early morning wherever she was in the world, but she wouldn't mind the call. Even when she was gallivanting around the world with her boyfriend, Devon, Mallory always made time for her older brother.

He crossed his fingers as he dialed, hoping she had some advice as she was an absolute treasure trove of useless, bizarre information.

It rang half a dozen times before she answered, sleep still in her voice. "Sonny?" She was the only person who still called him that nickname from childhood.

A smile bloomed across his face as soon as he heard her voice. "Did I wake you?"

"Not really, just rotting in bed."

He chuckled, "Where are y'all this week?"

Mallory and Devon were trying to visit as many countries as possible before settling down when they both turned 30 in a few years. Currently, they were working their way through the Asian continent, but Edison had no idea what country they were currently visiting.

"We're in Thailand for another couple of weeks. You should come for a visit. See the sites. This place is amazing, and the street food… oh my god. You'd love it." She sounded so happy.

Mallory was always a ray of sunshine, while Edison often felt like her complete opposite. Her loud and extroverted sunny disposition compared to his quiet, introverted brooding. Her dark raven locks and his blond hair. At just under 5 feet, she was tiny, almost elfish, while Edison had shot up to over 6 feet tall, packed with muscles. But the one thing they shared was the same stunning eyes from their mother that shined like flickering flames of light.

"Sounds nice." He muttered. He cleared his throat and tried to match her happy-go-lucky attitude. "I just wanted to check on you. See how you're doing. And..." His voice dropped off. He wasn't sure how to ask this. It was ridiculous.

"Okay, big bro, what's going on?" Mallory always knew when something was up when it came to Edison.

He huffed out a laugh. "This is probably going to sound crazy."

She laughed. "I think we can both agree I'm the crazier one."

He chuckled knowingly. He tended to play it safe while she was the one who jumped out of airplanes in the desert and hang-glided over the Amazon.

Edison took a deep breath, ready to give his sister some background. "Remember that girl I met when I first moved here?"

"Wait. The girl you brought to Pizza Verona?"

On a whim, he'd driven Claire an hour in the middle of nowhere to this secret outdoor restaurant where Mallory had worked as a teen.

"Yeah, that's the one." The words scraped against his throat, rough with unspoken regret.

"Did you run into her again?"

"Maybe? I don't know."

"Maybe?"

"Well..." His voice cracked. "I'm fairly certain I saw her a few days ago."

"Okay and?"

"Two things happened. First, I found this novel lying under a shopping cart at the grocery store. It was... strange and covered in handwritten notes. And then, a little while later, I saw her walking out of the store, and I ran after her."

"Did you talk to her?"

"No, by the time I got to the parking lot, she was already in her car. But I know she saw me."

"Then what happened?"

"That's it. She just drove off."

"What's the deal with the book? It's hers?"

"I don't know, but I think it might be. I found a photo in it, and she's in it. I think she's holding the book I found in the photo. This photo could be the key for me to get back to her. It's crazy, right?"

"Not that crazy. What's crazy is that you fell head over heels for a girl in three days, and you haven't stopped thinking about her this many years later." Dreamily, she added, "I don't know. Maybe fate is pushing you guys back together for another chance?"

"Sure." His voice filled with amusement.

"So what's the problem?"

He let out a sigh. "I need to find her, and I've tried everything—social media, reverse image search. I even went back to the coffee shop every day for weeks, and even now, I go there once a week just in case... Mal, how do I find her again?"

Mallory chuckled. "Well, you could stalk the grocery store daily until she returns. But that might make you look a little creepy."

"You think?" Sarcasm dripped from his words. He let out a frustrated sigh. "I'm desperate. Ever since I saw her again, I've been searching, trying to figure out how to find her again."

"Okay, okay. I have some ideas. We're going to find her."

"How?" He couldn't imagine what Mallory could come up with, which he hadn't already tried.

"So, I have this friend who met her husband on an app-"

"No," Edison interrupted immediately. "Please

tell me you're not implying I go to a dating app to find-"

"If you'd let me finish, you'd understand."

He let out a heavy sigh, "Fine."

"My friend Caroline. Do you know her? I don't think you've ever met. She met her husband online a few years ago on Lost Connections."

"Lost Connections?" This sounded like a ridiculous idea.

"Let me finish!" Mallory interjected, a rare spark of irritation flickering in her voice. She usually had the patience of a saint. "It's not a dating app. Lost Connections is for second chances, where you can find someone that maybe you met briefly or almost met or lost touch with. Caroline and Tyler were near each other at a concert and struck up a conversation, but they never exchanged information. Tyler posted a message looking for her. They got married a year later. Isn't that sweet? You never know. A lot of people read it. Just try it." She dropped her voice to a whisper, "Sonny, I have a good feeling about this."

His sister always had an uncanny intuition. When they were kids, she knew things like when someone was coming to visit unexpectedly or when something would happen. Once, they were walking home from school when a storm hit out of nowhere, and they ran under a big tree to escape it. A ladybug landed on Mallory's shoulder.

Her face drained of color, and she grabbed Edison's arm and yelled, "Run!"

Edison grabbed Mallory's arm, and they ran to the other side of the street, adrenaline pumping through his veins. Just as they reached a copse of trees, he threw himself over her and then felt, more than heard, the deafening crack, and a blinding flash came immediately after. Peeking out, his mouth gaped. In the place where they had stood moments before, a massive branch lay smoldering, sheared clean by a lightning strike.

Out of breath, she turned to him, her pigtails swinging as she shrugged, "Ladybugs bring bad luck."

"Sonny...? Are you still there?"

Shaking away the memory, he asked, "Seriously?"

"Just try it! Who knows, maybe she reads the posts every weekend for kicks?"

Edison hummed in agreement. Silence filled the phone before he decided it was now or never.

He muttered, "I guess I have nothing to lose. But...," He breathed, "if I do this, I don't want to sound like some creepy stalker."

Mallory snorted.

She asked him more questions about Claire and the book. He told her about the marginalia, purposely skipping the weird magic stuff. Based on her half-responses, he knew she was probably already scheming and writing the post for him.

A moment later, she cleared her throat. "How's this:

Henry seeking Clare

This is a long shot, but...Did you lose your favorite book in Denton? Would love to return it to you. Sometimes, people write the most interesting things in books. Don't you think?
To World Enough and Time because Time is nothing."

The knot in Edison's stomach unraveled a little, and a smile spread slowly over his face as she read it to him. It was a good start, but he had another idea.

"Yeah, okay. I'll do it." He swallowed, "but I want to write it myself."

She giggled. "Fine. I'm sure whatever you write will be way better than the crap that's usually on Lost Connections."

Edison deadpanned. "Really? I can't wait."

When they hung up, he downloaded Lost Connections and created an account. He took what Mallory had written and pasted it in a post, staring at it as he bit his thumbnail. But then an idea sparked, and he completely erased her post, deciding to go another way.

As he finished his post, he wondered if Claire knew about this app. Would she ever see this? It was such a one-in-a-million shot. He made a silent wish to the stars, hoping she'd find it, find him again.

Chapter 7 - Claire

My heart pounded as Darci toggled between two tabs. One was a picture from a different time, a college graduation ceremony at UT in Austin 10 years ago. It was a group of three young men. The blond guy had a very short haircut and a wide grin with dimples that I remembered vividly, beaming in his graduation regalia. He was listed as "Sonny Wright, Masters of Arts in English."

Identical but older was the man in the second tab. The photo was dated over a year ago, featuring a man with a neatly trimmed blond beard. The caption read, "Professor Edison Wright." His hair was longer on top and swept up, but that face mirrored the one I'd seen in the parking lot, down to the rolled-up sleeves on his button-down. He had a composed smile, no dimples in sight, that didn't reveal any of the warmth I remembered.

I was positive it had been him in the parking lot, and so many feelings washed over me. The man, who, for a fleeting moment, made me see colors I'd never seen with anyone else, was now a respected professor. A curious warmth bloomed in my chest, a bit of wonder and nostalgia, and I kept asking myself--who was he now, and who was I?

I blurted out, "That's him." I wondered aloud. "Is Sonny a nickname for Edison?"

"I don't know. Maybe?" Darci typed away, and sure enough, the nicknames for Edison were Ed, Eddie, Ted, Teddy, and… Sonny.

A teasing smile across her face, she said. "We found him."

My heart fluttered as I smiled at the prospect of seeing him again.

"What?" Darci smiled over at me.

"Do you think he recognized me?"

"Uh… yeah." She rolled her eyes. "Why else would he stand in the middle of a parking lot like some lovesick puppy?"

My smile widened. "Okay, okay. What else can we find about Fancy, Mr. Professor Edison Wright."

She laughed, "Oh, he's going to love that. Make sure you call him 'Mr. Professor' when he's plowing into you."

"Oh my god, Darci!" But I laughed, too.

"Let's see what else I can find on him."

Darci did a bit more sleuthing while I searched her pantry for snacks.

I found some microwave popcorn, and just as it started popping, Darci piped up, "Well, unfortunately, his social media all seems to be private."

"Damn. Anything else?"

"Hang on." Darci's fingers were flying. If the librarian gig didn't work out, she could open her own detective agency.

I grabbed two bottles of water and dumped the popcorn into a bowl. "Anything?"

"I'm trying to figure out where he teaches."

I nodded. "Good idea."

I set Darci's water down and took a long drink of

mine.

"I think I found him. He is an English professor at the community college here in town."

"Really? What does he teach?"

"I'm going to guess… English?" Darci grinned as she pushed the laptop over to me and shoved a handful of popcorn in her mouth.

Minutes. That's all that separated us. The college was just minutes from both here and the library. With a few clicks, his professional life unfolded like a map. He taught literature and writing courses, and his email address practically lit up on the screen. I glanced at Darci, then back at the screen, as I chewed my bottom lip. Did I dare?

"Do it," Darci offered. "Email him."

"What would I even say? 'Hey, it's me, the girl who ghosted you years ago?' I can't do that."

"You could sign up for one of his classes."

"It's the middle of the semester. And… I don't have time for that!" My cheeks flushed.

"Go audit his class." She shrugged, "It's worth a shot!"

"I don't know…"

"Do it," Darci whispered, peeking at me from behind the computer.

I gave her a tiny smile, forcing myself to leave my lip alone before it bled.

She shook her head. "Well? What's the plan?"

I tried to contain a huge yawn. "I- I don't know. I need to sleep on it."

Darci nodded and closed her laptop. "Okay, girlie." She squeezed my hand gently before she headed to the fridge to pull out my groceries. "Let's walk these over to your apartment."

Thirty minutes later, I was tucked in bed and drifting off to memories of Sonny from years ago.

* * *

A few days later, I called Darci early in the morning, knowing we both had the same day off. Her voice was raspy when she answered, but I couldn't wait any longer.

"Are you busy? Get over here and help me. I need to join Tinder or Bumble or something."

She immediately perked right up. "Tinder? But what about…?" Before I could answer, she said, "I'll be there soon," and hung up.

Five minutes later, she rolled in with a pan full of gooey cream cheese cinnamon rolls. Lifting them, she said, "I brought reinforcements."

"When did you make these? You were asleep when I called."

"I woke up in the middle of the night and decided to make these babies. You're welcome!"

I took them from her, feeling the warmth of the pan. "They smell heavenly! I'll make the coffee."

I needed it. The last few nights sleep had avoided me. I was too keyed up. He consumed my thoughts. This unexpected brush with the past had sent me into a tailspin. Every night, I'd lay there as images and what-ifs flickered behind my eyelids into the early mornings — a younger me, shared dreams whispered in a field of wildflowers, his body wrapped around mine in his bed. But that was then. People changed. If we reconnected, would it be like before?

Darci and I devoured half the cinnamon rolls and two pots of coffee at my tiny kitchen table, but we didn't talk about Sonny. It wasn't that I didn't want to reconnect with him. I just wanted a little practice, a date or two, to get back in the game before I made a fool of myself approaching him.

Three hours later, amid empty plates and cold

coffee, I was still trying to craft the perfect dating profile, realizing it wasn't just throwing up a selfie and a couple of sentences. From what I gathered, it was all about a witty opening line. Easy for them to say. After much erasing and agonizing, I settled for, "Do you hate it here as much as I do?" It wasn't exactly Shakespeare, but it got my vibe across.

Meanwhile, my best friend played stylist in my closet, going piece by piece through my wardrobe to find the perfect outfit for my profile pic. After taming my hair and adding some makeup, when it was all said and done, I looked pretty damn good if I did say so myself.

We ran around the apartment complex to find the best lighting for my pictures. By the time we made it back to my apartment, my stomach was loudly grumbling. I couldn't believe it was already lunchtime.

After my glow-up, I wanted to go out to lunch, so Darci ran home to shower while I added the last of the photos to my profile. We headed to our favorite diner, MacArthur's, on the square as soon as she was ready. They served breakfast all day and the best chicken fried steak in town, which I promptly ordered. Darci got her usual French toast.

After we ordered, she pulled out her phone and opened the Lost Connections app. Every weekend, this ritual unfolded like clockwork. She would curate the posts and read the best ones out loud to me. I pretended we were anthropologists studying the search for love, but more often than not, we ended up giggling like a couple of schoolgirls. There was some crazy stuff on that app. It was harmless fun, but I had discovered Darci's secret, and I'm not even sure she realized it, but I knew she longed to be the subject of a post on Lost Connections.

"Oh, this is the ONE!" Darci laughed.

I took a sip of water and rolled my eyes to prepare myself. "Dear lord. Okay, read it."

Darci put on a deep, sultry voice. "Hello. You were breastfeeding at McDonald's on Saturday during lunch. Our eyes met a few times, and yours warmed my soul, and I've only felt that one other time in my life. You are incredibly beautiful. I would love to get to know you better."

I scrunched my face and made a frown. "I don't even know what to make of this. Who thinks a nursing mother is making eyes at them? She's probably just trying to see what creepers are looking her."

Darci chuckled as she scanned the posts. "How about this one...

"Years ago, our paths crossed by the pond in the city, and we spent long days there together. We learned the secrets of the sacred water, and your aura and the magical, mystical scent of your hair enraptured me."

I nodded slowly. "That is certainly... a strange one."

Darci nodded absentmindedly, like she didn't hear me. She was still scanning the posts when she gasped and whispered, "Holy shit, Claire."

"Oh god. How bad is it?"

She shook her head, "No, I- I think it's about you." Darci looked up at me with wide eyes.

"What?"

"Seriously, listen. It's titled 'Henry Seeking Clare!"

"I don't know anyone named Henry. Why do you think it's about me?"

"Here." Darci handed me her phone with her eyebrows raised. I looked down and read the post.

* * *

Henry seeking Clare

*Found your well-loved copy of <u>The Time Traveler's Wife</u>,
complete with passionate scribbles about Henry and Clare.
They're safe with me. Please reply with your favorite quote
to claim them, and maybe discuss the merits of waiting
forever for someone you love.*

Time is nothing.

There it was, plain as day. My heart lurched. It had to be my book. The worn spine, dog-eared pages filled with underlined quotes, and messy handwriting that wasn't just mine.

I looked up at Darci, feeling butterflies dancing in my belly, their wings fluttering in time to my racing heartbeat. I took in a big breath and let it out.

Relief washed over me, sweet and sudden. I had convinced myself the book was lost, but now I realized how much I wanted it back. It was a time capsule when my life had changed so much this past year, anxieties and dreams scribbled in the margins. I had to get it back.

I shook my head. "Wow, I don't know. It does seem like it's probably for me. Maybe it's just the driver?"

Darci's brow wrinkled, "Wasn't he practically a teenager?"

I pursed my lips. "Uh… yeah.'"

She gave me a pointed look. "And you think he wrote this?"

I reread it half a dozen times. This wasn't written by some teenage kid who never read a book. No, this was written by someone who'd read it and loved reading. But who?

Darci gave me a huge grin and squeed with delight. "Are you going to reply?"

I hesitated. Should I? A thrill danced in my belly of nervousness and excitement. A stranger had found my book, read my thoughts, and held a piece of me in their hands. Thinking about the things I'd written about love and loss, I felt a flush creeping up my cheeks. Did I want to meet the person who'd seen all that vulnerability? I looked away, gathering my thoughts.

Maybe it was silly, but a part of me didn't want to meet the person who'd read my private thoughts. But that book... oh, that book. It was worth too much to let my fear stop me.

When I slid my eyes back to hers, that optimistic glow hadn't dimmed. Her eyes seemed to sparkle with a mischievous twinkle. I let out a soft chuckle, still considering her question.

I tilted my head. "Probably," I said in a playful hesitation.

She wrinkled her brow, "What? No. Not probably. You are doing this." She smirked, "Or I will!"

I gave her a flat look.

"Come on... just reply and see what happens."

"Or I could end up dead." I gave her my most incredulous face. "Remember that show we watched about the Lonely Hearts Killer?" I made air quotes with my hands, "What kind of Crimebrarian are you?"

"Really." She arched an eyebrow.

I couldn't hold a straight face anymore, and I broke out in a grin. I handed her the phone. "Fine, send me the link so I can reply on my phone."

Darci grinned, shaking her head, and quickly

emailed the link to me.

I dug my phone out of my purse as the email pinged and opened it to reply. My teeth sank into my bottom lip as my fingers hovered over the phone screen. My mind felt blank. "I'm not even sure what to say…"

With a shaky breath, I started typing. My fingers hovered over the send button. Was it too much? I bit my lip, then hit it with a silent plea.

I arched an eyebrow as I said, "It's sent. Happy now?"

Her eyes widened, and a slow grin spread on her face as the waitress set our plates down. As soon as she walked away, Darci clapped her hands like an overly excited toddler.

"Yay! This is going to end up way better than Tinder. I just know it!"

"I know what you're doing." I pointed a forkful of chicken fried steak drenched in gravy at her before shoving it in my mouth.

She shrugged. "Let's just see who it is and where it goes. Maybe it's nothing? Or maybe…" Her smile widened, "it's the start of something more."

I gave her a small smile, but adrenaline coursed through my veins, a hint of regret at sending the message without much thought. This person held a piece of me, but she was right. This could be the start of something new. And while I'd never say it out loud, I craved that.

Chapter 8 - Edison

Edison eyed the phone across the bed. Days ago, when he'd made the post, he'd felt that spark of hope tinged with fear. But now, it just felt like a big letdown.

At first, each notification sent his heart into a frantic rhythm, only to end in a dull thud as each message revealed yet another blatant sexual proposition or a ridiculous scam attempt. Lost Connections, it seemed, was more of a haven for scammers and fleeting encounters, not rekindled romances.

Disappointment coated his tongue as the replies dwindled every day like a whisper of defeat. He wanted to believe it would work, that she would see his message. But... was this just a fool's errand? It was supposed to be his lifeline, a fragile thread connecting him to a past he desperately yearned to reclaim.

In the last 24 hours, he hadn't had a single response, figuring his post had been lost in a million other desperate wishes. Giving up on sleep when the first light of dawn painted his bedroom in soft hues, he got up to take Bandit on his morning run.

Maybe a morning run would banish the memory

of a woman who still haunted him. He made a conscious choice to leave his phone behind and pounded the pavement until he was coated in sweat. Heading home, Bandit's tongue lolled as he ran alongside. Edison hoped a lunchtime nap could get him through the rest of the day.

After a quick shower, he was on the couch, reaching for his phone. The familiar weight was both a comfort and a curse. A moment after turning it on, he felt that tell-tale buzz, a jolt that sent a tremor straight up his arm.

He held his breath, unlocking the screen. There was one new message blooming on the display. As the words swam before him, he told himself this could be anything—another dead end, another proposition, or just another disappointment. But as he read, that little ember of hope he'd been holding onto for years ignited and sent a wave of nerves crashing over him, leaving him breathless for what fate had delivered.

To: fdajreq984-q3248-92@lostconnections.com
From: thelastbookmarker@gmail.com
Subject: RE: Henry Seeking Clare

"Oh my gosh, it's YOU! Because sometimes you just have to believe."

Sometimes, love is worth the wait, even if it feels like forever—especially when you've known it once before.

I think you found my book. I would love to get it back. Is your name Henry? Because surprisingly, I'm Claire. :)

* * *

Yours with world and time enough…

Air whooshed out of his lungs all at once. The words haunted him, *"Claire isn't looking for you, but she'll find you."* He was almost sure this was her.

What were the chances? The screen glowed with her words like stars guiding him home. "Oh my gosh, it's YOU!" It sent his stomach in a somersault, a rush of butterflies he hadn't felt in years.

This wasn't coincidence or luck. The universe was playing their song again, a forgotten melody resonating between them, even though it had been so fleeting the first time. This was the fates, the planets, and all the stars aligning for a second time, a second chance to rewrite the story they never finished.

His fingers itched to reply, but he glanced at the timestamp, realizing it had been just a moment ago. He didn't want to seem too eager. Sure, he was like a lovesick teenager glued to his phone, but he wasn't ready to admit that to her just yet. So he set a timer, forcing a pause to the symphony playing in his chest. Fifteen minutes. That was enough time to make a sandwich and ground himself but not enough to quell the excitement coursing through him. Heading to the kitchen, each step lighter than the last, he felt the promise of a new beginning.

To: thelastbookmarker@gmail.com
　From: edisonxwright@gmail.com
　Subject: RE: RE: Henry Seeking Clare

Claire, it is you! Sharing the same name as the main

character in the book? Is that why it's your favorite?

No Henry here, just a hopeless romantic who couldn't resist the story scrawled across your pages.

Are those notes in the book all yours?

Time is nothing.
Edison

After sending the email, he waited impatiently, his heart in his throat. All he wanted to do was check his email continuously for her response. Instead, he forced himself to watch a movie he wasn't paying attention to because his body was tuned to the buzz of his phone. He smiled when just moments later he felt it rumble through his fingers from the coffee table. He picked it up immediately.

To: edisonxwright@gmail.com
From: thelastbookmarker@gmail.com
Subject: RE: RE: RE: Henry Seeking Clare

Hi Edison!

Haha, maybe a little! It's a name that's grown on me since first reading it.

You have no idea how grateful I am you found my book. I thought I'd never see it again when I left it in that rideshare.

Most of those scribbles (and maybe a few tear stains) are mine. That book's been with me through a lot. But hey, at least you know I'm a dedicated reader!

What about you? Do you write in your books?

Yours with world and time enough,
Claire

In a car? How in the hell did it end up under the shopping carts at the store? His gaze slid to the book on the side table, and he swore it stared back, refusing to share its secrets.

He had so many questions. How was she? Where had she been all these years? Grabbing the book and flipping the pages, he couldn't help himself. He wanted to know her history, devouring every note, searching for clues to her life.

Each page was a little window into her soul. A note to call Mom whispered of a close-knit family. Did she have a cat? Doodles of cats were in so many of the margins, revealing a playful side. She liked lists. To do lists, work lists, grocery lists. The healthy groceries and doctor's appointments spoke of a woman who cared for herself, yet a smile tugged at his lips when he saw "cookie dough ice cream" perpetually on every grocery list.

He was drawn to her passion for quotes. Each one was copied and surrounded with little doodles with questions and notes to herself, like a story unfolding that he desperately wanted to be a part of. Lost in all of it, he glanced at his phone, realizing it had been over an hour as he hastily replied to her email:

To: thelastbookmarker@gmail.com
From: edisonxwright@gmail.com
Subject: RE: RE: RE: RE: Henry Seeking Clare

I love to read, but I also teach college English, so writing in books is a necessity. Truthfully, I like to study things people have handwritten in books.

Have you seen the marginalia in medieval texts? Some of it is downright bizarre.

Or Mark Twain's marginalia? He was absolutely savage, but it's pretty funny to read.

Time is nothing,
Edison

Rereading the message he'd sent quickly, he grimaced. Maybe nerding out on marginalia wasn't the smoothest move. "Geez, Edison," he thought, picturing her rolling her eyes.

Emails flew back and forth between them for hours. Edison barely registered his growing hunger, lost in the whirlwind of getting to know her. He no longer cared how eager he seemed. Every reply was a new piece to her puzzle—she finally became a librarian and was still a book lover. She was an Italian food connoisseur (not so much on the vegan cuisine), and she loved true crime. It was all so intriguing. He wanted to know everything.

He couldn't wait any longer, wanting to give her a nudge to a more personal connection simmering on his fingertips, a silent plea wrapped in a very short, casual question.

To: edisonxwright@gmail.com
From: thelastbookmarker@gmail.com
Subject: RE: Henry Seeking Clare

* * *

Text me?

Time is nothing,
Edison

He watched the screen, a nervous flutter in his chest. She replied almost instantly with her number. In minutes, he'd saved her contact info, and their texts flew, replacing emails with a quicker yet deeper conversation. Claire revealed she had been married and recently returned to town. She didn't give specifics, but she painted a picture of a woman who'd escaped a bad marriage. It ignited a protective fire in Edison's gut. Was her ex the reason she disappeared back then?

Yet beneath it all, her bubbly personality shined through. This was the Claire he remembered, making him feel like he could be himself. Every time he saw those text bubbles, butterflies danced in his stomach. He hadn't felt this alive, this hopeful, in what felt like an eternity.

He didn't want to wait anymore—the unspoken question burned in his mind. Meet me tonight? Was it too forward? He'd been dying to ask her her out, to dinner for the last few hours, but maybe he should start with something easier, like coffee. Hope bloomed in his chest as his finger hovered over "send." He refused to squander this second chance.

Edison: Meet me for coffee?

Chapter 9 - Claire

He wanted to meet for coffee. Oh god, it had been coming. I knew it, but seeing the words. After lunch, I'd been lounging across the bed as we emailed and then texted, but this. Like a fool, I leaped off the bed and danced around the room at his invitation, screaming "yes" from the rafters. I wanted to tell him to meet me right now. This minute. Was that ridiculous? I didn't care.

When he told me his name was Edison, I dared to entertain the thought. Was he... Sonny? Who else could it be? He taught English, and his name was Edison. How many were there in this town? This had to be some kind of cosmic joke. The astronomical chances that he found my book. The whole thing was unbelievable.

With shaking hands, I took a deep breath and called Darci because someone needed to talk me down.

"Hey! So...how's... it going?" She was out of breath.

Ignoring her question, I asked, "What are you doing? You sound like you're running a marathon." The entire time I'd known Darci, she had always avoided exercise.

She laughed nervously, "I...uh...had an... afternoon...date."

Oh god. "Am I... interrupting?"

She wheezed out a laugh, and then I heard the crunch of leaves and twigs. "Hell no." She sighed, "I guess I misunderstood because I thought we were going for a walk in the park. But he was with a huge group of people when I got here. He waved when he saw me and jogged over, handing me this hideous bright yellow t-shirt. I look horrible in yellow. He told me we were playing 'capture the flag' with a bunch of people." She chuckled, "I should have known something was up when he asked for my t-shirt size."

I cringed. "That's a thing... for a first date?"

"Apparently, so."

"Well, how's it going? Will there be a second date?"

"Technically, the date's not over. They still need to capture the flag." She lowered her voice to a whisper. "But I'm leaving. And to answer your question, hell no, I'm not seeing him again."

I barked out a laugh.

"Ssshhh!! I don't want them to know where I am."

"Sorry." I chuckled.

She whisper yelled, "I'm trying to figure out how to get back to my car without anyone noticing!"

I chuckled as I heard Darci's heavy breathing.

"So I need to know. What happened?"

"Well, after you went back to your apartment, he answered me, and soon after, we moved to text."

"Did you now?"

"Yep." I let out a pent-up breath and told her everything except my suspicions he was Sonny. "He just texted a few minutes ago and asked me to meet him for coffee. Is it too soon? What do you think?"

"I think it's great!"

"You do? Because I'm thinking about asking if he wants to do it tonight."

"Claire? What are you not telling me?"

"Well…" I muttered, "So…"

"Yeah?"

"Are you sitting down?" Here we go.

"No, I'm not sitting down. I'm hiding under some flowering… bush… thing. Spit it out, woman!"

"I think he's Sonny."

"What?!"

"Why are you yelling? Aren't you in hiding?"

She dropped back into a whisper. "Shit. I'm going to have to make a run for it. Don't hang up!"

"I won't."

There was more crunching as her breathing picked up. Was she actually running?

"You okay?"

A beep sounded, and then a car door opened and closed, along with heavy breathing. "I made it to the car. Hang on." There was some crinkling and noises I couldn't identify. "Okay, I'm lying across the backseat. I should be good now. Tell me everything!"

"Unless he walks up to your car."

"Crap, you're right. Hold on." There was more crinkling and a grunt just as the car started. "Yay, I'm out of this bitch. You think he's Sonny?"

"Yeah," A trembling breath escaped my lips, "He told me his name was Edison, and he taught college English. Who else could it be?"

"Oh my god, it has to be him!"

"I know!"

Darci murmured. "But wait, you said tonight? I can't do it tonight."

"Why would that matter?"

"Because I said I'd go with you. Remember your whole rant about being his next potential victim?"

I laughed. "It's fine. We both know he's likely not a serial killer."

Darci mused, "I don't know... it's been years. People change."

"Who's been watching too many true crime docs now?" I teased.

She chuckled, "Text me where you're meeting him and..." Darci clicked her tongue. "We need a phrase or something if he ends up being crazy, and I need to come get you."

"Okay...?"

"Hmm." She paused briefly before blurting out, "My Spoon's Too Big."

I cackled. "What? Are you kidding? How am I supposed to casually work My Spoon's Too Big into a conversation with you if he's trying to murder me?"

"I believe in you. You'll figure it out."

"That's reassuring." I swallowed audibly, "Wish me luck."

"You aren't going to need it. Something tells me that you two were meant to be." In a sing-song voice, she said, "Hopefully, you don't come home til morning."

"Darci!"

"What?" She broke out in laughter as we hung up.

Excitement hummed through my body. My heart was a drumbeat, pounding away any doubts. I was going to ask him to meet me tonight. Something told me he'd agree to it. Maybe he was what I'd been waiting for all this time.

I checked our messages, but he hadn't said anything else. That's when I realized he was still waiting for my reply. Shit, he probably thought I didn't want to meet him at all now. I hurriedly wrote out my question, feeling guilty about leaving him hanging.

Claire: How about tonight?

A wave of nerves hit my belly as my finger hovered over "Send." What if he said no? Would he? I tapped the button, feeling as if time was standing still.

Immediately, the text bubbles popped up. Oh god. My heart leaped into my throat as I turned the phone over, setting it on the bed and stepping back, staring at it but too scared to see his response. I jolted when the phone buzzed a second later, grabbing it with a shaky hand. I let out a breath before flipping it over.

Edison: Let's do it! Where do you want to meet?

Butterflies shot through my belly. My brain ran a mile a minute trying to think of a single coffee place in town, and then... it hit me. Why didn't we meet at Alchemy, where we had our blind date? It was perfect!

Claire: How about Alchemy around 7 pm?

When I pictured myself walking in the door and seeing him again, my breath hitched, and the butterflies in my belly turned to dive-bombing wasps. How was I going to remember to breathe in his presence?

Edison: Sure, that sounds perfect. Their blackout cake is to die for! I'll be the tall blond guy with a beard. I'll be in a red Henley and jeans. And I'll have your book with me.

A forgotten memory came to the surface. Wasn't that... wasn't that the same thing Sonny wore on our blind date? It felt like a lifetime ago. I had been such a ball of nerves, flustered from arriving so late. This had to be him. Please, please remember me.

Sliding the closet door open, a crazy, desperate idea took root. What if I wore the same dress? I used to wear it all the time back then. It was blue floral, and everyone said it made my eyes sparkle.

My fingers flicked through to the back of my closet, going back in time to senior year, that carefree time when life held so many possibilities. Did I still have that dress? I offered up a frantic prayer just before I found it nestled between some winter sweaters I hadn't worn in ages, still as vibrant as I remembered. A wave of emotions washed over me as I held it up, wondering if it still fit. It was a tangible connection to a past I longed for. Memories from that weekend flooded my mind. My hands trembled as I slid on the dress. It fit just as I remembered. Staring at myself in the mirror, I smoothed down the wrinkles.

I was a ball of nerves. Tonight, I wasn't just meeting a stranger. I was meeting a memory, a moment I'd been too afraid to even dream of. This was the man I'd longed for, and the memories I held had been my secret solace during my troubled marriage.

I picked up the phone to reply.

Claire: I'll be the redhead in a blue dress. See you there.

* * *

He replied immediately.

Edison: Can't wait!

When I got to the parking lot at Alchemy, it was nearly empty. This place used to be packed when I was in college. Maybe it was the time? Did people usually get coffee at seven o'clock at night? I pulled in next to an older red truck, and I remembered kissing in his truck. Was he already here, waiting for me?

After parking, I flipped down the visor, fluffed my curls, and gave myself a mental pep talk before stepping out.

"Calm down," I whispered as I walked towards the door, but the words were drowned out by my racing heart like it was trying to escape. Pressing a hand to my chest, I could feel the frantic beating.

Two people were sitting at a booth, laptops open and mugs spread around the table. Apart from them, the place was empty. No one was in a red shirt. I let out a delightful gasp when I noticed the booth where we met back then was free. I slid in so I could watch the front.

I raised my head at the tinkling of the bell over the door, but it was just someone leaving. That same weird lady with the black hair and witch-core dress. I didn't need to see her face to know it was her. I ducked, hoping she hadn't noticed me. But where had she come from? This place was empty, and I hadn't seen her at any of the tables.

Every rumble of a car engine turned my head, and hope battled the knot forming in my belly. I kept my eyes glued to the door, my foot tapping nervously. A barista came to take my order, and I asked for a cup of coffee to keep my hands from trembling.

Minutes stretched, and when I looked at my watch, seven o'clock had come and gone. My nervous excitement deflated. Fifteen minutes later, a knot of anxiety twisted in my belly, tightening slowly as the seconds ticked on. Did he change his mind? Was this some kind of joke? We had just planned this a few hours ago, but the edge of doubt crept into my mind. Still, I clung to hope, remembering he had waited over an hour all those years ago on our blind date.

A few minutes later, the shrill ring of my phone startled me. I dug it out of my purse, and seeing Edison's name flash across the screen, panic ran through my veins like ice. My heart kicked up a notch as my mind buzzed with a million scenarios. Why was he calling? My fingers shook as I swiped to answer, unsure what to expect or what to say. What would he say?

"Edison?" The question slipped out little more than a confused whisper.

"Claire?" He let out a sigh. "Yeah, it's me. Look, I am so sorry. Something happened." His voice was deep and a little rough but familiar. He cleared his throat.

"Are you okay?" The knot in my belly twisted. Please let him be okay.

"I took my dog for a walk before coming to meet you, down to the dog park, and h-" His voice caught. "He was attacked."

I wanted to hug him. "Oh my god, that's awful. Is he alright?"

"I don't know. I got him to the ER vet as fast as I could, and now I'm stuck in the waiting room while they're examining him. They won't let me back there."

A pang of empathy shot through me, hearing the defeat in his voice.

"I'm so sorry. Do you—" I debated whether to ask him this. "Do you want me to come there? You shouldn't be alone if it's... bad."

"I think he's going to be okay. Can we talk while I wait?"

I wanted to reach through the phone and offer comfort, but all I could do was listen. Maybe that would be enough.

"Sure. Anything you need. Tell me about your dog."

His voice softened. "His name's Bandit. He's a Boxer." He sniffled. "I got him from the pound about two years ago."

"Do you want to talk about what happened..." I heard a dog barking through the phone. "Or something else?" I waved the barista back over, ordering a larger coffee and a slice of cake. I was going to be here a bit longer.

"There was an unfamiliar dog, big, white, and fluffy, still on a leash." He let out another sigh. "There's a huge sign at the entrance that says all dogs are off leash inside the dog park. It can cause aggression. The guy hadn't read it." He let out a frustrated sigh.

"Okay."

"Bandit ran up on the dog to sniff him and say hello because that's what dogs do." He grumbled. "I don't know what happened, but all hell broke loose. It bit Bandit clean through his ear."

"Oh, poor Bandit."

"The frantic barks of other dogs alerted me that something was wrong. But when I ran over, the guy seemed oblivious, still holding the leash, as his dog tried to bite Bandit's face off."

"That's horrible!" Who doesn't stop their dog from attacking another dog?

"So I pull the dog off Bandit. His muzzle is bloody. His ear has a hole in it, dripping blood. I scooped him up and ran home as fast as possible, considering I had a 90-lb dog in my arms. Then, I drove up here as fast as I could." He blew out a breath. "But guess who walked in a few minutes after we did? That asshole and his dog. He said his dog was also injured and tried to instigate a fight with me in the waiting room. They finally had to put him in an exam room so he'd leave me alone."

"He sounds unhinged."

"Yeah," He scoffed, "Bandit's never been in a fight. His aggression is limited to enthusiastic slobbery kisses." He chuckled, making me giggle.

"He sounds like a sweetheart."

"He really is."

The silence stretched between us, but it didn't feel awkward.

"Claire?" He breathed out my name so quietly I almost didn't hear him.

"Yeah?"

"Thanks… for this. I felt a little crazy when it happened, especially since I was supposed to meet you. I didn't want you to think I stood you up. I would never do that. Not with you."

I winced, the guilt gnawing at me for ghosting him back then. "I can't imagine how upsetting this was for you." A quiet laugh escaped my lips. "Bandit's not even mine, and I want to kick that guy and his dog in the balls."

"You and me both."

There was some muffled speaking before Edison came back to the phone. "Hey, I need to go. I'll talk to you later and tell you how it goes."

"Sure. Good luck. I'm sorry about Bandit. Give him a smooch for me."

Chuckling, he said, "Will do... Bye."

"Sure. Good luck. I'm sorry about Bandit. Give him a smooch for me."

Chuckling, he said, "Will do... Bye."

83

Chapter 10 -Edison

Edison trailed the vet tech, his footsteps heavy with worry, into an empty exam room and flopped down in a chair for another round of waiting. Again. He let out a long sigh, the knot pulling tighter in his stomach. He reached for a magazine, the words blurring before his eyes.

A smile flashed across his face. Talking with her had calmed his frazzled nerves after Bandit had been injured. Missing their date had been the least of his concerns, but the pang of regret was still a dull ache in his chest.

An eternity later, the vet walked in, followed by the vet tech and a hesitant Bandit, his head wrapped in several layers of purple self-stick bandage wrap. Seeing Edison, his tail thumped a fast rhythm on the tile floor. He lunged forward with a burst of energy, his injuries doing little to stop his exuberant tail wag. Edison met him halfway, rubbing along Bandit's rump, offering a familiar comfort.

The vet extended his hand, offering a reassuring smile, "Mr. Wright, Bandit's going to be fine. His injuries were minor." As the vet continued, Edison released a pent-up breath he hadn't realized he was holding, "He needed some stitches in his ear, which will need to be removed in about ten days." Edison nodded as Bandit, feeling emboldened, peeked out from under Edison's chair. "His face looks worse than it is. We cleaned it up as best we could. The scratches might leave scars. " Edison winced. "Keep them clean while they heal over the next few weeks. When your vet removes the stitches, have them check his muzzle."

"Thank you. I'm glad it's not as bad as I thought." Edison paused and looked at Bandit again before raising his eyebrows at the vet. "Was the other dog injured at all?"

Pursing his lips, he shook his head, "Didn't have a scratch on him." He tilted his head and gave Edison a pointed look. "But I would caution against dog parks. I don't take my dogs simply because of owners like.... like that."

"Yeah." Edison grimaced and nodded.

"They'll have your discharge papers at the front desk."

Coaxing Bandit out from under the chair, Edison gently slipped the harness on, avoiding Bandit's ear and muzzle. His stomach twisted as he opened the door. Was that guy out there? He pushed the door open, his eyes darting around the waiting room as he headed to the desk. But it was empty. Relief crept in as he walked to the desk to check out.

At home, he pressed a pain pill into a hunk of cheddar as Bandit watched warily. Edison grabbed his takeout bag of tacos and a glass of water before settling Bandit on the bed. He carefully climbed into bed himself, sitting up against the headboard. Bandit snuggled against Edison's leg and fell asleep as Edison flipped through the TV channels as he ate.

Mindlessly flipping the channels, his eyes kept

glancing at the clock, wondering if it was too late to text her. It was nearly ten o'clock. Would she be up? Would she mind if he called? Edison pulled up her number, typing out a quick message.

Edison: Still awake?

He set the phone down, finishing his last taco while only half paying attention to a home builder show, eyes sliding to his phone every few seconds. A moment later, while cleaning up the remnants of his late-night taco binge, her message popped up, warm and reassuring, erasing his doubts.

Claire: I'm up. How's Bandit? Everything go okay?

Warmth bloomed through him. She was still worried about his dog. He immediately dialed her number.

"Hi." She sounded tired, her drawl a little stronger, but there was a smile in her voice.

"Hey." The tension in his shoulders eased just hearing her voice. "Have an exciting night?"

She chuckled, "Just reading. Your night seemed a lot more exciting than mine."

"Nothing like breaking up a dog fight." He joked.

"Is he okay?" Her worry tugged at his heart.

Edison breathed out, "He's fine. He needed some stitches in his ear and had some scratches on his snout."

Her voice softened, "That poor baby. Give him some pets from me."

A wave of tenderness washed over him. "You're sweet. He's passed out on pain pills in my bed. I have to keep his face clean while the scratches heal, and he'll need to get his stitches out in a week or so.

Other than that, he's fine."

"That doesn't sound too bad." Relief was evident in her voice.

"Yeah. So..." His voice trailed off.

"So...?"

"I'm sorry I stood you up." He knew it was ridiculous but still felt guilty for not showing up.

"Oh." She was silent for a beat. "Don't worry about it. What could you do? I feel terrible for Bandit."

"I wanted to meet you tonight. I haven't connected with anyone like this in..." He murmured the last word. "...forever."

"Me too." They sighed at the same time.

Quietly, he asked, "Are you busy tomorrow?"

"I just have to work in the morning, but I'm free in the afternoon. But what about Bandit?"

He thought for a moment. "How would you feel about meeting both of us in the afternoon for ice cream at Sugar Rush? We could sit outside?"

She giggled. "They do have the best ice cream. And I'd love to meet Bandit."

"But not me?" He teased.

Teasing right back, she said, "As long as puppy cuddles are included."

They both laughed.

Edison asked, "What's your favorite flavor of ice cream?"

"I'm not sure I want to tell you. You might make fun of me." She said in a playful voice.

He feigned indignation, "I would never!" Then, he quipped out of the side of his mouth, "Unless it's vanilla."

"How dare you, sir!" Her fake English accent amused him. "Vanilla is far superior."

"Hmm..." He let out a chuckle. His voice dipped an

octave, teasing and playful, "Is it really vanilla?"

A light and airy laugh tinkled from her lips, "No, I was kidding."

He laughed, startling Bandit, who gave him the stink eye before sighing and closing his eyes again.

Edison put his arm behind his head.

"Don't get me wrong. It's good, especially vanilla bean, but it's not my favo-"

"Wait! Let me guess it!"

"Okay."

He chuckled mischievously and said, "I'm getting a strong vibe of Unicorn Sparkle with sprinkles. Am I onto something here?"

Her cheeks flushed a hint of nervousness in her giggle. "I don't think I've ever had unicorn as an ice cream flavor."

Remembering her notes, he asked, "Hmm…what about cookie dough?"

"Excellent guess! I do like cookie dough, but my favorite is… bubblegum." She chuckled nervously. "Is that weird? I tend to love kid flavors like grape soda, cotton candy, and, most of all, bubblegum ice cream. 'Childish' as my ex liked to say."

He let out a breathy laugh and looked at the dog, hoping he wasn't waking him again. "Well, I guess I'm a little childish, too, because I love flavors like that. I'm not a big fan of fancy ice creams full of nuts or weird add-ins. My favorite is root beer float."

"Oh, that sounds delicious."

"Yeah. Sugar Rush is one of the few that makes all their ice cream in-house. They have all kinds of crazy flavors, and their root beer float ice cream is so good. We could share? Tomorrow? 4 o'clock?"

"I'd love to."

They sat in a quiet silence for a moment. Neither felt the need to say anything. Neither wanted to hang up. Then, Bandit let out the loudest snore Edison had ever heard. They both laughed.

"Sorry about that." He muttered, "Must be the pain pill."

"I figured." She yawned. "He's had a horrible day, the poor little guy."

"He's not a little guy." He gently patted Edison. "This big boy takes over half my king-size bed. He'd probably try to sleep on top of you."

She didn't say anything. He winced, worried he'd offended her at what he had just said. "I'm sorry. I probably shouldn't have said that. I wasn't—"

She breathed out a quiet laugh. "No, it's fine. I wouldn't mind... sleeping in your bed."

"Yeah?"

She murmured, "Yeah."

He let the silence fall between them again, imagining things he probably shouldn't.

She yawned again as he gave Bandit a gentle pat. "You sound sleepy, so I'll let you go and..." He swallowed, "thanks for being on the other end of the line tonight."

"Anytime." She said quietly, "I'm looking forward to meeting you and Bandit tomorrow."

"Me too." He murmured. "Good night, Claire."

"Sleep tight, Edison."

He set the phone down on the nightstand, clicking the TV off. Staring at the ceiling, his mind went straight to memories of Claire in his bed back then. He imagined her in his bed right now, against his chest, his arms wrapped around her. His pulse quickened, desperately hoping the connection he felt would still be there tomorrow.

Chapter 11 - Claire

Letting out a long sigh, I sagged against the seat of my car after work. As one of the newbie librarians, I worked most weekends in an endless monotony of re-shelving, dusting, and reorganizing books. But today had been a whirlwind of chaos. Shortly after opening, the library was plunged into near darkness with a massive power outage—the only light filtering from the wall of windows along the front of the building. I don't know what we would have done without our phone flashlights illuminating the labyrinth of shelves.

Thankfully, our patrons were great. They embraced the old-school experience, using their phone lights and requesting books I found solely from memory. We had to be creative and use paper forms to check out books.

I was so busy that I didn't have time to even think about seeing Edison and Bandit this afternoon until I was on my way home. A nervous flutter took root in my belly as I pulled into the parking lot of my apartment complex, but it gave way to an edgy anticipation. Maybe it was all that talking we did last night.

Walking in the door, I tossed my things on the

entry table and headed for the shower. Under the hot spray, I could only think I hadn't seen him in almost eight years. What if I was wrong, and it wasn't him? Please let this be him. Of course, it was him.

I was driving myself insane with the what-if game. What if I hadn't said yes to Pete? What if I had kept that date with Sonny? Where would I be right now? Where would *we* be right now? Married? Kids?

Even my hair seemed to hum with nervous energy, defying every attempt to tame it with mousse. I was vibrating with a nervous energy I hadn't felt in a long time, maybe since we first met. Out of the shower, I hesitated, eyeing the dress from last night. Something drew me to it as I ran my hand down the silky fabric, a silent whisper echoing, "It's meant to be." A second chance to rewrite our ending. It was so close. Taking one more look in the mirror, my hair a wild mane of damp curls, I glanced at the phone, hoping there was enough time to let it air dry.

I got to the square with 10 minutes to spare since parking was never guaranteed. It looked like everyone was downtown this sunny afternoon as I circled like a vulture for what felt like an eternity. Finally, a spot opened up two blocks away.

I hoped the walk to Sugar Rush would chase away some of my nerves. But my stupid inner monologue screamed every possible way this could go wrong. Was this really a good idea? Doubt gnawed at me. What was I doing? Another panicked thought ran through my mind. Was I supposed to call him Sonny or Edison? I reminded myself — what if... what if this turned out to be something amazing? A smile tugged at the corner of my lips. Taking a calming breath, I focused on the sunshine warming my face, the melody of laughter drifting around the square, and the possibility of what this could be. My eyes automatically began to search for a golden glint of hair and a Boxer dog.

A wave of deja vu crashed over me when I spotted him from behind. He was half a block away, his back turned towards me, but there was no mistaking him. He sat at one of the colorful metal tables outside Sugar Rush, a brown dog curled beneath it.

Edison, clad in a blue long-sleeve t-shirt, was nestled in a chair, his posture loose and easygoing, sleeves pushed up, revealing muscular, tanned forearms dusted with golden hair. He leaned back, turning his head slightly, showing his profile, sunlight glinting red and gold off his beard. He was even more handsome than memory, setting off a swarm of butterflies in my belly. As I came up diagonally, I saw his ankle resting casually on his knee, my book on the table before him. His grin flashed before I reached his side, his phone screen showcasing a familiar conversation—ours. The flutters in my belly had morphed into a full-blown hurricane.

Taking a deep breath, I swallowed the nervous giggle threatening to escape. This had to be a dream. There he was, tangible and real, bathed in the afternoon sun. With a surge of courage, I approached.

"Sonny?" I ventured, hesitantly voicing the name that had haunted my memories. "You're... Edison?" His name slipped out on a breathless sigh.

There was a hitch in his breath, a shift in his posture—his head turned, his eyes rising to meet mine. He stood, towering over me. His eyes flashed with surprise before melting into soft recognition. Up close, he looked a little older and a little more rugged, with lines at the corners of his eyes, but with that gentle boyish charm, I remembered. I liked the beard—a lot. The thought of running my hand across his cheek sent a flutter of heat through me.

My breath caught in my throat, and I instinctively put my hand on the table. His eyes. I had forgotten their captivating blend of green, gold, and blue. They were full of warmth, hope, and a spark of something else. A memory hit me, and I saw the two of us lying side by side, his eyes holding mine. The intensity was almost too much, forcing me to avert my gaze. Did he notice the flush rising to my cheeks?

I craned my neck to see the warm smile spread across his face. "Claire?"

I nodded, unable to speak.

His voice softened, "I had hoped it was you." There was a twinkle of amusement in his eyes as his head dipped down. "It's been ages since anyone's called me Sonny except my sister. When I became a professor, I felt like I needed to drop the nickname, so I started going by my full name. But..." His smile widened, revealing his dimples. He nodded and blinked slowly. "Sonny is fine."

He pulled out the chair next to him and gestured for me to sit. We sank into our seats, eyes meeting in a wordless conversation. Stupid smiles stretched across both our faces. His mirrored the disbelief buzzing through me as his Adam's apple bobbed. Was this really happening? Time seemed to stand still in this tiny bubble, stretching into an eternity.

I needed to confess the regret I'd been holding onto for years. Looking down, his hands rested on the table, so I gently placed my hand over his. Searching his eyes, my smile dropped as I let out a pent-up breath.

"I'm sorry I disappeared on you all those years ago," my voice trembled slightly as I blinked back tears. "I regretted it so much. I was trapped on the path I had chosen, but I always wondered and wanted..."

He looked down at the table, clenching his jaw, a muscle ticking at the corner of his mouth. The air hung heavy with his silence, but I didn't stop, hoping it wasn't too late.

"When I saw you in the parking lot the other day, I didn't recognize you with the beard." My other hand instinctively rose to caress his cheek, a smile playing on my lips as the coarseness of it grazed my fingertips. "Sonny...," I breathed out his name.

"Funny," he murmured, "I thought I saw a ghost that night." He looked up, his eyes locked on mine, shimmering with unspoken questions. But almost imperceptibly, something shifted. He leaned into my touch, eyelids fluttering closed for a fleeting moment.

"Later, I realized who you were, and I was suddenly flooded with memories from that weekend."

When he opened his eyes, there was a glint of shared understanding, and the corners of his mouth tugged up in a secret smile like we were sharing an inside joke. It was as if he knew every part of the movie replaying in my head from all those years ago.

"That same night, I found this." He reached over, grabbing my book.

None of this felt real, and I shook my head. "When I saw your post, and you signed your name, I had hoped..." My voice was thick, "The whole time we were emailing and texting, I kept hoping, afraid to ask. I wanted it to be you so badly."

His expression softened, his hand turned over, his fingers enveloping mine, cradling my hand to his heart. His voice, thick with emotion, rumbled with sincerity, "Claire, I lost a part of my heart when you disappeared. I've searched for you for a long time."

Tears welled up in my eyes, blurring his face. "Can we try again?" I whispered, my voice catching with vulnerability. "Is it too late for a second chance?"

His grip gently tightened, his eyes filled with tenderness that touched my soul. "It's not too late."

He tilted his head, a crooked smile revealing his dimples. A warmth bloomed in my chest and spread like wildfire. "There's nothing I want more." He murmured, his voice full of emotion.

Relief washed over me, tears streaming down my face. He hauled my chair closer to him, wrapping me in his embrace. His other hand gently brushed away my tears as he guided my head to his shoulder. We were content to exist in the quiet comfort of each other.

I closed my eyes, inhaling the scent of citrus and sandalwood that clung to him. Memories rushed back to me—days searching for that same intoxicating scent in countless stores, a futile attempt to hold onto a piece of him, even though I had been the one to let go. Now, enveloped in his warmth, I wanted to drown in it, taste his kisses, feel the scratch of his beard against me—it was all-consuming.

A warm slobbery nudge against my knee startled me. A choked giggle escaped through my sniffles as I peeked under the table.

"Is this Bandit?"

He was a fawn-colored Boxer dog with white

markings down the center of his face and the tip of his tail. There were no bandages, but I could see a small row of stitches on his right ear and two angry red scratches on the right side of his muzzle. He showered my knee with puppy kisses, and a sound like a purr came out.

Sonny chuckled, leaning over and giving him a pat on his rump. "The one and only. He's still groggy from the pain meds, but he's a sweet boy."

After sniffing my hand, Bandit immediately put his front paws in my lap, and I couldn't help but bury my face in his neck and snuggle him. Avoiding his injuries, I rubbed his chest and back. "Aren't you the cutest? Yes, you are. Yes, you are!" The more I rubbed him, the crazier his tail wagged.

Sonny grinned and shook his head. "My dog might like you better than me after that greeting."

A giggle escaped as I flashed him a playful smile. "Watch out, I might just take him home with me."

Sonny's eyes filled with delight, and his smile widened. He leaned close, his playful eyes locked onto mine, and whispered, "I was hoping I'd get the chance to steal your heart first."

My eyes widened, our lips mere inches apart. I couldn't tear my eyes away from him, desperately wanting to kiss him. "He's pretty irresistible. But..." I felt my cheeks heating up as I said softly, "I wouldn't mind that."

He cocked an eyebrow, flashing me a devilish smile, and cleared his throat, gesturing towards the doors, "Ready for ice cream?"

I nodded before blurting out, "What about Bandit?" My concern was etched on the sweet, floppy-eared guy under the table whose gaze was fixed on me.

"He'll be fine. I knotted his leash to the table, and

we'll leave your book to mark our spot."

I raised my eyebrows, looking at Bandit, "You're sure?" I glanced at the book, wondering if it might walk off again.

He nodded, a confident glint in his eyes. "Trust me. He'll be fine."

With a final "Stay" command to Bandit, Sonny reached for my hand. His touch sent a thrill through me as his fingers intertwined with mine, guiding me toward the door.

My heart skipped a beat as I stepped through and felt his hand brush against the small of my back. A shiver danced down my spine as I looked back to meet his gaze. And there it was, that crooked smile I had missed so much, the one that sent butterflies fluttering in my belly. But there was something else there, too—a promise of something sweeter, something deeper, just for me, and I couldn't wait.

Chapter 12 - Edison

As they got in line, Edison clenched his fists, digging them into his pockets to stop the urge to constantly reach out and touch her. They were finally together again, a dream he'd held onto for far too long. Every detail about her - the freckles dancing across her sun-kissed shoulders, the echo of her melodic laughter, the lingering sweetness of her scent - flooded his senses. A yearning he couldn't ignore coiled in his stomach, a desperate need to touch her, feel the warmth of her skin.

His mind drifted to holding her close, tracing the outline of her smile with his fingertips, maybe even stealing a kiss somewhere out of the way. With her near, the world seemed brighter and lighter, his breathing easier. But the memories of her disappearing without a trace still haunted him. The very thought of it happening again ripped at his heart.

Both Claire and the girl behind the counter were looking at him expectantly.

"Sorry, I was just..." He wasn't sure where to take that.

"You still wanted root beer float, right?" Claire asked, giving him a shy smile as she tucked a stray curl behind her ear.

He blinked a few times to clear his thoughts, nodding as he looked at Claire and then the girl. "Yeah. In a waffle cone, please."

"And for you?" The girl asked Claire.

Edison caught Claire's eyes darting around the room before lowering her voice to a whisper. "A scoop of bubblegum in a sugar cone, please," she said, her cheeks red.

He lifted his eyes from the wall of ice creams, unable to mask the smile tugging at the corners of his lips as he chuckled softly.

She met his gaze, amusement and a little vulnerability in her eyes. "I know it's ridiculous. Who cares what ice cream I like? But it would be easier to order if I had kids."

He shrugged, remembering that his thoughts went right to their future together just minutes after meeting her the first time. Now, he had a vision of two little girls: a blond one with Claire's freckles holding her hand and the younger one, a redhead with bouncing curls, on his hip as they chose ice cream flavors. The desire hadn't faded, but this time, it felt grounded, more real than it ever had.

Without thought, he wrapped his arm around her waist and pulled her toward him, tucking her unruly hair under his chin. She pulled back just enough to look up at him with the corner of her mouth hitching upwards. He hadn't even realized what he was doing until she was against him. He held his breath as she folded herself back into him, snuggling even closer while they waited for their ice cream. The moment she relaxed, settling into him, Edison sighed, feeling as if everything was finally falling into place.

Before stepping back outside, Edison snagged a sample spoon. Claire playfully grabbed it from his hand, smiling, "Bandit looks like he could use a little treat."

Returning to their table, they found Bandit sprawled peacefully beneath it and her book still on the table. But the moment Claire sat down, he popped up as if he'd never been asleep, tail wagging furiously. The big flirt nudged his head into her lap, begging.

She rewarded him with gentle pets down his neck, giving him tiny bites of ice cream on the sample spoon. "You're the sweetest, most handsome boy ever!" Bandit lapped it up, and each affectionate pat spread warmth through Edison's chest.

Edison hadn't had a relationship in a long while, but since rescuing Bandit a couple of years ago, he'd wondered how the dog would react to someone in his life. Bandit seemed utterly smitten with Claire, forgetting Edison even existed. He watched, a smile slowly spreading across his face as Claire encouraged Bandit's bad habits, cooing over his clumsy attempts to climb into her lap. Finally, unable to resist any longer, Edison chuckled and gently issued a "down" command.

Long after their ice cream was finished and Bandit snored quietly under the table, Edison and Claire lingered, their conversation flowing easily as if it hadn't been years since they were together. The question of why she disappeared hung between them. He was afraid to ask, not wanting to mess up the blossoming connection growing between them.

That warmth continued to bloom through him as he watched her, the way she talked with her hands fluttering around as she told him stories about her life, the way she wrinkled her freckled nose before she laughed. Her smile could light up a room, and those crazy curls of hers went wild every time she moved her head. It suddenly hit him hard how much he had missed this.

He wanted to touch her again, but he held back. Instead, he savored the moments, memorizing her.

Edison cleared his throat, "Can I ask you something about this book?"

Claire opened it, running her fingers over the handwritten notes. She looked up at him, her gaze catching his. "Sure. What'd you want to know?"

"I remember you mentioning you left it in a car?" He gave her a questioning look.

"Yeah. I left it in a rideshare of all places. I don't even know how it fell out of my bag. When I was out of the car, I saw it on the backseat floor as the guy drove away. It makes no sense." She smiled as she shook her head.

He watched her curls bounce, wishing to run his fingers through them. Would they still feel as soft as they did before? As the breeze rushed over them, he caught her scent, the same comforting sweetness, like a mixture of brown sugar and vanilla. His dick twitched, and he shifted in his seat.

Edison inclined his head. "I don't think I told you where I found it."

Claire's eyes widened. She leaned forward, waiting with a quizzical look. "I just assumed you found it in the same car I had been in?"

"Not even close." He shook his head. "It was under the carts outside the grocery store on University Drive." He gave the book a wary look. "I was getting one, and it wouldn't budge because it was stuck on something. The book was wide open when I looked, pages flipping in the wind, under the carts."

Claire gasped. "How did it even get there?"

Edison shook his head. "I have no idea, but when I saw all the handwritten notes inside, I couldn't just leave it there."

Claire's face softened, and she gave him a grateful smile.

"I had to crawl under the carts, laying on my belly to grab it."

Edison laughed as he acted out the belly crawl over the table. He dramatically rolled his eyes with his head and said, "That's not even the craziest part of my story."

Claire gave him a confused look as she leaned closer. "What do you mean?"

Just as Edison was about to tell her about the disappearing note, someone on a bike sped by, slowing just briefly to grab Claire's purse right off the table in front of them.

Claire immediately stood up and looked at Edison, who was utterly shocked. "That guy just stole my purse!"

Edison jumped up at the same time, turning and yelling, "Hey! Come back here, motherfucker!" He looked over at Claire and said, "Be right back." He took off in a sprint after the thief.

The biker rounded the next corner, and Edison wasn't far behind. He ran nearly daily, so it wasn't a stretch, but he lost the guy after six blocks. Disappointed, he slowed to a stop, hands on his knees, catching his breath before he turned and jogged back to the square.

When he returned to the table, he was out of breath and sweaty, and his shirt was soaked.

She stood up, dropping Bandit's head off her lap and grabbing Edison's forearm. "Are you okay?"

His heart was beating fast, but he felt it kick up more from her touch. His hands were on his hips, and he was heaving air. He nodded before saying, "Let me…catch my…breath, and…" He took a deep breath in. "We'll call the police."

"Are you sure you're okay?" She looked so worried, searching his eyes.

He nodded as his breathing slowed, but she disappeared into Sugar Rush before returning with some water for him. Edison finished it, crumpling the cup and tossing it on the table as he paced back and forth, taking a deep breath. Pulling out his phone, he sat down to call the police. Claire sat with him with Bandit's head resting in her lap, nosing her hand. She sighed, looking more resigned when Edison told her it would take at least 30 minutes for an officer to arrive.

Resting her head in her palm, she said, "What am I going to do? I had everything in that purse—my phone, keys, wallet… my life."

"I'm so sorry. What can I do to help?"

She looked over at him as she slumped back in the chair. Her eyes were wide, rimmed in red. "I honestly have no idea. This has never happened to me before. I don't know how I'll get my car home or even get into my apartment."

He took her hand, running his thumb over her knuckles reassuringly. "Don't worry. It'll work out." A smile half hopeful, half genuine bloomed on his face. "Are you hungry? Can I take you to dinner, and we'll figure it out together?" He was famished, but he'd rather starve than let this end on a sour note.

A hint of a smile shined through her tears as she sniffed, "I'd like that."

He laced their fingers together, bringing her hand to his lips, and kissed it. He lifted his eyes to hers, seeing some of that stress melting away into heat and desire. He didn't want to let go.

Chapter 13 - Claire

After talking with the police officer, I went with Sonny to his house to drop off Bandit. Riding beside him, I ran my hand along his truck's well-worn tan leather bench seat, watching him drive. I wondered if this was the same one he took me home in years ago.

His home was exactly what I imagined when I thought of him. A tiny bungalow just a few blocks off the square. It was dark wood with big, beautiful trees all over his property. A subtle blend of leather and citrus with sandalwood wafted through the air as we walked in the door, and I wanted to pick up a throw pillow and inhale deeply.

His home was a drastic change from when we first met. Back then, it was a studio apartment decorated like someone just starting out—stark and cheap. But this place was what I imagined a college professor's home would be like—neat, minimal, and bookshelves everywhere. My eyes took it all in, especially the books. I walked right up to the nearest bookshelf. Several shelves were full of fantasy and sci-fi. He had an entire shelf dedicated to Brendan Cross's hugely popular spy thrillers. I was surprised, but who was I to judge? I read smutty romance like it was going out of style.

He took Bandit down the hallway, shutting a door. A moment later, he returned, his eyebrows raised.

"Ready?"

As we drove away, he caught my eye and grinned, picking up my hand across the seat and rubbing his thumb across my knuckles. A shiver ran through me. Did he know what his touch did to me? Watching the road, one corner of his mouth hitched up like he was lost in thought.

He said, "I'm glad we found each other again. It feels like a twist of fate, doesn't it?"

I hedged, a smile playing on my lips, "I don't know. It almost feels like the universe is up to something."

He chuckled, glancing at me. "When can I see you again?" His eyes quickly darted back to the road.

I blushed as my grin widened. I played it coy, "When are you free?"

He looked back over at me, an eyebrow cocked. "What about Tuesday?"

My smile widened. He was just as eager as I was.

"Lucky you." I tilted my head, still smiling, "Tuesday is my day off. I work a lot of weekends at the library. A few Saturdays from now, I have a superhero escape room for the teens at the library." I twirled a curl, looking over at him. "I'm going to dress up like Belladonna Nightshade."

"Really?" His gaze darted back to me, eyebrows shooting up. "Have you done other escape rooms?"

I took a deep breath, relaxing into the seat. "I love scavenger hunts and escape rooms. Those are a few things I plan for the teens at the library."

"Is it always just for kids? Or can adults come, too?"

"Unfortunately, it's just for kids." I looked over at him. "Why? You want to escape my room?"

He cracked a smile as he glanced at me before his eyes went back to the road. "I wouldn't mind being trapped in it... but I'd love to come see it all, especially Belladonna Nightshade."

"Well, you could come before it starts... to check it all out?"

He grinned, "I wouldn't miss it."

I smiled, "Really?"

"Yeah, I love escape rooms."

"I'm excited for you to see it. It's going to be something! The teen room will be decorated like supervillain lairs, and some library staff will be in superhero or supervillain costumes. It's the biggest one I've created so far."

He gave me a wicked grin. "I'm looking forward to it. I don't want to miss getting tangled with some poisonous plants." He wiggled his eyebrows.

We stopped at a little Thai place and discussed what I should do. I realized I had given Darci a key to my apartment a few months ago. After dinner, I called her, hoping she was home.

"Ugh, Darci, you wouldn't believe it," I hissed. "Right outside the ice cream place, my purse was stolen."

Darci's laugh crackled through the phone. "You sure the dog didn't grab it off the table?"

I chuckled nervously, flicking my eyes to Sonny staring out the windshield, looking lost in thought.

I scoffed, "No, seriously, it was..." My voice trailed off when I felt a warm touch brush against my hand resting on the seat.

Sonny, still focused on the road, had reached over, his fingers brushing mine in a silent gesture of comfort. A jolt went through me, a strange current of something I couldn't explain. My breath hitched, the stolen purse momentarily forgotten.

"Hang on, Darci," I mumbled breathlessly.

"Hello? Are you still there?"

I didn't answer. I couldn't answer as the city lights became a shimmering kaleidoscope out the window. Sonny's touch was like a warm anchor in the chaos.

"Actually," I finally managed, my voice thick, "my spare key?" The sentence hung unfinished, lost in the sudden rush of the intense heat blooming in my chest.

"Claire? Everything okay?" Darci's voice was laced with concern.

I cleared my throat, forcing my gaze from Sonny's hand back to the road. The burn in my chest receded into a faint tingle and a confusing knot of emotions. I winced, thinking about all I needed to do with my purse gone — credit cards, a new phone, spare keys, new locks. The tasks were endless. The police officer told us things like this rarely get recovered.

"Uh, yeah," I lied, my voice back to its usual tone. "Just… lost my train of thought for a second. Listen, can you find the spare keys I gave you?"

"No worries, Smitten Kitten. I know exactly where they are."

I forced a laugh. "Thanks, you're a lifesaver. We'll be there soon."

I hung up, the phone feeling heavy in my hand. I stole a glance at Sonny, who was now focused back on the road. His hand was back on the steering wheel, but the phantom warmth lingered on my skin. What on earth had just happened?

He shifted in his seat, meeting my eyes. "Everything okay?"

"Yeah," I replied, my voice a touch breathless.

My purse felt like a distant memory, another lifetime. Instead, there was a sharp awareness, the thought of this night ending, his truck pulling away, him leaving me behind. It felt... wrong.

When we got to the parking lot, Sonny hopped out and rushed to my door to open it. It was so sweet and old-fashioned, and I loved it.

Taking my hand to help me out of the truck, I asked him, "Do you want to come up to meet Darci?"

He grinned, "Of course. I'd love to meet her."

We intertwined our fingers like we did this every day and walked towards Darci's building.

He smirked, "It's always important to make a good impression with the best friend."

I grinned as we climbed the stairs, suddenly feeling very nervous. We stopped on the landing, and he squeezed my hand, encouraging me to keep walking. We stopped in front of her door, and I looked over at him, my brow slightly wrinkled. Why was I so nervous?

"Deep breaths, beautiful. I'm right here with you."

I took a breath, and just as soon as I knocked on her door, Darci yanked it open with a giant glass of wine in one hand. "What the hell happen-" She stopped mid-sentence when she saw Sonny behind me, opening and closing her mouth like a fish. I couldn't remember the last time she was speechless.

Sonny took a step up next to me, "Hi? You must be Darci?"

I cleared my throat. I motioned toward him. "This is Edison."

She stepped back, indicating for us to come inside, "Come in, come in!"

We followed her to the kitchen. She held out her hand, her voice turning to honey. "It's very nice to meet you. I've heard a lot about you."

He chuckled, his eyes full of amusement, sliding to mine as he shook her hand. "The pleasure is all mine."

Her smile widened, still shaking his hand slowly. "You are quite the Viking, aren't you?"

He shook his head as his cheeks pinked. "I don't know about all that."

I didn't need to look in a mirror to know a flush was creeping up my neck, "Really, Darci?"

She dropped his hand and looked at me, "What?"

I rolled my eyes as I tried to steer the conversation to something else. "Did you find my spare key?"

She ignored me, still sizing up Sonny. I loudly cleared my throat, arching an eyebrow. She glanced at me. "What?... oh yeah." She slid my key out of her pocket. "Here you go."

I took it from her, realizing it was attached to a keychain.

"Um, Darci? What in the world is this?" I held up the keychain, my eyebrows nearly at my hairline. It was a little stick man with both middle fingers raised. When I hazarded a glance at Sonny, his lips were pressed together like he was trying not to laugh.

She chuckled. "Someone gave it to me years ago, and it reminded me of you."

I raised my eyebrows and put my hand to my chest. "Me?"

"Don't you remember that night we went to the Taylor Swift rave at Andy's?"

I twisted my lips. "Vaguely. Why?"

She arched an eyebrow. "Do you remember how drunk you got from all the Swiftie themed drinks we tried? I think you had like six Midnight Rains."

I could feel the flush crawling up my neck as I darted my eyes at Sonny. He looked at me expectantly.

"What does that have to do with this keychain?"

"Well," her smile stretched a mile wide, "You, my darling, started flipping everyone off while you were dancing. I had to drag you out of there before you got in a fight with some girl in a sequin mini dress who was ready to throw down with you."

I could feel the heat in my cheeks as I crossed my arms. "Hilarious, Darci." But the corner of my mouth twitched. Trying desperately to hold my ground, I narrowed my eyes, but that twitch grew as I fought the tiny, traitorous smile tugging at my lips. Before I knew it, a strangled snort escaped my mouth, and my cheeks heated even more.

I glanced at Sonny, a big grin on his face, "Sounds like you had one wild night. Flipping people off at a Swiftie rave? What a rebel!"

I doubled over laughing.

Darci wiped the tears from her eyes, "Now that we've both made a terrible impression on Edison, go make sure this key works."

I pocketed it and leaned forward, whispering to Darci, "I'll be back." Her eyes darted between Sonny and me, a ghost of a smile on her lips as she nodded.

Sonny, still chuckling, extended his arm. "Lead the way, wild child. Just promise to keep your middle fingers to a minimum."

I linked my arm through his and smiled. "No promises, but I'll try."

As we crossed the parking lot, she shouted from her door, "Don't do anything I wouldn't do!" Looking up, her smirk was a mile wide. I rolled my eyes at Sonny as we headed to my apartment.

Walking up the steps, a knot formed in my belly.

When I left today, I hadn't even considered the possibility we'd come back here. I wasn't the tidiest person, and for the life of me, I couldn't remember how messy my apartment was. I just knew we would walk in, and a bra might be hanging off the couch.

I inserted the key, praying it would work, and quickly unlocked the door, flinging it open to scan the room before Sonny came in. Surprisingly, everything was in its place, and there was no laundry in sight as I flicked the lights on.

I watched Sonny take in my space, scanning my bookshelf before walking over to a painting on the wall. It was from one of those paint-and-sip places. Mine had come out pretty good since I was the designated driver for the night. On the other hand, Darci's painting looked like a child had painted it.

Looking back at me, he pointed at the painting. "Let me guess….Hogwart's Castle as Starry Night?"

I laughed. "Yeah. How did you know?"

He walked over to me, so close I had to crane my neck to look up at him. "My sister is addicted to those paint-and-sip places." He chuckled quietly, "We go every year for her birthday."

Heat radiated off him, warming me. I murmured, "That sounds like a fun birthday."

A hesitant smile, barely a whisper, played at my lips. The closer we got, the more my excitement tangled with fear, leaving me breathless and trembling. I knew he wanted to kiss me, and while I wanted it, too, I was terrified.

He put his hands on my hips and pulled me gently toward him. I came willingly, pressing myself firmly against him, my hands on his chest.

His voice was rough, "It always is." He looked at my mouth, and all I could do was lick my lips, the anticipation building in my belly. He purred, "I've wanted to kiss you all day."

The air around us crackled with electricity. It had been years, but the attraction between us was just as magnetic, maybe even more potent than it had been. I glanced at his lips, my breath hitching.

The tension between us grew, and without a word, Sonny gently took my chin in both his hands. He leaned in slowly, his lips brushed against mine, a soft, tentative kiss. My heart pounded. His tongue parted my lips before tangling with mine. My hands twisted in his shirt, running over his arms, his shoulders, caressing the back of his neck. I couldn't get enough, so I wanted more. I nipped his bottom lip, and as if I'd pulled a trigger, he groaned and took my mouth like he owned it.

One of his hands slid down and wrapped around my waist, pulling me even tighter against him. Oh my. I felt his hardness between us. His other hand tilted my head, kissing down my neck to my collarbone. I moaned. A smoldering fire was building deep in my belly, and I could barely contain myself. My fingers worked down, trying to find my way underneath his shirt. I dipped my fingers into his waistband, a desperate need to feel his bare skin.

He slowly made his way back to my mouth. I savored the burn of his beard against my cheek, marking me. Another growl escaped him as soon as his mouth was back on mine, stoking my fire, and I let out a whimper. His fingers tangled into my curls as he deepened the kiss. I sucked his tongue into my mouth and swallowed his groan. Pulling his shirttail out, my hands ran under it, feeling his stomach, a light scattering of hair traveling up his belly to his chest. A feral part of me wanted to feel all of him, skin to skin.

Something snapped in my head, and I pulled my head back abruptly, removing my hands from under his shirt. My eyes popped open. We needed to stop this before it went too far. I wasn't ready for where this was headed or even confessing my embarrassing secret.

He instantly took a step back, searching my face. "Everything okay?" His eyes were still glazed with lust, but I could see the worry.

"I'm sorry." I gave him a shaky smile and took a deep breath. "I just… need to take things slow."

I avoided his gaze, looking down. I was never good at hiding my feelings. I had ached for him, for this, for years, and that kiss was a reminder of everything I dreamed about. I stole a hesitant glance, my gaze catching his, but all I saw was tenderness and longing shining back at me. He pulled me tight against him, resting his chin on my head.

"Don't apologize. I'm in no hurry."

We swayed to our own music, lost in the moment like we were the only two people in the world. I wanted him to be mine. I wanted to melt in his arms. I pulled back to look at him. That easy, crooked grin spread across his face, his dimples showing through his beard. I took a deep breath, forcing myself to let go of his warmth and that intoxicating scent that was wholly Sonny.

I raised my head, smiling up at him, patting his chest. "You better get home to that cute puppy before I steal him."

His hand covered mine as he smirked. "He may be cute, but I think I'm better at cuddling."

I shot him a playful smirk and purred, "Oh, I remember," before stepping back and opening the front door.

He leaned down and gave me a lingering kiss before stepping into the hallway. He started down the stairs before turning back, a playful glint in his eyes as he said, "Goodnight, Poppy."

I was startled at the nickname, remembering Fireflower Farms on our last day together. Memories from our picnic there ran through my mind as I stepped out into the hallway. My smile spread as I watched him get in his truck. He rolled down the window, looking over at me with a wide grin, giving me a quick salute as he drove off.

I glowed as I headed over to Darci's apartment, dying to tell her about my night. My stolen purse could wait until tomorrow.

Chapter 14 - Edison

Edison kept the windows down, letting the wind whip through his hair as he drove home. His mind whirled. He was crazy about her, like a shooting star chasing the moon, and couldn't keep the grin off his face. He had been floating on air this entire time and had no intention of coming down.

He played their date over and over in his head. When she first walked up, it simply took his breath away. His heart lurched when she called him by his childhood nickname. Every word she spoke, every glance she gave him, filled him with a hope he hadn't felt in years. The entire time they were together, all he could think about was how, somewhere, someone had finally granted the wish he'd been making for years.

Edison chuckled, recalling how worried he'd been that she wouldn't be the woman he so clearly remembered. But the moment he set eyes on her, those doubts disappeared. Her smile was as charming as ever, and she still had that infectious laugh. Her hair was longer, but those curls still defied gravity. From the moment she walked up, Edison's hands itched to touch her and hold her close.

The kiss they shared had been a revelation. Tasting her and feeling her soft curves ignited something in him. Their bodies spoke volumes, fitting together like puzzle pieces designed by the fates, like they'd never been separated. He'd tried to forget her. Years had passed, but something whispered that she was it for him. No one ever felt as right as Claire had in his arms.

He replayed their initial conversation, savoring the honesty, even if the reason for her past disappearance remained a mystery. Today had been a reset, erasing all that time apart and dropping them right back where they were supposed to be.

His street loomed up ahead, the darkness mirroring his turmoil as if a shadow lurked. He wanted to confess, needed to, but he couldn't bear the thought of another sudden heartbreaking goodbye. They teetered on the edge of something beautiful. If she disappeared again, it would truly break his heart. Could he risk it? He knew the truth had to come out, the truth he never confessed even back then. If he finally told her, would she still trust him? Or call him a liar? Vanish again? The uncertainty was crippling.

When he got out of his truck in the driveway, he stopped and looked up to take in the stars. Seeing a shooting star fly past, he did a double take and made a wish, hoping it had already come true.

Before getting ready for bed, he texted Claire goodnight, telling her how much he enjoyed spending time with her. He took off his shoes and let out a contented sigh, but he paced the room, too antsy and hyped up to sleep. Adrenaline and desire flowing through him, he stripped down and turned on the shower. The water was nearly scalding when he stepped into the stream as he slicked his hair back.

He pictured Claire standing before him as he caressed her wet curves, slowly washing her, kissing every inch of her. His eyes drifted to the fold-out bench against the back wall, and his blood heated, knowing it was the perfect height to taste her on his knees.

A bolt of heat rushed through him, and he was instantly hard. As he gripped the wall, jets cascading down his back, his mind soared with images of her. Her laughter echoed in his ears, sweeter than any song. He could almost see how her eyes shimmered, starlight melting into something molten.

He pressed his forehead to the cool tile. He couldn't stop thinking about her smile, the flush of her skin, the way it teased him, sending shivers down his spine. He needed her as he stroked himself over and over, feeling the coiling growing deep in his belly. His balls tightened as a groan escaped his lips with her name, exploding into his hand. He craved a different release, buried deep inside her, but for now, this would do.

A wave of exhaustion overcame him as he climbed into the bed and checked his phone, finding a text from Claire wishing him sweet dreams. He picked up her book, having asked her tonight if he could keep it a little longer. Truthfully, it wasn't the story that captivated him, but the possibility of more hidden messages, whispers about Claire and their connection.

He reread the quote about Claire from the store before slowly leafing through the book again, finding more notes written in the margins. Deeper in, someone had written upside down in the bottom margin. He didn't remember seeing it before. Was it hers? He cautiously flipped the book over to get a better look. It looked like a riddle... or a clue.

***

Chance encounters, a timeless reflection,
A moment reborn, defying detection,
Is it infinite love in a cosmic direction?
Or will it break apart a heart's protection?

Was this about him and Claire? A breath caught in his throat. The secret he'd kept could ruin them. He'd held it so long. He wanted to confess, but he didn't know how. Keyed up, he called his sister.

"Hey Mal," a hint of anticipation in his voice.

"Sonny! Did you find her?"

He chuckled. "You knew, didn't you?"

"Knew what?" He could hear her muffling a laugh.

"You knew it would work."

"You found her?"

"I don't know how, but it worked. We met up earlier today." His mind immediately went to Claire's smile, and he couldn't stop his own.

"How was it?"

"It was good. I can't believe I found her again." A flush went up his neck as he lowered his voice. "She told me she wanted another chance... at us."

"Sonny! I'm so happy for you! Tell me everything!"

"We talked all day yesterday and were going to meet last night until Bandit got hurt."

"What?"

"Yeah, a dog attacked him at the park. But he's okay, just some stitches in his ear." He relayed the whole story, from Bandit's injuries to the date he missed with Claire. "So we met up today."

Relishing every detail, he told Mallory everything except the stolen purse fiasco.

"I'm thrilled that you've found her again. She was

married? Why did it end?"

"Yeah, she was married." He sighed, "She hasn't outright said, but I get the impression he was... abusive."

She sucked in a breath. "Oh no..."

Edison clenched his jaw. "If I ever see that guy..."

Mallory's voice was nearly a whisper, "If that's true, she's still healing. Give her time."

"I know." He swallowed, "We're taking things slow." He sighed, "But Mal, I'm scared. I want this. I want her, but she disappeared last time."

"Do you know why?"

"Not really." Edison ran his hand through his hair as he took a breath. "You know how I told you it was a blind date? I let her mistake me for... her blind date." His voice cracked on the last words. He quickly said, "We just hit it off so well, and I never told her. We ended up spending the entire weekend together with plans to see each other again just a few days later, and that's when she just disappeared. I thought maybe she figured it out..." He trailed off.

"You did what?"

He winced, "Mallory... this was years ago. It's not like it just happened. I was at a coffee shop, and she sat down in my booth and thought I was whoever she was supposed to meet. And, well... I just went with it."

She snorted, "Holy shit! Edison Xavier Wright, I never would've expected you to do something like that." She was teasing him, but her voice was filled with genuine concern.

He muttered, "Yeah."

"I can't believe you did that!" She lowered her voice, "Are you ever going to tell her?"

That was the million-dollar question. He let out a

pent-up breath. "I want to. I just don't know how. I hate keeping this from her. I feel like a liar. But… would I lose her all over again?"

The air hung heavy with his confession.

"I don't know, bro. You should tell her, and the sooner, the better."

"I know." There was a beat of silence before Edison asked, "How's Devon?"

She sighed, "Who knows? He's just started a band with two guys he met here in Thailand. He's never home anymore."

"Well, that sucks. But you're okay?"

"I'm okay."

"You know, you can always come here."

"Seriously, I'm fine."

"I know, but you're my little sister. I'm always going to worry about you."

A yawn surprised him, and he suddenly felt drowsy, so they soon said goodbye.

In the darkness, he stared at the ceiling, his mind wandering to that strange note in the book before he drifted off into a dream with Claire sitting next to him in the truck, windows down, a smile on her face, and her curls blowing in the wind.

Chapter 15 - Claire

Darci's front door was open a crack as I knocked. Pushing it open, I found her on the couch, a bowl of chips in her lap and some fancy pink drink in her hand. Another full glass was on the coffee table, waiting for me.

She turned off the TV, looking over at me as she raised her eyebrows with a big smirk. "God, you're adorable. You practically have heart eyes right now." She patted the seat next to her, "Tell. Me. Everything."

I laughed as I kicked my flip-flops off and settled onto the couch with my feet tucked under me. She immediately handed me the drink. I took a sip and winced at the sweetness before setting it down.

Changing positions, she asked, "How in the hell did your purse get stolen?"

I sighed, taking another drink of the super-sweet cocktail. "Some guy on a bike just pedaled by and grabbed it while we were sitting outside Sugar Rush."

"That's crazy!"

I shrugged, "Sonny gallantly ran after him but couldn't catch the guy."

"Really?"

I nodded as I took a sip.

Darci sighed. "Damn. I bet he could throw you over his shoulder and run a few blocks without breaking a sweat."

I smirked.

Darci's eyes widened as she gasped, "Did you kiss him?" She leaned forward, waiting for me to answer.

"We did..." I took another sip and smiled into my glass, looking at her over the lip. I set it down as I let out a long sigh. "I had to slow it down. One minute we were kissing, and the next..." I felt my cheeks heating as I continued, "I found myself trying to pull his shirt off so I could run my hands up his body."

Darci nodded with a knowing smile. "I'm telling you. It's like riding a bike. You still know what to do."

"I know. It's just..." I looked down and felt the heat in my face.

"You're scared."

"I feel like a damn virgin."

She patted my leg as she hopped up to refill her drink. "But you remembered how to kiss him, didn't you?"

I had no idea how this tiny woman held her liquor so well. I was feeling tipsy from the three sips I took.

I giggled and nodded. "I did."

Sitting back down, she asked, "I'm guessing he remembered you?"

I smiled to myself, remembering it all. "We had *that* conversation as soon as I walked up to him."

"And how did it go?" Darci raised her eyebrows.

I shrugged, "Good. I cried." I picked up my glass and took another sip. "He said he'd been trying to find me for a long time."

Darci breathed out, "Wow… does Edison have a brother?"

I laughed. "I think he has a sister. I'm not sure."

"So then what happened?" Her eyes were wide.

I smiled, thinking back to this afternoon. "He practically wrapped himself around me in the ice cream parlor."

Darci pointed her drink at me. "You probably won't believe it, but that man is in love with you. It's written all over his face. He's probably been in love with you this whole time."

"It felt so right, you know? Like we picked up right where we left off, but at the same time, it also feels new." I blushed, feeling a mix of excitement and nervousness. Darci just grinned at me. "I just worry it's too fast. I want to be careful. Sonny and I are different people now." I sighed, "After everything with Pete, I don't want to rush into anything."

Darci's expression softened, and she reached out to hold my hand. "Just take your time. Listen to your heart. You deserve to be happy."

Finishing my drink, I squeezed Darci's hand and stood up.

"I've got to get home and deal with the fallout from my purse." I let out a sigh. "What a nightmare. Credit cards, my phone, keys, the bank—it's never going to end."

She shook her head, "I'm so sorry."

"Yeah." I opened her front door and said, "See you tomorrow."

The next day, the sun had barely peeked through my window when the first notification popped up. Sonny had sent me a playful GIF with a teasing caption that made me smile despite the early hour. With a chuckle, I fired back a retort before getting ready for the day.

After yesterday's power outage, work was a blur, filled with shelving books, answering emails, and creating my part of the monthly newsletter, but Sonny's messages kept me buzzing. As the day dragged on, his messages became bolder, laced with double entendres and suggestive emojis. A constant flush crawled up my neck towards my cheeks, and I'd steal glances around the library, imagining the whispers if anyone saw my replies to Sonny's daring texts.

Thankfully, my colleagues were blissfully unaware as I giggled at our conversations. He was a master of saucy teasing. His words painted vivid pictures in my mind, giving me one delicious thrill after another with each message.

Our words danced a fine line between playful and provocative, hinting at unspoken desires, keeping me on edge, and sending butterflies fluttering in my belly.

Every task I completed and every interaction I had with anyone was just a distraction from the indecent thoughts that consumed me. Heat swirled down to my core, and I constantly replayed that kiss we had yesterday, my fingers going to my lips. I wasn't sure how I could just go home alone tonight. How was it so effortless with Sonny? How did I ever think I could live without wanting someone this way?

I still felt that pull between us, even though we weren't anywhere near each other. It was wild that in just a few days, he had once again become such a source of comfort and excitement in my life, and the mere thought of being with him made my heart skip a beat.

When I got home, his texts had stopped since he

was teaching a class. My body vibrated with a deep need I hadn't felt in a long time. Each passing minute felt like an eternity. I had no desire to sleep after what we'd been doing all day. I started the shower, turning it as hot as possible, and shucked my clothes in a pile on the floor. Standing under the shower head, I tried to stop the thoughts racing in my mind. I reached up to pump body wash into my hands, rubbing it all over my arms, neck, and down my breasts, imagining Sonny here with me. I pumped more soap, washing down my abdomen between my thighs, letting the soap wash away as my core heated. My fingers ran down to my center, slipping inside and back again. I needed a release.

I grabbed the shower head and set it to the high-intensity massage setting. Spreading myself, I pulsed it between my legs and rode that wave to ecstasy, whispering his name like a prayer.

As I got into bed, not entirely satiated from my climax, I was drowsy, falling into sleep. My dreams that night brought us together, tangled in pale pink silk sheets, a recurring dream I had many times over the years. He caressed me, kissed me, and whispered something against my ear that I could never make out, no matter how hard I tried.

The following day, I woke up feeling this warmth about me as if he'd held me all night, but I was still puzzled over what he'd been telling me in the dream. Blinking a few times before realizing I was alone, I closed my eyes tightly, wishing to return to the dream, back to him. But it was hopeless.

I climbed out of bed and walked into my closet. I tensed, the warmth I'd felt shifting into a mix of fear and doubt that settled into my belly. In just a matter of days, Sonny was consuming me. Did I need to take a step back? Did I want to?

Chapter 16 - Edison

Edison wanted to take Claire somewhere special for their first official date, and he knew the perfect place —Matteo's. With the aromas of simmering sauces and roasted garlic, this place was just a few blocks from his home. It was nestled on the lower floor of a beautiful turn-of-the-century home that was now a bed and breakfast.

It was one of his favorite places. After he lost his parents, the owners, Tate and Noelle, had become like family to him. Tate was like a father to him, often taking him back to the lone booth in the kitchen, where Noelle would feed him plate after plate of homemade Italian food. Tate would settle in next to him, giving him advice, which usually was to find a good woman to settle down with. Edison looked forward to it and often walked over for dinner at least once a week.

He imagined Claire bathed in the glow of a candlelit table. Plates piled high between them with a home-cooked Italian meal. The menu offered no choices, just an abundance of deliciousness. Everything was served family-style, with bowls of pillowy ravioli, classic spaghetti, savory meatballs, crusty garlic bread, and more brought right to the table.

As he got ready, Edison realized it was as if he were bringing Claire home to meet his parents. Nerves fluttered in his stomach. He wanted this to be perfect after what happened at the ice cream shop.

He changed clothes six times before finally settling on a dark purple button-down shirt with a black undershirt. It stretched across his chest and arms but looked good. His mom used to tell him the green in his eyes glowed bright whenever he wore purple. He rolled his sleeves up, exposing his forearms, to look a little more casual, finishing with dark jeans and his favorite lace-up boots.

A nervous flutter replaced his heartbeat when he got to her door. The click of the lock, barely a sound, sent a tremor through him as though the earth had shifted. And then he saw her, and the world was whole again. There she stood, framed by the doorway, her curls like a halo of fire around her. Her radiant smile, mirroring his own, made him fall hopelessly under her spell. As their eyes met, his anxiety dissolved, replaced by a warm anticipation. Her hands fidgeted as she greeted him, and he wondered if she was feeling the same overwhelming feelings.

She was beautiful in jeans and a red flowy bohemian top that somehow made her dark blue eyes glow like sapphires. It was hard to look away. Her hair was half pulled up in a twist behind her head in some kind of clip that he wanted to pull off so he could run his fingers through her hair and kiss her senseless.

Inside her apartment, he couldn't keep his hands to himself. After they were practically sexting yesterday, he wanted her lips on his. He reached for her, wrapping her up in his arms. Her hands pressed against his chest, a seductive smile spreading across her face. Edison leaned down and gave her a long, lingering kiss before his hand slid down to hold hers, leading her outside. He knew they wouldn't be leaving her place tonight if he let himself take anything more. Instead, he leaned over, brushing his lips across hers again as he helped her into the truck's passenger side.

When they arrived at their destination, his heart kicked up again. This place was like another home for him. He wanted her to love it as much as he did, but mostly, he wanted Tate and Noelle to love her. Edison had never brought a girlfriend or date, but Claire... He knew she was more than that. Usually, he came alone, but on a rare occasion, he brought a friend or some colleagues from work. He had brought his parents and sister a few years ago during one of their visits.

Edison caught Tate's eyes as he and Claire walked in, hand in hand. He felt a flush rise up his neck as a huge grin lit up Tate's face. Edison smiled, pressing a hand to the small of her back, and led Claire to his friend.

"Tate, I would love for you to meet Claire."

With a timid smile, Claire extended her hand. "It's nice to meet you."

Tate, who could pass for Santa Claus with his long white beard and big belly, took her hand in both of his. His eyes lit up, and a genuine laugh erupted from him.

"It's my pleasure." He glanced at Edison, "I've been looking forward to meeting the woman who captured his heart."

Claire's eyebrows shot up as she glanced over at Edison. "Oh really?"

Edison blushed and rubbed the back of his neck

before busting out a big grin that went clear up to his eyes. Tate wrapped her hand into the crook of his arm and led them toward the dining room while Edison followed.

She leaned towards Tate. "I've never been here before, but it smells amazing. I can't wait to try everything."

He looked over at Claire and winked, a warm smile on his face. "You're definitely in for a treat tonight."

She squeezed his arm, "Wonderful."

Edison's eyes crinkled at the corners as he watched Claire and Tate click instantly.

Tate leaned over and whispered, "I have to tell you. My friend here hasn't stopped talking about you since you met."

Claire looked over her shoulder and caught Edison's gaze, a small smile on her lips. He couldn't quite decipher what she was thinking. Did she realize what Tate had meant? After they were seated, that same smile was still tugging at the corners of her mouth.

He shrugged as he grinned. "Can you blame me? You're pretty incredible."

She released a gentle laugh, her hand on his forearm.

Tate handed them each a drink menu. "Well, I can certainly see why he's smitten. You two make a great couple."

Tate squeezed Edison's shoulder, smiling at him like a proud father. It warmed his heart to get Tate's approval.

He winked one more time at Claire. "Don't forget to save room for dessert."

Claire's eyes widened as she smiled up at Tate.

Dinner was amazing. Claire and Edison stuffed

themselves with piles of salad, homemade ravioli, garlic bread, and spaghetti. When Tate brought out a slice of tuxedo cheesecake covered in chocolate ganache with two forks, neither could pass it up.

Edison leaned back in his seat, feeling the relaxing effects of the wine they'd had during dinner. Claire cut a bite of cheesecake, leaning toward him, and gently placed it in his mouth. He savored the flavor, closed his eyes, and moaned quietly.

She caught his gaze, flashing a playful smile. "Good?"

He hummed in agreement.

Using her finger, she swiped a dollop of ganache off the corner of his mouth. Tilting her head to the side, she teasingly licked it off her finger, maintaining eye contact with him the entire time. She was playing a dangerous game.

He smirked and grabbed the other fork, cutting a bite and offering it to her. She slid the bite off with her teeth, taking her time to chew, licking her lips, and keeping her gaze locked on his. He shifted in his seat, his jeans feeling too tight.

His tone had a hint of amusement, "You know just how to tease, don't you?"

With a playful sparkle in her eye, she held his gaze and said, "So do you…"

A devilish grin spread across his face as he signaled for the check, wanting to ravage her right here on the table.

After they left, he opened the door to the truck, and she turned to him with a glint of lust in her eyes and said, "I don't want to go home."

He leaned in and gave her a long, lingering kiss. It felt like she was his missing piece, finally found after all these years.

He pulled back and said, "Come home with me."

"Is that a good idea?" She asked against his lips. Her question caught him by surprise, but she deepened the kiss. The world fell away, and she pulled back before they both remembered they were in a public place.

She whispered, "We did agree to take it slow."

"We will. I just... I want to spend more time with you."

She met his gaze and whispered, "Okay."

"Yeah?" The corner of his mouth hitched up in a half smile.

"Yeah." She nodded, swallowing.

Bandit was thrilled when Edison walked in the door, but the dog went crazy when Claire walked in behind Edison. She couldn't contain her giggles.

"Do you remember me, big guy?"

She squatted down and rubbed him all over. Bandit's tongue was half hanging out of his mouth, and he was eating it up.

Edison grabbed Bandit's harness on the hook by the door and said, "Mind if we walk him?"

She stood up, nodding. "Yeah. That's fine." Bandit leaned against her legs, looking up at his new best friend, his tail wagging furiously.

Edison put the harness on Bandit, who eagerly helped.

"Dog park, okay?"

She shrugged, "Sure."

Edison and Claire walked hand in hand while he kept the leash taut to prevent Bandit from getting too far away from them. The park was a few blocks away, and Bandit tended to get overexcited the closer they got.

Edison unclipped the leash when they arrived, and Bandit raced around the perimeter in a big circle. Edison led her to a bench in the middle of the park. This late, there were just a couple of other dogs in the park, but Bandit ignored them, repeatedly running from one side of the vast fenced-in area to the next, showing off for Claire.

Edison waited for her to sit down before he scooted in close, their thighs touching as he wrapped his arm around her. He leaned toward her, her scent filling his nose, and kissed the top of her head. She reached up to her shoulder and laced her fingers into his hand, letting out a contented sigh. He felt a weight lift from his chest, and a sense of calm came over him as if he could finally breathe like this was how it should have always been.

Chapter 17 - Claire

When the sun had dipped down on the horizon and the park lights came on, Sonny whistled for Bandit. He ignored Sonny, playing a game of tag with his new doggie friends. Sonny chased him from one end of the park to the other, and I failed miserably at hiding my laughter. He smirked and rolled his eyes while chasing Bandit for another 15 minutes. Finally, he gave a command I couldn't hear, and Bandit shamefully cooperated, allowing Sonny to clip the leash back on his harness. I was impressed.

They came trotting back to the bench, and Sonny offered his arm to walk back to his place. My heart raced when I saw the way he looked at me. I couldn't shake the nervous feeling in the pit of my stomach.

Thank god he'd offered the crook of his arm so he couldn't feel how sweaty my palms had grown. We talked on our way back, but I avoided looking at him the entire time. The few times he caught my eye, a concerned look crossed his face, but he never asked what was wrong.

My mind wandered back to our past. The way he touched me, the way his lips had felt all over me, the way his body moved against mine. His hot breath was on my neck as he whispered such sweet, dirty words against my ear, knowing exactly what I needed. Goosebumps erupted down my arms just remembering how we were back then.

In my heart, this was the man I had dreamed about and ached for for a long time. Countless nights, I had thought about the passion we shared from that perfect weekend. I remembered how we lost ourselves in each other for hours. He had worshiped me like nothing else existed except us. I wanted that back, but I needed… I didn't know what I needed.

How many times had I wished I could relive those moments again? And now I was so close to it, and I was… terrified.

When we got to his house, I stayed in the living room looking at a wall of photos while he put Bandit to bed. I took off my shoes and pulled my feet up under me on the couch. When he came back, he was barefoot. Seeing him like that sent a rush of heat through me.

He sat down next to me and stretched his arm behind me, gently pulling me towards his chest as he kissed my temple. My head against him, I relaxed as he let out a sigh. There was a comforting silence between us.

My mind drifted back to those memories of our past. He made me feel so alive. It was ridiculous how worked up I had let myself get. I hated myself for staying in a sexless marriage for so long, turning into a shadow of myself. Pushing those thoughts away, I reminded myself that Sonny was kind and gentle, and I felt safe with him. I wanted to tell him my shameful secret, no matter how humiliating it was. He needed to know.

He pulled me closer, so I straddled him, my hands

on his shoulders.

"Everything okay?" I felt the rumble of his voice against my hands.

I took a breath and looked at him as my eyes burned. I whispered, "Can I confess something?"

"Always."

"On our walk back, I was feeling very nervous because...." I trailed off and looked away. I couldn't look at him, say my most embarrassing secrets, and see the pity.

He gently took my chin, turning my head so I would look at him. His eyebrows raised, and his eyes were filled with such tenderness that it made my heart leap.

"What are you trying to tell me?"

I let out the breath I was holding. Our eyes locked.

"My, um, marriage was bad." I swallowed, fidgeting with his shirt collar. "Really bad. Pete and I were not... intimate for most of the marriage." I breathed out the last few words. "I can't even remember the last time he even kissed me or held my hand. It's been a long time. Years. And now..."

I looked down, still messing with his collar, trying to will myself to look back at him, not knowing his reaction. Please don't pity me. I tried to hold the tears in, but one escaped and ran down my cheek.

My voice was nearly a whisper. "I'm scared."

I felt his thumb catch my tear and wipe it away. Looking back at him, I just saw tenderness, no pity. He brought his forehead to mine and gently kissed my lips.

He whispered, "You don't have to be scared. I would never..." This time, he looked away, and a flash of something I didn't understand crossed his face. His eyes came back to mine. "There's nothing wrong with taking things slow and only doing what you're comfortable with."

I nodded, more tears brimming over my lashes. "I don't want you to think I don't want you. I'm just..." I shook my head.

He leaned closer and kissed my tears as his thumb rubbed against my cheek. "That's not what I think. I want you for who you are, not just for what we may or may not do together."

I nodded, a lump in my throat.

He gave me a lingering kiss before he said, "I want you to feel safe with me. You'll always be safe with me."

I took a deep breath, trying to calm myself.

He grabbed my hips, pulling me against him. I laid my head on his shoulder, closing my eyes, his warmth radiating into me. It wouldn't be tonight, but I knew one of these days, I would soon give myself to him, body and soul.

"Do you want to stay the night?" His eyes searched mine. "We don't have to do anything. Just let me hold you in my arms tonight."

I nodded. "I'd like that."

Walking into his bedroom, my eyes first settled on Bandit curled up in a ball on his doggie bed, but as I took in his room, my eyes widened in surprise. This was not the room I had imagined. The bed was large and inviting, with fluffy pillows and a cozy duvet in whites and pastels. I ran my hand along the pillows and imagined myself curled up there with him, feeling safe in his embrace.

The walls were a soft, soothing blue, complementing the warm wooden floors and bed linens. The room was spacious and airy, with large windows along one wall that, I imagined, let in a lot of natural light when the sun was shining. He had put a lot of thought and care into creating a calm and comfortable space. I could just tell this room was a haven for him, where he could shut out the world. Something told me it would become a place where we would share many intimate moments.

On one wall, there were a few framed photos of people. One caught my eye, taken on a beach with a woman with dark hair, and Sonny's same smile and dimples.

He walked over, his hands in his pockets. "That's my sister, Mallory. It was taken in the Dominican Republic when I met her and Devon, her boyfriend, there a couple of years ago. They're currently traveling the world until they hit 30, and then they plan to move back here. Right now, they're in Thailand."

"Wow, that sounds amazing." I turned towards him, reaching my palm to his cheek. "You two share the same smile. The same dimples."

He chuckled, "I always felt like we were complete opposites."

He stepped back, and I inwardly groaned at the loss as he went to the dresser, opened a drawer, and pulled out a T-shirt.

"Want to sleep in this?"

I nodded, taking it from him to hold against my chest. It smelled like Sonny and his home, and I couldn't wait to put it on, enveloping myself in him.

He headed toward the bathroom, rummaging around while I looked around the bedroom. I felt at ease and relaxed. A few books, including mine, were stacked on the bedside table, with a lamp and a tarnished old pocket watch. I picked up the watch and turned it over, running my finger over the engraving on the back.

* * *

I suppose it's like a ticking crocodile, isn't it?
Time is chasing after all of us.

Sonny returned to the bedroom with a toothbrush still in the package. His shirt was unbuttoned and open, his black undershirt sculpted to his firm chest. He had turned into a mountain of a man, not in the imposing sense but in the quiet strength of his presence. He smiled, noticing what was in my hand. He handed me the toothbrush and gently took the pocket watch from me, rubbing his thumb across the engraving.

"When I was young, my grandfather moved in with us. This was before Mallory came along. He was my mom's dad and was getting up there in years, needing more help."

"What about your grandma?"

Looking up from the watch, he said, "She passed away a few years before."

He looked back down at the watch, chuckling. "He insisted I call him Arthur - not Grandpa or Grandad or anything like that. He wanted me, this little kid, to call him Arthur."

I smiled, feeling a warmth blossom in my belly during this peek into his life.

"He loved books, loved to read. So every evening, Arthur would come to my bedroom, books in hand, and read me a bedtime story." A wistful smile playing on his lips, "I loved it. We worked through all the classics — 20,000 Leagues Under the Sea, Robinson Crusoe, Treasure Island, Peter Pan..." He held up the pocket watch, catching my gaze. "Every night, he would pull out this watch and hand it to me. I felt so important. He even taught me how to tell time with it."

I offered him a small smile. "I'm glad you got that

time with him."

"Me, too." He turned the pocket watch over and clicked it open before closing it and turning it over to look at the engraving again. "He loved this quote. He was always telling me to make the most of every moment."

I nodded.

"Before he passed, he had my mom promise to get it engraved and give it to me when I graduated high school. When I opened it, I cried when I realized what it was." He carefully set it on the bedside table, giving me a bashful smile.

"He sounds like he was an exceptional man."

"Yeah." He let out a sigh, a smile still on his face. "He made me fall in love with books. He had been an English professor. I wanted to be just like him. When I was little, I'd sneak into his room, and my mom would find me wearing his fedora and blazer."

I breathed out a laugh. "I bet you were adorable." Something told me Arthur was a big part of why Sonny grew up to be such a kind and thoughtful man. He didn't take things for granted and relished the little moments.

Sonny looked away for a moment and said, "You know? I might have a photo album from my parents somewhere with me in his clothes. I'll see if I can find it soon."

"I would love to see you as a little boy."

He grinned, running his hand along my arm. "Let's go brush our teeth."

He pulled off his jeans, revealing black boxer briefs, and heat pulsed down to my core.

It had been a long time since I shared a bathroom with someone, just doing mundane things like brushing our teeth together. When he was done, he walked out and sat on the bed, plugging in his phone while I shut the door and changed. His shirt hung loosely on me, nearly to my knees, but it was full of his scent. I lifted the neckline and breathed in deeply. I wanted to steal it and take it home to hide under my pillow, to keep a little piece of him with me.

When I returned to the bedroom, Sonny was sprawled lazily in bed. His eyes met mine, and he raised the covers, inviting me in. His hand brushed mine as I slid in, a shiver running through me. We both scooted closer, facing each other, our legs barely touching. His eyes were locked on mine in a deep gaze, that magnetic pull strengthening. I wanted him down to my core, but fear snaked through me. My cheeks heated as he brushed a curl off my forehead, and I smiled.

He leaned in, brushing my lips in a soft kiss before he rolled over, his arm effortlessly guiding me to his side. My head nestled against his chest. The steady beat of his heart was like a soothing lullaby. We lay there, lost in whispered conversations and shared quiet laughter, the space between us electric with unspoken desire—each touch, each gentle graze, sent bolts of heat straight through me.

My fingers found their way under his t-shirt, and I cautiously trailed up his bare chest. I was caught off guard by the firmness of his muscles beneath his skin. My hand couldn't help but explore further, feeling his heartbeat surge as I traced down the trail of hair to his stomach. He lay perfectly still, just letting me explore him. I marveled at how his body felt like an ancient oak's quiet strength.

Somehow, we resisted the urge to take things further. I wiggled, angling my body against his, my head up into the crook of his neck, breathing in his clean scent. He felt so safe. His gentle fingers ran soothing circles on my back, lulling me towards sleep. As I drifted off, his steady heartbeat, a comforting rhythm, was the last thing I heard as I closed my eyes and fell asleep.

Chapter 18 - Edison

Edison and Claire were a chain reaction—an undeniable force reigniting with the same unstoppable intensity as before. She soothed something deep in him, just as he did for her, their connection magnetic and consuming. They spent their weekends and days off wrapped in each other's worlds—romantic dinners, long walks, and getting lost in the aisles of dusty old bookstores.

Somehow, time passed differently for them. Hours felt like minutes. More than a day apart felt like an eternity. Edison couldn't keep the grin off his face when she was beside him. She felt so right in his arms. This was something he'd never known. He wanted more, so much more. It worked its way into the back of his mind.

But whenever things began to move toward the bedroom, she would pull away, and he worried. Was it more than just the years of neglect from her ex? Was it him? Did someone hurt her? Just the thought sent a rage through him. He wanted to give her everything, and it killed him that this was something she had to work through on her own.

On Tuesday afternoon, Edison planned a surprise date and told Claire to be ready for some adventure.

On the way, she was fidgety, but she paused when they arrived at their destination, The Witchery, an occult shop near the downtown square.

She arched a brow, "What are we doing here?"

"I thought it might be fun..." He trailed off, watching her, unsure what her reaction might be.

But when a smile lit up her entire face, he relaxed. She asked, "Remember when we went to the witch market?"

His eyes softened. "I remember that entire weekend."

Edison hopped out. When he opened the door, nervousness flickered across her face as she looked at the shop. He held his hand out for hers.

She leaned towards him and whispered, "Do you believe in this stuff?"

"I don't know anymore. It could be harmless fun and wishful thinking, but I thought it might be fun to try again." He gave her that crooked smile revealing his dimples. "I even brought the book." He held it up in his other hand.

She chuckled, "I wondered if I'd see it again," she teased.

He'd been holding onto it for weeks, and truthfully, he'd finished it a while ago. But for some reason, he couldn't bring himself to return it, like giving it back would shatter the magic that had been building between them.

"Someone had to keep an eye on it. You know how it tends to walk away." He grinned and winked as he said, "And I needed an excuse to keep seeing you."

She bit her lip as her cheeks reddened, and then she took his hand and hopped out.

"You know," Her eyes rose to him, "you never need a reason to see me."

He pulled her close and murmured, "I know, but... the real reason... the only reason I need... is because spending time with you feels like coming home."

She smiled, her cheeks still pink, as she stood on her tiptoes and kissed him before turning towards the store and tugging him behind her.

The store was lit with only candles, which should have given it an ominous vibe, but it felt inviting. It smelled of sage and incense and was empty except for a man with a long dark beard peppered with gray and a black eye patch behind the counter, shuffling an ancient deck of tarot cards.

Edison grabbed her hand again, her bracelet tickling his wrist. He looked down, catching a glint of it, and did a double take. His breath hitched as he rubbed one of the charms with his thumb. It was the bracelet they had bought together at the witch fair all those years ago.

They had stumbled on a booth selling bracelets and tarot card charms just after leaving their tarot card reading. Claire's eyes lit up, and she immediately gravitated toward a silver one.

"This one," she said, wrapping it around her wrist as Edison reached for the clasp.

Beside the bracelets were small tarot card charms on a velvet cloth. Edison selected the charms for cards from their reading. With a warm smile, the seller attached the three charms to the bracelet still on Claire's wrist. Edison still remembered her laughter as she held it up and swished it back and forth.

It was such a simple thing, yet knowing she had kept it all these years made him fall for her even harder. He squeezed her wrist slightly, leaning over to whisper against her ear, "I can't believe you kept it all this time."

"It always made me think of you," she confessed softly.

Edison felt a warmth bloom in his chest, a slow burn spreading from his heart. Claire had been wearing the bracelet all this time, a tiny, constant reminder of him tucked against her skin, and it was a revelation. He had never dared believe she'd thought about him as much as he had her all these years apart.

But a flicker of fear crept in. What if he messed this up? He still wasn't sure when to confess the secret eating at him, but knowing she still had the bracelet gave him a bolt of bravery.

"Claire, I..." She looked up at him with such sincerity.

"Can I help you?" The man called out to them.

He'd have to do it later. They both turned and walked up to the counter. Edison said, "Yes, I had an appointment at 4 o'clock?"

The man eyed them both up and down, and a smirk flashed across his face. "Just a moment." He turned away to grab something behind him and then opened what appeared to be an ancient appointment book with gold leaf on the page edges. Running his fingers down the names, he stopped. "Ah, Edison Wright?" The man looked up with a cunning smile.

Edison smiled politely. "Yes, that's me."

The man closed the book abruptly, sending a small plume of dust into the air. Then, just behind him, he pulled a curtain aside, revealing a long, dark hallway.

"Right this way."

They followed him, walking through the dark corridor lit with torches like something from a video game. They continued walking, arriving at the last door on the right. He opened it, gesturing for them to go inside.

It was a tiny room painted entirely black, no bigger than a broom closet. In the center was a small round table draped in purple and black velvet. Three wooden chairs were around the table. A smaller table against a wall held a lamp draped in red silk scarves. It was the only source of light in the room. They crowded against the wall as the man followed them inside, swiftly shutting the door.

He held his hands out towards the table, "Please sit." He rubbed his hands together before taking the third seat before them. His hands went to the velvet top of the table.

"I'm Dirt. Welcome!"

He had a deep, booming voice with the hint of a strange accent Edison couldn't place. Dirt pulled out the same old deck of cards he'd been shuffling earlier. They looked ancient as if they could disintegrate just from his touch.

Claire caught Edison's eye and mouthed, "Dirt?" Edison pressed his lips together to prevent a laugh from bubbling up and wondered what they were in for.

Dirt finished shuffling the cards and raised his eyebrows as he looked between Claire and Edison. "So, what brings you here?"

A memory hit Edison from that enchanting night at the witch market they happened upon. The market had an ethereal glow from lanterns illuminating the path to the booths, giving it a magical feel. In the middle of the fair were two tents for psychic readings.

"Let's try it, Sonny," Claire said, nudging him playfully. "I want to see what the cards have in store for us."

Edison chuckled, raising a shoulder, feeling a bit skeptical. "Sure, let's do it."

They chose one randomly and walked in, settling in front of a young woman with flowing tendrils of black hair that had fallen loose from the braid that rested over her shoulder.

"Welcome." She gave them a cryptic smile that seemed to shift with the light. She offered a tarot card reading for the future of their relationship.

Claire's eagerness was palpable as the psychic began shuffling her worn deck of cards. The woman laid out a three-card spread. Her brow wrinkled slightly as if sensing something mysterious in the reading.

"This is… an interesting set," she said, glancing nervously at Edison as she stared at the cards. "Your bond appears to be intertwined with the fates, where destiny and time hold greater significance than ever."

Claire leaned forward. "What does that mean?"

Edison sat back, watching the psychic carefully.

"The future is paramount," the psychic continued, pointing to the first card. "The present is the hidden thread in your journey. It's significant — but it's also… out of time?"

Edison caught the way her voice lifted on the last word. Was she asking a question?

Her finger moved to the second card. "The winds of change are gathering, and one of you is about to have a drastic transformation."

Claire's eyes widened with curiosity and a touch of uneasiness. "A change? Well, I'm graduating college in a few days. Could that be it?"

The psychic tilted her head as if that was a possibility. She offered a reassuring smile.

"Perhaps."

She ran her fingers over the third card. "Your path will realign with the one meant for you." Edison still remembered the unsettling way the psychic smiled at him before she turned back to Claire. "Patience and trust in the universe's timing are essential."

When they left the tarot card booth, Claire seemed deep in thought, processing the cryptic fortune. She looked at Edison with a mixture of wonder and excitement. "What was that? I have no idea what any of that meant. But I hope the future holds something amazing."

He smiled, recognizing the spark of hope in her eyes. "I have no doubt about that." He wrapped her hand in his, kissing her knuckles. He quietly said, "The universe often works in mysterious ways." Especially the way it dropped her right into his lap.

Claire squeezed Edison's thigh and flicked her eyes to him. "Sonny?"

He blinked away the memory, clearing his throat before he said, "Um… we wanted to do a couples reading?"

"Yes, yes. Let me guess. You are seeking… something about love?" Dirt's eye had a hint of mischief as he looked between them.

Edison nodded and narrowed his eyes. "Well…" He set the book on the table, and Dirt narrowed his eye at it. "We wanted to know…" Edison caught Claire's eyes, and she gave him a wary look, subtly shaking her head. Pressing his lips together, he said, "Um, we wanted to know… about us?"

"Let's see what we can do." Dirt nodded as if to himself. "The spirits are telling me to try this another way. Give me your hands."

Dirt held his hands out, his elbows resting on the

table, and Edison and Claire each placed a hand in his. He looked at both of them and barked, "You as well. Hold hands!" He closed his eyes and began to hum.

Claire jumped and took Edison's other hand. The lamp began to flicker. Edison wanted to roll his eyes. At least they were getting their money's worth.

Dirt gripped their hands tightly as his humming became louder. Claire leaned back, her eyes widening. Edison gave her a small reassuring smile and tenderly squeezed her hand. She smiled back at him and turned to watch Dirt.

A moment later, Dirt began to speak in a hair-raising monotone that didn't sound like his voice. It was unsettling.

"Sometimes the future echoes to the past..." Edison felt his stomach drop. "Twin flames... two halves... one soul... reconnecting through time..." He and Claire looked at one another, both wide-eyed. He could feel a prickly sensation running down his body.

Edison spoke up. "What does that..."

But, before he could say anything more, Dirt dropped Edison's hand and held his hand up to stop Edison from speaking, releasing his breath like a loud hiss. Edison recoiled.

Dirt kept speaking. "This fate... began long before you..." He began moving his free hand in a hypnotic zig-zagging motion as he continued speaking. "The universe doesn't wait. It sends future echoes to the past..." He took a huge breath in. "The future sends echoes to the past." He opened his eye, and his iris glowed silver, almost otherworldly. Dirt's eye locked on Claire, and he pointed at her. "You... you are the key."

Dirt's eye closed, and his chin fell to his chest. The

light stopped flickering as he dropped Claire's hand. Was this an act? What the fuck was that?

Claire's hand was still clasped in Edison's as he lowered it to his thigh, looking between her and Dirt, unsure what to do. It took Dirt nearly a minute to raise his head again. He wrinkled his brow in confusion and looked around the room.

He smiled politely and began to stand up. "Thank you for coming. I'm sorry I couldn't help you. There is no charge."

Claire looked just as puzzled as Edison. They both stared at Dirt. She spoke first, "What just happened?"

"This way, please." Dirt cut her off and opened the door, leaving the room. He was nearly at the end of the hall, going through the curtain as Edison and Claire walked out of the room. They quickly followed him down the hallway.

Edison had so many questions, and Claire looked just as confused. But Dirt wasn't there when they entered the store's main room. At another counter, a woman in a long dark purple dress with black lipstick and pentagram hoop earrings was helping a customer choose a tarot deck.

Edison walked over to her, Claire behind him. "Excuse me. Do you know where Dirt went?"

"Who?" The woman looked over at them.

"Dirt? We just had a reading with him."

"You mean Roy? He does the weekday readings here." She looked around the store before glancing at the customer still choosing tarot cards. She looked pointedly at Edison. "But we don't do readings today."

Edison looked exasperated. "No, he said his name was Dirt. Eye patch? Dark beard? Does any of that sound familiar?"

The woman shook her head. "No, we don't have anyone who works here with that description."

Under his breath, he said, "What the fuck?" He pointed towards the thick black brocade curtain where they came from. "Surely, you saw us walk out of that hallway?"

She looked at the curtain and then back at them. "Hallway? What are you talking about?"

Edison walked between the counters and over to the heavy curtain. "This…one?" But, as he pulled it to the side, there was no hallway, just a solid brick wall. His eyes widened, and he looked at Claire.

"Sorry to bother you. We'll be going now." Claire grabbed Edison by the hand and led him to the front entrance. She looked over her shoulder to see the woman glaring at them before whispering, "Let's get out of here."

Edison took one last look around before opening the front door, and they walked out.

Out front, Claire laughed. "That was so crazy!"

Shaking his head, Edison, wide-eyed, asked, "What was that?"

"I have no idea what just happened." She playfully grabbed him by the belt loops of his jeans, pulling him against her. "Come on, let's go have an early dinner. I need a drink after that."

He laughed out an "okay" and snaked his arm around her waist, letting her pull him down the sidewalk.

Chapter 19 - Claire

As we made our way to The Taco Shop, I was lost in thought. It seemed we both were because we barely spoke the entire way there. I just kept replaying what had just happened in my head. After we ordered and grabbed a table, I raised my eyebrows, looking at Sonny, who was taking a long drink of his mineral water.

"We didn't imagine all that, right?"

"Yeah, that was... weird." He grimaced and stared out the front window of the restaurant. His voice dropped to a low whisper. "So weird..."

I thought back to what Dirt had said. "What do you think he meant by future echoes to the past?"

Before he could answer, the waitress dropped off my peach margarita and a basket of chips with fire-roasted queso. Sonny drug a chip through the queso, popping it in his mouth. He chewed and swallowed before shrugging.

I leaned forward, whispering. "Do you think...?"

He gave me that crooked smile. "Yeah, I do."

I narrowed my eyes, a playful smile on my lips. "How do you even know what I was going to ask?"

He cleared his throat. "I think he meant the first time we met—the blind date? Maybe we weren't ready back then? Maybe we met before we were supposed to?"

My eyes widened as I slowly nodded. "Yeah, that's what I was thinking."

He chuckled, "I thought so."

"Do you think it could be true?"

He looked thoughtful before meeting my eyes again and slowly nodding, "I do." His smile was wistful.

A memory came to me from when we were at the witch market. "Wasn't that similar to what that psychic said back then? Something about out of time?"

He nodded again, "I remember that, and she said something about my path would realign with the one meant for me."

I gave him a shy smile and looked away. I offered, "Maybe she meant me? Since we're back together again."

He shrugged as he crunched another chip. "I want to show you something." He took a drink before brushing off his hands. "I never told you this when I found your book, but a photo slipped out." He pulled the photo from the book and handed it to me.

I gasped, taking the photo. "Sonny, this is crazy." I shook my head, a smile blooming on my face. "If I didn't see it right here, I'd swear it was on my fridge." I laid it on top of the book and stared at it. "It was the first conference I'd attended with the other librarians. We were in Florida. A rain burst caught us by surprise, so we were all stupidly hiding under this tiny awning, trying to stay out of the rain." I looked up at him, "I'm surprised you could even see me in the photo. I hid behind Bert."

Sonny picked the photo up and huffed out a

laugh. "You were the first thing I noticed. I instantly knew it was you, making me wonder if this was your book." Setting it down, he smiled and ran his fingers loosely through some of my curls. "All I could remember was your first name and these red curls." He leaned back and tapped the book. "I just felt that this book was the key to finding you again."

I grinned as I shook my head, "This is getting weird. But I'm glad it brought us back together."

He got up and slid in next to me in the booth. He murmured, "Me, too," as he took my hand in both of his, a tender look in his eyes. I wanted to melt. "Claire, I have to tell you something else."

I chewed my lip, my eyes darting around the room before they found him again. "Okay."

"I remember everything from that weekend."

He gently put his hand to my cheek.

"Everything. You were unforgettable. When you canceled on me later that week and disappeared, I wondered if I had imagined it all. If I had imagined you. Did you know I looked for you?"

Feeling so much regret, I looked down and shook my head, a tear slipping down my cheek. Looking back at him, I whispered, "I never forgot you either." I took in a deep breath. "I dreamed about you all the time. I never could figure out where we were. It was always the same place, and I was always in your arms in a dark room with gauzy curtains blowing gently and..." I swallowed, our breath mingling.

"Pink silk sheets." We both said it at the same time.

I wrinkled my brow and said, "What?"

He raised his eyebrows. "Pink silk sheets?"

"How did you..."

Before I could finish my question, he interrupted

me. "Do you remember Dirt mentioning twin flames, two halves of the same soul? I never knew that could be real, but I've read that twin flames can walk in each other's dreams. "

My eyes widened, "Is that true? Are we? But how…?"

He shrugged, "I don't know, but I've been in that same room. I remember those dreams."

I let out a breath, "This is crazy."

He shook his head. "I don't know what any of it means. It just makes me think about fated mates in fantasy books. Maybe that's us?"

"Maybe…" I gave him a small smile. "I would wake up and try so hard to get back to those dreams, to get back to you." I leaned forward and said quietly, "Sometimes I would swear I could smell you on me when I woke up."

With a mixture of surprise and intrigue in his eyes, he asked, "Really?" His voice was tinged with curiosity.

I nodded, a faint blush creeping up my cheeks. "It seemed so real."

After a drink, he looked like he wanted to say something more, but the waitress set our food down, and the moment passed.

I stared at my plate, thinking about everything — the dreams, Dirt, the psychic at the witch market. I looked up at Sonny. "He said I was the key."

"Wha-?" Sonny looked over at me quizzically with a mouthful of taco.

"Dirt looked at me and said, 'You're the key.' What could it mean? Maybe it's the books?"

"Books? There's more than this one?" His eyes flicked to the book on the table.

I nodded as I swallowed. "I thought I told you about this? I got a very strange box of books months ago." I picked it up. "Including this one."

"From where?"

"Did you ever go to this odd bookstore out in Ponder? It was called The Enchanted Attic?"

He tilted his head, shaking it. "I don't think so. It sounds familiar, though."

"Oh, you'd know. It's gone now, but it was in this Gothic Victorian house that was painted bright pink. The bookstore is gone, but the pink house is still there. It was a secondhand bookstore that was just… odd."

"Yeah?"

"I don't think I can do it justice by just describing it. We should drive out there sometime so you can see it. The whole place was just… weird—the bookstore, the little man who ran it, even the way I got that box of books."

"Weird, how?"

I started talking fast with my hands. "I never saw another soul in there, ever. It was like it was my own secret bookstore. The last time I was there, the owner took me to a back room and practically shoved this box of books at me. Didn't want me to pay for them and sent me on my way with a wink and a smile." I took a drink of my margarita. "When I got home, I went through the books. It was all these romance novels. I thought he just noticed I often bought romance novels and wanted to get rid of them." I shrugged, "But when I went through the box at home, every book was covered in notes. And… I found this strange riddle written on a torn-out page at the bottom of the box."

"Notes?" Sonny had finished his tacos and folded his napkin on his plate. His chin rested in his palm over the table, and his brow was wrinkled.

I nodded to the book on the table. "I'm sure you

saw all the handwritten notes in that book." I hooked my thumb towards it. "Imagine an entire box of books like that."

He tilted his head. "What did the riddle say?"

I give him a dismissive wave, "I don't know. It's stupid. It seemed to allude to finding true love with these books."

"I'd love to see both the riddle and the box of books."

"Of course." I leaned in, "But that's not even the weirdest thing about it all."

He eyed the book before giving me a questioning look. "Okay?"

I guess the most straightforward way was to say it and hope he didn't think I was nuts. I shrugged and shook my head, curls going every which way. I lowered my voice. "This is going to sound crazy, but... the books tell me to do things."

He raised his eyebrows. "Uh... like what?"

I grimaced. "Sometimes, the books urge me to write in them. It's like an itch I have to scratch or a whisper in the back of my mind that won't quiet until I do. And the strangest part? Sometimes, I don't even remember writing them."

He studied me for a moment, his brow furrowing. "What kinds of things do you write?" His voice was careful like he was unsure if he wanted to know the answer. "Just notes? Or... something else?"

"Sometimes it's quotes about love. Other times, it's doodles or... random names. I don't know. It just comes out of me, and I can't explain it."

He raised his eyebrows.

Heat climbed up my neck. I gave him a tight smile and wrinkled my nose. This was so embarrassing. He probably thought I was crazy. "But that's not all... the books tell me to leave them places." My voice dropped to a whisper on the last word.

His eyes went to the book on the table. "So you purposely left this one in that car?"

I shook my head. "No."

"Okay...?"

I looked over at the book, a smile tugging at the corner of my mouth. "It's one of my favorite books. I'd been dragging it around in my bag for months. I'd had no plans to leave it anywhere, but sometimes they have a way of... disappearing on me. It's like they walk off. But until you, no one had ever tried to contact or find me when I left a book."

Sonny shook his head in disbelief. "Okay, wait. So, sometimes the books tell you where to leave them, and sometimes they just... disappear?"

"Yep." I nodded while I slurped the last dregs of my peach margarita.

He looked over at the book. "I have so many questions." He chuckled to himself. "How do the books tell you where to leave them? How many books have you left? Where do you leave them?"

"I know it's crazy." I shrugged and rolled my eyes. "First, it starts with dreams. I'll dream about a place multiple times. Then, people around me start talking about that same place."

"Is it always nearby? Like it's not some far-off place or something?"

I nodded, "Yeah, it's always around here, around the city. This anxious feeling builds up until I just have to go there. It could be a restaurant, a park bench, a coffee house... Anywhere, really. Once, it was a church."

His brow wrinkled. "A church?"

"Yeah, that was one from a couple of months ago. I left it on a pew."

"Really?" He pulled his head back and wrinkled

his brow again. "What happened?"

"Well, this woman came running up to me at the end of the service asking if I left the book, but I just told her it wasn't mine. She opened the book as she walked away, smiling and hugging it to her chest."

Any minute now, he was going to tell me I was nuts.

But he surprised me when he asked almost shyly, "Could I go with you the next time you do it? Leave a book, I mean?"

I smiled. "I'd love for you to come."

He grinned, his dimples showing. "Cool, I want to see how it all works."

"I'm just glad you believe me."

"I believe you." He hooked his thumb toward the book. "I had a rather strange dealing with that book."

"You did?"

"Oh yeah. It freaked me the fuck out."

"The photo?" I wrinkled my brow.

He shook his head, "No, not the photo." He took a drink. He bit his lip as if he was trying to figure something out. "Standing in line at the checkout, I thumbed through it and found a grocery list. It caught my attention because it was a little strange to find something like that in a book."

I chuckled and nodded because I remembered writing that list when I couldn't find any paper.

"But... while I looked at it, the list began to fade. At first, I thought maybe it was lighter than I remembered, but then I watched it disappear. The crazy thing was..." He leaned towards me and lowered his voice so no one else heard him. "The crazy thing was that it didn't just disappear. It changed right before my eyes to something about... about you." He looked so serious. "I swear to god,

Claire." He visibly swallowed. "It scared me, and I dropped the book. It was so loud when it hit the ground, everyone in line turned to stare."

"Was that the night I saw you in the parking lot?"

"Yeah." He nodded. "It was."

"You found my book while I was there?"

"I guess so." He shrugged.

We both looked at the book. I was almost afraid to ask as I slowly whispered, "Sonny, what did it say?"

He grabbed the book and flipped to the page, placing it in front of me, his finger marking it. I gasped, a cold shiver running down my spine as I read it several times. I couldn't help it when I reached out, running my fingers over the words to make sure they were real.

Claire isn't looking for you, but she will find you.

What kind of strange magic had I unleashed?

Chapter 20 - Edison

Claire stared at the words. She hadn't moved or said anything for more than a minute.

"You okay?"

Edison thought she was scared as she stared at the page for a long time. Her brow wrinkled. Her eyes narrowed the more she read. Her nostrils flared, and he realized she seemed... angry.

She raised her hand to her forehead, smoothing it out with her fingers as she looked at Edison. "Why didn't you tell me about this before?"

Edison rubbed the back of his neck as he raised a shoulder. "I don't know."

Claire let out a big sigh and pinched the bridge of her nose. "Let's talk about something else."

It felt like the air had been sucked out of the room. Claire seemed different, closed off.

Edison studied her before nodding slowly as he let out a pent-up breath. "Sure." He leaned forward. "Did you always want to be a librarian?"

She smiled, but it didn't reach her eyes as she told him the library had always been her favorite place as a kid, and she had spent countless hours volunteering there as a teenager. She'd come home with stacks of books and sit outside on the front porch reading until the streetlights came on. Edison had never met anyone who enjoyed reading as much as he did.

As the night progressed, Claire's usual talkative nature was quieter. She reminded him that she would be putting in long hours this week with the supervillain escape room this weekend, but he couldn't wait to see her in her element. After leaving the restaurant, Edison steered Claire out of the foot traffic, worried something was wrong. She looked up at him expectantly, but he could see the tension in her face. He tucked a loose curl behind her ear.

Searching her eyes, he asked, "Is everything okay… between us?"

He wasn't ready to end their date, but Claire seemed different tonight. Something flashed across her face when he asked. What wasn't she telling him? Was it the book? Something else? He knew something wasn't right. She looked over his shoulder, avoiding his gaze. He rearranged his face to hide his disappointment before her eyes returned to his.

Claire gave him an apologetic smile. "Yeah, everything is fine. It's just… Sonny… I need to go home."

Everything was not okay.

He let out a sigh, "It's okay. I understand. I do."

She squeezed his hand, her eyes softening. "I'm sorry. It's just…" She took in a breath. "I have a bunch of chores I've been neglecting, and I need to finish some work on the escape room. I hope you're not mad at me." She looked down.

"Why would I be mad at you? Maybe a little disappointed, but I get it." He smiled as warmly as he could.

She peeked up at him under her lashes. Her voice

was a whisper. "I'm sorry."

"Poppy, it's fine." Edison ran his hands down her arms reassuringly. "Are you sure it's not something else?"

She shook her head, and he brushed his lips against hers, offering his arm as they returned to his truck.

As he pulled into the parking lot of her apartment, a wave of anxiety washed over him. Claire had already told him she didn't need him to walk her up, but he'd always done it. This time, though, something felt different. He could feel her pulling away, and it was killing him. Worst of all, he wasn't sure why. It was like déjà vu, a repeat of the last time she'd disappeared on him. He refused to lose her again.

He turned toward her and put his hands on her hips, waiting for her to pull away. But instead, she leaned toward him, and he pulled her against him. What was happening? This whole day, it just confused him.

He kissed her forehead and rested his cheek on top of her head. "I can't wait to see your escape room on Saturday."

Quietly, she said, "I'm excited for you to see it."

When she looked up at him again, he dropped his gaze to her lips. They were just so kissable. Her eyes closed as if she were waiting for his kiss. Her lips curved against his as he gently tilted her face, catching her mouth with his, parting her lips with his tongue, and deepening the kiss. Her hands went to his shoulders and around his neck, clinging to him like this was their last kiss. He nipped her bottom lip as one of his hands ran to the back of her head, his other wrapping her tighter and pulling her into his body.

He pulled back, breath ragged. "Claire..."

She didn't say a word, just smiled, locked her gaze with his, and yanked him towards her. She swallowed Edison's moan. He ran his hands down her arms, feeling the goosebumps prickling her skin. A fire built in the pit of his belly. He needed this to feel her. He kissed down her neck and felt her shiver, almost convulsing.

She breathed out, "Sonny... fuck."

She moaned against his ear before sucking his earlobe, causing him to groan. He nipped at her collarbone, marking her before kissing back up to her mouth, his hand caressing the back of her neck.

She put a hand on her chest, looking dazed and out of breath. "That was... you are..." She locked eyes with Edison, and they both laughed softly.

He knew what she wanted, needed, what her body was begging from him, but he fought the urge to keep her in his arms and moved over to the driver's side, his hands white-knuckling the steering wheel.

He choked out, "You sure you don't want me to walk you up?"

She shook her head. "I'm okay."

His hand shot out to her arm as he said, "Goodnight, Poppy."

Her eyes were on his hand as it slowly slid down, letting her go before rising to meet his eyes again, nodding once as if she'd just made a decision.

She slid out of the truck and gave him a small smile. "Have a good night, Sonny."

He waited in the parking lot, watching as she walked up to her apartment, not driving off until her door finally shut. It was getting harder and harder to leave her. Was he reading too much into this? Did his confession about the book scare her? He reached under the seat and tossed the book on the bench, not wanting to forget it when he got home. Maybe he'd find a clue about what was going on with her.

As he drove home, he passed The Basement, the dungeon-like bar he frequented years ago. It was in the basement of a club on the square, complete with flickering torch lights and battle axes on the walls. For old-time's sake, he was so tempted to stop and drink, see if any of the regulars from years ago were still there. But that was a bad idea. He didn't want to ever go down that path again. Luckily, fate stepped in when every parking space was full, so he drove back home to Bandit. Edison felt guilty when Bandit whined and paced at the garage door, looking for Claire.

After their run, he sat on the couch with Claire's book and started paging through it. He wasn't quite ready to admit this book had some magic, but he was hopeful that it might give him a clue about what was going on with her. He flipped through the pages, trying to remember where the quote with her name was, but this time he couldn't find it. He was sure he knew the exact page, primarily since he had found it a million times, but that page was blank. There were no notes on it at all. Slowly, he went through every single page repeatedly, looking for it. He even tried opening and closing the book a few dozen times. But every time, it remained blank. No quote about Claire. No grocery list. Nothing but an empty page. What the hell did that mean? Had he lost her? Was it an omen of things to come? Did the magic wear off? He had no idea.

More than anything, he wanted to drive straight back to her apartment and wrap her in his arms just to be near her. But he knew that was the last thing she wanted. She needed some space, even if she hadn't outright said it, and he'd give it to her. But he just needed a clue, a hint, some reassurance, so he didn't feel like he was losing her again.

Chapter 21 - Claire

Darci pounced when I walked into the library offices the next day. "Oh my god, woman! You never called me. I am dying to know what happened!"

I blushed, a smile playing on my lips.

"So, what was your surprise date?"

"He took me to a psychic."

"Really? How did that go?" Darci's eyes widened.

I sighed and gave her a knowing look as I put my stuff on a counter. "It was...something."

"As in what? It was stupid and fake or... something else?" She flicked her eyes towards me and loudly rapped her fingernails on the desk.

I wanted to tell her everything, but it was a lot to unpack.

"Why don't we get started on the escape room? I'll go grab Melody and Anna to help." She shrugged, raising her hands as I chuckled. "I'll tell you all about it at lunch."

In between helping patrons, we worked for half the day creating props and set pieces out of cardboard boxes and craft paper until Darci's stomach let out a loud rumble heard across the room.

I stood up and stretched. "Who's ready for

lunch?"

Darci popped up from where she'd been painting a piece from one of the supervillain's lairs. In a sing-song voice, she walked over to me and said, "I am starving, and you promised to tell me everything at lunch."

As soon as we were all seated at a table in the tiny kitchen in the back of the office, Darci immediately asked, "Okay, Claire, I'm dying over here. Tell us what is going on with you and Edison. Because something is definitely going on."

I looked at Anna and Melody and immediately shoveled a giant bite of salad into my mouth. I gave Darci a wide Cheshire cat grin, satisfaction sparkling in my eyes.

Darci rolled her eyes. "Fine. I see how it is. I guess I won't be sharing my sweet treats with you."

Anna giggled, and Melody smiled like she wasn't sure if she should be there or not.

I took a big drink from my water bottle and wiped my hands on a napkin. "I was going to tell you. Where do you want me to start? Dirt, the psychic? Or maybe the magical book that writes messages? Or the kiss-"

"Hold up. Your psychic was named Dirt? Like dirt on the ground, like dirt, dirt?"

"But that wasn't even the strangest thing about him."

Darci purred, "Do tell."

"Well, I'm not even sure he was real."

Everyone looked confused. Darci choked on her tea. "What?"

"Have you ever been to The Witchery?" I asked.

"No." Darci and Anna answered at the same time.

Melody shrugged and quietly said, "I've been a few times. They have nice candles."

"Sonny had made an appointment for a reading. We got there, and Dirt introduced himself and led us behind a curtain down a long hallway to a tiny room painted completely black. It was... spooky." They all leaned closer, waiting for me to go on. "He had us hold hands, and before I knew it, his voice changed—deep, eerie, and nothing like his own. It sent a chill down my spine. Honestly, it was downright unsettling."

Darci blinked, wide-eyed. "Jesus, Claire, what did he say?"

"He said something about twin flames and the future echoing in the past. He kept repeating the same things over and over." A shiver ran through me. "Honestly, if he hadn't disappeared, I would have chalked it all up to theatrics. Even the light was flickering in the room."

Melody quietly piped in, "He disappeared?"

I nodded. "He stood up and said in his regular voice that he was sorry he couldn't help us and that there would be no charge. Then, he ushered us out of the room and back down the hallway to the shop. Then, he vanished."

Darci narrowed her eyes.

I nodded, "Just as we walked back to the front of the shop from behind the curtain, the guy just disappeared."

"That's crazy!" Darci took a drink.

"Yeah. We saw another employee and asked her if she knew where he went. She said no one worked there with that name, and then she told us they don't even do readings on Tuesdays." I looked between all three of them before I continued. "We pointed to the curtain and said he took us down the hallway behind it. She looked at us like we were crazy, so Sonny pulled the curtain open to show her. And… it was a freaking brick wall! There was no hallway."

Anna flinched and leaned back in her chair. "What?"

I shrugged. "Believe it or not, but things got even weirder." I stood up to rinse my container before putting it back in my tote bag.

When I returned to the table, Darci opened a container of homemade brownies topped with crushed Butterfingers.

I cooed, "These look amazing," and immediately picked one up and took a bite.

Anna and Melody each took one, and Darci grabbed another, moaning as she bit into it. She quickly shook her head, sending her short, choppy hair into a playful dance.

"You both saw the guy, so where did he go?"

"No idea." I finished my brownie and said, "You know that book I lost that started this whole thing?" I lowered my voice, "I think it's magical."

Melody squeaked out, "What does that even mean?"

I gave Melody and Anna a quick run down on the box of books, the notes, and Sonny finding my book.

"While we were at dinner, he told me about this strange thing that happened when he found it, and I don't know what to make of it."

Darci raised an eyebrow, putting the lid back on the brownies.

"Trust me, it freaked me out." I finished my water bottle and tossed it in the recycling before continuing, "Remember how I left the book in that rideshare I took to the courthouse? Well, Sonny found it at a grocery store." I gave them all a dramatic shrug. "He had to get down on the ground and yank it from under the carts. And… y'all remember that photo of all of us from the library convention? It just conveniently fluttered out of the book into his lap."

Darci tilted her head. "Hasn't that photo been on your fridge for months?"

"That's what I thought, but when I got home last night, it wasn't on my fridge. I don't know how it got in the book."

She wrinkled her brow.

"It gets even better. I had written a grocery list on a certain page, but it disappeared before his eyes, and something else appeared."

Anna gasped, and Darci exclaimed, "What?!"

I nodded. "Crazy, right?" I gestured with my hands. "It happened the same night I saw him in the parking lot at the store, which means he found my book. When. I. Was. There."

Darci sucked her teeth and said, "Yeah, this is getting stranger by the minute."

"But what did it say?" Melody asked in a hushed whisper.

I leaned forward, my gaze catching each one of theirs, "'Claire isn't looking for you, but she will find you.'" Cue the mic drop. I pushed back from the table and stood up.

Three pairs of wide eyes raised to meet mine. Darci wrinkled her brow, "Your name was in it? How does that even happen?"

"No clue." I blurted out as I paced the small break room like a caged animal. I stopped, throwing my hands up, unable to stop the words spilling out, "Do I even have a say anymore?" I tried to contain the emotions. "I mean, I'm so glad I found him again. But... I barely had a say in my marriage, and now this..." I trailed off, memories of my controlling mother and my suffocating marriage swirling in my mind.

Melody and Anna exchanged worried glances before quietly retreating to the workroom. Darci stayed.

"Look," she said, catching my eye with a surprising softness as she stood up and approached me, "It's weird and a little frightening, but... it's also a little romantic. All these coincidences putting you and him together..." Her voice trailed off, leaving the thought hanging in the air.

"Maybe," I murmured. Was it romantic? Or, once again, I wasn't getting a say in my life? Something unsettling took root in my stomach. "But what if it's not just this," I whispered as I talked with my hands. "What if the universe or whatever has already decided everything?"

Darci squeezed my shoulder, her touch grounding me for the moment. "Hey," she said, her voice firm yet reassuring, "even if there's something bigger at play, that doesn't mean you don't get a say. The universe might have pushed you together, but you can still go your own way."

I nodded as I swallowed.

But there was no way I could avoid the pull between me and Sonny. I was falling for him, and I was falling hard. It scared me. But the question still lingered in my mind—was I truly in control of my life and destiny, or was something else already playing out its grand design? And what did those books have to do with it?

I sighed as we made our way back to the workroom. I didn't want to think about this right now. I just wanted to get back to work, get back to my quiet boring life before the universe butted its nose in. But that was impossible. I couldn't go back to my quiet, lonely life, a life without Sonny. Maybe the universe wasn't trying to control me. Maybe it was just giving me a second chance. A chance for something real, even if it was terrifying.

Chapter 22 - Edison

Edison was caught in a whirlwind of what-ifs. Days had passed, and Claire had primarily gone radio silent. She denied it, but something changed when he showed her the book. He should have never told her what happened. What if she disappeared again?

Their constant messaging and stolen moments had dwindled to almost nothing. The one-word replies and the delayed texts were such a stark contrast to the sexually-charged exchanges they'd been having.

The knot in his stomach tightened. He just wanted to touch her, kiss her, exist in her orbit. He kept reminding himself that Claire had warned him about a busy week and all her preparations for the escape room. But it felt like more than that. Logic urged him to calm down, but when did love ever follow logic's rules?

Each day stretched into an eternity, his mind replaying every moment, every word, every stolen glance. What had he missed? He could barely sleep, didn't want to eat, didn't want to do anything. Work barely kept his attention. His students were bearing the brunt of it all.

He had assigned a paper a few weeks ago, and the

due date was fast approaching. Today, he'd been trapped in his office after nearly every student showed up with a litany of questions. He began to wonder if he'd ever get to leave campus. Finally, during a lull, he sneaked out, practically running to the parking lot before one more person could stop him. Nearing his truck, Edison pulled his phone from his pocket, dialing her number before realizing what he was doing. He had a desperate need to talk to her.

"Hello? Sonny?" Hearing her voice, the storm building in his gut calmed.

"Hey, I just…" Trying and failing to hide his desperation, he wasn't even sure what to say. "I called because…" He chuckled nervously.

"Are you okay? Is something wrong?" The sound of a drill was in the background.

He took a deep breath. "I just… hadn't heard from you. Things didn't feel right between us the other night, and I… and I missed you."

"I'm sorry. I just…" She let out a sigh. "I've been putting work off, and I… I just needed a minute to breathe."

His stomach clenched like a fist. It hadn't been his imagination.

"There's just been a lot of work for the escape room." Exhaustion coated her voice, her drawl coming out stronger.

"Do you need anything? An extra set of hands?" He yearned for a chance to prove himself to her.

Her voice muffled as she spoke to someone else before asking him, "How good are you with power tools?"

He smirked as his voice dropped an entire octave. "I'm pretty… handy."

She cleared her throat. "Oh really?" Her voice

was like honey, and he could hear her smile. "Do you want to come help out tonight?

He sighed as a weight lifted off his chest. "I'd love nothing more."

He stopped by the house to take care of Bandit before sending a quick text to let her know he was on the way. When he pulled up, he could see Claire in the window, a smile blooming across her face when she spotted him. As she opened the door to let him in, she reached for him, and Edison grabbed her around the waist, planting a kiss on her lips. He pulled her against him like it had been months since he'd seen her, not just a few days.

Her face was buried in his neck when she said muffledly, "I'm glad you're here."

He squeezed her tighter before letting her go.

As they walked to the teen room, she asked if he could put some old shelving units together they had stashed in the storage room. She handed him a drill and showed him where to find the shelves before heading to paint set decorations.

Hauling the shelves to the teen room, he looked around at what they had already done, and the transformation was unbelievable. He couldn't wait to see the final setup tomorrow. In one corner, Crimson Hammer's Sanctuary of Solace was taking shape. Two librarians were working in another area that looked like it was becoming a laboratory. He couldn't believe how creative Claire was. She had this vision, and it was coming alive before his eyes with just paper, cardboard, and a few shelves.

He got to work, but he could feel Claire watching him. He'd look up and catch her gaze, and she'd give him a whisper of a smile. Every single time, it sent a thrill shooting through him.

Here, in her element, he wasn't the only one

captivated by her. Everyone in the room was drawn to her, needing to gravitate in her orbit, asking her questions, giving her smiles. They'd cast curious looks at him, but she seemed focused solely on him, their eyes meeting every few minutes like a secret language between them.

As he finished the last of the shelving units, he looked up to find Claire and Darci whispering like two school girls as they glanced at him. He walked over, but before he reached them, Darci gave a quick wave and went to a laptop on one of the larger tables.

"I finished the shelves. What else can I do?" His tongue felt thick, the unspoken plea hanging in the air. Please don't send me home.

She smiled and motioned with her head for him to follow, leading him over to piles of greenery.

"Want to help me untangle all of this?" She asked as she sat down in the middle of it.

He grinned, amusement in his eyes as he sat down next to her, his thigh brushing against hers, and began untangling the mess.

Smirking as he untangled the long strips of ivy next to her, he asked, "Is this for your character?"

She laughed, and he'd do anything to hear it every day of his life. "You remembered?"

He leaned over, his breath caressing her ear, whispering, "I never forget anything you tell me."

Almost imperceptibly, her breath hitched, her reaction forcing his eyes from the greenery.

She swallowed and nodded slowly. "Some of these are going to be my backdrop."

As he untangled the mess, Edison carefully laid each garland, piece by piece, in front of Claire while she stapled them to a long swath of craft paper.

A few minutes later, they heard a banging on the

front door. Claire was startled, "Who the heck is that?"

Edison stood up, rubbing his hands together, a conspiratorial smile spreading across his face. "Probably my little surprise." He took off jogging towards the front door.

Darci perked up. "A surprise?" Everyone trailed out of the teen room and followed him to the foyer.

A moment later, he turned around with pizza boxes and a 12-pack of sodas in one hand.

Claire ran towards him, reaching for some of the pizza boxes. "Oh my god, Sonny, this is amazing!"

"You are just full of surprises, Edison." Darci followed right behind Claire and took the drinks out of his hand, a big smile on her face.

Claire led the way. "Let's take this back to the kitchen." She flicked the lights on with her shoulder as they walked into the dark depths of the library.

Setting the pizza boxes on the counter, he leaned towards Claire, lowering his voice. "I hope this is okay."

She kissed his cheek, whispering, "Are you kidding? This is more than okay."

"This looks so good!" Anna exclaimed as she and Darci helped themselves to slices.

A smile tugged at his lips as he pulled Claire into him. Turning in his arms, she leaned back to meet his gaze. The urge to kiss her bloomed in his chest, taste her lips, feel the silkiness of her hair, her skin against his. Instead, he gently squeezed her before letting go and stepping back.

She grabbed him, pulling him back, going up on her tiptoes, pressing her lips against his. "This was so sweet. How did you know pizza was my love language."

Edison picked up a slice and held it out for Claire

to bite. "Lucky guess? But the way your eyes lit up when you took those pizza boxes is the same way they do when you look at me." He waggled his eyebrows before taking a bite of the same slice.

Claire blushed and broke out in a shy smile as she chewed.

Darci rolled her eyes as she grabbed another slice. "Oh my god, y'all get a freaking room."

Everyone else had already sat down when Claire and Edison came over, and just one chair was left. Claire set her plate down and turned to find another chair when Edison pulled her down on his lap, his arm wrapping around her waist. Her eyes widened, the blush creeping up her cheeks, but she shrugged, amusement dancing in her eyes as she picked up a slice and took a bite. Biting into his, he raised his eyebrows, daring her to get up. She narrowed her eyes, smirking at him as she took another bite.

The curve of her ass against his lap caused his dick to thicken, pressing painfully against his zipper. Apparently, she had also noticed this... predicament. Her eyes slid to his as she slowly arched her brow. Was this a bad idea? Worth it, he thought, the corner of his mouth ticking up in that crooked grin as their eyes locked. He wrapped his arm tighter around her waist, gently lifting her and repositioning himself in the chair.

He didn't care what they did. Just being with her, near her, it was what he craved. Her presence sent waves of comfort washing over him. Tonight had erased all that worry and heartache he'd felt this week. Yet beneath it, a shadow lurked. Would she pull back, and disappear on him whenever something went wrong?

Chapter 23 - Claire

This was turning out to be our most intricate escape room, and I had grossly underestimated how long everything would take us. Thankfully, Sonny and a few extra employees got us through. I wasn't sure how I could repay him for all his help tonight. Without him, we might have been here all night. Not only did he help us get so much done, he even had dinner delivered to feed everyone. His enthusiasm and genuine excitement for the escape room had been contagious, spurring everyone.

I had this kind, thoughtful, and gorgeous guy who was really into me. And I was pushing him away? What was wrong with me? When he'd called, the familiar warmth of his voice had an edge of worry. It tore at me. I'd disappeared on him years ago. Now, he probably thought I was doing it again. The last thing I wanted to do was hurt him.

Granted, I knew exactly why I was pushing him away. It was scary. I'd never clicked with anyone so completely like I did with him. We just... fit together. It was almost too perfect, too good to be true, like, at any moment, the other shoe would drop, not to mention the whole idea of the stars or fates or whatever was pushing us together, something I didn't understand. It all scared me.

The escape room this week had been a welcome distraction from this dizzy whirlwind I'd been in with Sonny. But I still couldn't stop thinking about how my name appeared in the book. I had my suspicions about that strange box of books. But now? What did it all mean?

Sure, everyone wants to believe in soulmates and twin flames and the idea of destiny or fate finding your true love. It all sounds great, but what do you do when it's happening to you, and you feel like you're not in charge of your own life? Was I supposed to sit back and let it happen? I just needed space to wrap my head around everything, take it all in, and figure out what I wanted. I needed to be in charge of my own destiny. I didn't want to be swept up in someone else and forget myself. I got swept up in Pete, and look where that got me.

But tonight, with Sonny near, the ache of his absence over the past few days hit me like an avalanche. I didn't realize how much I missed him, his touch, his very presence. I wanted to throw caution to the wind, dive headfirst into what we had together, and finally let it consume me.

We'd finished as much as possible by midnight, and I couldn't stop yawning. I'd been here since early this morning. Melody, Anna, and some volunteers left while Darci and I moved the art supplies to the workroom with Sonny's help. After Darci said goodbye, we packed up the leftover pizza. I knew what I was having for breakfast tomorrow.

He walked me to the car and helped me put everything in the trunk. As I shut it, the streetlight above us felt like a spotlight shining down on us, like we were starring in a romantic movie. He leaned back against my car, smirking as he reached for me and dragged me against him. My hands splayed across his chest, and I wished I could feel his bare skin against mine.

His forehead went to mine, and he growled, "Poppy, I thought I was losing you again."

Instinctively, my hands slid to his back as I pulled myself tighter against him. My heart hammered against my chest. A small sigh escaped my lips. This. Being in his arms. I felt safe, and it was where I was supposed to be.

In a hushed tone, I confessed, "You never lost me."

My words held a deeper truth about all those lost years when we could have shared a life.

His hands came up to my face, cradling my cheeks. Before I knew it, his lips were on mine. He dove into my mouth, and I followed. He kissed me hard like he needed so much more. His hands ran down my arms, wrapping his fingers into mine. He pulled my hands behind his back and let go. Tangling his fingers in my hair and kissed down to that place between my neck and shoulder. My knees nearly gave out.

He whispered my name. "I need you. I want to do so many dirty things to you."

A breath caught in my throat. I wanted him to do those dirty things. All the things. I breathed out his name.

He smiled against my collarbone, dropping his voice. "Yes?"

His fingertips teased along the edge of the hem of my shirt and jeans, just a whisper of touch, and goosebumps bloomed on my skin. I arched my back, pressing my breasts into his body, begging him, willing him to touch me. He caught my bottom lip in his teeth and kissed me deeper, our teeth nearly colliding.

I wanted everything from him—his mouth, his

touch, his skin bare against mine. Molten heat swirled in my belly. I felt him stiffen as I untucked his shirt, my palms finding their way underneath to his warm skin.

I heard the catch in his breath, and then, he devoured me. I loved the scratch of his beard against my skin, marking me as his. I ran my fingers through a smattering of chest hair as my lips trailed to his neck. He let out a growl, tangled his hands into my hair, and pulled my lips back to his.

I was ready. I wanted to give him all of me. If I could, I would have gone home with him right then. We would have kept each other up all night. But… I had an early day tomorrow. If I went home with Sonny, I wouldn't get any sleep.

I released him, stepping back even though I desperately wanted to press myself against him. Instead, I lifted my eyes to his and offered a smile of regret.

He narrowed his eyes, still glazed with lust, as his hands continued to roam my body. "What's wrong?"

"Nothing's wrong. It's just… getting late." Do I confess? I bit my lip before whispering in his ear, "You have no idea how much I want you right now."

I felt a rumble in his chest as he wrapped his hands around my waist, pulling me against him again.

"I'm yours. You can have me. Body and soul, Poppy."

"I know, but…," I leaned back out of his grasp, "I have to be up early to finish a few things in the morning."

He let out a dry chuckle and ran his hand through his hair, looking up at the dark sky. He nodded and quietly said, "I know. I just want..." A frustrated sigh escaped his lips.

I nestled against him again. He rested his head on top of mine. This was torture.

He choked out, "It's hard... to let you go."

I went up on my tiptoes and gave him a kiss that spoke volumes before I said, "I know." Our lips lingered, neither of us wanting to part. I purred, "After the escape room tomorrow, we could, you know, create our own little adventure. I bet we could find some... intriguing ways to pass the time."

My breath came a little quicker as I let the words hang between us, the invitation unmistakable. I saw how his jaw tensed and his fingers flexed like he was holding himself back. He wanted this—wanted me—but he wouldn't take that step unless he knew I was ready.

His hand traced a slow, deliberate path along my arm, sending a shiver through me. "Are you sure?" His voice was low, rough with restraint, but something else was beneath it—something deeper. "Because when we do this, I want it to be because you're ready. Not just because you think I want it."

I held his gaze, letting him see everything I felt—no fear, no hesitation, just certainty. A small smile played on my lips as I leaned in, my fingers curling into his shirt. "I'm sure," I whispered. I want this. I want you."

His eyes softened, the tension in his jaw easing as his thumb brushed gently over my cheek. "You have no idea how much I've wanted to hear that," he murmured. "But more than that, I just want you—however you want to be mine."

Sonny caught my bottom lip between his teeth before kissing me hard and pulling me into him, my face against his neck as his scent filled my nose. He inhaled my hair before kissing the top of my head. He opened my car door so I could climb in, leaning down for one more gentle kiss.

"Sleep tight, Poppy." He dipped his head, his lips barely grazing mine as he whispered, "After the escape room, I plan to take my time with you." He tucked a curl behind my ear, his voice like a quiet promise. "Because you deserve to be cherished, every part of you."

A lick of heat fluttered down to my core, and my breath hitched. I was so close to saying fuck it and going home with him right now, but I knew I couldn't do that. He shot me that crooked smile, his dimples peeking out as he nodded. Then, he moved out of the way so I could shut the door.

Driving home, I should have been going through my checklist for the escape room, but he was the only thing running through my mind.

That next day, Sonny found me in the foyer, panicking. He hugged me before interlocking our fingers as I quickly led him to the escape room. But he halted me just before we reached our destination.

"Claire, what's the matter?" he asked, his voice filled with worry.

Tears shined in my eyes as I tried to blink them back. "It's going to be a disaster."

"What? Why?"

"One of the librarians, Bert, was supposed to be a supervillain in the escape room, but he called in sick. He's had a stomach bug all week."

Sonny rubbed his hands up and down my arms. "It's going to be okay. Is there someone else who can fill in?"

"I haven't found anyone else who can do it. We

can only spare so many people to help out. Everyone else is running the library."

He shrugged, raising his hands, and grinned with a mischievous glint in his eye. "What about me? I've played through lots of escape rooms. I could do it."

He and Bert were about the same height. "Really? You want to? Are you sure? You'll be here all day."

"Yes. Absolutely." He nodded with a smile that went all the way to his eyes. "What do I need to do?"

Maybe this wouldn't be as big of a disaster as I had thought. I let out a sigh of relief and beamed up at him. "Okay. Let's get your costume. You can change in the bathroom."

As we walked to the back room, a knot of anxiety tightened in my belly as I slid my eyes over to him. He might take one look at the costume and refuse, but he didn't even look in the bag when I handed it to him. He just turned toward the bathroom.

For a moment, a weight lifted from my shoulders. But I wanted to ensure he knew exactly what he was getting into, so I quickly followed him, touching his shoulder.

"Sonny… hang on a second."

Chapter 24 - Edison

Edison had barely stepped towards the bathroom when Claire said his name, grabbing his shoulder.

She bit her lip as she reached for the bag. "Um… let me show you all the parts."

Edison wrinkled his brow as soon as she pulled the costume out of the bag. He was hoping for some cool, sexy superhero like Crimson Hammer, but it was a green morph suit mottled with gold and black scales.

His voice cracked as he asked, "What is this?"

She took a deep breath and smiled a little too wide, her cheeks red as she continued removing things from the bag, including a latex frog head with huge, bulbous, bright yellow eyes from the shopping bag.

"Ta-da!"

Edison shook his head. "I'm a… frog?"

"Technically, you're a toad. You know The Quantum Heroes?" She handed him the head and tilted her head. "Dr Toad? He's a mad scientist who turned himself into a huge toad and became evil? Haven't you seen the movie Crisis of Power?"

She pursed her lips as if she was expecting him to hand back the costume and refuse to do it, but there was no way he could let her down. He didn't care if he had to wear this ridiculous costume. He was putting on this costume no matter what.

He shook his head. "Sorry, I haven't kept up with the latest superhero movies." He didn't watch much television or movies, preferring to read. Whenever he did end up at the movie theater, he'd stare at his watch and think of all the other things he could be doing.

He huffed out a breath with his hands on his hips and gave her a determined smile. "But don't worry. I won't let you down." He jerked his thumb over his shoulder and said, "Gotta go turn myself into Dr. Toad."

She grinned and handed him back the bag.

Cuddling on the couch with Claire as they watched a movie sounded like something he wanted to do. Just as Edison headed off to the bathroom, he quickly turned around.

"Maybe tonight we could watch it together?"

A warm smile bloomed on her face as she nodded.

He walked into the bathroom, set the bag on the counter, looked at himself in the mirror, and sighed.

"What in the hell have I got myself into?"

Fifteen minutes later, he was mostly dressed, standing in the middle of the men's bathroom, looking at himself and wondering how anyone would wear this costume in public. He felt naked. It was tight, very tight, and while his body was fit, this outfit did not hide a thing when it came to his crotch—not one thing. While he looked himself over, it slowly dawned on him, to his horror, that the morph suit had huge airbrushed breasts on the chest. Dear god. He swore Claire said a guy was supposed to wear this. He breathed in through his nose, wondering how he would walk out there looking like this.

A middle-aged man entered the bathroom while Edison put on the frog shoes. The guy did a double-take and started to turn right back around.

Edison quickly lifted a hand as if that would make this less awkward. "It's not what it looks like!" Then he glanced down at the oversized webbed feet he was shoving on and winced. "Okay, maybe it is what it looks like, but I promise, I'm doing this for the children!"

Edison could hear the man's maniacal laughter echoing outside the bathroom. Well, this was going to go... swimmingly.

After putting on the gloves, Edison looked at himself again as he paced in front of the mirror. How in the hell was he supposed to walk out there?

He rechecked the bag and sighed in relief when he realized he missed the white lab coat folded at the bottom. Thank fuck for that. He put it on. It barely hit the tops of his thighs and was a snug fit over his chest, but at least his crotch wouldn't be on display. Before walking out, he slid on the latex mask and hoped none of his students were at the library that day.

Peering through the minuscule eye holes, he looked at himself again before walking out of the bathroom. Making his way to the teen room, he quickly realized that seeing through the eye holes was nearly impossible. He bumped into two tables, a bookshelf, and finally, a person before he gave up and ripped it off.

As soon as he pushed open the doors to the teen room, she called for him on the far side of the room. "Sonny! Over here! You look great!"

He plastered on a smile as his eyes darted around the room. He felt like a trapped animal searching for an escape route. He reminded himself he was doing this for her and released a pent-up breath. He'd do anything for her, including wearing an embarrassing costume. She reached for his bag of clothes and set it behind one of the shelving units before he gently grabbed her by the elbow and led her over to the far wall for privacy.

"Um, Claire?" He set the mask down and took off the frog gloves to unbutton the top buttons of the lab coat, pulling it open. Edison lowered his voice to a whisper, "I think this morph suit has breasts. Didn't you say a guy was supposed to wear it?"

Claire looked at his chest, and her eyes widened. A blush rose in her cheeks. She doubled over and started to shake. Was it that bad?

"Are you okay?" He leaned over, a gentle hand on her back, when he realized she was silently laughing, tears running down her face.

She raised back up, trying to control her laughter. "I'm so sorry. I know it's not funny, but…" She fell into another fit of giggles, which caused Edison to break out in a smile and chuckle.

Claire wiped her face and put her hands on her hips, taking a deep breath. "Okay, okay. No more laughing."

She snorted out another giggle and shook her head again. He grinned.

"That's what happens when I let Mrs. Peterson order the costumes. She's been here since the 60s. She insisted on helping out with this project. Most of us had put together our costumes, but Bert was one of the few who didn't have one."

She moved closer to Edison, rebuttoning his lab coat and smoothing it across his chest. Even through layers of clothing, her touch did something to him. He took a step back, hoping she didn't notice.

"Just..." She cleared her throat and dropped her hands, raising her gaze to his.

He smirked, seeing the desire in her eyes.

She took in a deep breath and let it out before giving him a reassuring smile. "Just keep this buttoned, and you should be fine."

She led him to the area for Dr. Toad's laboratory. It was a pond made with blue craft paper and a painted cardboard lily pad in the center containing fake moss and some of the ivy they had separated last night. There was a table with test tubes and beakers full of colored water. He saw a fog machine under the table.

"This is where you'll be." She handed him a stack of sealed clues. "The kids need to tell you a secret passphrase, and you'll give them one of these for their next clue to save Crimson Hammer. The passphrase is..." She suddenly broke out in an evil supervillain laugh, "MWAHHAHA!!!"

He waited for her to give him the passphrase, before realizing what she meant, "Uh... wait, it's the evil laugh?"

She chuckled, "Yep, the clue has letters circled that spell out M-W-A-H-A-H-A."

He nodded, feeling excited. "Cool, that seems easy enough."

Claire turned to face him. "I really appreciate you doing this." She grabbed his hand and squeezed. "I owe you one."

As he slipped on the frog gloves, Edison leaned in, his voice a warm rasp against her ear. "Oh, you definitely owe me," he murmured. "But don't worry —I plan on collecting tonight. And something tells me our adventure will be a lot more fun than this one."

Her cheeks flushed a lovely shade of pink as she

tucked a loose strand of hair behind her ear. "I, um, should go get changed into my Belladonna Nightshade costume," she said, her voice a little unsteady.

Weeks ago, when she told him she was going to dress up like Belladonna Nightshade, he looked up the character and was surprised to see she was a sexy siren with sleek curves accentuated in a black and purple body suit with fiery red curls like Claire's.

Edison smirked, his gaze lingering on her. "You know," he murmured, low and teasing, "you could just wear it home. Might make things a little more interesting tonight."

For a brief moment, Claire's eyes widened, and her lips parted like she wanted to say something— maybe a witty retort, maybe a breathless laugh. Instead, she pressed them together, fighting a flustered smile as her blush deepened. Then, with a shake of her head and a pointed look that couldn't quite hide her amusement, she turned on her heel and walked off to change. He chuckled softly to himself.

After she left, Edison looked around Dr. Toad's lab, unsure what he should be doing.

"Hey!" Darci came behind him dressed like a sultry black cat.

Claire had told him Darci was the supervillain Foxy Feline. She wore a shiny black latex bodysuit with cat ears and a tail. Her patent leather boots went above her knees. Her makeup was dark and smoky around her eyes, and what looked like real whiskers came out of her face.

"Hi, Darci. You look amazing! How are you?" He waved, but she hugged him awkwardly, making them both laugh.

"I'm good. So she talked you into Dr. Toad, huh?"

He grinned shyly. "I offered to help when she said y'all were a man down. But this costume is something else."

"Oh yeah, it's something else, all right," Darci smirked and gave him a once over.

Edison asked, "So, do I stand on the lily pad or sit? I didn't see a chair..."

"Can you pop a squat?" She showed him by squatting into position over the lily pad, a mischievous grin on her face.

"Seriously?" Edison ran his hand through his hair.

She stood up laughing, brushing her thighs with her hands, "No, no. I'm kidding."

"You had me there for a second." Edison smiled, a blush creeping up his neck.

"Hang on a sec! We do have one cool prop for you."

Darci ran to a storage closet and returned with a small cooler, a pair of tongs, and a hammer.

She held up the cooler, smiling, "Dry ice!"

"Cool. What do I do?"

She set the cooler under the table and opened it. Grabbing the hammer off the table, she started beating something inside.

"What... are you doing?"

"Breaking up the dry ice." She grabbed the tongs and lifted a small pebble of dry ice. "It's for the beakers." She dropped it in the blue-colored one with a plop. It immediately started to bubble, and steam rose. It added a cool effect to the mad scientist lab. The kids were going to love it.

She closed the cooler, setting the hammer and tongs on it. Turning to face Edison, she put her hands on her hips and said, "Two rules."

"Okay…"

"Number one—don't touch the dry ice with your bare hands. It will burn the shit out of you. And number two—keep the lid on the cooler, or the dry ice will evaporate and disappear."

He nodded along. "I think I can handle that."

"Perfect. Now you'll look like a real mad scientist." She patted his chest and chuckled as she walked around the table. "Oh, and turn on the fog machine under the table when a group of kids start to go through the escape room. Then, turn it off in between."

Edison nodded. "Got it."

He leaned down to see how to work the fog machine when he heard Darci let out a whistle. "Girl, look at you!"

He righted himself and did a double take as Claire walked over in costume. His jaw dropped, and he couldn't take his eyes off her. With her sexy sway and smirk, she seemed to have adopted her character's attitude. He wasn't subtle as his head tilted ever so slightly, a smirk on his face, as his eyes followed her movements, sweeping down her body and back up again.

Claire had a dark purple bodysuit covering nearly everything but left nothing to the imagination. Her shoulders were bare, and he could see the galaxy of freckles over each of them. Her waist was cinched with a black corset that not only enhanced it but made her breasts the centerpiece of her outfit. Her lips were dark purple, almost black. She had a small black mask covering her eyes, which practically glowed sapphire blue with her dark smoky eye makeup. To complete the look, she had a pair of black gloves that went to her elbows and black knee-high boots lined with buckles up her legs with a dagger in the top buckle of each one. Her curls were interspersed with greenery and round blackberries.

Darci looked up at Edison and smacked his stomach, "I think there's some drool on your chin."

He reached up towards his face as Darci and Claire laughed.

"I think I'm ready." Claire looked between Darci and Edison. "Do I look okay? I haven't worn this one before."

A huge smile spread across Darci's face. "Oh my god, woman. You look gorgeous. Doesn't she, Edison?" She twirled her finger around, and Claire did a quick spin.

He nodded quickly, "You look incredible, Poppy."

Claire blushed.

Darci backed away with a little wave. "I'll see you two in a minute."

Claire called after her, "Can you make sure Anna, Melody, and Calvin are ready?" She tapped her watch as Darci nodded and walked away. "The first group shows up in 15 minutes!"

She looked up at Edison and asked shyly, "I look okay?"

Edison's brows lifted slightly, his gaze sweeping over her with a mix of awe and something unmistakably heated. His lips parted as if he'd forgotten to breathe for a second, then curved into a slow, reassuring smile. He couldn't believe she'd ever doubt how incredible she looked.

"Like I said... you look incredible... just stunning."

She grinned and inclined her head. "You ready for this?"

Edison ran his hand over his mouth, raising his shoulder as he grimaced. "As I'll ever be."

Chapter 25 - Claire

I had to hand it to Sonny. He got into his character. He kept up with the first group of kids, handing out clues and telling jokes. He even made a few kids laugh when they were too shy to make the evil laugh for the clue. There were three more groups to get through, and our escape room was on its way to being our most successful yet.

During a break between groups, I walked over to check on him. When he saw me, he pulled his mask off and met me halfway. His face was flushed and sweaty, and I could feel the heat radiating off his body. Desire fluttered through me when I remembered the promise I gave him last night. I desperately wanted to touch him, kiss him, anything to get back to where we were last night. I took a deep breath, hoping to quell my need, and smiled at him.

"How's it going?"

His hand brushed mine, but he kept his distance. "It's good. But... you wouldn't believe what the last group was saying."

I frowned. "What was it?"

"Um..." He stifled a laugh. "I, uh, I overheard the kids calling me Dr. Chode instead of Dr. Toad."

"What?!" I looked around, hoping no one was around to hear this conversation. I inclined my head for Sonny to follow me to the far wall, away from everyone.

He huffed out a laugh, and amusement lit up his eyes. As we walked, he leaned over and whispered in my ear. "Claire... you do know what a chode is, right?"

I stopped abruptly and said quickly, "Of course I do," but refused to make eye contact with him as my cheeks reddened.

He leaned against the wall with a playful smirk on his face. "What is it?"

I looked around to ensure we were completely alone. He had one eyebrow cocked, mirth all over his face.

I shook my head. "I'm not..." I wasn't sure how to answer this in the middle of the library. I stepped closer to him and held my hands up in a circle. I tried to keep a straight face and said quietly. "Like a tuna can?"

He broke out in quiet laughter. "Do you know how hard it was to keep a straight face with them calling me that? God, to be in middle school again." He laughed again.

"I can only imagine." I nodded and giggled, holding my hand over my mouth.

He leaned closer and lowered his voice. His hot breath caressed my ear, and it caused a prickling of goosebumps down my arms. "Do I look like I have a chode?" His voice cracked.

Heat flared to my cheeks again. I took two steps back. My eyes slowly traveled down his body, but the lab coat hid everything.

He held his hands out. "Hold on." He squatted down into a frog pose. "At one point, I dropped a bunch of the clues and was crouched down like this when I first overheard them." Once he was squatting, he looked up at me expectantly.

I couldn't stop giggling, "Oh my god… Sonny, we cannot be doing this right now."

He loudly whispered, "It does, doesn't it? I look like I have a chode?" A look of worry flashed across his face, but there was a glint of amusement in his eyes.

I waved my hands around as I whispered, "No, of course not. But… seriously! Someone is going to hear you!" I couldn't stop giggling. "Hold on. I'm still looking."

He muttered, waggling his eyebrows, "I'm sure you are."

I couldn't see his crotch from where I was standing. I walked around him nonchalantly to see him from different angles. His gaze followed me, a puzzled look on his face.

I choked out a laugh, "Hmm, maybe…."

He gave me a skeptical look, "Maybe what?"

I shook my head, unable to control the laughter as I spluttered, holding my hands over my mouth. I lowered my voice. "Sonny, I can't see anything… chode-like."

He stood up immediately, releasing a breath and stretching his legs again. "Thank god."

I arched an eyebrow and asked him, "Were you really worried?"

A slow grin spread across his face. "No."

I rolled my eyes and shook my head. I took a step closer to him and leaned towards him.

"So what did you do?"

"About the kids?"

I nodded.

"What was I going to do?" He shrugged. "They

were just getting back at me because I was teasing them. I'd tell them their laughs weren't evil enough. Then, I'd make them do it repeatedly before giving them the clue." He laughed.

"Ruthless." I chuckled. "You're brave, teasing teenagers."

"Those kids are the ruthless ones." He chuckled, "At least they aren't saying it to my face. It's hard being a supervillain."

I laughed again and brushed my fingers against his forearm. "Alright, Dr. Toad, it's time for another group of kids to come through."

He puffed out his chest. "Let's do it." He gave me a smirk and a salute before putting his mask on.

I couldn't help myself. I ran my hand up under his lab coat and lightly smacked his ass before I walked away.

He turned, his voice muffled from the mask, but I could still hear the glee, "What was that?"

I shrugged, giving him a wink as I walked backward to my spot. Then, as the next group of kids filtered in behind me, I gave him a big smile.

Two hours later, we were finally done. The last group had come through and saved Crimson Hammer from the supervillains. The escape room had been an enormous success. More kids had attended this one than any other we'd had before.

"Please tell me I can take this off now."

I chuckled. "You've completed your service as Dr. Toad."

"Awesome!" He found his bag of clothes hiding behind the shelves and jogged towards the bathroom before turning around. "Wait for me?"

"I'm not going anywhere." I motioned to the supervillain lairs. "We have to clean everything up and make it look like a library again."

"Don't start without me, Poppy."

I blushed as he grinned and walked backward towards the bathroom. His eyes roamed my body again before he turned around and headed into the bathroom with his clothes. I sat down on a bench, pulling my boots off and massaging my feet.

My mind wandered as I thought about how different Sonny and Pete were. When Pete bothered to communicate with me, he never called me anything but my given name. Most of the time, he kept his distance in another room, completely closed off. There were week-long stretches where we rarely spoke to each other. It was a lonely time. I talked to him until I was blue in the face about marriage counseling, but he didn't see the point.

Those last few months of my marriage, I was constantly crying. My breath hitched when I remembered how close I'd come to doing something terrible. I had been reading _The Virgin Suicides_, and I was a little obsessed with the scene where Cecilia is in the bathtub and slits her wrists. I read it repeatedly and romanticized it in my head for weeks. It seemed so... easy, peaceful, and warm, like I could do that, and it would fix everything.

One day, my mom showed up, took one look at me, and said, "We're leaving. Pack your stuff."

We packed my bags that day, and I moved in with my parents for a few months before I moved to Denton alone. Emotionally, it was hard. Sure, I was grateful to be out of a loveless, sexless marriage. Starting over again gave me some hope where I'd had none, but seeing couples together, even doing mundane things like grocery shopping, sent me into tears.

But eventually, I broke out of my despair. Slowly, I came back to life again. I started working out, and I met Darci. I loved my new job at the library. I went back to doing what made me happy—the things Pete always hated, the ones I gave up just to please him. I went back to reading smutty romances again, dancing around the house to my favorite Taylor Swift songs, and finally feeling like me again. It took some time, but I found myself—the bubbly, upbeat girl who had always been so full of life and energy. Surprisingly, I wasn't the only one who noticed my transformation. People started to gravitate to me more than ever, and even my mom said she could see the sparkle in my eyes again.

Walking to the back room to grab a roll of trash bags, I let those memories fade. When I returned to the teen room, I handed out trash bags to Darci, Melody, Anna, and a few volunteers. I started in Dr. Toad's lab and tossed the painted display into a bag. I finished it just as Sonny walked back in, looking way too delicious in dark blue jeans, boots, and a purple t-shirt. Every time he moved, his shirt tightened around his chest and shoulders just the right way. Watching him swagger over to me, I felt my body heat up.

"Cleaning up without me?" He playfully pouted.

He grabbed the trash bag from me as we continued cleaning. I shrugged and gave him a smirk.

"Just getting a head start so we can get out of here sooner."

He wrapped his free arm around my waist and tried to kiss the top of my head but got a face full of belladonna berries from my headpiece instead. I laughed as he batted them away.

"Smooth, Mr. Wright. Very smooth."

He chuckled while pushing down the trash in the bag to add more.

Thirty minutes later, we were done. Sonny and a couple of guys from the reference desk moved the empty bookshelves to the storage room, and before we knew it, the teen library room was back to normal. Darci and Melody took the trash bags to the dumpster, and I went to change clothes.

I removed my headpiece and mask, and it took me forever to remove the heavy eye makeup. I reapplied a little mascara and lip balm before slipping into a short green peasant-style dress and black wedge boots.

I found Sonny casually leaning against the wall in the foyer, one arm above his head and his eyes glued to his phone. Even in that pose, he was effortlessly sexy as his shirt rode up, revealing a hint of a dark blond trail leading south. But my eyes snagged on his arm, and the edge of an intricate tattoo peeked out of his left shirt sleeve. How did I never notice it before? I didn't remember him having any tattoos years ago, and I was suddenly dying to see the rest of it.

His gaze met mine as he lowered the phone. A slow smile spread across his face as he scanned my body. The heat in his stare sent a thrill rushing through me. I was suddenly desperate to feel the heat of his skin against mine, surrender to him. That familiar rush of desire no longer scared me, and nothing would hold me back.

All those years ago, we had been a supernova, a fiery collision that burned so bright. Those memories had been playing on a loop in my mind for so long, and I needed him. Sonny had been so patient, too patient, waiting for me. Now, I was consumed by a primal need. I wanted him. Over me. Under me. On me. In me. I wanted him woven into the fabric of my very being. Something told me that tonight had been etched in the stars, a moment that would change everything.

I stopped in front of him, craning my neck. I wasn't sure who kissed whom, but it sent a jolt of electricity coursing through me, erasing any doubt or fear. It didn't even occur to me that we were still in the library foyer or if anyone saw us.

Chapter 26 - Edison

All those years of wanting, waiting, and dreaming of her coalesced into this moment, and while Edison had imagined it countless times, nothing had prepared him. Her gaze was a gravitational pull drawing him in.

She nearly jumped into his arms, wrapping herself around him. Gone was the hesitation and fear, replaced by a new raw urgency. Whatever she figured out in those days apart, she had needed it.

Claire melted against him, and his body came alive at the sound of her quickening breath, the feel of her frantic pulse. She nuzzled his jaw up to his ear. Claire traced a finger along Edison's arm, sending shivers down his spine.

"Remember what I whispered last night?" Her voice was a husky murmur.

He couldn't help but grin, a flicker of amusement in his eyes. "I think it was something about making our own adventure?"

A slow smile spread across Claire's face, her lips teasingly close to his. "Something like that."

"The only adventure I have in mind right now," he murmured, his voice barely a whisper, "involves getting you alone and exploring every delicious inch of you."

He brushed his thumb across her cheek, his gaze holding hers with a promise of what was to come.

"Take me home, Sonny," she murmured, each word igniting the desire for their connection. "Let's make up for lost time."

Hesitantly, he pulled back, searching her eyes. "You're sure?"

Claire nodded a silent promise. Her eyes reflected his longing, and he wanted to lose himself in her gaze.

Tucking her against him, he kept her close as they stepped outside. After he helped her into the truck, he slid in, and she scooted against his side. The drive felt like an eternity and a heartbeat all at once as Edison drove home. The silence was like a taut cord, tense and electric, while she traced slow, deliberate circles on his thigh, the feather-light touch going straight to his thickening cock.

Taking her hand, he led her into the house, straight to the bedroom, where he gently pushed her to sit on the bed. Bandit jumped up and gave himself a shake.

Edison kissed her softly on the lips. "I'm going to let Bandit out and feed him. I'll be back in a few minutes." He gave her a mock, stern look, kissing her again. "Don't move."

She giggled, "Okay."

He returned a moment later, grabbing the dog bed to take to the living room. "Bandit's going to hang out in the living room."

She arched her eyebrow, "You think that's going to work?"

He raised a shoulder, "A guy can hope."

"He seems a little… needy. Knowing we're here, won't he scratch and cry at the door?"

He grinned, pulling a couple of chicken jerkies from his back pocket, "Not if I give him these."

She laughed. "If you think so..."

"Well, we're going to try."

He walked back out and returned a moment later, shutting the door and locking it.

She stood up as he prowled over to her, his lips on hers instantly, swiping his tongue against her mouth. She responded, and their kiss deepened, soft but quickly becoming something more. Edison's hands found their way to her waist, up to her shoulders, her cheeks, and then tangling into her hair. She melted into him.

He pulled away, breathless, reaching behind him and pulling his t-shirt over his head. His gaze held hers, searching for a flicker of doubt, a retreat. But there was none. Her eyes snagged on the expanse of his chest. It was broad and more defined than years ago, covered in a light dusting of blond hair.

As her gaze drifted down, she stopped, lingering on his upper left arm. He drew in a shaky breath and let it out. This was it—the moment he'd both dreaded and craved. She'd see the hidden bloom, a silent confession etched on his skin. The poppy—its petals impossibly delicate, blooming against his skin. The vibrant splash of crimson with its black center, the veins and tendrils of the stem snaking down his bicep, a secret only revealed in moments of intimacy like this. It had been a foolish desire years ago, a reckless promise. But now, it bloomed into something so much more. What would she think?

Her eyes widened in surprise, like a sunrise. A deeper emotion flickered beneath. Recognition or something more? Shimmering with unshed tears, her eyes met his again, a silent conversation passing between them. She hesitantly reached up to caress the petals. The hitch in her breath sent a shiver down his spine.

She breathed out, "Sonny," as he leaned down and kissed across her collarbone. "Is that... a poppy?"

She gently traced the labyrinth of swirls with her fingers down the intricate stem, goosebumps spreading from her touch.

He kissed her neck and breathed, "Yes," before daring to meet her gaze again. "I lost you once... but I never wanted to forget."

Edison's smile flickered just briefly, heat rising in his cheeks. Her eyes searched his. He felt so exposed, laying bare a part of his soul, a piece of her, permanently etched on his skin.

He took her hands in his, placing them over his heart. "Tell me," he whispered, a hint of nervousness.

Claire's breath was warm against his skin as she leaned forward and kissed his chest.

"It's..." she began, her voice barely a whisper, "breathtaking." Her hand, drawn by an invisible thread, returned to the intricate lines, tracing them with such reverence. Another kiss, soft and lingering, landed where she had touched, igniting a spark that danced between them.

He gave her a loving smile, running his fingers to the tops of her shoulders, sliding each sleeve of her dress down, revealing those constellations of freckles he had fantasized about countless times. He raised his eyebrows, silently asking permission before she helped him push her dress down until it dropped to the floor. She was in nothing but a lace bra and matching panties, so delicate and hugging her curves in all the right places. The color was nearly identical to her creamy skin.

Edison took in an audible breath, "Look at you."

He couldn't help but stare, wistful at the sight before him. A flash of memory took over when he remembered those fleeting nights she slept bare, pressed against him as he tried to count the galaxies of freckles all over her body. He traced the curves of her body with gentle fingertips, a half smile on his face, savoring her softness. He walked her back until her legs hit the bed and gently laid her back, hovering over her and caging her in.

Her eyes were heady with desire. She reached down, cupping him through his jeans.

He hissed, "Fuck."

Claire slipped her hands into the waistband of his jeans, moving her hands to open the button and slowly pulling the zipper down. Edison felt instant relief as his cock sprung forward.

"Off," she said before his lips found hers again, kissing her hard and chaotic as she slid her hands into the waist of his jeans, slowly working them over his ass, down to his thighs. He kicked them off, tossing them aside. The only thing separating them was his black boxer briefs and her scrap of lace underwear.

Edison kissed down from her lips to her neck, goosebumps rising on her skin as he smiled against her. His mouth was at the valley between her breasts, licking up one side to the edge of her bra cup and then tugging it down with his teeth to expose her rosy nipple. He nibbled it, suckling it into his mouth, pulling and tweaking with his teeth.

She moaned, "Yes."

He found the front clasp, flipping it open with one hand, allowing her breasts to fall from their weight as he pulled it off, tossing it somewhere. His fingers pinched and twisted the nipple he'd just left while his mouth licked the other one, suckling it into his mouth, flicking it with his tongue.

Claire's eyes were closed, heat staining her chest, a look of ecstasy across her face. She whispered, "More."

Her hips pulsed under him, but he needed a taste of her. He kissed his way down her stomach, tickling her with his beard as she giggled, pulling off her underwear as he went. He stopped at her pubic bone, just above her tight red curls, right where he knew she wanted him when something caught his eye on her left hip—a small yellow sun outlined in black with words written in a feminine script around the edge. "I wish I had known that the sun would never shine without you."

"Poppy?" He looked up at her face, his voice thick. "Is this...? What is...?" Overcome with emotion, his hand brushed across her hip.

"I guess we were both thinking the same thing," she said with a ghost of a smile. She nodded with tears in her eyes. "My biggest regret..."

The emotions filling him up felt too strong, too fast, too soon. He wanted to say the words he'd been feeling for too long.

Instead, he crawled back up to her, kissing her fiercely before saying, "We found each other again, and this time, I'm holding on."

Edison kissed back down her body and gently kissed the center of her tattoo, staring at it for one last beat before licking his way back to her pubic bone, his desire overwhelming. He kissed down her inner thigh, nipping with his teeth, marking her as his.

"Sonny, please." She pleaded.

"Please, what?"

"I need-"

He smiled up at her, and in a teasingly seductive tone, he asked, "What do you need, baby?"

Her hands found the back of his head, guiding him towards her center as she whispered, "I need... your mouth."

Her legs opened wider. She glistened, so wet, so turned on. She couldn't hold still, writhing with need. His arm across her hips pressed her body into the bed to keep her still. Her scent was intoxicating, musky, and sweet. His mouth watered, remembering how he devoured her repeatedly that weekend.

He looked up at her as she opened her eyes and found his. He smiled tenderly. "There you are. Look at me, baby. When you come on my tongue, I want to see those beautiful blue eyes."

She locked her gaze to his as he flattened his tongue and gave her a long lick, relishing the look on her face. It was even better than he remembered. He flicked and sucked her clit, steadily increasing the pace, watching her pant, feeling her hands pressing his head deeper into her center. He sucked her clit into his mouth, harder, nipping it, feeling her squirm as memories flooded his mind from all those years ago. She moaned his name. He pushed one, then two fingers, into her slowly, curling them, finding her g-spot, pumping in and out, while his tongue played with her clit.

Her eyes, still locked to his, were pools of black. She was consumed by desire, barely able to form words. "Sonny, I... going...come."

He grinned with a flash of dimples. "I want to watch you come undone, Poppy."

That was all it took before she clenched around his fingers and came all over his tongue. He lapped her up, not stopping, even when she begged, wanting her to ride it out as long as possible.

Those dark blue eyes were windows to her soul, and he just glimpsed a part of her that no one else had ever seen, a part he selfishly wanted just for himself, forever. He kissed and licked every part of her as he crawled his way back up, pushing his boxers down while she came down from her euphoria. His beard was still slick with her orgasm when he kissed her deeply, allowing her to taste herself.

She smiled against his lips as she whispered, "How do you make me feel so good?" She breathed out, "I had forgotten."

He grinned before kissing her again. If only she knew how often he had played the memories of their lovemaking in his head over the years. There were times he wondered if it had all just been a fantasy. But after this, he knew, he remembered, it had been real. With her in his bed, one word flashed over and over in his mind—mine. Mine. Mine.

He raised, hovering over her. "Are you on birth control?"

"Yes."

"It's been a long while since I've been with anyone. I'm clean and want to feel all of you, Poppy."

She lovingly caressed his back. "Yes, I want that."

His tip nudged against her thigh as he guided himself to her entrance. He went cautiously slow as he entered her, knowing it might be painful for her. She grabbed his broad shoulders, bracing herself, trembling against him, fear overtaking her.

He ran his lips against her jaw, down to where her shoulder met her neck, and then up to her ear. "Is this okay? Do you need to stop?"

She shook her head, her eyes tightly closed.

He kissed behind her ear as he whispered, "Relax, baby. I won't hurt you. We'll stop if that's what you need."

She bit her lip and nodded, letting out a pent-up breath. She whispered, "Don't stop."

He continued to slowly push into her, peppering her with tiny kisses down her neck.

As he seated himself, the heat and pressure felt so good. Too good. Like she had been made just for him. His missing puzzle piece. It had never been like this with anyone else.

Relaxing, she let out a breathy sigh as she began to move her hips against him.

"Poppy, let me... Wait, just... Just let me feel you." He choked out a chuckle, "I don't want this over before it starts."

She stopped moving and grinned. Their eyes met, and hers danced with a hypnotic energy he couldn't resist as she whispered, "I'm sorry. You just feel so good."

Her lips found his again, and he got lost in the passion of the moment and felt the beginning of the coiling low in his belly. They moved in sync slowly at first and then gained speed as he pumped in and out, her hips meeting his every time.

Her breath stuttered in his ear, and everything else lost significance. Time stopped, and minutes blurred into each other. The universe collapsed and was reborn. Stars and galaxies died and scattered into nothing. All there was... was her.

As his pace quickened, he dragged his hand between them, finding that bundle of nerves, running circles around it, flicking it with his finger. Her breath hitched in his ear.

"Oh god, Sonny. Right. There. I'm. So. Close."

He grunted into her neck, feeling her convulse and clench around him.

"Poppy, come for me again."

She wrapped her legs around him, digging her nails into his shoulders, the pain so good, marking him as hers. She clenched tighter, her moans addictive, euphoria washing across her face. She screamed out his name.

He wrapped his hand into her curls, holding her against him. His cock swelled from the intensity of her orgasm as his own built and coiled even tighter until he could no longer keep it at bay, releasing with such ferocity his heart raced, fighting to leave his chest. He growled her name and saw stars as he fell against her.

He rolled them so they were facing each other, not wanting his weight pressing down on her. He kissed her tenderly and tucked a curl behind her ear. She smiled at him.

He asked, "You okay?"

She gave him a languid smile. "Perfect. This was... You're so... perfect." She caressed the side of his face.

He grinned and kissed her again. "I saw stars. Never had that happened before."

He hopped out of bed, washed himself quickly in the sink, and grabbed a warm washcloth to clean her up before returning to the bed to snuggle against her, their legs entwined.

Emotions welled up in him—big ones, overwhelming ones—ones he was afraid to say out loud. They stared into each other's eyes. She seemed as awestruck as he was. Nestling against him, she closed her eyes, and he found himself tracing the contours of her face with his gaze, memorizing every detail as she drifted off to sleep, a contented smile on her face.

Watching her sleep, he marveled at his incredible fortune, but a whisper of doubt clouded his thoughts, the secret he'd been afraid to tell her. He pushed those thoughts aside, recognizing them as just his fears. Things were different this time, and tonight, as he held her, it felt like he was holding everything that ever mattered.

Chapter 27 - Claire

The morning light painted the room as I woke up, still wrapped in Sonny's embrace. I couldn't help but smile, seeing him still asleep beside me.

Feeling the need to stretch my limbs, I gingerly moved out of his embrace before scooting back into him as the little spoon. He nuzzled his chin into my neck, and a raspy whisper sounded like "I love you" mumbled in his sleep. It didn't scare me.

I pressed myself tighter into him and sighed. Last night, it was as if my soul had finally woken up and recognized its other half. Were we always destined to collide? I didn't know, but it didn't really concern me anymore. If the universe brought us together or if we'd been destined since the beginning of time, I was choosing him. There was this certainty, this clarity that Sonny was mine, and I was his in more than just a physical connection. My heart swelled when I realized I truly loved him. Was it too soon? Did he feel the same way? Should I tell him?

The more I thought about it, the more I needed to tell him. I couldn't hold back the dam of emotions that was about to burst.

I rolled over to face him. The need to touch him, feel him, kiss him was overwhelming. It consumed me. My fingers brushed against the rough texture of his beard against his cheek, and he stirred, a sleepy smile playing at the corners of his lips. My heart fluttered as he reached for me.

His voice was rough with sleep, "Come here, Poppy."

He hauled me against him, turning me so my back was against him again. The warmth of his skin next to mine and the strength of his body pressed completely against me made me feel safe, cherished... and loved. He pressed a sleepy kiss against my shoulder as his arm pulled me tighter into him, wrapping protectively around my belly.

He relaxed, and his breath slowed as he fell back to sleep. I wanted to stay in this cocoon with him, away from the world forever. His steady breath brushed against my skin, each rise and fall drawing me deeper into the warmth of sleep.

I woke again, unsure how much time had passed, but the light outside was brighter, not the gentle glow from earlier. Sonny's erection was pressed firmly against me, his hand now cupping my breast, my nipple between his fingers. He was still asleep, but I couldn't hold still, moving my ass up and down against him. The wetness between my legs let him slip along my center as I pressed backward into him to the right spot.

Sonny woke up with a start, breathing out my name as I reached behind me.

His hand massaged my breast, tweaking my nipple. His lips went to my neck, sucking gently, and his body began to move against me until he slid in deep, right where I needed him. I hooked my leg around his hip as his hand slowly migrated down, and his fingers parted me. He pressed his thumb into my clit as he slowly pumped in and out. With each thrust, I pressed against him, and our hips moved faster together. As my climax built, I squeezed against him, and we raced toward bliss.

I came hard, reaching up and wrapping my hand behind his neck, moaning his name. Seconds later, his breath stuttered as he fell off that same cliff, and his warmth filled me. He whispered my name so reverently my breath caught. I turned to find his lips and wrapped my hands around his back, pulling myself against him. His hand reached behind my head, tangling in my hair as he gently kissed me.

Those three little words were on the tip of my tongue, but a whisper of caution held me back. I worried it would be too much too soon. When our eyes met, I saw those same feelings reflected back at me. No one had ever made me feel both safe and vulnerable at the same time the way he did. Every confession, every shared secret, every glance, every touch made our connection stronger.

Breaking the kiss, my voice was barely a whisper. "There's something I need to tell you," I confessed, a blush creeping up my neck. Tears welled in my eyes, threatening to spill. "But I'm afraid it might be too soon." Hesitantly, I met his gaze again, letting out a shaky breath. "Is it?"

Sonny gently placed his palm on my cheek, his eyes full of tenderness. "You can tell me anything." He nodded, "I want to hear what's on your heart."

His eyes twinkled in the light streaming in from the window, full of warmth and affection, and I couldn't help but kiss him again.

"I... I love you. I worry it's too fast. We've only found each other again, and I don't want to rush things or scare you away, but these feelings are overwhelming if I keep them in any longer."

A smile bloomed across his face as his eyes crinkled like I was cherished and adored. "Claire... you've cracked open a part of my heart that I thought was lost forever. I didn't realize I fell in love with you that weekend until you were gone. I'm not sure I ever stopped loving you all this time. I'm desperately in love with you, Poppy."

My tears fell. "I don't want to be too much."

He swiped my tears before tucking one of my curls behind my ear. "You are never too much. Falling in love is terrifying. You willingly leave yourself open and vulnerable to someone else. There's always a chance of getting hurt, but that won't happen with us." I laid my head on his chest, and he kissed my forehead. "We got a second chance, Poppy, and I won't waste it."

Silence stretched before he said, "You were always it for me, even when I thought I'd lost you."

My breath hitched. "All this time?"

He nodded as he pulled me over his body to straddle him. He intertwined our hands, pulling me down. He leaned in to kiss me as we slid together. Our lovemaking was unhurried, like we had all the time in the world. I pulled our hands up over his head, using them as leverage to move against him as our kiss deepened. Our bodies slick with sweat, we moved together as one, slowly, passionately, and stayed intertwined—our hands, our mouths, our bodies. I needed him everywhere.

I pulled back from our kiss, my breath ragged as he locked his eyes with mine and said, "I love you, Claire," like a vow, just as I fell over that cliff, whispering his name as a prayer as the rush of ecstasy overtook me.

A moment later, I felt the heat of his release, and my love for him overflowed, burning brighter than a thousand stars. This felt like more than just a four-letter word. It was as if our paths weren't just meant to cross. They were sewn together with the threads of fate itself.

I nuzzled my face against his neck and whispered, "You're mine, Sonny, and I will always be yours."

Chapter 28 - Edison

They'd been together for weeks, but the night of the escape room had changed everything. What had always been an undeniable pull between them deepened into something more—something unspoken yet understood in every glance, every lingering touch. Edison couldn't get enough of Claire, and neither could she. They sought each other out constantly, drawn together by an invisible force. Their nights blurred into shared breaths and tangled limbs, falling asleep wrapped around each other, fingers instinctively laced together.

Mornings became his favorite part of the day—waking up to her warm body pressed against his, the scent of her shampoo lingering on his pillow, the way she sighed softly in her sleep. When she wasn't there, the bed felt empty, the silence too heavy, her absence something he could feel down to his bones. He wanted her beside him every night, to wake up to her sleepy smile every morning, to build something real, something lasting.

If it were up to him, she would've moved in already—yesterday, last week, years ago. But the ink on her divorce was barely dry. Would she see his invitation as security or a sacrifice of her newfound independence? He wouldn't risk pushing her away. So instead, he showed his intentions in quiet gestures—a cleared-out drawer, a corner of the closet, a spare key left by her purse. And every time he noticed another trace of her claiming space in his world—a stray hair tie on the nightstand, her perfume lining the bathroom shelf—his chest tightened with something he couldn't quite name. But he knew what it meant. She wasn't just becoming part of his life—she was becoming his home.

One lazy Saturday, they spent all morning in bed together. Edison relished the feel of her soft skin against him as they lay wrapped in the sheets in the late morning light. She slipped out of his arms, and he couldn't help but watch her beautiful backside sway out of the room, Bandit following her. He chuckled, wondering how in the world did she get freckles on her ass.

"Where are you going?" Edison mock-whined, his voice rising playfully at the end. "I need you back in this bed."

She popped her head back in the doorway. "I'll be right back." She smiled and gave him a wink before disappearing down the hallway. She was back in seconds, a book held against her chest.

She asked, "Want to do something with me?"

Edison sat up in bed, the covers slipping down, exposing his eagerness. Her eyes roamed his body.

He smirked, wiggling his eyebrows. "Always. Get over here!"

She rolled her eyes, a smile tugging at her lips. "I meant something else."

"What?" He turned, his legs hanging over the side of the bed as he reached for her, never having his fill.

She came over, standing between his thighs. "You know I want you in as many ways as possible, but this is different."

"So what exactly are we doing?" He murmured against her neck, his hands running up and down her hips and backside.

She leaned into him, his arousal pressing against her stomach. He let out a dark chuckle, his hands roaming further down, finding her ready for him as she moaned and struggled to keep the conversation going.

When she said they needed to go to the downtown square, he turned to lay her on the bed. Hovering over her, he suggested they have a picnic lunch on the courthouse lawn between kisses, and she readily agreed.

"Now, where was I?" He asked as his eyes roamed her body. She giggled. "Oh yes, I remember. I think I was about to..." he sucked her nipple into his mouth, and she moaned, her hands lifted to run through his hair.

An hour and two orgasms later, they were ready to go, having packed up a blanket and a cooler full of drinks. Bandit was patiently waiting by the door after Edison put his harness on. On the way, they stopped to grab some sandwiches at a deli.

Edison drove around the square looking for an elusive parking space near Hearth & Grain, the restaurant where Claire wanted to leave the book. She'd been having dreams about it for days.

Across the street, they found a nice shady place under a big oak tree on the courthouse lawn for their picnic. Edison set out the food while Claire filled a water bowl for Bandit and got their drinks out of the cooler.

Once they settled into their picnic, Edison

wondered aloud what might happen next. "So you leave books for people to find, and then what?"

She chuckled, "I've never stuck around long enough to find out."

Edison pinched his brows together. "Really? Don't you ever wonder?"

Claire took a huge bite of her meatball sandwich, chewing as she thought about Edison's question before answering.

"I'm curious, but at the same time, I'm not sure I want to know." She shrugged.

Edison nodded as he chewed.

She popped a chip in her mouth. "I don't know. I like the mystery."

Curiosity danced in his eyes as he leaned in, whispering, "Ever wonder... if maybe the books bring people together? Like us?" He shoved a bite in his mouth, eyebrows raised, eagerly awaiting her response.

"I don't know. Maybe we're different?" She smiled, shrugging. "I wondered about it when that girl at the church found my book. There was something about her that just made me feel like that book was going to lead her to love."

Edison took her hand in his. "Whatever it is, I'm just thankful that book brought me to you again, and we're doing this together."

She looked up at him shyly. "I want to do everything with you." His stomach turned over as he leaned in to kiss her.

After eating, they cleaned up and walked Bandit around the square before walking to the restaurant. They sat outside at a table under the awning and ordered drinks since Bandit was with them. When they were done, Claire left the book in one of the chairs at the table.

Walking away, Edison leaned down and whispered in her ear. "Want to see if someone finds it?"

Giving him a conspiratorial smile, she nodded. "Sure."

Edison led her back to the old courthouse to a staircase on the side. "Let's sit on the steps. We'll have the perfect view to see what happens."

Nestled comfortably on the steps, Edison's arm circled Claire's shoulders. Bandit claimed the shade above them, sprawled lazily across an entire step. Edison's gaze darted toward the table they had occupied earlier.

"Claire," He whispered, "look!"

She whipped her head around and saw a woman alone at the same table in a vibrant red sundress with golden blond hair cascading down her shoulders. Her server had just walked away when the woman leaned over to set her purse on the seat where Claire had left the book.

Claire's eyes followed the woman's every move, a curious silence filling the air. They watched as the woman found the book on the seat next to her. She picked it up, scanning the surrounding area as if searching for its rightful owner.

Suddenly, Edison cupped Claire's chin, turning her head towards him. He leaned in, their lips meeting in a soft, unexpected kiss. Claire's breath hitched at the surprise before she melted into him. Pulling away just as quickly, his forehead rested against hers.

"I didn't want her to see us staring," he murmured.

"Oh." Claire's eyes had a playful glint as she met his gaze with a small smile. "Wouldn't want that."

Their attention shifted back to the woman, who

now had the book on the table and thumbed through the pages. She stopped flipping suddenly, finding something of interest on the page.

Edison spoke softly in Claire's ear. "What do you think she's reading?"

"I don't know, but..." Claire's eyes widened as she turned to Edison, "What if it's something like what happened to you?"

A shiver went up his spine, remembering how the words changed before his eyes. "Should we stay and watch?"

Claire raised a shoulder before relaxing against him again. His arms tightened around her as she let out a contented sigh. He ran slow circles along her skin with his thumb just under the hem of her shirt.

"Do you think she's waiting for someone?"

"Well... she seems nervous, and she keeps looking around."

Edison's gaze darted around the square, trying to gauge if anyone else looked like they were meeting someone. Half a block away, he spotted a man dressed much nicer than most, in navy blue dress pants and a white button-down shirt with the sleeves rolled up. He was wearing sunglasses and a brown fedora. He nodded in the man's direction.

"What about that guy?"

Claire followed his gaze and chuckled. "He's pretty fancy. Love the hat."

"You do? Should I wear a fedora?"

"Still have Arthur's?" She giggled as he put on an imaginary hat. "Maybe you could wear it," her voice lowered, "and nothing else?"

His eyes were full of delight. "Hmm, I bet you'd like that." Following the man with his eyes, Edison's eyebrows shot up when he watched the man make his way to the restaurant and walk inside.

Against her ear, he quietly said, "He just walked into the same place."

They checked on the woman again, who was still reading the book and smiling.

Claire shrugged. "Could be a blind date?"

At that exact moment, the door to the restaurant opened, and the hostess led the man in the fedora to the woman's table. She smiled at him as he took her hand before sitting across from her.

Edison leaned close to Claire's ear, whispering, "I think you might be right."

Claire broke out in a wide grin as she met his gaze. "Sonny, do you know what this means?"

With one eyebrow raised, he waited.

"Could they...? What if those books set off a spark or chain reaction for falling in love?"

"Well..." he shrugged, "look at us."

Chapter 29 - Claire

I blurted out, "Let's go talk to them!" It was a crazy, stupid idea, but I wanted to do it.

Sonny narrowed his eyes as he searched mine. Slowly, he said, "You want to talk to them?"

I nodded as I whispered, "I think I do."

We made a plan. Sonny would walk Bandit around while I approached them alone and asked them a couple of questions, and we'd go from there.

Sonny laced our fingers together as we made our way across the street. "You're sure you want to do this?"

I nodded. "I'm sure. Just wait for me over there." I pointed to the closed furniture store two storefronts over.

He nodded but grabbed my hand, "Give me a sign if something goes wrong and you need me. Okay?"

I wrinkled my nose, "Like what?"

"I don't know." He grinned and reached over to tuck a stray curl behind my ear. Amusement flashed in his eyes. "How about finger guns?"

"Yeah, that won't seem weird at all." I laughed.

He blushed, shrugging his shoulders as he chuckled. "I had to think fast."

I smirked. "Well, what if... instead of that, I just tug on my earlobe? How's that?"

He nodded, "Works for me."

I breathed and said, "Okay, here I go. Watch for my sign, babe."

He pressed a quick kiss to my lips before walking off with Bandit, leaving me to head toward the restaurant. But just as I neared it, I froze. A chill curled down my spine.

There she was.

That strange woman in those eerie Victorian clothes sat in a booth just behind the couple, her presence too unsettling to be a coincidence. My pulse quickened as her gaze flicked toward me, her lips pressing into a thin, unreadable line.

Something about her made my skin crawl.

I hesitated, torn between turning back and pushing forward. She suddenly rose from her seat as I forced myself to keep going. My stomach lurched—was she coming toward me? But the moment I took another step, she slipped away, vanishing down the sidewalk like a shadow before I could even process what had just happened.

I let out the breath I'd been holding and put on a friendly smile as I walked over to the couple, giving them a little wave.

"Hi! I hope I'm not bothering you, but can I ask you something? Is that okay?"

The woman in the red sundress smiled up at me, a puzzled look on her face. "Um...okay?"

I looked back at Sonny with his reassuring smile before I said, "I'll be quick. Promise."

The man gestured for me to take the seat.

"This might sound weird, but I saw you guys from across the way, and I just had to know. Are you two on a blind date?"

They both looked surprised, but as their eyes met, their smiles softened.

She turned toward me and asked, "How did you know?"

I grinned, waving a hand around. "Oh, I just have a sense about these things. How did you meet?"

The man cleared his throat. "On social media." He continued, "I never would have guessed my posts would play a part in bringing me and Emily together."

She smiled shyly at him and murmured, "Aaron..."

"Really?" I leaned closer, curious to know their story.

They reminded me of us. My eyes darted around the square, spotting Sonny near the old furniture store. I had to hold back a laugh. Somehow, he'd found a newspaper and peered over it, watching us. Cloak and dagger, he was not. I looked away before I lost it.

I smiled at them and said, "Tell me more..."

Aaron took Emily's hand over the table. "It turns out that this lovely woman stumbled on one of my posts through a mutual friend. And well... I guess she liked what she saw."

I turned to Emily, who raised her eyebrows.

A blush heated her cheeks as she chuckled. "Oh! He was just so funny and clever but thoughtful, too. I found myself chiming in on his posts. We ended up talking back and forth for days in the comments."

Aaron interrupted excitedly. "I felt like Emily and I had a connection. Checking out her profile, I took a chance and sent her a DM, hoping to turn our conversations into something more." He looked back at her with an adoring smile. "Incredibly, we both lived right here in town. A small world, huh?"

I gave them an encouraging nod. "Indeed." It was hard to believe this was their first date. They were like two magnets about to collide.

Emily gazed at Aaron and continued their story. "We started messaging, and something there felt like more than a friendship."

He nodded as he gently rubbed his thumb across her hand, "I knew I had to meet her, and here we are."

"Here we are..." She murmured, smiling at him like no one else existed.

When the server came to the table with their drinks, that was my cue to leave.

I grinned. "I'll let you get back to your date. I have a good feeling about you two."

As I walked away, I searched for the dark-haired woman, surprised she was lingering near the crosswalk. I hesitated, debating whether I should go to Sonny or follow her. Sonny was already walking towards me, wearing a big smile, but it slid from his face when he saw the worry etched on mine. With Bandit in tow, he reached out, pulling me toward him.

"It looked promising from here, but..." He searched my face. "Did something... happen?"

I looked behind me to see the woman crossing the street by the secondhand bookstore. I made a split decision.

"Come. I'll explain as we walk." I picked up the pace, headed toward her, and motioned for Sonny to follow.

We hurried, quickly gaining on her, as I told Sonny about the strange encounters with her and how I felt like she was always watching me around town. When I finished, Sonny's mouth was pressed into a tight line. I couldn't shake the feeling that this woman knew something, and somehow, it involved me.

Sonny handed me the leash. "Here. Hold onto Bandit. I'll stop her." He took off towards her. I hurriedly followed behind, with the dog padding along beside me.

Sonny slowed as he approached her and said something. She turned towards him, a strange smile on her lips and what looked like a glint of recognition in her eyes. Did Sonny know her? They continued talking, and it looked heated. But I was too far away to make it out.

As soon as Bandit and I got near, they stepped away from each other. Sonny gave me a tight smile, inclining his head and eyes towards her, and said, "This is… Elodie."

Elodie looked at him almost expectantly before offering me a smile that didn't reach her eyes.

I blurted out, "Are you following me?"

She chuckled sarcastically as she rolled her eyes. "You're not in danger, Claire."

My eyes went wide. Her voice was… melodic and different than I expected. Why did Sonny tell her my name?

"Why… why would I be in danger?"

Elodie's dark gaze met mine. That fake smile still plastered on her face was almost predatory. She tilted her head as if carefully considering her words before speaking: "Something tells me we were always destined to meet."

My annoyance flared at her response. She wanted to talk in riddles. Before I could press her further, her eyes focused on something behind me, but I didn't see anything when I looked back.

She said, "I must go," giving Sonny one last look, her nostrils flaring, as she brushed past him. A block down, she turned towards an alley, giving us one last look before disappearing. What in the hell was that about?

Sonny turned toward me, his expression mirroring my confusion. "That was... weird."

My eyes narrowed. "Do you know her? What were you two talking about before I got here?"

Sonny stiffened. "I just asked if we could talk to her for a moment."

"Did you tell her my name?"

His brow wrinkled. "What? No." He swallowed. "What happened with that couple?"

I sighed, not answering right away, looking over at the restaurant. They were still there, Aaron sitting next to Emily as they looked through the book together.

I cleared my throat, moving closer to Sonny and trying to shake the thoughts of Elodie running through my brain. "Yeah, it was a blind date."

"How did they find each other?"

"Their story is a bit like ours. They met online. She liked his posts, and they started talking through social media. One thing led to another, and they decided to meet in real life. Surprisingly, they both lived here in the very same town."

"Wow, that's uncanny." Sonny squeezed my hand, his touch warm and grounding. He leaned in his voice barely above a whisper. "It does remind me of us... maybe that riddle from the books actually means something after all."

"Maybe," I hedged. When I first found it, that riddle seemed a little far-fetched. But now? My mind was reeling. Was it a coincidence? Or were these books catalysts for something more? Aaron and Emily were already meeting up when she found the book. It's not like it led them to find each other. But

Sonny and I met long before I got the books.

It was curious, but I couldn't stop thinking about Elodie and how she was involved. Something told me she wanted something from me, but what?

Back in the truck, Sonny squeezed my thigh. "Everything okay?"

"Yeah. Just thinking about… everything." An idea popped into my head. "Let's go by my apartment. I need to grab some clothes for work, and I want to get the books."

"Yeah, of course."

When we got to my apartment, the parking lot was full. "Just wait here. I'll be fast."

I jogged through the parking lot, taking the stairs two at a time to the second floor. As soon as I got to my closet, I grabbed the first tote bag I saw and started packing. But something dawned on me when I looked at everything in my closet. My closet was half empty. For weeks now, I was spending most of my time at Sonny's. I'd practically taken over his bathroom with all my stuff.

I slowly walked backward until my legs hit my bed, sitting down stunned. This apartment was where I found my independence and found myself again. But now, it didn't feel like home anymore. I exhaled as I walked back into the closet, grabbing my favorite skirt and a few extra things I threw in the bag. I heaved the heavy box of books in my arms and headed downstairs. As soon as Sonny saw me coming down the stairs, he hopped out of the truck to grab the heavy box, setting it in the truck bed.

On the short drive to his place, I thought about where it felt like home. Did any place? But my first thought was Sonny's place. I smiled to myself, thinking about how much I loved it there. It was warm and inviting and just made me feel calm.

When we got there, that's when it really hit me. This place, Sonny's house, something about it, felt like home to me. From the first time I was here, every time I walked in the door, a peacefulness and a sense of belonging washed over me.

But it wasn't just the place. It was him. We had somehow woven our lives together in such a short amount of time, and I hadn't even realized it was happening. The evenings we spent curled up on the couch, watching a movie, playing a game, or deep in conversations that stretched into the night. Dancing in the kitchen while we cooked together, our laughter mixed with our favorite songs, how he made me feel loved and cherished when we were tangled in bed.

But an inkling of doubt crept into the back of my mind, and I couldn't shake it. We were practically living together and hadn't even discussed it. Were we moving too fast?

Chapter 30 - Edison

As they settled into bed, something, or rather someone, invaded Edison's mind. Elodie. Just showing up out of the blue. He thought he'd put that mistake behind him years ago. As he nestled beside Claire, he could feel her anxiety simmering. After they stopped at her apartment, he'd brushed it off as a passing thought, but now, it radiated off her like heat waves.

While she read her book, she chewed her bottom lip. He found himself tracing patterns down her freckled arm, hoping to draw her attention as he tried to find the right words to reach out and soothe her. Easing himself on his elbow, he leaned in, pressing a soft kiss to her lips, buying himself some time.

His gaze met hers, his only desire to ease her burden, "Poppy," He murmured, his voice laced with concern, "something's on your mind. I can feel it."

She glanced at him, surprise flickering in her eyes before she went right back to her book. "It's nothing," she mumbled, turning the page.

He wrapped his arm around her, pulling her closer. "Tell me," he urged, his voice laced with gentle persistence.

Claire sighed, setting her book on the nightstand, "I don't know. It's probably ridiculous." She lifted her eyes to him, her fingers reaching to intertwine with his. "It's just... when I walked into my apartment and saw my closet was nearly empty, I realized that we practically live together." She swallowed, "I'm here every night, and we never..." she swallowed, "we never really talked about it, and I just... worried what it meant."

Her words hung in the air, a question seeking an answer. This wasn't just about clothes or living arrangements, but everything that came next.

His eyes twinkled when he smiled. He had no doubts. "It means I want you with me. I want to go to sleep next to you and wake up to you every morning. Don't you want that?"

She gave him a small smile. "After my marriage, it was important to me to be completely independent. I didn't want to depend on anyone ever again. I was trapped in that marriage for such a long time because I didn't have anything of my own. I'd gone straight from college to him. And..." She dropped her voice to a whisper, "I'm just afraid of losing everything again. I don't want to make another mistake. Are we... is this moving too fast?"

Edison rolled to his back, letting her hand go. He let out a frustrated sigh. "I'm not him, Claire. I don't know what he did to you, but I'm not him."

She reached for him, "I know."

He sat up. "I don't want you to lose any part of yourself. I love you the way you are, for who you are." He motioned between them, irritation in his voice. "This here. This is about you and me, not the past. Pete can go fuck himself. The more you tell me about that guy, the more I want to punch him in his fucking face. He did a real number on you, and I-." He hissed, "I hate him for that." He ran his hand through his hair, trying to contain his anger.

He leaned over, gently stroking her hair. "Because he should have loved you and revered you..." He took in a deep breath "and worshiped you." His eyes shined as he motioned between them again. "This... this right here is about us supporting each other. I want you to be everything you want and have your independence."

As her gaze met his, Edison could see a sense of relief softening her features, vulnerability glistening in unshed tears.

He flopped back down on his back, holding his arm out for her, "Come here." She didn't hesitate, laying her head on his bare chest. "Poppy, I am so grateful we got a second chance. I'm not sure I can put it into words, but I cherish every moment we spend together. I love you."

She snuggled closer to him and whispered, "I love you, too." Her hand ran up to his chest, her fingers gently caressing him before moving to his arm and tracing the lines of his tattoo. Edison relaxed into her touch.

"I'm just as scared as you are. This is fucking terrifying, but you feel like... like home. My home."

A smile spread across her face as she looked up at him. "That was something else I realized at my apartment."

"What was it?" He asked, his fingers running lazy circles on her hip.

"It just didn't feel like home anymore."

Their eyes met as he held his breath and waited.

"I mean..." She pushed herself closer to the headboard so they were face to face. "I think I've known it awhile, but today it seemed so obvious.

When we walked in the door today, I just knew... this was home." A quiet chuckle escaped her lips, "I can't explain it, but... I picture my life here with you."

Edison's heart stuttered as he took in a breath. "Yeah?"

She nodded as a smile bloomed across her face. "Yeah."

He decided to ask her tonight, his heart pounding in anticipation.

"Poppy..." his voice filled with tenderness. "Move in with me?" Edison continued, his voice filled with sincerity. "I know it's fast. It's just been a few months, but I want to wake up to your smile each morning and fall asleep next to you every night." A tender smile played on his lips. "I want us to share our lives, our dreams, all of it. What do you think?"

Her eyes widened. While they were almost living together now, he knew asking her to give up her place was a huge step. He could see the answer in her eyes as soon as the words were out. She wasn't ready.

"Sonny," she replied softly. "I love you and want a future with you, too. I don't know. Are we rushing into this?"

He reached out and put his hand over hers. "Claire, there aren't any rules. There aren't any timelines. What matters is how we feel and the connection we share. I don't want to live without you."

She searched his eyes like she was looking for the right answer. "This is a big step. I just need some time... time to think. Can we sleep on it tonight?"

He nodded, a tinge of disappointment on his face. "Of course," he replied, trying and failing to mask the worry in his voice. He audibly swallowed, "Take the time you need."

Edison understood, really he did, but he couldn't stop the doubt creeping up, making him wonder if this was more one-sided than he thought. He kissed her before laying back down and rolling on his side away from her, facing the wall. The silence between them was heavy as Edison's mind swirled. Despite the soft rhythm of her breath, Claire seemed unnaturally still. He sensed sleep wasn't finding her any more than it was him.

After an eternity, Claire's voice finally broke the silence, barely a whisper, "Sonny?"

A wave of relief washed over him as he turned to her, his voice raw with emotion. "Yeah, baby," he whispered, a flicker of hope sparking in his eyes.

She whispered, "I'm sorry."

He was too tired to hide his disappointment as he let out a long sigh, but the last thing he wanted was to make her feel guilty. "You have nothing to be sorry for, Poppy."

Claire exhaled and started speaking slowly as if looking for the right words. "I've been thinking… about everything you said… and you're right." She scooted closer, putting her hand up to caress his cheek. "I don't want to be without you. I can't… be without you." She moved closer, leaning on Edison's chest to face him. "I love waking up to your raspy voice every morning and falling asleep in your arms every night. There's nowhere else I want to be. I want this. You. Us."

Edison closed his eyes for a moment, wondering if he was dreaming. She kissed his shoulder.

"Let's do it. I want to move in with you."

He wrapped himself around her, rolling them as he held himself over her. "Are you sure? I don't want you to feel guilty or like you must decide this right now." The words came out with boyish excitement.

She smiled and nodded. "I'm sure. I know what I want. And I want a life with you."

His eyes sparkled as his smile lit up his face, those dimples peeking out of his beard. "You have no idea how happy you've made me."

Their lips collided, and the kiss began slow and lingering. It quickly turned heated as Edison swiped his tongue against her lips, which she parted readily, allowing their kiss to deepen.

The little sounds she made shot bolts of heat down his body, and he was instantly hard. His hips convulsed against her as her hands roamed his body. He needed to be inside of her.

His hands went to her panties, pushing them down her legs as she helped kick them off. He grabbed the hem of her t-shirt and pulled it over her head, tossing it aside. Feeling her naked body against him, her breasts pressed against his chest, his desire rose infinitely higher. He slid his hand down, grabbing her thigh and hooking her leg around him, pressing his erection against her wetness. He could feel the sweet heat of her center against him.

Her fingers dipped into the waistband of his boxers, pushing them down his hips. His cock sprang forward as he quickly kicked them off, her wet heat spreading along his length as he moved against her. Slowly, he ran his cock up and down her slit, teasing her as she pressed harder against him.

"Please, Sonny."

A slow grin spread across his face as he pressed into her to the hilt. He fit like a glove like they were made for each other.

"Fuck, Poppy." He closed his eyes, muttering, "So

tight." She felt so good, too good.

Their hips slowly began to move in sync, their lips locked in a wild kiss. She held onto him, wrapping her arms around him, holding him against her. It was slow and passionate, their lips never parting. He just wanted to stay this way, deep inside her forever.

He ran his lips against her neck, peppering her with kisses, slowly making his way up to her ear, nipping it before whispering, "You're so fucking sexy."

Her breath stuttered. "More. Harder. Please."

In one swoop, Edison raised up and flipped her over, putting her on all fours. He grabbed her hips and pulled her back against him, filling her up in one hard thrust.

He growled out, "You never have to beg, baby."

Claire screamed, "Oh god."

One hand still gripping her hip, he leaned over her, wrapping his other hand around her breast, rolling her nipple between his fingers. His strokes increased harder, faster, deeper, her muscles squeezing him. Knowing she was close, his dick swelled, his own orgasm coiling in his stomach.

Barely holding back, he choked out, "Where… are you?"

"Right… there. God, right there. Fuck, I'm going to come." She clenched his cock so tight he barely held on as she screamed.

He couldn't take it anymore, releasing her name in a breath. "Poppy…"

Fireworks exploded in his vision before everything went black as he pressed his body against hers until he regained himself. Out of breath, he laid on his side, pulling her back to his front, legs still tangled together.

Her hands wrapped around his on her belly as she whispered, "I love you."

He kissed her shoulder before nestling his chin in the crook of her neck, breathing her in.

"You weave a magic around me, Poppy, that words can't express like a secret language between our souls."

After laying with her for a few moments, he scooted backward off the bed, leaving the warmth of their nest to get a warm washcloth to clean them both up before settling back in. He wrapped his arm around her as their legs intertwined again. Sharing hearts and bodies in a tangled mess, they fit together so perfectly.

He didn't want to know how late it was, how little time they had to stay wrapped up in each other before the inevitable dawn of morning. Instead, he relished these fleeting moments with her in his arms. Claire relaxed against him, her breath settling into a slow rhythm, and Edison finally surrendered to the drowsiness creeping up. Feeling completely satiated, he drifted off, all at once, wrapped around her.

Chapter 31 - Claire

It felt like just yesterday that Sonny and I made the leap to move in together, and now, my lease is ending in a few weeks. It was crunch time. My apartment was a jungle gym of cardboard, with boxes stacked precariously high everywhere, creating an obstacle course for anyone brave enough to navigate it.

The hardest part wasn't the logistics of the move but leaving Bandit at doggie daycare for a long weekend. It was Sonny who had the worst separation anxiety, so we found a place with fancy webcams and live video feeds where he could check on Bandit all day long, which he did at every opportunity.

When we dropped him off, Bandit couldn't contain himself. He disappeared into the playful chaos before we even had a chance to say goodbye. Sonny watched him go like a proud papa, a mixture of excitement and nervousness flickering across his face. I couldn't help but wrap my arms around him as we left. As we stepped outside, he reached for his phone, pulling up the live video feed. It tugged at my heart whenever Sonny pulled up the app on the drive back to my place.

He was still watching it when I pulled into the parking lot, so I leaned over his shoulder and asked, "How is he?"

He fumbled the phone, cheeks red, "I, uh, wasn't..." His gaze caught mine as I cocked an eyebrow at him. He shrugged, a bashful smile played on his lips, and a flash of dimple appeared. "He's sleeping," he mumbled, feigning nonchalance.

I chuckled amused at his attempt at acting like it didn't kill him that Bandit wasn't with us.

He let out a long sigh. "I know. I know," he confessed, tucking the phone back in his pocket as we exited the car. "He'll be fine. I'm being ridiculous."

Walking up to my apartment, I squeezed his arm. "You're not being ridiculous." I reassured him, "You're just a good dog dad." His eyes softened.

"He's probably having the time of his life."

Watching Sonny worry over Bandit, an image bloomed in my mind of him cradling a sleeping newborn against his chest with his gentle nature. I glanced at him. The picture was so vivid that it felt like a premonition. A flush crept up my neck as I quickly looked away, a whirlwind of emotions swirling inside me. Was it too soon to imagine that future? Did he?

Swallowing those thoughts, I concentrated on the tasks at hand. I planned to tackle the kitchen and bathroom while Sonny worked on my closet and bedroom. Today, we needed to divide everything into donations or things to take home.

Home. Every time I thought about it, a wave of excitement coursed through me. I had no hesitation, just joy at the thought of spending my life with Sonny.

Sonny grabbed the tape dispenser and the boxes

we carried in and started putting them together. I decided to start the party with a bit of music. It always helped me get things done. Grabbing my phone and a wireless speaker from my bag, I settled on a playlist with fast-moving songs to motivate us.

I danced to him, grabbing boxes and high-stepping over to the kitchen counter before returning for a roll of tape. Just as he finished the last box, he grabbed my hand and twirled me to the song.

As it finished, he pressed a soft kiss to my lips. "I can't believe this day has finally arrived. You've made me so happy, Claire."

"I'm glad." I kissed him back, my lips curving against his mouth. I danced backward as I said, "Okay, let's get to work."

While I worked through the kitchen, Sonny grabbed a couple of boxes and headed to my bedroom.

A little while later, Sonny yelled from the bedroom. "Do you need all these sweaters? We live in Texas, and it's like a sweaterpocalypse in here!"

I laughed as I walked into the bedroom, finding him surrounded by sweaters in the closet.

I nodded slowly, "I do seem to have a thing for cozy sweaters, even if it's 90 degrees outside. But you're right. Which ones should I keep?"

I ran to the kitchen and grabbed a trash bag for the donated ones. We were surprisingly efficient. After just 20 minutes, my sweater pile was down to just a handful, and the donation pile was an avalanche on the bed.

He held up an extremely oversized and very brightly colored sweater and smirked. "What about this one? It looks like a crayon factory exploded on it."

My eyes lit up as I ran my hand across it. "I can't believe I still have that one. It was a gift from my Aunt Jackie when I was in middle school, but I haven't worn it in years."

"You wore this in public?"

I laughed. "Well, not exactly… but there was that one time I'd been feeling sorry for myself because of a breakup," I winced, not wanting to bring Pete up. "And my roommates pushed me out the door to the bar down the street. I forgot I was wearing it when we left."

He chuckled, "I would've loved to have seen that."

Putting my hands on my hips, I said, "I'll have you know I was the epitome of fashion that night. I'm pretty sure I was wearing plaid leggings with shark slippers, and I don't think I had showered in days." I smirked.

He broke out in a wide smile when he admitted, "Honestly, Claire, you could be wrapped in a potato sack and still be the most beautiful woman in the room."

Feeling exposed, I chewed my lip, a blush reaching my cheeks as I tried to stop the shy smile tugging at my lips.

"Let's donate it."

Instead of putting it in the donation pile, Sonny decided a fashion show was in order. He slipped the rainbow sweater on and struck a supermodel pose, walking across the room and swaying his hips.

"What do you think?"

I couldn't help my giggles. "Very sexy. I want to peel it right off of you."

He sashayed up to me, popping his hip out, a flirty smile playing on his lips. "Do you now?"

I stood on my tiptoes, kissing him before slowly pulling away. "Very much so. But we need to pack."

I looked at my watch, "And Darci will be here soon."

He let out a loud exaggerated sigh as he rolled his eyes before winking at me. "But when we get home, you're definitely peeling it off me."

I looked over my shoulder, giving him a playful smirk before heading back to the kitchen. "I can't wait."

Awhile later, Sonny emerged from the bedroom. "Hey, Claire, what's this? It looks like an old diary."

He clutched a leather-bound diary.

I quickly walked over and said, "I'll take that. Thank you very much," grabbing the book from him, hugging it against myself as I made my way back to the bedroom with Sonny hot on my heels. We sat on the bed as I ran my hand over the diary in my lap.

"I can't believe you found this. I completely forgot about it. It's my high school diary."

He leaned over, trying to open the pages. "Can I read teenage Claire's diary?"

My cheeks heated. "Absolutely not!" I smirked at him, clutching the diary even tighter in my grip. "My little brother was notorious for reading this thing, so I filled it with stories I made up to scare the crap out of him."

Sonny leaned in, a conspiratorial smile on his face. "You did?"

I smiled and nodded, "Yep." I tilted my head, "And then there was my crush on David Parker."

A broad grin spread across Sonny's face. "David Parker, huh?" He reached for the diary as I snatched it away again. He feigned a pout, "I can't read about him?"

My gaze slid away as I smiled bashfully. "I had the biggest crush on him."

"I'm dying to know how he captured your heart."

I shook my head, "He had no idea I existed. I was the quiet girl. I poured out all my feelings in this diary. There's probably quite a few pages with Mrs. Claire Parker written all over them." One corner of my mouth hitched up. "Well... there was one year."

Sonny arched an eyebrow, a crooked smile pulling up the corner of his mouth, "Yeah?"

"English had assigned seating, and I was in the desk right next to him in junior year. I admired him from afar and never talked to him before, but he was just as charming as I imagined. By the second week of school, we had some stupid inside joke about Christopher Marlowe."

Sonny laughed. "That is so cute! Did you ever tell him how you felt?"

My eyes widened, "Are you kidding? He was way too popular for me, the quarterback with the cheerleader girlfriend."

I felt the heat in my cheeks as a mixture of embarrassment and amusement swirled in my belly. I flipped through pages, landing on a section filled with the bubbly handwriting of my teenage self. There it was, a shrine to the boy whose memory still brought a smile to my face.

"Here," I said, trying to suppress a chuckle, "you can read all about the boy I was convinced was my soulmate back in high school."

Sonny leaned in, his eyes dancing over the words, wrinkling his brow with feigned seriousness. "Let's see... 'In English class, we're practically partners in crime, cracking inside jokes about Christopher Marlowe faking his own death and whispering about Mr. Thompson's questionable toupee. But the moment the bell rings, it's like a switch is flipped. He's swept away by the tide of his usual crew, leaving me stranded on the shore of invisibility... I just wish the boy who finds me so fascinating in English class would notice me in the real world...' Aww, Poppy."

My heart fluttered in my chest like a hummingbird as I avoided Sonny's gaze. I shrugged taking the book back and hugging it to my chest, "I was an incurable romantic."

His gaze softened, "He doesn't know what he missed. You were clearly special, even then."

He wrapped his arms around me, pulling me close. "I can't help but feel a little lucky that boy never figured it out. Otherwise, I never would have had the chance to discover how incredible you are, and that's something I wouldn't trade for anything."

Heat crept up my neck as I leaned back to look up at him. I gave him a small smile. "I think you were always meant to be the one to figure it out."

I stood up and handed him back the diary, and he tucked it into a box labeled "Miscellaneous."

"Your teenage secrets are safe with me."

I looked over my shoulder when I got to the door, giving him a small smile before walking back to the kitchen. Sonny had this way of seeing right through me like no one else ever had. He stripped my defenses, making me feel so exposed, yet he made me feel safe to be vulnerable.

A couple hours later, we took a short break. Sonny had packed my entire bedroom except some things in the closet, and I had the entire kitchen pretty much boxed up.

I found Sonny laying across the couch watching Bandit's video feed.

"Let's order pizza."

"Januzzi's?" He asked, pulling the app up on his phone.

"That sounds perfect. Just don't forget the Italian dressing."

He rolled his eyes, "It was one time!" Shaking his head, he tried to hide a smile, "You're never going to let me forget that."

"Nope." I chuckled before I took some of the empty boxes to the bathroom.

A few minutes later Sonny leaned into the tiny bathroom, his hands holding up the door frame. "Pizza's ordered. It'll be here in 30 minutes or so." He bobbled his head back and forth as he added, "And... I didn't forget the Italian dressing."

I smirked, "I bet you didn't." I turned around and gave him a quick kiss before going back to tossing more things into a box.

Bending over to grab the last few things from the cabinet under the sink, a sudden hardness pressed against my ass, making me jump. Strong arms braced themselves on either side of the sink, effectively caging me in the tiny bathroom. I straightened up slowly, a shiver trailing down my spine. In the mirror, he towered over me, his gaze locked on mine. Desire flickered in his eyes, and a spark ignited a heat in my core. His breath was warm against my ear, and his entire posture spoke of a hunger that had nothing to do with the pizza on its way.

Sonny brought his hands to my waist, turning and lifting me up to sit on the counter before caressing my face. In a rough whisper, he said, "I need to kiss you again. That little taste wasn't nearly enough."

The things he said to me could set me on fire. A dangerous, intoxicating feeling bloomed in my core that left me wanting and breathless. He pressed his lips to mine with such longing, and I savored it. Our mouths moved in harmony. My hands found their way to his chest, as I fisted his shirt, pulling him even closer, wrapping my legs around him. His hands cupped my ass, kneading it, pulling my pelvis up and into him, his hardened length pressed against my belly.

Our kisses became more urgent, a fire burning out of control between us. His hands roamed my body, working their way under my shirt, tracing the curves of my breasts through the lace of my bra. He pulled me down, moving us out of the bathroom toward my unmade bed. Darci would be here any minute, but I didn't care. I wanted him bare again,st me.

I had just unfastened his jeans when we heard the knock. Reluctantly, I pulled away, my breath ragged. Straightening our clothes, our eyes met, a silent promise of more when we got home. I stopped to look in the mirror, finger combing my hair, but I knew my flushed cheeks and swollen lips would tell a story Darci wouldn't miss. I headed to the living room leaving Sonny to adjust himself before following me out.

Opening the door, I cleared my throat and put a smile on my face. "Darci! You're here!"

She walked in with a grocery bag in one hand and an armload of boxes in the other with a big grin on her face. "Of course, I'm here! I come bearing gifts —boxes, beer, and bubble wrap!" She smirked as she looked me up and down, "By the looks of it, you've been busy with other things."

I tucked some curls behind an ear and chuckled. "We've just been… packing."

"Sure, sure." She clicked her tongue, one corner of her mouth pulling up as she turned to set things down. "Where's Edison?"

I hooked a thumb towards the bedroom just as he walked into the living room.

He said, "Thanks for helping us pack up."

She wrapped her arm around my shoulder and said, "Well, it's not every day my best friend moves in with the man of her dreams!"

I felt the flush rising up my neck as I turned to hand him the boxes she brought. He took them to the bedroom.

She set her other bag down, turning to grab my hands. "I'm thrilled for you, Claire. Truly. But I'll miss having you just a few doors down."

I hugged her back. "I know, but I'll only be 10 minutes away."

She chimed in, "And we'll still see each other at work."

"Don't forget about 'Murder Nights.'" I gave her a mischievous grin. "And maybe we'll find a tatted-up musician destined to be your soulmate."

She rolled her eyes and huffed out a laugh, "I'm not sure he exists…"

Sonny walked back into the living room with a big smile on his face. "Wait, wait, are we trying to find Darci a date?" He stroked his own beard, looking to the side, deep in thought. "Maybe I know someone?"

Darci's cheeks heated. "Yeah, let's not get carried away. I can find my own dates."

I smirked, nudging Darci. "Didn't you literally hide from a bad date in the park?"

Darci opened her mouth to answer just as there was a knock at the door. Sonny answered the door to find a pizza delivery guy with a full sleeve tattoo and a very nicely trimmed beard. Sonny slid his eyes to us, breaking out in a big grin, and I giggled as I elbowed Darci.

The pizza man smiled at all of us. "Pizza from Januzzi's?"

"Excellent timing!" Sonny looked over at us quickly and winked, his playful grin getting bigger. "Tell me, are you in a band?"

Darci threw her hands up and groaned as she walked away. She muttered, "Tell lover boy I don't need help finding a date."

The pizza delivery guy chuckled. "Actually, I am! How'd you know?"

I put my hands over my face. "This is too much."

Darci turned back around, feigning nonchalance, but I caught a flicker of interest across her face.

Sonny shrugged. "Lucky guess." He handed the pizza guy cash and took the food. "Keep the change. Do you play around here?"

"Oh yeah, man. I play bass in Dishrag Swill. We're playing down at Andy's next Friday night." He pulled out a folded-up flyer in his back pocket and handed it to Sonny. "Come check us out."

The pizza guy looked Darci up and down, a smirk on his face. "You should all come. It's going to be a great show!"

Darci gave him a ghost of a smile and nodded.

Sonny unfolded the paper and looked it over as the pizza guy headed to the stairwell. Before he got down the stairs, Sonny leaned out and yelled, "Cool, man. We might just be there. Thanks for the pizza!"

Darci headed to the kitchen to grab a lone roll of paper towels while Sonny set the pizzas on the coffee table, and I pulled out the drinks from the grocery bag.

Darci let out a sigh, "Can we stop trying to find me a date?"

I chuckled, popping the lid off a cup of Italian dressing and grabbing a cheese stick. Dipping it in, I took a bite.

"I was just trying to help," I defended. "You never know where you'll find love. Who knows, maybe you'll meet someone when you least expect it."

She mumbled, "Sure… where I least expect it… like the dumpster down in the parking lot."

Chapter 32 - Edison

"I didn't get a chance to tell you about my nightmare date from a few days ago." Her voice was brimming with amusement. "I met up with this guy, and he was hot—like drool-worthy hot, totally my type—big guy, tattoos, beard, the whole package. But... he had this weird obsession with Air Supply."

Edison exchanged a curious glance with Claire, clearly intrigued by the bizarre turn of events.

Edison asked slowly, "Air Supply? The band from the 80s?"

"Yep," Darci nodded in between bites. "I mean, seriously, it was strange."

Claire asked her, "How old was this guy?"

Darci twisted her lips. "Maybe around 30? Why?"

Claire shrugged. "I don't know. Aren't they before our time? How do you know anything about Air Supply?"

"My mom. She's a mega stan for Air Supply. She even took me to their concert when I was a kid."

Edison smirked, "Maybe you could set him up with your mom?"

Darci pursed her lips. "Yeah, I'm not doing that. Just what I want, that guy as my stepdad." Darci rolled her eyes, and Claire nearly choked on her pizza. "From the moment we met, he found a way to steer every conversation back to Air Supply. He wouldn't stop talking about them—their songs, their history, how many times he'd seen them in concert. Which... did you know they're still touring?" She waved around a slice of pepperoni and mushroom pizza as she talked with her hands. "Every time I tried to talk about anything else, he'd bring it right back to freaking Air Supply. At one point, he started singing Lost in Love."

Claire burst into laughter, her red curls shaking back and forth.

Edison chuckled, "That sounds awful."

Darci's eyes went wide as she nodded furiously. "And then... for some dumb reason, I agreed to go with him to the bookstore next door. When we walked in, and he wanted to see if they had any Air Supply albums, I realized I was trapped in the fifth circle of hell." She took a bite of pizza and pointed the crust at Edison. "Do you know what I did? I hid from him."

Edison looked over at Claire, who just shrugged at him like it was typical for Darci.

Picking up a cheese stick and dipping it into some dressing, Darci continued, her voice filled with excitement. "I was killing it in my stilettos and that tiny green dress, but did he notice? Nope, just Air Supply this, Air Supply that. Blah, blah, blah. So when he went to the bathroom, I ducked behind some bookshelves, evading him for nearly half an hour. When I spied him back by the entrance near the restaurant, I ran out through the mall exit and took the long way back to my car."

Claire lifted a shoulder. "Sounds like your typical date." Her voice dripped with sarcasm. "But why on earth were you dressed like that for a first date?" she asked a hint of disbelief in her voice.

Darci shrugged, grabbing another cheese stick, a sly grin on her face. "Well, I was hoping maybe I could get some... action. It's been a while," her cheeks pinked as she looked away. "He had a body like a god but ruined it with the weird Air Supply obsession."

Claire just shook her head. "I can't believe you did that." She took a bite of pizza, a twinkle in her eye. "Well, that's not true. I can totally believe you did that. Isn't that the third date you've had to flee?"

Darci laughed, shaking her head. "Nope, the fifth."

Edison grimaced as Claire said, "That's what you get when you stalk Missed Connections for potential dates."

"Excuse me, lady." Darci pointed at Claire teasingly with a slice of pizza and inclined her head toward Edison. "But did you not meet him there, too?"

Claire bobbed her head from side to side. "Technically, we had already met."

Darci rolled her eyes. "Whatever." They both laughed. Darci took a bite of her pizza, still grinning from ear to ear.

After finishing the pizza, they packed the rest of the apartment while Darci told them about her other bad dates. Edison hadn't laughed that much in a long time.

Darci let out a dramatic sigh as she fell on the bed. "I swear, I have the worst luck when it comes to dating."

Claire turned toward her. "That's why you need to let us find you a date. Could it really be any worse than the Air Supply guy?"

Darci shook her head as if trying to erase the memory. "I don't know. Remember footie pajama guy?"

Sitting on the bed, sorting her clothes for donations, Claire snorted. "Oh god, I had forgotten all about him. Tell Sonny about footie pajama guy."

He asked, "Footie pajama guy?"

Darci nodded, "Yeah, so this guy wanted to meet in the Target parking lot. I thought we were just meeting there and then going to dinner or something. No, he decided it was a brilliant idea to take me to Target for our date to shop for footie pajamas for himself in the children's department."

Edison couldn't help but laugh. "That's a little creepy."

"You're telling me," Darci continued, her voice laced with disbelief, wildly gesturing with her hands. "There I was, walking through the children's clothing at Target, surrounded by moms with kids, and we're searching for footie pajamas for a grown man."

Darci continued, "I didn't see a way to escape that time, so I just made up a story that I had an appointment I forgot about. He grabs some random pair of footie pajamas, and we head to checkout. He pays, and then, without any warning, in the middle of the entrance, he grabs me and starts kissing me and trying to grope me."

Darci shuddered at the memory, the disgust evident on her face.

"It was the wettest kiss I've ever had, like he had forgotten to swallow or something, and the taste..." Darci continued, a mixture of horror and amusement in her voice. "I swear, I nearly threw up in his mouth! I just left him standing there and never saw him again."

Edison wrinkled his nose, "That sounds horrible. I feel like I need to apologize on behalf of all men."

"That's not even the weirdest date I had in the last couple of months," Darci said, her voice filled with anticipation. Looking at Claire, she says, "I don't think I told you about the guy who took me to the Renaissance faire." She picked up another box, taping it together. "We were meeting at the entrance, and he came completely dressed as a satyr! Shirtless, a magical staff, horns, and fur pants with high-heel hooves. But he didn't mention wearing a costume when he asked me out. So I was in shorts and a t-shirt on a date with a seven-foot-tall goat man. And he would only speak in Old English. Can you imagine?"

Claire doubled over in laughter while Edison struggled to keep a straight face.

"Don't get me wrong, he looked incredible—abs like a Greek god." Darci sighed wistfully, her eyes glazing over for a moment.

Claire flicked her eyes to Edison.

"And I appreciate someone who embraces their interests," Darci continued, smiling. "But seeing him prancing around like a mythical creature and having no idea what he was saying half the time... let's just say it wasn't exactly what I had envisioned for a first date."

By 10 p.m., nearly everything was packed into boxes. They called it a day, walking Darci back to her apartment before heading home—their home. Edison savored the sound of it.

Turning into the neighborhood, he glanced at Claire. She seemed content but exhausted. He reached across the seat and ran his hand up her thigh, finding her hand and linking their fingers together. She caught his eye, and he smiled and winked at her.

He was finally getting his chance to make a life with her, but doubt crept in every time he daydreamed about their future together. What would she do when he finally told her about that blind date? He just wanted to confess. He was tired of the fear, of keeping it from her, and most of all, feeling like a liar. He wanted this weight off his chest, but it was too late to get into it tonight. They were both exhausted, and the next few days would be busy. Edison made a promise to himself to tell her after the move.

She squeezed his hand, looking over at him. "What are you thinking about?"

He couldn't confess the one thing that lingered in his mind, so he said something sweet. "Just how beautiful you are."

He couldn't see her blush in the darkness of the night, but he could see it in the way her head dipped with that shy smile across her lips.

"I don't feel very beautiful. I feel like I'm covered in a layer of dust. As soon as we get home, I'm taking a shower." Claire sighed, rubbing her tired eyes.

Edison flashed a devilish smile and leaned in closer, his voice filled with flirtation. "I could help you with that," he teased.

A playful smile on her face. "Could you?" Claire replied, her voice filled with a hint of excitement. "And what exactly do you have in mind?"

Edison's eyes twinkled with playful desire. "To get you naked, wash every inch of your body, and then have my way with you, of course." His voice was laced with seductive anticipation.

Pulling into the garage, he could see the effect his

words had on her when she licked her lips and squeezed her thighs together. Desire coursed through him, and he felt that gravitational pull between them.

A coy smile tugged at the corners of her lips as she leaned toward him, her voice barely above a whisper. "Well, Mr. Wright, that sounds very tempting indeed."

Edison put the truck in park before turning towards her, gently brushing his fingers against her cheek.

"Consider it a promise," he murmured, gently pulling her by the hand out of the driver's side.

Chapter 33 - Claire

The exhaustion I'd felt melted away into a desperate need for him. Sonny led me through the house to the bedroom and into his bathroom—our bathroom—stopping briefly to grab towels and candles from the linen closet.

That bathroom had quickly become my favorite room. I loved the shower so much that sometimes I took multiple showers a day. I was obsessed.

Sonny told me that when he bought the house, the bathroom had a small glass shower and a separate clawfoot tub. He had the whole thing gutted and upgraded it into one huge glass-enclosed shower with multiple oversized rain shower heads on the ceiling and two handheld shower heads on the wall. It was luxurious. The first time I saw it, I silently wondered how many people he had expected to shower together.

When we got to the bathroom, he gently pushed my shoulders down to sit on the closed toilet seat. He leaned over and kissed me, then in a playfully stern whisper, said, "Don't move."

He started the shower, and the steam immediately filled the bathroom. I watched as he lit six short pillar candles, placing them around the room before turning out the lights, creating an ethereal atmosphere.

He knelt, kissing me softly on the lips, pulling my shirt over my head, and then took my shoes and socks off before pulling me up with him to slide my jeans and panties off. Locking my gaze to his, he reached down and ran his hand between my legs, feeling the wetness pooling between my thighs.

He ran his beard against my cheek before his mouth captured mine in a ravenous kiss. His lips trailed down my neck as his hands slid up my back, unhooking the clasp of my bra and letting it fall to the floor. Between kisses, Sonny pulled his shirt over his head while I quickly shucked his pants and boxer briefs down his legs.

He opened the shower door and followed me in. Standing under the steady stream of hot water, I relished how the warmth melted away the tension from packing all day. The soft, warm glow of the candles illuminated Sonny's body. A slow smile spread across my lips as I turned towards the water. He followed and pressed against my back. My heart skipped a beat as the steam surrounded us, creating a magical atmosphere.

The water mingled with my skin, heightening my senses and sending a shiver down my spine as he wrapped his hands around my waist, pulling me into him, his erection pressing into the small of my back.

I turned to face him, that crooked smile hitching one corner of his mouth up. My hand instinctively reached up to caress the dimple in his cheek as he reached over me, grabbing my soap and lathering his hands. He worked his way slowly down my body, taking extra care to thoroughly wash my breasts before lathering his hands again and working his way down my stomach, between my legs, down my thighs, leisurely washing me before rinsing me. The soap and hot water acted like conduits, amplifying his touch. He gently turned me and did it all again down my shoulders and back, taking extra care with my ass and legs before rinsing me clean.

I leaned back against him, feeling the rumble in his chest as he murmured, "Poppy." He kissed down the side of my throat to my shoulder, growling, almost in a whisper, "I love these fucking freckles."

His hand ran down to my ass, around to my stomach, and further down into my wetness until I felt one finger press into me and then another while his thumb circled my clit. My head fell back against him as I moaned. I needed to touch him, feel him, so I reached behind me to stroke his cock, his arousal slick in my hand.

He hissed, "Fuck, Claire."

I pulled away, smirking, wanting to take care of him before he got me off. I grabbed his body wash, lathering my hands, the scent intoxicating as I began with his shoulders. I tenderly washed his arms and then his chest, running my soapy hands down to his stomach, following the trail of hair before grabbing his cock in one hand, his balls in the other, and gently stroking him as I washed him clean.

"Baby," he breathed. "if you keep doing that..."

I gave him a devilish smile as I kept stroking, gently tugging his balls in the way that drove him crazy.

Innocently, I asked, "Keep doing what?"

He took my hands off of his body and rinsed himself with the handheld shower before pushing me up against the wall and turning it on me. He spread me wide with one hand, allowing the pulses to hit my clit in the most perfectly delicious way. Seconds before I thought I'd explode, he pulled it away, kneeling and licking down my core before sucking my clit into his mouth. As he sucked harder, I writhed against the wall, moaning his name, running my hands through his wet hair, pulling him into me, and holding him right there. Right where I needed him.

I didn't think I could take another second, but he let go and put the shower head back on my clit. He ran his hand up my thigh, inserting two fingers into me, pumping slowly. The intensity built in my belly, the euphoria circling about to wash over me. I chased it. I wanted it. I craved it.

"Sonny, I'm… I'm going to come."

He stood up, his fingers still pumping, our eyes locked. I could see my desire reflected in his flame-filled eyes.

"Come for me, Poppy."

He wrapped his hand in my hair, kissing me hard, and I let go. I clenched hard against his fingers, screaming from the intensity. Ecstasy coursed through my veins. It was intoxicating and a high I wanted to chase forever. I craved more of it, of him, desperately, like a moth drawn irresistibly to a flame.

Sonny gently wrapped his arms around me, holding me up and kissing me slowly. He walked us to the center of the shower. As we stood there, warm water cascaded over our bodies, time blurred as if nothing existed but us, savoring the simple pleasure of being together in that moment.

He turned the water off, helped me out of the shower, and gently dried me and himself before we went to bed. He threw the covers to the side, allowing me to get in first. He climbed in and scooted in close, holding me from behind, and I felt his hardness pressing against me as he pulled the comforter back over us both.

I turned my head, but Sonny rumbled in my ear, "Sleep. You're exhausted." He kissed the back of my neck.

I could barely speak, drowsiness pulling me under. "But..."

Kissing my hair, he said, "Sleep, Poppy. I'll be okay."

I woke up early the following day, still in Sonny's embrace as the sun rose. My thoughts drifted to the dream, still lingering from sleep. It had been about this strange little coffee shop on the other side of town, and that little voice in my mind said it was time to leave the book I had just finished.

But before I did anything else, I wanted to take care of the man wrapped around me. Trying not to wake him, I drug the covers down to the bottom of the bed. I slid my hand down his body and gently played with his balls, running my finger against the seam as I stroked him with my other hand.

He stirred awake, a sleepy smile as he asked, "What are you doing?"

I smirked. "Oh, I think you know."

"So good, baby." He rolled onto his back, giving me better access.

I kissed his lips and made my way down, kissing and licking his chest and his belly, running my breasts against his thighs before taking his cock in my mouth. I ran my tongue along the underside before swallowing him deeper, sucking hard as I came back up to the tip, over and over, until his leg muscles began to tighten. I ran my tongue down the seam of his balls, gently sucking one into my mouth, swirling it with my tongue, before taking the other, all while stroking his cock from root to tip. His balls began to tighten.

"Poppy… baby, I'm close. Come up here." He looked down and reached for me.

I continued stroking as I smiled and shook my head. "Nope, this is all you."

He relaxed back into the bed, his hands fisting the sheets. After sucking just the tip of his cock, I ran my lips to the underside, teasing it with little nips before I wrapped my lips back around him, taking him deep. My hand went to the base and squeezed as I sucked until he convulsed.

"Fuck! Claire. Please."

I didn't stop as I traded off between stroking and sucking until I felt his hot release hit my mouth, squeezing his base as I sucked. When he was spent, I crawled back up over his body, straddling him and kissing him deeply, letting him taste himself on my lips. His tongue entwined with mine, diving deep into my mouth, his hands twisted into my curls.

He pulled back, a hint of amusement mixed with the desire in his eyes. "You are so dirty."

I kissed him one more time before hopping out of bed. Looking over my shoulder, my lips curved into a smile as I met his gaze.

"And you love it."

I grabbed some clothes from the closet and laid them on the bed before heading to the bathroom.

Sonny put one of his hands behind his head and lazily looked at me. "Where are you going? We're supposed to finish up your apartment today."

"I know, but we need to take a little detour to leave another book," I made jazz hands, "maybe that whole love thing will happen again."

Chapter 34 - Edison

Edison quickly dressed in jeans and a plain gray t-shirt, skipping a shower until they finished at Claire's apartment. He had no idea where Claire wanted to go but was anxious and excited to test their theory.

Bandit was at doggie daycare for two more days, and Edison was still obsessively checking the video feed. Every time Claire found him doing it, she'd sidled up to watch along with him. Over the last few months, Bandit had become their dog, not just his, making him think about the future. He pictured a miniature version of Claire, maybe with his eyes, climbing into bed with them on Saturday mornings to snuggle. He wanted that, and he hoped she did, too.

When they got to the truck, Claire plugged the address for Viva Coffee into Edison's phone. It was a newer coffee shop on the south side of town known for its cozy atmosphere and oversized servings. Twenty minutes later, they had arrived.

When they entered, Edison's stomach grumbled from the sweet scent of sugar and cinnamon that permeated the cafe. Claire chose a table near the entrance with a good vantage point to see the whole place. She took the book and discretely slipped it into a booth at the back on the way to the bathroom, ensuring it was in plain sight for anyone heading to the counter to order.

When she returned to the table, Edison went to order coffee. A few moments later, he returned with a tray containing two super extra large mugs of coffee and a cinnamon roll the size of a dinner plate.

Claire's eyes went wide. "Sonny, what in the world is that?"

He grinned. "Can you believe the size of this thing? This place is famous for its giant cinnamon rolls. It's like the Mount Everest of cinnamon rolls. "

As he set it on the table, Claire asked, "How are we supposed to eat this?"

Edison picked up both forks, handing one to Claire. His eyes twinkled, "Step one: Dig in. Step two: Keep digging."

"I hope you have a map because I might get lost in this thing." Claire deadpanned as she speared a gooey bite dripping in cream cheese glaze.

Edison leaned over the cinnamon roll, digging into the center. "I think I just found the lost city of Atlantis... made entirely of cinnamon and sugar."

Claire laughed before taking another bite, closing her eyes, and moaning.

Edison shoveled another piece into his mouth, a satisfied grunt escaping his lips.

Claire took another bite and groaned. "If we finish this whole thing, I'm going to explode. Tell everyone I went out like a hero—drowned in a sea of cinnamon and cream cheese, no regrets."

Edison nearly choked on his bite, laughter shaking his shoulders. "Noted. I'll make sure your tombstone says, 'Death by pastry, zero shame.'"

As they devoured the colossal pastry, their eyes

occasionally darted between the cafe entrance and the table with the hidden book, wondering who would find it.

Claire set her fork down, barely making a dent in the giant pastry. A big smile lit up her eyes. She leaned towards Edison and whispered, "I'm excited this time."

A grin spread across his face. "We're staying, right?"

"Of course." Her cheeks turned pink when she caught his gaze. She picked up her fork again. "And we have to finish this cinnamon roll monstrosity."

The minutes ticked by as people entered and exited the cafe. Claire and Edison exchanged hopeful glances as some people noticed the book but passed by without picking it up.

He wanted to witness another potential love story, proof that their second chance was something more than just coincidence. He wanted it to be true. He felt it down to his bones that they were meant to be like it had been written in the stars for millennia. He'd never forgotten the visceral reaction he had when they met the very first time. She had changed his destiny, his everything—a lifeline thrown to a drowning man.

Their patience paid off when a young woman in a dress the color of dark chocolate walked in a few minutes later. She was striking with skin the color of mocha and freckles across her nose. Her eyes wandered around the room as she entered the coffee shop, but she stopped when she spotted the book. Her face was piqued with curiosity as her eyes darted around before she hesitantly picked it up, examining the cover and flipping through the pages.

Edison let out a breath he'd been holding in anticipation. He sneaked a glance at Claire, who was watching the woman intently. Excitement brewed around them as the woman paged through the book, her expression shifting from curiosity to intrigue. The world seemed to fade around her as she became completely oblivious.

A server, a man with dark brown locks tied back in a ponytail, wearing a black apron and a name tag that said Jack, came to the woman's table, pulling her attention out of the book. As he took her order, his face was hidden from view, but Edison noticed immediately how the woman's eyes sparkled with emotion as she smiled at Jack. Was this it? Were they seeing the magic of these books working firsthand?

Edison overheard the woman tell Jack her name was Grace. He said something else, and she laughed like a cascade of pure joy. Claire gasped and grabbed Edison's forearm, sliding her eyes to his as she grinned. He raised his eyebrows and shrugged because it seemed like something extraordinary was about to happen.

Jack walked away, and a few minutes later, he returned with a giant mug brimming with whipped cream. Did they only have giant-sized servings at this place? Jack lingered, leaning over the chair across from her as she took a drink. His eyes crinkled as he grinned when he handed her a napkin from his apron pocket when she pulled back with a line of whipped cream above her lip. Grace's chest heaved when their hands touched, and her cheeks reddened.

After an hour, Grace had three empty mugs on her table and was chapters deep in the book as Edison watched Jack steal glances at her from behind the counter while he made other customer orders.

Edison was sure Claire had forgotten all about packing up her apartment. He was just about to ask what the plan was when he spotted Jack walking back over without his apron and holding two more mugs in one hand and a plate with a sandwich in the other. Jack leaned over and whispered something to Grace. She smiled and nodded as she closed the book, gesturing for him to sit closer. He set a mug down in front of her and then the other for himself before sliding the plate between them, offering half his sandwich. Her eyes widened as she gladly took it, and they started murmuring, her gaze filled with longing and a mix of wonder as Jack sat down.

They fell deep into conversation, and neither one could stop smiling. Their voices carried snippets of laughter and teasing. Edison couldn't believe the connection growing between Grace and Jack right in front of everyone. When she handed her phone to Jack, and he promptly punched in his number, Edison glanced at Claire. This had to be more than a coincidence. It had to be the books. Edison was sure of it.

The bell above the door made a tinkling sound, and Claire was visibly startled when she looked towards the entrance. When she grabbed Edison's hand under the table, his gaze swung back to see what scared her. Fuck. It was Elodie, looking like she was playing a villain in *My Fair Lady*.

Claire wasn't kidding. She really did seem to be following her. Elodie glanced around the cafe, but as soon as she saw them, she walked towards their table with a determined purpose.

Great. Just great. His lips pressed into a line. They were going to have to deal with her again. What did she even want?

She wore another Victorian-style dress in black and dark navy stripes, thick black tights, and knee-high boots. She gave them a tight smile in her signature blood-red lipstick. Edison swore the corner of her mouth twisted into a sneer when she made brief eye contact with him.

"Hello Claire… Edison." She nodded, looking Edison up and down, before raising her eyebrows at Claire. "Mind if I sit?"

Edison mumbled a "Yes" but forced a strained smile, trying not to look as uncomfortable as he felt. Claire, wide-eyed, shot him a look as if to ask, "Are we really doing this?"

She stumbled over her words, "Um… sure… Have a seat." She gestured towards the chair next to her, a friendly smile on her face.

Edison felt her eyes on him, searching for some kind of cue, but he had no idea how to handle this either. He gave her a small shrug, hoping she'd somehow read "I'd rather be anywhere but here" from his expression. Instead, she shot him a pointed look before rolling her eyes, the silent "Seriously?" loud and clear.

Before Elodie sat down, she turned slightly, her gaze drifting toward Grace and Jack. Edison followed her line of sight—Grace and Jack were still deep in conversation, soft smiles playing on their lips, the book between them untouched. But it wasn't just curiosity in Elodie's expression. There was something colder. Contempt.

Edison watched as she studied the couple, her lips pressing into a thin line. She sneered when she caught him watching her, flicking a dismissive hand in his direction.

"I suppose your husband can hear this, too."

What? She knew damn well they weren't married.

Claire's eyebrows shot up as she exchanged a look with Edison before turning back to Elodie, shaking her head. "He's not my—"

Elodie's eyes widened, feigning innocence. "Oh?" Her smirk deepened as she tilted her head toward Edison. "I guess I was… mistaken."

Goddamn, that woman. Edison clenched his jaw, his protective instincts flaring. Every part of him wanted Elodie away from Claire, as far away as possible. But Claire wanted answers—needed answers—and Elodie had them. He forced himself to stay put, fists tightening beneath the table, biting back the urge to drag her out of the café himself.

Elodie raised her eyebrows at him, that smirk still on her face, daring him to say something. God, she brought out the worst in him, and she relished it. Claire's lips twitched into a slightly annoyed smile. He relaxed his hands, sliding one hand to Claire's lap, gently squeezing her thigh.

Elodie inhaled sharply through her nose before turning to Claire. "I'm not sure if you're aware, but The Enchanted Attic was mine—my bookstore, my baby."

Claire's eyebrows lifted. "I had no idea. I only ever saw a man running the store."

Elodie's lips curled slightly. "That was my ex-husband, Donald."

Edison's jaw tightened, his eyes narrowing. "Small world," he muttered, the words laced with skepticism.

Elodie sighed as if bracing herself, then turned fully to Claire. Her voice dropped to a low, almost conspiratorial whisper.

"There's something you need to know. Those books you have in your possession? They're mine. And they're cursed."

Chapter 35 - Claire

What the fuck?

I whispered, "Cursed?"

Elodie flashed a quick smile, a touch too bright. "Honestly, cursed might be putting it mildly."

Sonny caught my eye, then shot a sharp look at Elodie. "What aren't you telling us?"

Elodie leaned toward me, completely ignoring Sonny. In a dramatic tone, she said, "I'm sure Donald never mentioned where they came from when he gave them to you. Hmm?"

I shook my head. "No. He just said they were mine for the giving, which didn't make much sense."

She clucked her tongue and huffed out a breath, "I swear that man..." She didn't finish her thought. She looked through me as if she was seeing something in the past. "Years ago, as I was collecting books to start the store, the daughter of a matchmaker brought in some very special books. Supposedly, her mother kept this secret stash of romance books."

It seemed like Elodie was being dramatic, trying to reel me in, but I had to ask, "Secret?"

She raised her eyebrows, raising a shoulder. "Her mother had a special gift for playing... cupid." She tilted her head, "It was rumored she could find anyone's true love." She said the last two words in a sing-song voice. "But... her daughter didn't inherit her gift. While she saw her mother give those books to clients, she never learned the secrets kept in that box."

She paused as if she was waiting for me to ask something else. I waited for her to continue.

She shook her head. "In their condition, I couldn't sell them, so I set them aside and forgot all about them. But one day, I was doing inventory and found them again as if they had just reappeared. So I took them home, and that's when things got... interesting."

Sonny inclined his head, a look of skepticism on his face. "Interesting how?"

The corner of her mouth pulled up. "Like some puppet, I found myself writing notes in the books I couldn't explain. Notes I didn't remember writing. And then, I started leaving them around town."

My hand flew to my mouth as I glanced at Sonny. This all seemed very familiar. I let out a shaky breath.

My voice, barely above a whisper, wavered. "But why do you think they're cursed? Did something happen?"

Elodie's gaze darkened. "What happened..." She shook her head, drumming her long crimson fingernails on the table as she chuckled sarcastically. "I was naive. I'm sure you've found that ridiculous riddle about true love," she said, rolling her eyes.

As she told her story, it sounded eerily similar to mine, finding that strange riddle at the bottom of the box, writing in the books, leaving them places. It was unnerving. She'd been giddy with anticipation as she left books everywhere—a park bench, next to a fountain, on a bus—hoping fate might take its course. But it was never in the way she envisioned and certainly not the way that riddle seemed to promise. Her story made me question everything I knew about the books.

One of the last times was the worst. A young couple seemed enamored with each other, stealing kisses and holding hands—utterly in love. They stumbled on the book, and Elodie said she couldn't resist following them.

They found a quaint little outdoor cafe. The book sat on the table between them. At first, they were wrapped up in each other. Elodie's heart swelled, convinced she was witnessing the magic of the books at work. But then, something changed.

Another woman walked up to their table, recognizing the man. She looked between the couple as if she was confused. Their conversation escalated. Voices rose, accusations flew, and the once affectionate couple fractured like a broken mirror before her eyes. The man's face turned red, full of rage. He slammed his fist on the table as the first woman blinked back tears. Finally, with a heart-wrenching sob, she grabbed the book, hugged it against her, and stormed off. The other woman sat down, the man apologizing and caressing her.

Elodie watched with a sickening feeling twisting in her gut as the first woman hurled the book into an overflowing trash can as she walked out of the restaurant. Unable to bear it, Elodie ran to the trash, fishing the book out before it was lost in a sea of rotten food.

"That day," Elodie finished, her voice heavy with regret, "I realized these books weren't bringing anyone love. They shattered relationships instead of creating them." Her solemn gaze held mine, her eyebrow arched. "Be careful, Claire."

Her eyes glazed over, and a distant look took hold as she looked back at Grace and Jack. A flicker of something like jealousy crossed her face.

Sonny spoke up, "Maybe it was just a fluke."

I piped up, "Maybe the first woman was the 'other woman'."

"I don't know. I just know her heart was broken." Elodie sighed, "I did see her again weeks later. I couldn't forget her face." She shook her head, "Her entire demeanor had changed. I was sitting outside at Hearth & Grain and watched her walk down the street. She looked so sad, and then, she just stopped suddenly, dead in her tracks." Her eyes flicked to Sonny. "I looked around, trying to figure out why she froze." Elodie swallowed. "That's when I saw him, the same guy. He was sitting outside at the Oak Street Bar with that other woman. They were kissing."

I raised my eyebrows.

"I don't think he saw her. But it was like she folded in on herself as if everything had just been taken from her."

I blinked back the sting of unshed tears, my breath unsteady. Sonny's hand remained firm on my thigh, grounding me.

Elodie's gaze locked onto mine. "Other things happened before that, but that's when I knew something was wrong with those books. I don't know what kind of magic was at play, but it was nothing good." She straightened, her voice crisp with certainty. "Mark my words—those books are cursed."

She exhaled, shaking her head as if recalling a memory she'd rather forget. "I went home, boxed them up, and put them in the storage room at the bookstore, planning to destroy them. But then, the curse got to me. Days later, my husband served me with divorce papers—completely out of the blue. It was like those books poisoned everything around me. A few weeks later, my doctor found a tumor in my lung. And then... I lost the bookstore."

For a fleeting second, her mask slipped. Beneath the sharp edges and bravado, I glimpsed something raw—grief, regret, something heavier than she'd admit. But just as quickly, she smoothed it over with another practiced, hollow smile.

I murmured, "I'm so sorry, Elodie," reaching out I put my hand over hers. She grimaced and recoiled, curling her fingers, almost like claws and pulled away. My cheeks heated as she rubbed her hand like it'd been burned.

"To make matters worse, my husband—without telling me—gave away boxes of books from the storage room to customers. I had no idea until recently that the box was even missing. And, of course, he refuses to take my calls."

I bit my lip and nodded, a quiet understanding settling between us.

Elodie sighed, shaking her head. "With everything that happened, I let it go. But a few months ago, I felt the magic of those books again. This time, it was... different. I can't explain it. Something keeps pulling me to the places where you leave them, like today."

Sonny narrowed his eyes, suspicion etched into his features. "What does that even mean?"

Elodie barely spared him a glance, her expression cool and detached, before leaning in toward me. Her voice softened, dripping with honeyed venom.

"If I were you, I'd be careful. Those books have a way of worming themselves into you... like roots burrowing deep into your soul."

A shiver ran down my spine as her gaze lingered on me.

"And it seems you're their new plaything, Claire."

Sonny squeezed my thigh before he spat, "Don't you have anything better to do? Why are you even here?"

Elodie's laughter echoed in the room, laced with a twisted amusement. She locked her eyes with mine, "I just wanted to warn you. Those books don't play by human rules."

I cleared my throat. "Maybe. But that's not what's happening here." I inclined my head towards Grace and Jack. Elodie arched an eyebrow, skepticism on her face.

Sonny sat up straighter as he said, "One of the books even brought us back together."

She looked between us in annoyed disbelief. "Really?"

A smile lit up my face when I looked over at Sonny and nodded.

He said, "We met years ago. But we lost… touch." He smiled back at me and gave my thigh another squeeze.

I shrugged my shoulders. "Somehow, one of the books fell out of my bag. He found it, and it led us back together."

Elodie smiled like a Cheshire cat. "Well, isn't that a sweet story."

There was something about her I couldn't quite put my finger on, but I didn't like it.

Sonny added, "Claire's left books for other people, and it was nothing like what you describe. It's been the exact opposite.." He gestured towards Grace and Jack, gazing at one another and holding hands across the table.

"Do those two look like they're cursed?"

Elodie rolled her eyes before looking towards the new couple, rapping her nails on the table as if annoyed.

I blurted out, "Do you know how the books work?"

Sonny squeezed my thigh and I glanced at him. He shook his head almost imperceptibly.

She shrugged before she suddenly stood up. "Just know, happily ever after might come at a cost." She sniffed before saying, "I have another appointment. Claire, I'll see you around."

Sonny muttered, "God, I hope not."

She stared daggers at him before leaving.

As she walked towards the door, my mind raced. I looked at Sonny, wondering if this curse she spoke of might affect us, too.

I felt his hot breath on my ear as he whispered, "Don't trust her. We need to stay far away from her."

"She seems like she's just trying to help."

He shook his head, releasing a dry chuckle. "She is not trying to help. She's up to something."

Suddenly, a memory came to the surface, my eyes wide with realization. A few years into my marriage, I remembered finding a book on a park bench. But shortly after that, there was a turning point where everything just fell apart. My heart raced. What if that book had been one of Elodie's?

"Claire?" Sonny looked alarmed, "What is it?"

I took a deep breath but hesitated before speaking, "What Elodie said made me remember something," I said, my voice shaking with uncertainty.

Sonny's expression shifted from alarm to reluctance. "There's something off about her. You know that, right? She's full of shit." He leaned in closer as he studied me. "But what is it?"

I recounted the memory that had resurfaced. "When I was married, I found a book on a park bench, and things between us started to fall apart right around the same time. The timing just seems… I don't know." I took in a deep breath, "Maybe if I never found the book…"

Sonny's brows wrinkled. "You think that book might have been one of Elodie's?"

I shrugged, my heart pounding in my chest. "It's possible. I remember it had a lot of notes written in it. And if it was, then… maybe I should be more careful with these books."

His eyes held mine with both understanding and worry. "We'll figure this out." He looked down at the table before looking up at me again. "But do you really think a book could cause your marriage to end? You said yourself that y'all had a lot of problems. He lied all the time, and his anger…" Sonny clenched his jaw, a lethal calmness coming over him. "Was he… ever physical with you?"

Sonny's question pierced right through me. He was asking things I hadn't allowed myself to acknowledge fully. I looked away, feeling shame building in the pit of my belly. I had avoided talking about it, even admitting it to myself, for so long, but I wanted to be honest with him.

I opened my mouth, but no words came out as my throat tightened. A single tear trailed down my cheek.

Chapter 36 - Edison

Edison's eyes locked on that tear, following its path. His jaw clenched, a muscle ticking in his temple as he balled his hands into fists. The mere thought of hurting a woman disgusted him. If he ever crossed paths with that fucker, he didn't know what he might do. He huffed out a breath, shielding Claire from the full force of his anger.

Quietly, he said, "Maybe we should go home and talk about things."

Claire nodded. "Okay."

They drove home in silence, and Edison's anger sat between them. Once home, Claire sat on the leather couch, warily watching him pace the living room. His eyes softened as they locked on hers. He came and sat down next to her, letting out a sigh.

He picked up her hand, his own trembling as he said, "I love you. I've loved you for a long time. I can't believe..." He stood up, unable to finish his thought, and paced in front of the couch before stopping and kneeling in front of her. His face darkened, "I need to know. I need to know what he did to you."

She opened her mouth to speak, but before she answered, Edison stopped her. "Wait," He said, "I don't know if that's a good idea. The thought of someone hurting you... It's... I don't know if I could stop myself from finding him and making him pay for what he did." His gaze clouded with anger and sadness.

Claire went to him, wrapping her arms around his shoulders. "Sonny, please. It was a long time ago. This won't change anything."

He hugged her, his face buried in her hair. His voice muffled, "What you said back there..." He pulled back. "It terrified me. I want this life with you and the thought that it might all crumble before us... I don't know if I can bear it."

Claire gave him a puzzled look, "I don't understand. What are you talking about?"

He locked his eyes on hers as he gestured wildly. "At the coffee house? You sounded like you wanted to go back... to him." He spat out the last words.

"Where did you get that idea?" She asked.

He told himself she hadn't intended to hurt him, but it still sent a chill straight to his heart. She reached for him again as her eyes welled with tears.

"Sonny," she began, her voice thick, "I knew from the first moment we met. I knew we were going to be something special. It was you. It was always you. After that first night, I knew you were my soulmate, but now..." She exhaled, "It's so much more than that."

She closed her eyes for a moment before opening them, those dark blue eyes shining like sapphires. "That weekend we met? It was life-changing, and I wasn't ready." She looked down as tears fell, shaking her head. Her voice was a mere whisper, "I wasn't ready for you."

She lifted her eyes to his. Taking a breath, she steadied her voice. "It scared me so much that I ran back to Pete. He was the worst decision of my life, and it took me far too long to realize it. You have nothing to fear because my heart, my everything, belongs to you. I think it always has."

Edison blinked back tears, relief coursing through him. His heart hammered against his chest as he pulled Claire into a tight embrace, holding her close. He pressed his forehead against hers, closing his eyes.

"Sometimes, I wonder if we've been finding each other over and over, lifetime after lifetime—two parts of one soul destined to meet, no matter how the world shifts around us." His fingers brushed her cheek, his voice thick with emotion. "Words could never capture the joy of finding you again. And if it takes eternity, I'd wait through every lifetime just to be yours."

Claire's breath hitched as she met his gaze, emotion swelling in her chest. She reached for his hand, lacing their fingers together as if anchoring herself to this moment. "I'm yours, Sonny. I always have been. In every lifetime, in every way... it's always been you."

Without thought, his hands caressed her face as they kissed. Between kisses, they both whispered sacred promises to each other. Her hands roamed from his back to his hair to his chest just before he laid her against the couch, hovering over her.

As their lips met again, she asked, "You felt it, didn't you?"

Curiosity danced in his eyes, "Felt what?"

"That first night. That we were something... more," she breathed. Her pulse was visible across her chest, her heart pounding as fast as his.

"I don't know," he replied, "But I felt an instant connection the moment this mysterious redhead sat down at my table like this was going to turn into something way more than I could know."

His lips curved against hers. "Can I confess a secret?" He didn't wait for an answer, "One of the first thoughts that crossed my mind when we first met was this would be the story we'd tell our children."

"Our children?" A smile bloomed on her face, warm and comforting. Edison was willing to move mountains if he could make her smile like that every day.

"Yes," he whispered, sealing his words with another tender kiss before trailing his lips down her neck.

She breathed out his name, "Sonny..."

If she only knew what it did to him when she called him that old nickname. His lips found their way between her neck and shoulder, and the world faded into the background, leaving only them, lost in each other, two souls entwined and bound by a force beyond understanding.

He came back up and gazed into her eyes with such tenderness. The tears glistening in her eyes made him want to confess something else.

"I've never felt this way for anyone. It's like everything in my life led me to you. Did I ever tell you?" He swallowed, a look of vulnerability across his face. "When I moved here, it was simply because I had an unexplainable urge to do it. I'd never been here before, never visited. I didn't have a job. I didn't know a soul, but something pulled me here."

A shiver went down her spine as she smiled against his lips. "Or someone."

He whispered it back to her in confirmation, "Or someone."

"It makes me wonder if we were always meant to

find each other."

He stood up, holding his hand out. "Let's go to bed, Poppy."

She took his hand and led him back to the bedroom.

Claire was nestled against his shoulder, his arm wrapped around her firmly at the hip. She had quickly fallen asleep after they had made slow, passionate love together. How did three hours of lovemaking feel like only a moment in time? But it was always like that with her. He lost himself in her, and he marveled at how it was possible as he lazily ran his fingers down her hip to her thigh and back again.

There was nowhere else he wanted to be, but Edison couldn't fall asleep. He couldn't stop replaying their earlier conversation when he said, "This mysterious redhead." God, he'd nearly confessed and hadn't even realized it. He was living in a house of cards. What would that have done to everything?

He looked at the clock, realizing it was afternoon, and they still hadn't returned to the apartment to finish packing. He gently slipped out from under her and went to take a shower.

After getting dressed, he sat on the bed and gently shook her to wake up. "Poppy? Claire? Wake up, baby."

She stirred, giving him a sleepy smile as she rolled over to face him. "Good morning, my love."

"You mean, good afternoon."

Claire gave him a confused look before wiping the sleep from her eyes and sitting up to look at the clock. Her eyes widened. "Why'd you let me sleep so long?" She scooted to the end of the bed and grabbed her jeans. "We have so much to do and haven't even made it to the apartment today. We need to leave. Now."

Chapter 37 - Claire

Sitting at my desk, I was lost in thought, replaying Elodie's conversation at the coffee house. It had been on my mind for weeks, but I had no idea what to make of it. Was she just being helpful? I wanted to believe her, but I just kept questioning her motives.

Sonny was convinced she was trying to scare us into giving the books back. Should I give them back? But more importantly, was that all she wanted? I couldn't figure her out.

I was so lost in thought that I didn't hear when Darci came over.

"Hey, girl!"

I jumped but stood up, offering a friendly smile. "Darce! You need something?"

Darci hesitated, her expression uneasy. "A woman is asking for you over at the checkout desk." She made a face. "She seems… intense."

My eyes widened in recognition as I grimaced, "Like she could play the part of a villain in a Disney movie?"

Darci chuckled, "Uh, yeah."

Elodie. It had to be. Her penchant for drama and gothic fashion was unmistakable. What in the world did she want now?

"Did she give her name?"

"Uh, I think it was Eliza or something?"

Of course, it was her. Who else would it be?

"Elodie?"

Darci looked surprised. "Were you expecting her?"

I chuckled knowingly. "No, but I'm not surprised. She has a... distinctive style."

"That's an understatement." She chuckled, "Ask her what lipstick she uses. It's like... the reddest red I've ever seen."

I couldn't help but grin. "Like fresh blood?"

Darci nodded. "Who is she?"

"Honestly, I don't really know. But I'll tell you what I know at lunch."

"Looking forward to it." Darci offered a sympathetic smile. "I'll be over here if you need backup or anything."

I chuckled. "I might. Thanks for the heads-up."

As I made my way to the checkout desk, I smoothed down my skirt, wishing Darci had come with me, but I reminded myself that Elodie had been nothing but cordial to me. Still, I couldn't shake the feeling that she was up to something.

Standing at the desk, she wore a large black hat to complement her black lace Victorian dress. Where did she get all these outfits? They must have cost a fortune and been custom-made for her. I straightened my spine, feeling like a fly wandering into a spiderweb.

She approached me with that hollow smile she always wore, asking if we could talk. I led her to a quiet corner and wished Sonny was with me. Was she going to demand the books back? I had an odd feeling she was about to unleash a storm.

We sat at a small table by a window, and I gave her a polite smile. "What's on your mind?"

She smirked. "There are things, Claire, that I shouldn't know. But I do. About your ex-husband, for instance. He was quite the liar, wasn't he?"

My breath hitched. How did she even know I had been married? I narrowed my eyes, "How did you...?"

Elodie leaned toward me as her eyes softened. "I know more than you might think, my dear. And I worry about you."

"You don't even know me." Where was this going?

She lowered her voice and looked around before her gaze returned to me. "How well do you really know Edison?"

I wrinkled my brow. "What? Why are you asking?"

She leaned back casually in her chair, raising a shoulder. "Edison is more than he seems. Has he told you what he does?"

"I'm not sure what you mean. He's a professor at the college."

"That he is, but he's also a very successful writer, behind some of the bestselling novels out there. His books have been made into movies."

My eyes widened, "What? How do you..."

She interrupted, her brows raised, "He's never told you, has he? Why do you think that is?"

"I... I don't know." I tried and failed to hide the tremor in my voice as I asked, "Are you sure?"

Her eyes lit up. She leaned toward me, shaking her head. "That's not all. That little blind date, years ago?"

"My blind date with Sonny?" What in the hell was she talking about?

Her head inclined. In a sing-song voice, she said, "Your perfect man has been keeping a big secret."

"What secret?"

"Claire, do you want to know the truth?" Her smile seemed warm, but I saw a sharp glint when I looked into her eyes.

"The truth?"

She rolled her eyes, her voice full of irritation. "Is there an echo in here?"

That sent my blood boiling. I'd had enough. "Just say it. I need to get back to work." I snapped at her.

She shook her head, a smile playing on her lips. She walked her fingers along the table towards me. I couldn't look away from those dark red nails as she spoke.

"Remember how you were over an hour late to your blind date? He wasn't who you were supposed to meet." She paused, waiting for my reaction.

"What are you talking about?"

"He had no idea who you were. He just… played along when you came over."

Her smile turned into a predatory grin, stretching across her face. Her eyes mirrored the same darkness. Laced with such chilling confidence, her words sent a shiver down my spine.

"That's not true..."

Even with my denial, a seed of doubt, tiny and unwelcome, began to take root. The memories from that afternoon ran through my head—Sonny's smile when I sat down at his booth, the recognition in his eyes, was it just wishful thinking on my part?

She whispered in my ear, her nails on my shoulder. I jumped, realizing she was now sitting beside me, her lips at my ear.

"Do you see that man over there, the one at the desk with the laptop?"

I followed her gaze to find a man who reminded me too much of Pete. He had salt and pepper hair parted on the side and dark eyes, and he was muttering to himself as he picked lint off a blue polo shirt.

"That's Dave. He was supposed to be your date. You could go say hello."

I pulled away and looked at her like she was out of her mind. "Why would I do that?"

"Do you really want to be with another liar? I just can't help but think it's related to those cursed books. Maybe if you gave them back..." Her voice trailed off as she looked at me expectantly.

I felt a flush of heat rising up my neck. Would he lie to me like that?

I sniffled, blinking back the burn of tears behind my eyes. "So that's it? You just want those books. You really will say anything to get them back, but you're not getting them."

Elodie put her hand over mine. Her voice softened, "Claire, it's all true. Just... think about it. I don't want you to go through what I did."

I looked down at her hand over mine. The black lace at her wrist pulled back slightly to reveal part of an intricate tattoo peeking out.

I jerked my hand away as the tremor in my voice gave me away. "I need... I need to get back to work."

I looked up at her, wiping an escaping tear before standing up. Goddammit, I did not want to cry in front of her. I took a deep breath, trying to calm myself before I said, "I'll walk you out."

She shrugged as she stood up, smoothing her dress down. At the doors, she turned towards me. Her voice was overly sweet. "I'm only telling you these things because I care, Claire. I don't want to see you hurt."

I looked down and nodded. When I met her eyes again, she didn't look worried. Her eyes remained cold and calculating, flitting around the room as if looking for an audience. The corners of her mouth twitched slightly as if struggling to suppress a smile.

I forced a polite smile, but I could feel the tension in my face. "Thank you for coming."

As Elodie walked away, my mind reeled. Maybe she was trying to be helpful, but my eyes stayed on her, wary, searching, waiting for whatever game she was trying to play to reveal itself. Walking back to the teen room, I felt exposed and vulnerable. Was anything she said true? How could she know any of it?

I was never good at hiding my emotions, so during lunch, I confessed everything to Darci—how Elodie once had the books I have now, how she'd show up when I left the books, the weird way she behaved around Edison, and all the stuff she said today.

Darci took in every word. "She seems like a real piece of work. We need to..." She stared off into space for a moment. "We need to figure out who she really is."

The early afternoon was always slow, so Darci and I turned to the internet, determined to uncover the truth about Elodie. It wasn't long before we unearthed one revelation that didn't seem surprising—Elodie was a practicing witch, and she liked to dabble in dark magic.

Darci came back to the teen room and picked up my phone. "I found her social media."

"Okay..."

"Lilith_Bloodgood." She typed in the username and returned it to me with her profile pulled up.

I chuckled wryly, "It doesn't seem like she hides who she is online."

"No, she seems to thrive on it."

The account came up immediately, and I scanned through a few of her posts.

Darci was scrolling through something on her phone. "I think I found her Etsy store where she sells readings and spells."

"Really?" Her profile had a link to her store. I followed it.

Darci pulled up a chair as we huddled behind my desk, determined to unravel who exactly she was. The screen refreshed, revealing the homepage of an Etsy shop named "The Raven's Quill." The description read: "Handcrafted spells, readings, and rituals for those seeking guidance on the hidden path." Scrolling through the listings, I kept returning to the same question. What did she want with me?

"Lunar Binding Ritual? Shadow Binding? The Pact of Rituals? These sound... intense," Darci's voice dripped with mock horror.

"Right?" I replied, forcing a smile, but a shiver ran down my spine despite the warmth of the room. "I can't imagine anyone needing some of these... interventions."

"Who knows?" Darci shrugged, her playful demeanor fading slightly. "Maybe someone desperately wants to win the lottery." Her voice dropped to a whisper. "Or maybe they have something a little more... sinister in mind."

"What the hell is all this?"

My eyes scanned the details of the "Lunar Binding Ritual" kit – dried wolfsbane, a silver chalice tarnished with age, and a worn leather-bound book filled with symbols. Each item seemed to whisper of a power I couldn't fathom.

"This is getting creepy," Darci admitted, shifting

in her chair. "Maybe we should just... stop looking."

"I'm starting to wonder if Elodie has something a little more sinister in mind regarding me and Sonny." I wanted to figure her out, but after everything, she scared me. What was she capable of?

"Let's go back to her Instagram," I said.

Darci nodded slowly. "Yeah, it might give us some insight about her," she said, her voice grim. "Maybe we can figure out what she's up to."

I took a deep breath, trying to quell the rising fear. I didn't want to turn back now. Not until we understood the truth, however unsettling it might be.

"Okay," I said, my voice firmer than I felt. "Let's see what sweet little Lilith Bloodgood is up to."

I reopened the app, and we went down a rabbit hole. The profile picture was a grainy, black-and-white photo of a woman with flowing dark hair and piercing eyes that seemed to hold a thousand secrets. The bio simply read: "Seeker of shadows." Below were three pinned posts, each a single cryptic image: a weathered hand holding a worn book, a circle of flickering candles casting dancing shadows on the wall, and a close-up of an intricate astrological chart.

"Interesting," I muttered, scrolling through the feed. "But not exactly smoking gun material." I continued, clicking on old posts. I held up my phone. "This was when her marriage fell apart. She said it was a total surprise."

Darci leaned over. "Is that a sonogram video? Was she... pregnant?" We both leaned in closer as I pulled up the post. Darci took a sharp intake of breath. "Oh no, it's... cancer. Can you imagine going through something like that while dealing with a divorce?"

I shook my head. "I can't imagine, but it looks like she went into remission."

Darci pointed to the pink house in one of the posts, "Is that...?"

I opened it and smiled softly. "Yeah. Can you believe it was her bookstore?" My eyes widened as I looked over at Darci, "She owned it."

"Are you serious? That's a weird coincidence."

I let out a sigh. "Yeah, but look," I said, opening another post announcing the bookstore's closing. "Within a matter of months, she lost everything—her husband, her health, and then the bookstore."

Darci mused, "Maybe that's why she's into dark magic? Life dealt her one blow after another. Scroll back a bit more. Let's see what she used to be like."

"Sure." I swiped my thumb back, looking for Elodie's happier time. Soon, there were posts with her goth 'fit checks and strange occult items. I stopped when I saw a post with a familiar sign and lanterns down a path of canopies.

I breathed out, "Darci."

"What is it?" She leaned closer, searching the images, looking confused.

I opened the post for the Witch Market. The caption had the correct dates. "I think... she was the psychic who read our tarot cards that weekend I met Sonny."

"Okay, this is seriously too many coincidences."

"I'm almost positive. I first saw her a few months ago at that church. I thought she looked familiar." I zoomed in on the post with the lanterns. "I still remember the cryptic words she said back then. "She kept saying we were 'out of time.' I thought she meant we'd run out of time for the reading, but now I wonder..."

Darci shrugged. "Anything's possible, I suppose."

"I think she saw our future. I have this sneaking suspicion there was more to it than she told us. But she looked like she had seen a ghost when she flipped our cards over." That memory sent shivers down my spine.

I scrolled through more posts, watching her change from a girl into a woman. Her look changed from a homespun hippie into the polished Victorian witch-core she had going on now. One post caught my attention. Most were taken outside, but this one stood out — a picture of her inside a restaurant... or maybe a bar. A man's arm beside hers triggered a strange sense of familiarity, though I couldn't quite place it.

I zoomed in and noticed the short sleeve of a t-shirt, and on the inside of the arm was the edge of a tattoo, the stem of a very familiar flower—one I'd traced many times. Sonny knew her. Why hadn't he told me?

Chapter 38 - Edison

When Claire moved in, everything just clicked—as if the universe had been waiting for this moment all along. In his wildest dreams, Edison never imagined waking up to her smile, making love to her as the morning sun streamed through the curtains. Some days, he wanted to pinch himself, unable to believe that every unspoken wish had come true.

It was nearly noon when he finally rolled out of bed, taking full advantage of his late-starting classes. Claire had left for the library in the early morning, but he missed her, knowing they wouldn't cross paths again until late tonight. She'd likely be asleep by the time he got home. He rolled onto her pillow, inhaling her lingering scent, a quiet ache settling in his chest.

On nights like this, Claire would make dinner, take Bandit for a walk, and tuck herself into bed before he even stepped through the door. Edison would find them curled up together, fast asleep, the soft glow of the bedside lamp casting warmth over them. And every time, without fail, the sight unraveled him—reminding him just how lucky he was.

Later that night, as he pulled into the garage, he

chuckled, wondering where he'd find Claire and Bandit tonight. Last week, he walked into the bedroom to find Bandit curled beside Claire on the bed, the two of them practically spooning. She had been fast asleep, a book in her hand open across Bandit's back. Another time, he'd found them on the couch, both asleep, with Bandit lying between Claire's legs.

Tonight, as Edison walked into the bedroom, Bandit opened his eyes, his head resting on Claire's hip as he curled up behind her. He didn't move a muscle as he watched Edison enter the room, probably because he was supposed to be in his bed on the floor. But Edison couldn't bring himself to make Bandit get down. The dog closed his eyes again, immediately falling asleep, his snout twitching as his paws gently moved in rhythm with his doggy dreams. Edison grinned, taking a photo of the two of them snuggled together.

Midterm week had drained Edison. Testing days were always the worst, and tonight had been especially brutal—exams in both of his evening classes. Hours of sitting in silence, watching students scribble away while he played the role of an ever-vigilant hawk. It wasn't just exhausting, and it was mind-numbingly dull.

Taking off his shoes, his stomach rumbled. He was ready to eat and then crawl into bed with Claire. He headed to the kitchen in search of leftovers. He found a wrapped plate with chicken tikka masala, steamed rice, and a note set on top. He popped the plate in the microwave and unfolded the note, finding Claire's bubbly cursive.

My love,

Just thinking about you makes me smile. You

always have a way of brightening my day. I can't wait until you get home.

With all my affection,

Poppy

As Edison read her note, warmth spread through him, easing the tension from the day. A slow smile tugged at his lips, the exhaustion of the day momentarily forgotten. While his food heated in the kitchen, he went to his office and opened the desk drawer where he kept every note she had ever left him. With careful fingers, he tucked this one alongside the rest, a quiet reminder of her presence, even when they were apart.

His mouth watered as he walked back to the kitchen, the delicious aroma filling the air. He wasn't sure what magic she infused, but her chicken tikka masala was one of his favorites. As soon as it was ready, he went to the living room, sank onto the oversized leather couch, stretched his legs out on the coffee table, and watched a documentary.

After enjoying a second helping, he went back to the bedroom. With only a sliver of the bathroom light shining through the door, he stripped down to his boxers before sending Bandit to his dog bed and lying down with Claire. Watching her sleep, he couldn't keep his hands to himself as he stroked her hair, feeling overwhelmed with love. Breathing in the scent of her shampoo, he kissed her hair and knew he was a lucky man. He tucked himself behind her and snaked his hand around her middle, pulling her into him. Instinctively, she pressed back into his body before falling back into a deep sleep. Content, he let out a soft sigh and drifted off.

Later that night, he woke up suddenly, anxiety swirling in his stomach. It was too dark to see, but

Claire was no longer curled against him. He felt along the bed, finding cool sheets instead of her warm body. Sitting up, he looked around, rubbing his hand down his beard as he checked the clock to see it was four in the morning. Where did she go? Was she sick? He groaned as he climbed out of the bed, a chill against his bare skin, checking the bathroom before going to the living room, hoping to find her there.

Still looking, he headed to the kitchen. She was sitting in the dark at the table with her hands over her face as she sniffled. Fear coursed through him as he rushed to her side.

"What's wrong? What happened?"

She looked up, her face streaked with tears and tried to compose herself. He pulled her up against him, wrapping his arms around her. She leaned into him as she stood, his arms falling to her waist.

"I had a bad dream. It felt so real. My heart was racing. When I woke up, I had to do something and get it out of my head."

Edison reached up, caressing her cheek. "You should have woken me. Do you want to talk about it?"

She nodded, her eyes glistening with tears. "You were... You were with that strange woman, Elodie, like together. You didn't want me anymore."

His brows shot up as he huffed out a laugh. "Me and Elodie? Where did that come from?

"I don't know. I know it sounds silly. Maybe her visit to the library triggered it."

"She showed up at the library?" He tilted his head. "What did she want?"

"Well," She took in a shuddering breath. "She certainly had a lot to say... about you." Tears welled in her eyes.

He cocked his head. "Me?"

Claire sniffled as she nodded. "Yeah."

"What did she say?"

She said, "I need to show you something."

"Okay."

She picked up her phone. Claire opened Instagram and handed it to him. When he saw the photo, his stomach twisted in a knot. Elodie was a thorn in his side.

He closed his eyes, dreading the conversation he knew they needed to have. "Claire..."

She peered up at him, "Why didn't you tell me you knew her?"

"Because I don't. Not really."

She sat down, inclining her head. "Not really?"

He plopped down in one of the kitchen chairs. He let out a sigh, running his hand through his hair. "She was my... student."

"Oh god. Please tell me-"

"No!" He sat up, shaking his head. "No, that never happened. I knew she was interested. She made it blatantly obvious, even at school, but I kept my distance." He swallowed, "I used to go to this bar, The Basement. It was just a place to unwind."

Her eyes narrowed, "Okay?"

Edison fidgeted, running his hands through his hair again, unable to sit still. "She started showing up there, moving from guy to guy. She was always eye fucking me, but I ignored her until one stupid night." His eyes pleaded as he shrugged, "I was in a bad place, had too much to drink. I was... I was lonely."

She crossed her arms, "Go on."

He sighed, leaning over, his elbows on his knees. "She came over and made a pass at me. I barely remember it. I was really drunk, but I agreed to get coffee with her."

"Why didn't you tell me?" She gave Edison a death glare.

"It was a mistake. I had forgotten it ever happened until..." He grabbed the back of his neck. "I don't even remember how we ended up at Alchemy, but realizing where we were... where you and I met, memories flooded my brain. I wanted to forget. I didn't think I'd ever see you again." His gaze darted to her before looking away. "We were in a booth at the back, and... She kissed me, and for a second, I let her."

"And then what?"

He brought his gaze back to hers, his eyes full of remorse. "I was drunk, Claire, and at that point, she wasn't my student. Honestly, I don't remember much, but I know I scrambled out of the booth, regretting it immediately. I didn't want to be a jerk, so I gave him some stupid excuse."

He reached for Claire's hand, but she recoiled.

"And you never thought to mention any of this to me? What did you think I'd do?" She stood up and paced, stopping to look back at him, her hands dropping to her sides. "This. This is why she looks like she wants to kill you every time she sees you."

He shrugged. "I guess."

He walked to Claire, his hands gripping her hips and his eyes pleading. "It was a wake-up call. I stopped going there, stopped drinking like that... shortly after it happened."

"You should've told me. How do you think this makes me feel?"

"You're right. You're absolutely right. I should have told you. But honestly, I didn't remember until after we ran into her on the square. I didn't put it together seeing her in those weird clothes. She wasn't like that back then."

Claire backed out of his touch. Her tone was accusatory, "I knew something was off when you two were talking. Why didn't you tell me then?"

"I'm sorry. I didn't think it was important." He stood up, tugging on his hair.

She sniffled before setting her phone down on the table.

He stopped, standing on the other side of the table. "Is there something else? Did she say more?"

Claire flicked her eyes to Edison.

"She said you're not who you say you are."

"What does that mean? I'm exactly who I say I am." He laced his fingers together on top of his head while he paced.

"She said you're a super successful writer with movie deals." She looked over at the bookshelf in the living room. "Is that true?

He grumbled, "I swear to god...that fucking... How does Elodie know anything about me?" He walked over to the chair next to Claire and plopped down. He shrugged, raising his palms. "Yes! Yes, I write for Brendan Cross." He nodded.

"Like all those New York Times Bestsellers?"

How in the hell did Elodie know so much? No one knew this stuff. He forced himself to speak in a measured tone, the tension in his shoulders betraying the frustration simmering beneath the surface. "Yes, I wrote most of the recent ones."

One side of Claire's mouth ticked up. Her voice softened, "Seriously? Even the ones made into movies?"

He cleared his throat and nodded, feeling his stomach tighten into a knot. "Um, yeah. I've had four deals for film rights."

Claire looked away and mouthed, "Wow!" She

caught his gaze. "Why doesn't he write his own books?"

"It's a well-kept secret. He's nearly 90 years old and developed dementia about ten years ago. Initially, his family hired me to finish the book he'd been working on when he got too bad to finish it. It was a mess. It took me a year to fix everything, and then, the book sold like hotcakes. They wanted me to keep doing it." He shrugged. "The pay was good for someone fresh out of grad school."

She gave him a curious look. "Why don't you write under your name?"

"I wanted to. I still do. It's just…"

"Don't you want to make a name for yourself as a writer?"

He nodded, "Of course I do. But now that I've been doing this for several years, it's hard to get out from under it."

She went to the fridge, getting the pitcher of water. Before pouring her drink, she turned around suddenly to face him. "Why didn't you just tell me?"

Regret washed over him. Why hadn't he? Did he even have an answer? He should have done it weeks, months ago, but the words had always slipped away, pushed to the back of his mind. He never tried to hide it, but he hadn't told her either. He'd never reached that point in a relationship where he needed to reveal such a significant part of himself.

He ran his hand over his face, not sure what to say. The irony wasn't lost on him. He crafted stories for a living, yet he had made a giant mess of something ridiculously simple when it came to his life. A flush crept up his neck as he felt acutely aware of his shortcomings.

She sat back down, and he took a moment to

steady himself, then looked directly into her eyes. "You deserved to know. I should have told you a long time ago."

"You didn't trust me?"

His eyes softened. "Claire, no, that wasn't it at all." He sighed, knowing this whole thing made him look bad. "I signed an iron-clad NDA and never even told my parents. It's just... I didn't know how to tell you."

When he reached for her hand, she moved away.

Her gaze hardened. "She told me something else..." The words came out tight, and just before she finished speaking, her eyes flicked away.

Fucking Elodie. Edison didn't know how she always seemed to know just where to strike, but she took pleasure in twisting the knife. She had been out for blood from the moment he saw her in the square, her smirk sharp as ever. And when she raked her red nails against his skin, she had made her message clear—she hadn't forgotten, and she sure as hell hadn't forgiven. After all this time, she still resented his rejection.

He exhaled, steadying himself. "Claire, there's something I've been meaning to tell you." His voice carried a slight tremor as he met her eyes, his fingers reaching for hers. This time, she didn't pull away.

Chapter 39 - Claire

Dread bloomed in my belly as my hands started to shake. A breath was caught in my throat. This had to be a bad dream. This was a scene ripped straight from my marriage when I'd catch Pete spinning one ridiculous lie after another until his eventual confession, which was frequently just a prelude to a disaster.

I closed my eyes, shaking my head, "Whatever it is... just tell me."

I could almost hear Pete's voice, laced with a practiced remorse that promised another betrayal. I pulled my hands from his, reaching for the bracelet on my other wrist, twisting it in a silent plea for strength against this all-too-familiar fear.

What was Sonny going to say? Would it shatter everything between us? The anticipation coiled, freezing my insides as I waited for the other shoe to finally drop. From the very beginning, I feared this second chance was too good to be true.

He leaned closer, catching my gaze. Those fiery eyes that had always made me feel so safe—until now. I wasn't sure what they were telling me. He took both my hands, gently rubbing his thumbs over my knuckles.

"Remember our blind date?"

I nodded as I bit the corner of my lip. "Of course, why?" I narrowed my eyes as Elodie's words played on repeat in my mind.

"Afterwards, did you ever talk to..." He looked to his left before catching my gaze again. "Uh, what was her name?"

Slowly, I said, "Rebecca? My friend who set us up?" Please. Oh god. Please tell me what Elodie had said was true.

He nodded slowly. "Yeah... Rebecca. Did you ever talk to her after that weekend?"

I thought back to that time and shook my head, my curls bouncing. "No, we didn't talk after that. She moved out over the weekend before graduation. It was a busy time. When I got back together with Pete, I didn't reach out and tell them he'd proposed. They hated him. I knew they would try to talk me out of it." I shrugged.

Sonny exhaled, his fingers drumming lightly against the table as he studied her. "And... were they wrong?" His voice was gentle, but something else was beneath it—something knowing.

I narrowed my eyes, pulling my hand back. "What does that have to do with anything?" My voice came out sharper than I intended, but I was panicking—this wasn't what we were talking about. "I don't see how my past mistakes have anything to do with whatever you're trying to tell me." I crossed my arms, waiting. "Can you just say it?"

He grimaced, letting out a sigh. "I wasn't your blind date." His head dropped as soon as the words were out of his mouth.

"What? Yes, you were. Like Rebecca said, you were the blond guy in a red shirt. We were together the entire weekend."

I had prayed, wished, and hoped that what Elodie said was a lie. Even now, I wanted to believe it wasn't true.

He slowly shook his head, wincing as he confessed. "I wasn't supposed to meet anyone. I didn't know Rebecca. I had just walked in there a few minutes before you did after a long day of teaching."

I pulled out of his grasp. The knot twisted in my belly as I frowned, "You weren't my blind date?"

"No." Avoiding my gaze, he shook his head again, his mouth in a tight white line.

I scrutinized his face, looking for any sign he was joking. "Seriously?" His eyes were full of worry as I shook my head. "Then why did you..."

I was startled as Sonny's chair scraped against the floor as he shot to his feet, the force of it tipping back before he caught it. "You captivated me." His voice was raw and rushed, frustration bleeding through as he spread his arms wide, desperation flickering in his eyes.

His voice softened as he righted the chair, a slow exhale leaving his lips. "At first, it was your smile." He reached up with his thumb to brush against my lips, "Your smile is like the summer... But then... then it was something else, something deeper. From the moment you sat down, we had this... connection. It felt like..." He paused, his chest heaving as he fixed his gaze on me, "like I belonged with you." The last words came out in a whisper.

He sank back into his seat, his hand running through his hair again. "From the moment I had the urge to move up here, it was as if I was waiting for something, someone... and then there you were." He murmured, "There you were..."

His gaze fixed on mine, "You felt like... coming home. I can't explain it. I didn't know who you were, and yet, at the same time, I felt like I'd known you my whole life. I know it sounds crazy." His hand reached out, hovering near mine, the yearning in his eyes impossible to miss. "I know you felt it, too."

I stared back, caught off guard by the intensity of his confession. He wasn't wrong, but what could I say? I remembered it like it was yesterday—insta-love, soulmates, destiny, whatever you want to call it. When I slid into his booth and our eyes met, something clicked into place. A sense of recognition settled into my bones that defied logic, like I was exactly where I was supposed to be.

But his confession made me question everything, like I was trapped in the same situation I'd been with Pete, not knowing which way was up or what to believe. I wanted to trust everything Sonny was saying, but how could I? The floor had just been ripped out from under me. He knew Elodie. He didn't tell me he was a successful writer. And to make matters worse, all this time, he never admitted he wasn't my blind date.

I wrapped my arms around myself as I stood up and began to pace, thinking about our first meeting. Had I missed something? I stopped abruptly, turning around and glaring at him.

"But you..." I remembered when I asked him about the beard. "You said Rebecca told you to shave your beard when I asked why you didn't have one!" I glowered at him, feeling like I might throw up.

"Did you ever even have a beard back then?"

As soon as I called him out on his lie, his shoulders slumped, and a defeated look washed over his face as he looked down and shook his head.

He frowned and looked away, shame flashing across his face. But he didn't say a word.

"Oh my god, I should have known!"

The more it sank in, the more I couldn't believe it. He pretended to be my date, and fucking lied to my face. What else did he lie about? Pete lied all the time about the stupidest shit, and I'd be damned if I was dumb enough to fall for that again.

I let out a harsh breath. I was livid. I covered my face with my hands, taking a calming breath before tucking my curls behind my ears. I sat down on the other side of the table, as far away from him as possible, letting my arms fall. I was at a loss about what to do next. My face heated as tears overflowed down my cheeks. Why did I have to cry whenever I was angry? I hated it.

My eyes slid to him, my voice low, "You lied to me." I'm not sure he even heard me as I barely breathed it out.

I turned away as I tried blinking the tears away, but nothing could stop the dam from breaking. Fuck! I willed myself to stop crying. Sonny came over, getting down on his knees as he turned my chair to face him. He clasped both my hands in his and gave me a sad smile, his eyes full of regret and agony.

He sighed. "This wasn't how this was supposed to go. I was going to tell you—everything. You have to believe me. That blind date was the only time I wasn't truthful."

I chuckled dryly, "What about your job? Elodie? You weren't exactly truthful about those things, were you?"

He squeezed my hands, "What can I do to fix this? I wasn't keeping anything from you, not intentionally. I didn't know... how to tell you." His voice cracked on the last words.

He took a breath. "You have to know, this has driven me insane since you canceled and disappeared on me all those years ago. I thought you'd figured it out, and that was why you ghosted me."

Looking down at my lap, I couldn't meet his gaze. Hot tears dripped onto my legs, and I closed my eyes, shaking my head, my hair falling in my face.

He put his forehead to mine and whispered, "Please, Poppy. I'm sorry. I'm so sorry. For all of it." His voice hitched, fighting a sob. "Please. I can't... lose you again."

I raised my head. His eyes were so full of hope. I couldn't take it. A sob wracked my body.

He whispered, "It was always you. Always." Silent tears streaked down his face as he closed his eyes.

"You know what Pete's lies did to me. I can't..." I tried to swallow the lump in my throat. I can't what? Do this anymore? I wasn't ready to say that, but I needed to be alone, space to think. I needed clarity.

My heart pounded, my lungs tightened as if the air had been stolen from the room. I needed out—anywhere but here, away from him. My thoughts twisted into a tangled mess, panic and longing warring inside me. Numbness crept over me, at odds with the frantic beating of my heart. My legs felt unsteady, but somehow, they carried me forward, each step shaky as I stumbled toward the door.

Leaving was the last thing I wanted. I wanted to be in his arms. I wanted this to have never happened. But I couldn't stay. I opened the front door, staring out into the dark.

"Claire?" Sonny's voice hitched behind me, laced with confusion that mirrored my own emotions. "What are you doing? It's the middle of the night. Can't we just... go to bed? Sleep on it?"

Shutting the door, I turned around, looking at him and then at the clock, realizing the time. I sighed, "Yeah, you're right." I turned towards the hallway leading to the bedroom.

He took a couple of steps like he was following me.

I snapped, "No," shaking my head, "you're not sleeping in the same bed as me. I need to be alone."

He froze, his eyes wide as my words sunk in. "I understand."

His shoulders slumped, and the light dimmed in his eyes, and I felt a stab of guilt, knowing I had just broken his heart. I pressed my lips together. He nodded and went to the couch. I would cave if I stayed in this room with him any longer.

I softened my voice. "Just... just give me some time, okay?" I sighed.

"How much time?"

I shook my head. "I don't know." His eyes darted away, his jaw tensing before I left the room.

I tossed some clothes in a bag, setting my alarm for 7 a.m., though I knew sleep would be impossible. Lying in the dark, my mind spun relentlessly, my heart racing with a whirlwind of emotions. Why did he keep all of this from me? Was I running away? Were we really over?

When my alarm finally blared, I threw on some clothes and grabbed my phone, dialing Darci as I slung my bag over my shoulder.

After a few rings, she picked up, her voice warm and groggy but laced with concern. "Hey, is everything okay?"

I swallowed hard, struggling to keep the tears at bay. My voice wavered. "Those things Elodie told me? I... I confronted him, and it was all true. Can I stay with you for a few days? I just—I need to get away from here."

Darci's voice softened instantly. "Oh, honey, I'm so sorry. Come on over. Stay as long as you need."

"Thanks, Darce," I whispered, my voice filled with gratitude. I sniffled. "I'll be there soon." I hung up and wrote a note, leaving it on Sonny's pillow. My eyes went straight to my stupid box of romance books, and I leaned over to heave it into my arms. Maybe Elodie did know what she was talking about. Maybe those goddamn books really were cursed.

Tiptoeing through the living room, I found him wrapped in a sheet on the couch. He was sound asleep with tear streaks drying down his cheeks. My heart told me to wipe them away and kiss him, but my brain said something else.

I grabbed my purse on the entryway table just as Bandit came down the hall, nails clicking on the wooden floor. He rubbed himself on my legs like a cat, and I squatted down to say goodbye, "You're a good boy. Take care of him for me."

I turned around, surveying the room, and took one last look at Sonny. I thought he would wake up as I moved around, follow me, beg me to stay, or something. Why wasn't he fighting for me, for us? Then, I quietly opened the front door and walked out. He still had not appeared by the time I'd loaded my stuff in the car. Feeling disheartened, I drove to Darci's apartment as the tears fell.

Chapter 40 - Edison

Edison had hoped his confession would be met with understanding and forgiveness, but their relationship now felt fragile, like something delicate and unsteady, teetering on the edge of breaking. It was his own doing, but never in a million years did he think this would happen. How could a few words from Elodie turn everything into such a fuck up?

At least he had convinced Claire not to walk out in the middle of the night, even if she refused to let him come to bed. Knowing she wanted nothing to do with him was pure torture. If he had to apologize for the rest of his life, he'd do it. All he wanted to do was hold her, comfort her, and tell her everything would be all right.

Out on the couch, sleep never came. He was awake the rest of the night, falling into a fitful sleep shortly before sunrise. Just minutes later, the soft rustling of Claire moving through the living room pulled him from sleep. He feigned sleep, giving her some space, but hearing the door click shut behind her felt like a death knell. He nearly ran after her, begging forgiveness again, but he wanted to give her the space she needed.

Despair clung to him, and he found himself face down on the floor. Claire was slipping through his fingers again, except it was his own doing this time. He replayed the scenes in his mind like a broken record—the hurt in her eyes, the betrayal she must have felt, the click of the door as she left. Why hadn't he been honest from the very beginning?

He knew her marriage had been full of Pete's lies, and Edison had never wanted her to endure that again. Yet that's precisely what he'd done. Edison's heart ached with so much regret. He'd destroyed the trust they had built, and now he feared it was permanently broken.

He buried his face in his hands as the crushing weight of reality pressed down on him and let sleep take him. When he woke, he was still sprawled across the living room rug, now with a crick in his neck and a tension headache. He had no idea what time it was. The muted glow in the room gave no clue until he looked at his watch, realizing it was almost evening.

How many hours had they been apart? He wasn't sure if he could survive this. The worst part was he had no idea where she was, if she had somewhere to go, or if she was safe. He dragged himself to the bedroom, looking for his phone, but found her note on his pillow. The tight knot of dread coiled in his stomach loosened slightly now that he at least knew where she was.

He left the note on the bed and went to the shower, his despair morphing into seething anger as the scalding water fell over his body. It bubbled up like a roiling fire, consuming him. He was mainly angry at himself, but there was someone else he wanted to blame—someone who had instigated this entire nightmare.

He got dressed and paced the bedroom,

considering what to do. He couldn't just sit back and let Elodie's meddling destroy what he had with Claire. He grabbed his wallet and keys and flew out the door. It was time to confront Elodie.

Edison's eyes darted around the dimly lit bar. The Basement looked even more like a dingy dungeon than he remembered, with the stone walls and flickering sconces. He inhaled through his nose. He didn't want to be here. There were too many pathetic memories from years of loneliness he'd sooner forget, but this had always been one of Elodie's haunts. He hoped she'd be here. A moment later, he spotted her at a corner table, sitting in the lap of a huge bearded man. Her presence exuded an air of coquettish confidence.

Edison approached her, his voice laced with anger and frustration. "Elodie," he began, his tone sharp, "we need to talk."

She raised an eyebrow, a smirk on her face. "Edison, darling, what a surprise. I wondered how long it would take before you showed up here."

"What the fuck is your problem?" He wasted no time, his accusations tumbling out. "Why? How? How do you know so much about me? About Claire?"

Elodie untangled herself from the man and whispered something in his ear before he lazily stood up and walked to the bar. She gestured to his seat at the table. Edison ignored her, sitting in the chair furthest away.

Her smirk was mocking. "Oh, you overestimate me. There are so many ways people inadvertently reveal things. I just pay attention."

He pressed further, his voice tense. "Who told you about my writing? How did you know about the blind date?"

Her laugh was bitter and cutting, but she merely shrugged.

Edison's frustration peaked. "Why are you going out of your way to cause problems between me and Claire?"

Her eyes glittered with a spiteful glint. "You should have just convinced her to return the books."

He scoffed, "So that's what this is about?"

She chuckled. "Remember that quaint little witch market? The tarot card reading?" She paused, letting the memory settle in the air between them. "Do you remember who read your cards?"

His eyes widened, realization dawning. "You... That was you?"

Elodie tilted her head, that sinister smile widening. "I'm surprised you remembered. You sure didn't remember me when I took your class. You were still so wrapped up in... her." Her voice was mocking.

He heaved out a sigh, "Elodie..."

She murmured, "Though, I must admit, it was strange. I've never seen cards align like that." She shook her head. "Such the perfect pair, hmm?"

Edison's heart pounded in his chest. Her revelations left him stunned. "What do you want?"

Elodie's gaze turned steely, a vindictive glint in her eyes. "Do you remember? You didn't seem to be missing Claire that night."

"That... was a mistake." Venom laced his voice.

"Was it?" A cruel smile stretched across her face, the amusement in her eyes a chilling contrast to the venom in her voice. "Just a mistake, hmm?" She scoffed, "Funny, the cards didn't see it that way."

Edison's brow wrinkled. "What are you talking about?"

"After you... just left me at that coffeehouse,"

Elodie continued, her voice dripping with disdain, "I needed answers. So, I did another reading. And you know what it told me?"

She leaned forward, her dark gaze boring into his fiery gaze. "Your path with Claire wasn't as clear-cut as you thought. It hinted at... another possibility. A connection that could blossom, a new story waiting to be written." Her voice dropped to a seductive whisper. "Maybe you and I could have found our own happily ever after."

Edison's jaw clenched as Elodie's words hung in the air. "I'm sorry, Elodie, but that would never happen."

The mask dropped briefly, revealing the pain in her eyes. But just as sudden, a sly smile stretched across her face as she glanced past Edison's shoulder. Her voice took on a sickly sweet tone as she reached forward, brushing his chest. "Why, Edison, darling," she cooed, a theatrical flutter of her eyelashes accompanying the words. "You didn't mention we'd have company."

Her gaze locked onto someone behind him as she waved her fingers. He froze, a knot of dread forming in his stomach. He turned his head, his heart sinking as he caught a glimpse of red curls vanishing out of the bar. Fuck.

Edison snapped his head back around to Elodie, "What the hell is wrong with you? You think this is a game?" He demanded, standing abruptly.

Leaning back in her chair, Elodie smiled mockingly as she said loudly, "Seems like you've got some explaining to do, darling."

He caught up with Claire a block away, desperate to clarify the situation. "Claire! Wait! Please!" Edison pleaded, gently grabbing her arm.

Turning to face him, tears running down her

cheeks, "I can't believe you. You were with her?" She pulled away from him, "After everything?"

"What?" Edison's eyes were wild. "Goddammit! No, it's not like that. I came to get answers and tell her to stay away from you, from us."

Claire's gaze wavered between disbelief and hurt. "I saw your location. I was worried, so I came to find you. I wanted..." She looked away. "I wanted to talk about things. But seeing you with her... I... can't." She backed up.

Edison reached for her, attempting to cup her face in his hands. "Please. I love you. I was trying... to fix this." His face twisted in anguish, his eyes full of pain. "I would never... Claire, you have to believe me." His voice fell on the last words.

She pointed a finger at him, her face full of indignation, poking him in the chest. "Believe you?" She pointed toward the bar. "She's the one who told me the truth about you."

She pulled away, shaking her head as a sob escaped. "I... I can't do this."

Edison attempted to explain again as he reached for her, but Claire shook her head and backed away. She whispered, "I need to go."

He stood there, helpless, as Claire walked away. He had no idea how to get back to where they were. After she disappeared, he released a heavy sigh fueled by frustration and anger, turning around and storming back into the bar. His eyes bore into Elodie as he approached her with a quiet rage.

"Elodie."

She turned to look at him, an arched brow her only indication at the surprise of his cutting tone.

"I don't know what story you've built up in your head, but that night was a mistake—a one-time thing fueled by grief and bad decisions. It meant nothing. There is nothing between us." And there never will be.

She tilted her head, "You never wondered? Maybe question if destiny had it wrong?"

A sarcastic laugh escaped his lips. This was ridiculous. "Are you really this desperate?"

He saw a flicker of something in her eyes—maybe pain, maybe anger—but it vanished as quickly as it appeared. She leaned back in her chair, that predatory smile on her lips.

Edison slammed his palm on the table, and the sudden movement caused Elodie to flinch. The bar noise faded into a dull roar as he leaned across the table. "Let me be perfectly clear," his voice a lethal calm. "I love her. Claire is it for me. There is nothing, and never will be, between you and me."

She flinched, but a look of defiance crossed her face. "What a knight in shining armor," her voice dripping in sarcasm. "This isn't over, Edison. The cards never lie." She leaned in, her voice chilling, "You'll see." Her smirk deepened, a challenge in her eyes as if she reveled in the chaos she had ignited.

Edison's jaw clenched as his simmering anger grew, and his eyes narrowed with determination. "You're playing with fire, Elodie," Edison growled. "But mark my words. If you don't stay the fuck away, you'll regret it. I won't let you ruin what I have left."

He turned away, leaving the bar, determined to salvage what remained of his unraveling relationship with Claire.

On the drive home, a sense of unease pressed against his chest. What else did that awful woman have planned? A surge of worry and regret bubbled up in his stomach. If he'd only been more truthful with Claire...

Chapter 41 - Claire

When I walked in, Darci took one look at me, and her eyes widened as she followed me down the hallway.

"What happened? Is everything okay?"

I avoided her gaze, making a beeline for the guest bedroom. I didn't want to talk until I processed the storm brewing inside me. I was doing all I could to hold back the tears ready to fall.

"I'm… okay. I just can't right now. I need to be alone right now."

Shutting the bedroom door, I wiped more tears from my eyes and pulled my phone out. Walking away from Sonny had left a gaping wound in my chest. Every missed call and pleading message from him just added to the pain. I sank into the cool sheets, pulling the quilt over my head. I drifted off but tossed and turned most of the day. Sonny haunted my dreams.

That evening, I woke up just as miserable, the weight of everything pressing down on me. Restless, I grabbed my phone off the bed, my fingers trembling as I checked his location.

My stomach dropped. He wasn't home.

I zoomed in, my pulse hammering as the name of the bar appeared on the map—The Basement. My mind spiraled. Was he drowning himself in whiskey, trying to forget? Or worse... was he already moving on?

I couldn't sit here wondering. I had to see for myself.

Slipping out of bed, I cracked open my door, peeking out into the dim apartment. The only light came from under Darci's door. Keeping quiet, I slid on my shoes, crept down the hall, and eased the front door shut behind me.

The drive to the square felt like a blur, my thoughts tangled in the unknown of what I was about to walk into. When I pulled up to the bar, my fingers tightened around the steering wheel.

I hesitated at the door, my pulse hammering as I took a deep breath. Then, I stepped inside.

My stomach twisted. There he was. Seated at a table with her—Elodie. I couldn't see his face, only the back of his head, but that was enough. Enough to make my breath hitch, enough to send a sharp, burning ache through my chest.

What the fuck was this?

Elodie's eyes met mine instantly, her lips curling into a slow, satisfied smile. She reached across the table, her hand brushing against Sonny's chest as if staking some silent claim. Then, as if things couldn't get worse, she waved.

I didn't wait to see what Sonny would do. Why had I even come? I spun on my heel and walked out, the bar door slamming shut behind me.

Before I crossed the street, I heard him yelling my name. Fine, let him. I didn't turn around.

When he finally caught up to him, he touched my elbow, and I whirled around, tears running down my face. He pleaded, but I couldn't do this, not here.

I pulled away, shaking my head as a sob escaped.

"I... I can't do this."

He didn't follow me. Crossing the street, my heart twisted when I remembered that stupid smirk on Elodie's face. What in the hell was I thinking showing up there? I felt like such an idiot.

I had wrestled with the decision to find him even in the first place, but when I saw his location was at a bar... I just needed to make sure he was okay. We could talk or something. Fuck. I don't know what I thought, but seeing Elodie there... Was he telling the truth? Was Elodie just batshit crazy? How were we ever going to get past this?

I had the next couple of days off and no desire to do anything except sink into my misery. Even getting out of bed was too much as I leaned over, digging through my bag on the floor, looking for the book I'd been reading, but it wasn't there. Then it dawned on me that I had left it in the living room at home, so I grabbed the first book off the top of the pile in the box and started reading.

As if by Murphy's law, I had randomly chosen the saddest romance book ever. It ripped my heart out. Star-crossed lovers who were always meeting at the wrong times in their lives. Just as they finally confessed their love, a cruel twist of fate snatched one of them away. The whole story was just misunderstandings and missed opportunities.

By the time I finished it, I was a sobbing mess. I had to get out of this apartment and do something mindless to forget everything for a little while. I tucked the book in my bag so I could leave it somewhere—anywhere. I didn't want to think about it anymore.

I drove downtown and wandered through the Square, but memories of Sonny and where everywhere I looked. Were we like that book? I stopped into my favorite thrift store until they closed for the night. But even shopping couldn't stop my mind from reeling. Was this just a huge misunderstanding? Or was it more? Was I making a big deal for no reason?

Walking back to my car, I remembered the book in my bag and noticed a new Indian restaurant a block away. It looked just as good as any place to leave the book, and I was starving. I ordered a shawarma to go, and while I waited I pulled the book out of my purse, walked over to a table on the patio, and set it in a chair before leaving. I had no desire to wait around for whoever found it.

When I pulled into the apartment complex, I stayed in the car, devouring my meal in silence. By the time I made it up to Darci's apartment, the lights were out. Maybe she had a date tonight? Either she wasn't home, or she'd already gone to bed.

I didn't bother changing. I crawled under the covers, still in my clothes, and slept like the dead.

I called in sick for a few more days. Ever since I saw Sonny and Elodie at that bar, I'd been hiding out in the guest room. I'd barely seen Darci for days. She'd been giving me space, but the third day I called in sick, she showed up at the apartment during her lunch hour and barged in to the bedroom.

"What in the actual fuck, Claire?" With her hands on her hips, she looked like a pissed-off pixie.

I was still in the same clothes I'd had on the one day I'd left the apartment. I hadn't looked in a mirror in god knows how long. I was sure my hair was giving Medusa a run for her money, and I had zero fucks to give. Zilch.

Darci had a takeout bag in one hand, but before

she entered the room, she held her hand up, wrinkling her nose, "Are you actually sick?"

I just shrugged, a sad smile on my face. "No. It's more of a mental breakdown." I reached for the bag. "For me?" When she gave me a soft smile, taking a step in the room, she nodded and lifted the bag up to me. I took the bag from her, made my way back to the bed around piles of tissues and takeout boxes, and sat down. I sighed as I opened the bag and smelled a delicious burger inside. I pulled it out and took a big bite.

Darci followed me into the room and looked around wide-eyed. I'd ordered DoorDash the past few days while she was at work. Takeout containers were piled everywhere. The trashcan by the bed was overflowing with tissues. My books were spread out all over the floor, the box upended.

She gingerly picked up a takeout box, still looking around at the mess. "Claire, what in the hell happened?"

When I swallowed, I said, "Sonny. Sonny happened." I grabbed a tissue and blew my nose, tossing the tissue on the floor.

She arched an eyebrow, watching the tissue fall to the floor. "Well, duh. I knew that." She gave me a pointed look as she said, "Now that's just gross!"

My face heated. "Sorry."

She picked up the trashcan, tossing all the tissues on the floor along with any other trash I'd left. "This isn't like you at all."

Setting the trashcan down, she looked for a place to sit on the bed before throwing a pile of clothes off to the floor and sat down with a huff.

"So... Edison, huh? Is it over? Do you want it to be?"

"I don't know," I muttered.

"Was it like this when you left Pete?"

"No, that was a relief. I felt like I could finally breathe again." I sat up, taking another bite of my burger. "This... it's like the opposite. Like I can't breathe without him. My heart is folding in on itself."

Her eyes slid to me. "Are you ever going to tell me what set this off?"

I pressed my lips together, eyes wide. "I found him with Elodie!" I fell flat on the bed, and Darci followed me.

She looked at me incredulously. "At the house? What were they doing?"

"No, they were sitting together in a bar. She saw me and ran her hand over his chest. She... she gave me this look like she'd won, and he was the prize. So I left. But... he came running after me. Said he was there to tell her to stay away."

"And was he?"

"I don't know."

"So you saw him sitting with Elodie, and your first thought was he was what? Trying to get with her?"

"I don't know." I let out a sigh. "You remember that photo we found of his arm in a picture with her?"

"Yeah?"

"He told me one time he agreed to go for coffee with her after a night at the bar, and she... kissed him." I looked up at Darci after those last words to see her expression.

She gasped, "When was this?"

"I don't know, like years ago. He said he regretted it immediately."

"So what are you worried about?"

"I don't know. But when I saw them together, I

freaked out."

"Claire, you lovable dork." She tossed a pillow at me, "I think this is all a huge misunderstanding. That man has been in love with you for fucking years. Years!"

Darci sat up, and her eyes narrowed. "What exactly happened?"

I raised up and exclaimed, "He lied to me!"

Her mouth quirked to the side. "Yeah, you said. Was it everything Elodie told you?"

I nodded as tears overflowed my eyes. Darci leaned over, picked up the box of tissues, and handed them to me before she got up and brought the trash can over to me.

Her eyebrows lifted. "So you just left?"

I slowly nodded. "Yeah," I sighed. "I told him I needed time to think."

It felt like we'd been apart for months, years, centuries, even though it hadn't even been a week. Without him, I felt like I was missing a limb. But how could we get past this?

"What are you going to do?"

I stood up and paced back and forth. "How can I believe anything he says?"

Darci bit her lip as she nodded slowly.

"How is he any different than Pete? I don't want to go through that shit again." I couldn't be in another relationship where I couldn't tell the difference between a truth and a lie.

Quietly she asked, "Do you really think he's just like Pete?" She caught my gaze from the corner of her eye.

"Yes." I let out a heavy sigh. "No? I don't fucking know! What should I do?" I fell back on the bed and looked up at the ceiling, feeling deflated. I murmured, "I don't know what to do. I don't want to lose him again… but…" I trailed off, not knowing how to finish that sentence.

Sonny was nothing like Pete, absolutely nothing. He was sweet and kind, and he loved and supported me. I wasn't just a box to check in his life plan. But still… he kept so many things from me.

"Claire, I think this is a case of man logic. I don't think he deliberately hid things from you. He didn't know how to tell you and kept putting it off. I don't think he considered how that would look to you." She tenderly brushed a strand of hair off my face. Then she stood up and held her hand out for me to grab.

I took her hand and pulled myself up. "And what do I do with that?"

She led me to the bathroom and turned the shower on, shrugging. "Put yourself in his shoes." She gave me a hopeful look.

Reluctantly, I said. "Okay."

She opened the bathroom closet, pulled out a fluffy white towel and washcloth, and set them on the sink. "What if it was you? What if you just met him, and he thought you were his blind date? You didn't know who this guy was, but you immediately had this unexplainable strong connection. Would you have told him?"

I mumbled, "I don't know."

"You told me you couldn't get enough of him that weekend." She tilted her head to the side, raising her eyebrows. "Wouldn't you have worried he'd leave and find his real blind date?"

I squeaked out, "Maybe?"

"Just maybe?" She squinted at me. "What about the whole writing thing? He did say he had an NDA. Maybe he wasn't sure how much he could even tell you?"

"He did say he'd never told anyone, not even his parents, so he wasn't sure how to tell me."

"He fucked up, but can you see why he did it?

"Yeah. But what about Elodie? Why didn't he tell me he knew her?"

"Does he really know her? It was coffee years ago. It wasn't even a date, and he rejected her immediately. Maybe he was embarrassed about the whole thing."

"Am I making this a bigger deal than it is?"

"Honey, I don't know." She took in a breath and let it out slowly, "Clean yourself up, and let's go do something, maybe get some food."

An hour later, we sat at Alchemy as I drowned my sorrows in the largest caramel macchiato they served.

Darci let out a moan. "Oh my god, this chocolate cake is to die for."

She cut a bite of her blackout chocolate cake, and it made me think about that very first meeting between me and Sonny. I stared at the cake as I tried to blink back tears.

Her eyes softened when she looked at me. "Oh, honey. It's going to be okay." She sighed, "I know Edison didn't tell you everything, but that doesn't mean everything else was a lie." She said, "It's scary to trust people, especially when everything in your marriage was a lie. But Edison is nothing like Pete. Surely you can see that. The happiness you had… have together was real. None of that's a lie. I see it with my own eyes." She took a drink of her coffee, watching me over the lip of her mug. "Don't let this misunderstanding overshadow the connection you two have."

I pushed the barely-eaten chocolate cheesecake muffin away and said, "What if there's more he's not telling me?"

"Have you given him a chance to explain?"

"Not really. I just… left." I sighed.

"People make mistakes, and sometimes they do things out of fear."

I held my head, murmuring, "But it's making me question everything."

Darci squeezed my arm. "There's always a risk when it comes to love. Sometimes, it's worth giving someone another chance." She shrugged. "Yeah, you could get hurt, but you could also find the love of a lifetime, which I think you found. What you two have…" She shook her head, grinning, "doesn't come around often."

"But how do I let it go and trust him again?"

She slowly shook her head. "I don't know, babe. It takes time. Let your heart lead you." She gave me a warm smile. "But I'm here for you. Always."

Chapter 42 - Edison

When Edison got home after work, fatigue settled into his bones. He went straight to the bedroom and lay on her side of the bed, regret coursing through him. Her pillow still smelled like her, enveloping him in memories that felt so far away. He fell into a deep sleep almost immediately, Bandit curled next to him.

When he woke up, his stomach rumbled, and he couldn't remember the last time he'd eaten. He wandered to the fridge, but nothing looked good. He wandered into the living room, grabbing the remote off the coffee table, and just looked around the room, trying to figure out how to keep his mind occupied when something bright blue caught his eye. It was the book Claire had been reading before she left. He swore it had been on her nightstand, but it lay face down, under the coffee table. He leaned over and picked it up.

It was one of the books from that box of books she practically took everywhere. He flipped it over, looked at the open page, and read through the handwritten notes. There were quotes about love and loss. He lifted his eyes, and a breeze ruffled his hair, seeming to race through the room. What the fuck? He glanced around, checking the front door and windows, but everything was locked tight.

All at once, as if by some mysterious force, the book seemed to leap out of his hands. He wasn't entirely sure if it leaped or he dropped it, but the book felt warm and heavier when he picked it back up. He leaned over, feeling the floor where he had just picked it up, but the wood was room temperature, cool to the touch. He flipped through the book, trying to find an explanation for the heat.

A page caught his attention. There was a handwritten quote about love that stood out. It had red hearts doodled around it. He ran his finger over the indentions of the hearts, knowing Claire's bubbly handwriting anywhere. Those were her doodles, and they seemed to stand out from the page as he reread it.

Each great love story will find the way,
A path revealed, day by day.
A journey's quest, a heart's desire,
To find the one, ignite the fire.

Edison's heart beat wildly when he noticed it slowly fading. He closed the book, tossing it on the coffee table. He wanted as far away from it as possible, but as he stood up, a voice in his head reminded him of the last time this had happened. It had led him back to Claire. Maybe it was trying to help him fix what he'd broken.

He sat back down and picked the book up again, finding the quote fading, but not all the words disappeared. A few words were still bright and easy to read.

"Love... will... find... a... journey..."

* * *

"What the…?" He murmured.

Edison's eyes ran over the page, looking for some kind of clue. What was he supposed to do now? But as he scanned, the actual story text on the page began to flicker like a light burning out. Three words were left behind — "one," "twenty," "three." What was it? A time? A date?

He scanned the blank page, waiting for something to appear, those three words just staring at him. And then it dawned on him. A page number? He flipped to page 123. Another handwritten quote was written in bright pink ink, glowing on the page.

With love there's detours in the quest,
With hidden clues and hearts to test,
Yet love's true prize will never stray,
A treasure to keep, a guide to stay.
Buried deep, a gem so rare,
For those who seek and truly dare.

Again, the quote began to fade out, just a few words left behind. "Hidden…treasure… deep… heart… to keep… will… guide."

His brow wrinkled as he mouthed the words. What was this book trying to tell him?

The text flickered again before disappearing. He found "forty" and "eight" and turned to page 48, finding yet another quote, this time written in purple.

Love isn't found on a map, it's true,
A twist of fate, a chance for you.
It finds you when you least expect,
A journey's end, a sweet effect.

* * *

There were several quotes on the page, but only one glowed. Most of it faded away, but three words remained. "A... love... map..."

Edison waited as the text on the page dimmed out like the first one. A cold shiver ran down his spine. Still gibberish. Was this book... broken? Staring at the words and flipping back to the previous pages, he had an idea. He ran to his desk, grabbing a pen and notepad and copied down every word left behind as he waited for the text on the page to disappear, finding "nine" and "four." He nearly ripped the book apart as he flipped to page 94—another quote.

And the greatest prize?
A heart so true,
A perfect fit, for me and you.
No other choice, no need to find,
A love so pure, a peace of mind.

He read it repeatedly, even as it faded, leaving the words "no... to... a... prize..." He copied them into the notepad as the text on the page faded away, but this time no page number appeared. He laid the book down on the coffee table and studied his notepad.

This was it? None of it made sense.

"What the hell is this?"

Frustration washed over him as the words on the notepad blurred together. Were the fates just toying with him? He tossed the notepad on the coffee table next to the book.

He lay on the couch, rolling to his back, staring at the ceiling when he had an idea. Was this some kind of puzzle to solve? Maybe he needed to rearrange the words to figure out the final clue? He sat up as his breath quickened, each inhale increasing his anticipation. The answer, he realized, was right in front of him, waiting to be unlocked.

Two hours later, he threw the notepad down, that hopeful anticipation turning into something colder. He looked at the book as if it were sentient.

In a sputtering outburst, he asked, "You expect me to just to waste my time with this ridiculous puzzle?"

He threw his head back against the couch as he ran his hands over his face and through his hair. He was talking to a goddamn book now.

He muttered, "I think I've finally lost my mind."

Standing up to stretch his limbs, a strong breeze wrapped around him. The papers stacked on the coffee table scattered to the floor. His eyes darted around the room. The windows were still closed, but the front door was wide open. He rushed toward it as debris flew inside. As he shut the door, he noticed a dust devil swirling in the yard, heading toward the porch, leaves and dirt flying everywhere. He slammed the door shut, locking it.

Eyes wild, Edison turned around, glancing at the book on the coffee table. The breeze was gone, but the book's pages fluttered until it stopped as if it'd been caught in the act. He slowly walked over to see the book was open to a new page, another handwritten quote written in black ink.

Sometimes, the greatest treasures reside,
Not where you seek, but where the heart will guide.
Needed within, a path unknown,
A treasure found, one love your own.

* * *

Goosebumps ran down his arms when he noticed the doodle beside the quote. It was a poppy drawn in red, green, and black ink, just like his tattoo. He gently traced the lines with his finger. Had Claire drawn this? He picked up the book to get a better look. The ink was fading just like the others. Five words remained. "The... reside... where... needed... one..." He grabbed the notepad and wrote them with the others.

He shook off his doubts. He could solve this. He had to. He began rearranging the words in a desperate dance. Daylight bled into night, the room illuminated only by the harsh glow of the television. Crumpled paper was strewn all over the floor. Each failed attempt left him exhausted. Yet, he wouldn't stop, fueled by a stubborn hope that this was the key to fixing what he'd ruined.

Finally, as the first rays of the new day peeked through the window, he smiled. He'd rearranged the words into a message of sorts:

Love's a treasure, hidden deep,
A journey's end, a prize to keep.
No map needed, the heart will guide,
To find the one where love will reside.

Edison pinched the bridge of his nose, his eyes burning from lack of sleep. Was it another clue? Why did these books love riddles so much? He laid back on the couch, wondering what it meant until he started to doze, dreaming of her.

Claire was by his side with a crudely drawn treasure map. She smiled, speaking animatedly to him and pointing to the map, but he couldn't make out her words. She gently took his hand, leading the way down a path into the night, stars shining above them. Soon, lights appeared ahead, lanterns similar to the witch market marking the path. They stopped at a canvas tent, where he pulled the side open for them to enter. He expected a tarot card reader, but inside was a cozy bookstore that looked much bigger than the tent. They winded through stacks and shelves to a door hidden in the back. Claire went through, Edison followed, and when he turned around, they were in the middle of FireFlower Farms, surrounded by a tapestry of color, poppies everywhere. He whirled around, but Claire was gone.

He jolted awake, his heart pounding as he sat up. The dream felt so real, giving him a moment of clarity and a sliver of hope sparked in his chest. Could it be that simple?

He glanced down at the notebook again. For the first time in days, he was sure this was what he needed to do. Fueled by newfound energy, he grabbed a fresh sheet of paper and began meticulously detailing everything he could remember about places that had special meaning for him and Claire—now and from their past. Memories flooded back—sitting outside the ice cream parlor, the kiss they'd shared hidden in the stacks at a secondhand bookstore, dancing under the fairy lights, how her eyes sparkled when he'd slid the poppy in her hair at the wildflower farm.

He'd barely slept over the last two days, but a new sense of purpose replaced his exhaustion. For the first time since that horrible night he'd lost her, he wasn't staring at a dead end but at a new beginning.

He wasn't entirely sure it was the book, but he'd been challenged to remember, to connect the dots of their love story, and show her what she meant to him and what they were together. He had to believe, reliving their past, she'd see the future he hadn't forgotten.

After making the list, he grabbed some thick stationary paper and began to craft clues to the special places that held significant meaning for them. They would lead her on a treasure hunt through the places they fell in love, hopefully reminding her what they were together.

Now, he just had to convince Darci to help him. She was fiercely loyal to Claire, and there was a good chance she hated him right now. But something told him that underneath the sharp remarks and protective glare, she still wanted what was best for her best friend. And if he could prove that he was what was best for Claire, Darci just might be willing to help.

A bittersweet smile flickered across his face as he pictured Claire's reaction when she found the first one tucked into one of her books. Edison planned the final clue would take her to the wildflower farm:

"Find the bloom that mirrors your flame where a fiery sea whispers its name."

Darci had agreed without hesitation, but as Edison prepared to deliver the first clue a couple of days later, a knot of worry tightened in his stomach. This could backfire spectacularly. And yet, beneath the nerves, a spark of excitement pulsed through him. This wasn't just a love letter—it was a treasure hunt for their souls. Each clue held a memory, a reminder of why they were meant to find their way back to each other.

Chapter 43 - Claire

Since I had the afternoon shift at the library, I showed up a little after lunchtime. Darci had been here since this morning. I made a beeline for the teen room but slowed when I heard laughter in the children's area. I did a double-take when I caught sight of them. Elodie. She was with Darci. What the hell?

Darci caught my eye and waved me over with a tight smile. "Claire! Do you have a minute?"

A ripple of unease passed through me. What was Elodie doing here?

"Guess what?" Darci had a tight smile, relief in her eyes. "Elodie is our newest volunteer. Isn't that great?"

"Wow!" I turned toward Elodie, giving her a polite smile as a chill of unease ran down my spine.

"Darci's been an absolute angel showing me around." Elodie chimed in, her eyes gleaming with a deceptive innocence. "You know how I love books. What better place for me to share my time?"

I nodded, "We always need volunteers."

A moment later, I excused myself, but as I turned to leave, I covertly caught Darci's eye, raising my eyebrow and giving her an incredulous look. She shrugged, shaking her head.

I headed back to the teen room, and as I got to work, I mulled over Elodie's sudden appearance. If Sonny had confronted her, she knew she'd messed up my relationship with him. What else did she want? Was it all for the books? Or was she trying to get back at Sonny all these years later?

A few hours into my shift, there was finally a lull, and I decided to find Darci to discuss an email about an upcoming conference for children and teen librarians I wanted to attend. I hoped Elodie would have left by now, but when I approached, I saw Darci looking slightly exasperated as she patiently showed Elodie how to shelve books—neither noticed me walking up.

"Darci, darling, you know how appearances can be deceiving. People like Edison, they're never what they seem," Elodie insinuated, glancing at the teen room.

I ducked behind a shelf and continued to listen.

"Elodie, Claire is my friend, and this...," she lowered her voice, "isn't an appropriate conversation." She grabbed a stack of books. "Here," she said, handing her the books to shelve. "Can you shelve these over there in the biographies?"

Elodie took the books but clearly missed the hint. Leaning closer, she lowered her voice conspiratorially. "I've known Edison a long time— we used to frequent the same gin palace. He still spends a lot of time there." Her eyes glittered with feigned concern. "I doubt Claire even knows. He's quite the charmer. Women practically line up, and let's just say he doesn't exactly discourage them."

Darci's expression shifted to disbelief. "Are you saying he's cheating on Claire? There's no way that's true, Elodie. You shouldn't spread rumors like that—it could easily get back to Claire."

What kind of crap was this woman spewing? Sonny had warned me, but now I think I finally understood. My heart pounded as I came around the corner. Elodie flashed me a saccharine smile, and I returned it to her.

Darci, sensing the tension, waved at me. "Claire, hey. Did you need… something? Elodie was telling me, um, something you might find… interesting."

I feigned nonchalance. "Really? What's so interesting?"

Elodie grinned deviously, saying, "We were just talking about Edison. You two aren't together anymore, right?" She huffed a laugh. "I heard he's been frequenting The Basement, women hanging off him most nights." She leaned closer, dropping her voice to a conspiratorial whisper, "I hear he meets some of his female students there."

My heart skipped a beat. Anger and disbelief flashed through me. I had just about had enough of Elodie.

"Is that so? It's funny because he's been home every night this week. Alone. Except that night, I showed up. You remember when I came by, don't you?"

The smile plastered on her face widened.

I tilted my head, "Where do you come up with this stuff?"

She shrugged, "Maybe he didn't want you to know."

My patience hung by a thread, threatening to snap completely. "Elodie," my voice surprisingly steady, "this… whatever you're trying to do, it's not going to work."

As I spoke, a strange sense of calm washed over me. Her attempts at sowing the seeds of doubt had the opposite effect. Looking into her eyes, something shifted in me. I felt this fierce protectiveness for Sonny.

"I trust him," I whispered, more to myself than her. The weight of my own words surprised me. It was fragile, but it was still there. "Whatever you're trying to do is not going to work."

Elodie's smile morphed into a sneer. "You sure it's me and not those cursed books? If you just gave them back..."

Darci, attempting to mediate, said, "Maybe we should all take a step back..."

My gaze locked on Elodie as I held a hand up to Darci. "No, Darci. This has gone on long enough. I don't know why I didn't realize it until now..." I trailed off, my voice dropping to a conspiratorial whisper, "She just wants those damn books."

Darci raised her eyebrows and said dryly, "The cursed ones?"

I chuckled and nodded, and she snorted before turning towards Elodie.

"Look, if you want to cosplay as a fairytale villain, feel free." Darci's voice hardened as she walked towards Elodie, who stepped back, tripping over a table leg, "But do it somewhere else. You can't waltz in here and bully Claire into handing them over."

Elodie's eyes darted between us like a trapped animal. "Claire, you don't understand," she stammered. "Those books... I was looking out for you."

There wasn't a drop of sincerity in her tone.

"No. I'm done with this, Elodie. You didn't get to play these games with me anymore."

Elodie's smirk faltered. "Claire, just listen—"

"No. You listen," I snapped, my voice sharp and

steady despite my shaking hands. "I thought you were trying to help, but all you did was lie, twist things around, and try to ruin my relationship. For what? Some sick game?"

Before Elodie could respond, Darci stepped forward, arms crossed protectively, her eyes blazing with anger. "You aren't helping anyone—you're just hurting her."

Elodie's confident smirk vanished entirely, replaced by a flicker of panic. "Claire, please—I was only trying to protect you."

I laughed bitterly, shaking my head. "Protect me? From what?"

Her gaze dropped briefly to the papers I clutched tightly, and she hesitated, swallowing hard. "They're not safe, Claire. You have no idea what they—"

"Oh, I understand plenty," I said coldly. "I understand that you were never really trying to help me. I understand that you crossed lines you never should've crossed. This was all a game to you, and you need to leave."

She stared at me, mouth opening as if desperate to justify herself, but nothing was left for her to say. My mind was already made up.

"You're not welcome here anymore," I said firmly. "Get out of my library."

Elodie paused, breathing sharply. She looked between Darci and me, hoping one of us might relent. But our silence held firm. Finally, she turned and left, the library doors shutting behind her.

Darci exhaled heavily, her shoulders relaxing. "God, I thought she'd never leave!"

I nodded slowly, my heartbeat finally easing into something steadier. "I can't believe I ever thought she wanted to help me." My voice trembled with the realization. I had been so blind. How did I ever believe Elodie's charade of concern? Shame burned in my throat. I needed to set things right with Sonny.

After a long day at work, I finally made it back to Darci's. She'd already ordered us salads for dinner, and sinking onto the couch with a fresh serial killer documentary felt like the perfect way to unwind. But I could barely focus. My mind wouldn't stop spinning, anticipation coiling tight in my chest.

I needed to talk to Sonny.

The second the show ended, I headed to the guest room, shutting the door behind me. Sitting cross-legged on the bed, I pulled my phone from my back pocket, exhaling slowly as I opened our text thread. My fingers trembled. Butterflies fluttered in my stomach as I stared at the blank message field, trying to find the right words.

Claire: Hey, can we talk? Meet on Saturday?

I kept it short. This was a conversation that had to happen face-to-face. I just hoped Sonny wouldn't read too much into what I didn't say.

His reply came almost instantly.

Sonny: I've missed you. Are you okay? Saturday works for me. Can I take you to dinner?

My heart clenched. He didn't even try to hide how relieved he was. That soft concern, the way he asked if I was okay—a warmth rushed through me.

God, I missed him.

Claire: I'm okay. And I miss you too. Sure, let's do that. Where?

* * *

Matteo's popped into my head immediately. Tate and Noelle were wonderful, the food was amazing, and most importantly, it was quiet—perfect for the conversation we needed to have.

Sonny: How about Matteo's? I can pick you up at 7?

I chuckled, shaking my head. Of course, he'd suggest the exact place I was thinking. And he wanted to pick me up. My chest tightened at the thought of seeing him again.

Why had I chosen Saturday? Days away suddenly felt unbearable. I should have said tonight.

Claire: Sounds good.

As I hit send, a flicker of hope sparked inside me. Maybe this was just a bump in the road. We could fix this.

But then, like a dark cloud creeping in, Elodie's name slithered into my mind. I hated to admit I'd constantly looked over my shoulder since I kicked her out of the library. Something about her little games felt like a ticking time bomb, but I pushed her from my mind.

Darci and I were scheduled to work over the weekend, so we both had Friday off. I took full advantage of the slow morning and was still lounging in bed, absorbed in my book, when a knock sounded at the front door.

I barely registered it, lost in the pages, until a few minutes later, Darci appeared in my doorway, holding a package.

"No return address," she said, her expression curious as she handed it over.

"What's this?"

She grinned and said, "It's for you! Open it!"

"Is it from you?"

Her grin lingered as she shook her head. "Nope."

"Are you sure it's safe? Maybe it's from… Elodie?"

She waved her hand dismissively. "It's not. Just open it."

Opening the package, it was my book that I had left at home. I grinned, knowing exactly who had brought it.

I looked up at Darci, a puzzled look on my face. "Why do you think he sent this?"

She rolled her eyes and let out a pent-up breath as she sat on the bed beside me. "Claire, I swear… just… open the book."

"Okay…" I flipped through it until I found a single crimson rose petal pressed between two pages. Written in white ink across the petal was a single word—"Remember." What in the world was this?

Darci asked, "What is it?"

I lifted the petal, and she gave me a knowing smile.

I carefully flipped through more pages, wondering what else I'd find when a folded note fell on the bed. I opened it and read through it several times.

> *Your phone's the key, a digital map,*
> *To a message hidden on a certain app.*
> *To World Enough and Time…*
> *A longing plea,*
> *Can you see?*

* * *

As I read the clue, my breath hitched. "To world and time enough," I breathed.

A thrill ran through me. What was this? Had he really...? A giddy smile stretched across my face as I looked up at Darci. She grinned. My heart thumped against my ribs.

I whispered, "It's a clue."

I blinked, processing it. "He made me a... scavenger hunt?" I asked slowly.

Her smile widened as she nodded.

Sonny had created a scavenger hunt for me.

My face erupted with a smile, widening with uncontrollable excitement. I shot up in bed, stretching my arms. "Well... let's see where it takes us!"

Chapter 44 - Edison

Days ago, Edison nervously dialed Darci with his plan to create a scavenger hunt for Claire, his mind pinging with ideas like a hyperactive toddler. Thankfully, Darci had a mischievous streak a mile wide and was all for it. He thought he'd have to beg her to start the hunt with Claire, but surprisingly, she offered to help him do even more. They met one day, spending the entire afternoon weaving a trail of clues through the city.

He'd tucked the first clue inside Claire's book, which he'd found at home, and hand-delivered it—wrapped as a package—to Darci's house. The real fun began with a post on the Lost Connections app, leading her to a trail of clues hidden throughout the city in the places where they had fallen in love.

Darci offered to tag along with Claire, but she was a double agent, keeping Edison updated on Claire's journey around town.

After leaving the first clue with Darci, he waited at home, his heart pounding with nervous anticipation. Pacing the living room, he flexed his hands restlessly, second-guessing everything. Was this the dumbest idea he'd ever had? He'd poured so much time into creating this scavenger hunt, hoping it would remind her of all the good times they'd shared. But would she see it that way?

He took a deep breath, trying to calm his nerves. "She'll appreciate it," he muttered to himself. "That's the kind of person she is. It's one of the reasons I fell in love with her."

A couple of hours later, Darci texted, letting him know Claire was on her way to Matteo's, where Tate would give her the final clue.

Edison knew it was time to leave. He planned to wait at the end of the hunt at the wildflower farm, where they'd shared that fairytale picnic years ago. He pulled the truck into the parking lot awaiting her arrival, gripping the steering wheel, and just focused on his breathing for a moment.

He chuckled to himself, shaking his head. He hadn't been this nervous since they'd met at Sugar Rush months ago. He took a deep breath as he climbed out and approached the covered entrance with the ticket booth, a wrapped bouquet of crimson poppies clutched in his hand. She'd be here soon enough.

It was the very beginning of the season here at the wildflower farm. Not all of the wildflowers were in bloom, so there weren't a lot of visitors.

He ran his hand through his hair, praying silently that this would go as planned. He could only hope the look in her eyes would be worth the risk when she saw him.

Twenty minutes later, a red Civic slowed and pulled into the large, dusty parking lot. Edison's pulse kicked up as he spotted Claire stepping out alongside Darci.

Darci pointed toward the ticket booth, and Claire, wearing red heart sunglasses, shielded her eyes with her hand as she scanned the area.

God, she was beautiful. The sight of her in a pale blue daisy sundress hit him square in the chest, stealing his breath. For a moment, all the nerves, the doubts, the what-ifs faded. It was just her—the woman he loved, standing there like she belonged to him.

He clutched the flowers, letting out a shaky breath, standing up straighter, waiting, anticipating, hoping, praying. He couldn't help but wince at the pain of regret that brought them here. He desperately wanted to run to her, take her in his arms, get on his knees, and beg, but he waited patiently as she made her way to him.

He scrutinized her face, but with her eyes hidden behind those oversized sunglasses, he only saw a hint of a smile and the collection of folded-up pieces of paper in her hands from the clues. Was she happy? Upset? He couldn't tell.

As Claire walked toward him, Darci lingered for a moment before quietly slipping away. He wasn't sure where she went, but it didn't matter—his focus was locked on Claire.

Everything else blurred into the background as she approached, sliding her sunglasses onto her head. The breeze sent curls dancing across her face, and without thinking, he reached out, gently tucking one behind her ear.

She looked up at him shyly, cheeks tinged pink. Her breath hitched before she exhaled softly, "Hi."

"Hi." Edison let out a breath he hadn't realized he was holding. His heart pounded, and the words spilled out before he could stop them.

"I'm sorry. For everything. I'm sorry I didn't tell you about Elodie or my writing. I just... I didn't know how."

He swallowed hard. His voice wavered, but he

forced himself to go on. "I'm sorry I never told you about the blind date. I was scared, which sounds like an excuse, but I just didn't want you to walk away."

He searched her face, his voice raw with honesty. "And when we found each other again, those fears came rushing back. I was terrified of losing you all over again—I don't think my heart could take it. I just wanted you to finally be... mine."

"I get that." She smiled through her tears, her gaze never leaving his. "I'm sorry I overreacted and left. I don't know why I ever listened to Elodie. This week without you has been..." She shook her head and sighed, "I've missed you."

Edison was taken aback by her confession. Every part of him ached to pull her into his arms, but he hesitated, simply nodding instead—unsure if she wanted his touch.

A smile tugged at the corners of her lips. Although hesitant at first, it began to bloom slowly. She held up all the clues, "I can't believe you made me this scavenger hunt around the city."

He breathed out, "Yeah," offering her a shy smile as his Adam's apple bobbed, "It was my love letter to you."

As their eyes met—truly met—the hesitancy between them melted, replaced by a warmth that shattered the lingering awkwardness. Claire's smile softened, then bubbled into a light, airy laugh—the kind of sound he hadn't realized he'd been starving for. His heart pounded so hard he swore it might break free from his ribs, and before he could stop it, a grin overtook his face. Dimples peeked through his beard as he stepped closer.

Her laughter faded, but in its place, a quiet longing filled her gaze—one that sent a fresh wave of hope crashing over him.

Edison took another slow, measured step forward, the space between them shrinking with each deliberate inch. She didn't look away. Instead, she held his gaze, a silent conversation passing between them.

His smile softened, but his hands trembled as he dipped his head—an unspoken invitation he desperately hoped she would accept.

And then, she did.

She closed the final breath of distance, her lips meeting his, and that familiar jolt shot straight through him. A week of wondering—aching—if he'd ever feel this again. And now, with her pressed against him, he knew.

Some things never faded. Some things were worth fighting for.

He deepened the kiss, his hand reaching the back of her head, tangling in her curls, as she dropped the book full of notes and wrapped her hands around his neck. Her touch sent shivers down his spine. It was a kiss reconnecting their souls, of unspoken promises, and a silent oath that they were in this together.

Remembering the flowers in his hand, he reluctantly broke the kiss as he raised the bouquet. He stepped back and said, "These are for you."

A small sigh escaped her lips as she took them from him. "They're... beautiful."

She moved closer to him, and his arms instinctively wrapped around her.

"This is the most romantic thing anyone has ever done for me." She leaned down, picked up the book, and carefully checked that all the folded papers were still inside before looking back up at him.

Seeing the book, one corner of his lips tugged up,

"Well, I did have a little help."

"Sonny."

"Claire."

They spoke simultaneously, their voices overlapping, and they shared a smile for the first time in what felt like forever.

He placed his hand over hers, his touch warm and steady. "You go ahead."

Claire drew in a deep breath, steadying herself. "I want to come home. I want... *this*. I want *us*."

Edison didn't hesitate. He wouldn't waste another second.

Cupping her face in his hands, his gaze locked onto hers, fierce and unwavering. "Come home, Poppy. Now. Don't wait another second."

He leaned in, his voice a rasp of pure emotion. "Because you're everything I want. *Everything*."

She paused, looking down at the book. She ran her finger over its edges, worry in her eyes. Quietly, she asked, "What do we do about Elodie?"

Sensing her unease, Edison gently squeezed her hand. "I don't want to even think about her. She's not worth our time."

"You know, she did all this for the books. She's still so desperate to get them back." She looked off in the distance, "I think... we should just pack them up and hide them in the attic or something."

He nodded slowly, "Yeah, I think that's a good idea."

Claire looked at him with amusement in her eyes. One corner of her mouth ticked up. "I sort of threw her out of the library the other day."

Edison cocked an eyebrow. "Do I even want to know? She probably had it coming."

She leaned in, resting her head against his shoulder, and laughed, "She did."

He chuckled before kissing the top of her head.

Claire reached for him, pulling him into her. He lifted her chin and pressed a tender kiss to her lips, holding her tightly in his arms. He was bursting with so much gratitude. She broke out in a wide grin.

He leaned back, a devilish smile on his face as he ran a finger across her collarbone, his hand getting dangerously close to her cleavage. "Want to go home?"

His touch sent shivers down her spine. She tipped her head up. "More than anything," she purred, a playful glint in her eyes.

"Perfect," he replied, his voice low.

Claire found Darci in the small gift shop a few minutes later, her arms laden with souvenirs. Claire whispered something in Darci's ear, a grin on her face, and handed Darci the keys to her car. She'd come by to pick up her stuff and the car later.

Bandit was beside himself when they got home, nearly knocking Claire off her feet in his excitement. Laughing, she followed Edison into the kitchen, the dog glued to her side as if afraid she might disappear again.

She leaned against the counter, watching Edison lead Bandit out the back door into the yard. The second he shut it, he turned, eyes dark with intent, and prowled toward her.

She met him halfway.

And then he was on her, their mouths crashing together, the urgency between them electric. He wanted her with every breath in his body, with every fiber of his being. Their hands moved feverishly, shedding layers of clothing in a frenzied blur, whispered apologies, and desperate declarations of love tumbling between kisses.

There was no more waiting. No more hesitation. Just them—finding their way back to each other.

Too desperate to even reach the bedroom, he took her on the kitchen floor, laying her down on their discarded pile of clothes, his arms caging her head. Claire's hands lovingly ran through his hair. Just as quickly as they started, he stopped and whispered her name, his gaze locking to hers. She gave him a hint of a smile as desire built in his stomach.

She asked, "Yes?"

He shook his head, biting back the emotions welling up in his eyes as his lips found hers a heartbeat later, prodding her to open for him. Her tongue followed his, tangling together. She raised to meet him.

Breaking their kiss, she panted out, "I need you."

He kissed down her jaw, his voice dropping lower, "You have me, Poppy." His breath caressed the shell of her ear, "You. Have. Me."

There was a quiet desperation between them, frantic yet unhurried. He wanted to give all of himself to her.

She licked his earlobe, taking a nip and moaning in his ear as she nearly climaxed just from him kissing where her shoulder met her neck.

She moaned, closing her eyes, "Please."

He went utterly still, holding his body over hers. He murmured, "Poppy, look at me."

Their eyes met. Tenderness and love filled his flame-flickered eyes. He nudged her legs open, sliding between her thighs, the tip of his cock right at her entrance. He pushed in slowly, deeper until he was at the hilt, where he stayed, not moving. He wrapped his arms around her, his weight pressing against her, their foreheads touching.

"Are you okay?"

She nodded.

He began to move slowly, finding his rhythm, hitting all the right spots as she writhed under him. Her legs wrapped around his waist, and her hands instinctively went to his cheeks, angling his head as they kissed, swallowing his moans.

She was on the precipice of coming undone, gasping, begging him, "Harder, baby. Please."

He grinned like a devil, bringing her legs with him. He pulled out before slamming back into her over and over again. He felt the coiling deep in his gut and began to convulse when she blissed out. There was no warning as she clenched around him, screaming his name and milking him until he groaned with his own sweet release.

Both out of breath, he stayed inside her, not wanting to lose this connection. Claire held on to his shoulders for dear life as aftershocks rippled through her. Soon after, they both drifted off, still connected.

When Edison woke from Bandit's scratches at the back door, he was still half hard inside her as she stirred awake. He caressed her cheek, kissing her tenderly.

"I've missed you so much."

"Me, too." She leaned up, kissing him before snuggling against his chest. "We should probably get off the kitchen floor and let Bandit back in. I think he's complaining."

Standing up, he chuckled as Bandit whined against the door. "Oh shit. I forgot we put him out there."

"I'm sure he's fine, and it was worth it." She had a smirk on her face as Edison helped her up. "But I'm starving."

He let the dog in before coming over to kiss her

quickly. "Let's order something."

Sonny grabbed his phone, opened the app for their favorite pizza, and placed the order online. When he looked up, she'd put on his button-down shirt, only a couple of buttons buttoned. He broke out in a mischievous grin as he stalked over to her. He wanted to rip that shirt off her and go at it again.

"Poppy…" he purred.

Glancing down at the shirt, she questioned, "What? Is this alright?"

Sonny swallowed audibly, his hand gliding over his neck, "Wear my shirts anytime you want, baby."

Her eyes drifted down, noticing his desire had reignited.

"Oh," she murmured.

He set the phone on the table, grabbed the front of the shirt, and unbuttoned it quickly, pulling the sides open before leaning down and running his tongue around her nipple. She arched her back, moaning as she held onto his shoulders.

Her stomach had other plans and loudly gurgled.

He pulled back, chuckling. "Food's ordered." He glanced at the phone, arching an eyebrow, saying, "Though, I think we have about 30 minutes to waste until it arrives."

She chuckled. "If we must," she said as he led her back to the bedroom.

Chapter 45 - Claire

Six months later

It was Saturday morning, and Sonny was practically giddy with excitement, like a kid on Christmas morning. He was adorable, but he was definitely up to something.

He came up behind me while I was making coffee, wrapped his arms around my waist, kissed my neck, and said, "I've got a surprise for you."

I chuckled. Of course, he did. After that scavenger hunt he'd made me, he was always doing things like that. "You do? Do I get to know what it is?"

"Not yet." He kissed me again and laughed before heading into the bathroom to shower.

As we got ready, Sonny was restless—fidgeting, running his hands through his hair, tapping his fingers against his leg, pacing the room. I watched him with a mix of amusement and curiosity. Was he nervous about whether I'd like his surprise?

Honestly, it didn't matter. I didn't care what we did as long as I was with him. Besides, he had a knack for planning the best dates—I always loved his surprises.

"You okay?" I asked, tilting my head.

He stretched his arms, trying to play it cool. "Yeah, I'm good. You ready to go?"

Swiping on a final coat of lip gloss, I stood and flashed him a smile. "Let's go."

We said goodbye to Bandit and hopped in the truck. About 45 minutes later, we arrived at the biggest bookstore I'd ever seen. It was a secondhand bookstore, and I couldn't wait to go inside.

I looked over and grinned at him. "Is this the surprise? A bookstore?"

He offered me a cryptic smile, chuckling. "Yes… and no."

I swatted his arm as I smiled at him. "So mysterious today."

He shrugged and hopped out of the truck. Opening my door, he grabbed my hand and led the way. As we stepped into the giant bookstore, the scent of old books hit me. I could barely contain myself. This bookstore held two stories with miles and miles of shelves to explore on both levels. I felt like a kid in a candy store.

"This place is… amazing!"

He grinned, "I knew you'd love it."

The building was nearly the size of a Walmart, but somehow, it looked like it had once been a pirate boat. The floors and walls were wooden, and the wood creaked everywhere you stepped. On one side of the building was the entrance to a literary-themed cafe, and I could smell the scent of coffee and something sweet wafting towards us.

Sonny checked his watch. "We have another 20 minutes until our reservation. Want to explore?"

"Reservation?" Is it lunch?

He just smiled. "You'll see…"

Climbing the stairs, I murmured, "Sonny, this place is incredible."

Seeing the fiction section, I grabbed his hand and followed the shelves like a lab rat in a maze until I found a specific book in a series I couldn't find anywhere.

"This is the book I've been looking for!" I opened the cover to find it signed. I was ecstatic as I showed it to Sonny. "I can't believe it!"

He winked. "It looks like you've found a prize."

I nodded, running my hand over the cover. "Like it was here just waiting for me."

Checking his phone, he said, "It's time to go. Let's go pay for your book and head over."

He reached for the book, and I practically skipped to the checkout beside him, saying, "We have to go back here again."

After we paid, I put it in my bag, and Sonny laced our fingers to lead the way.

He turned to me, a grin spreading across his face. "You ready for this?"

I shrugged, smiling as he took my hand and led me toward the back of the store, anticipation buzzing in the air.

When I caught sight of the sign above the entrance, my breath hitched, and I stopped in my tracks.

I gasped. "Sonny!"

Spinning to face him, I found him watching me, his grin stretching even wider.

I didn't know how, but he found an escape room with _The Time Traveler's Wife_ as the theme in the most fantastic bookstore I had ever seen.

I looked around in wonder as I whispered, "How did you find this place?"

He pulled me close, his arms wrapping securely around my waist. A smirk played on his lips, those irresistible dimples acting like a direct line to my heart—or maybe something deeper.

"I'll never tell," he murmured, his voice teasing. "But I had a feeling you'd like it here."

I stood on my tiptoes, purring into his ear, "Do you know how lucky you're going to get tonight?"

He laughed.

The moment we stepped inside, it was like stepping straight into the pages of the book. It looked exactly how I had always pictured it in my head, and a determined thrill shot through me—we would solve this.

While we waited for the game master, I quickly tucked away every plot point, character detail, and quote I could recall. I'd read the book multiple times, but it had been months since my last reread.

When our turn finally came, the game master went over the rules and explained how the escape room worked. We had an hour to complete the challenge. Then, with a pointed look, he added that we were at a disadvantage with just the two of us.

Such a vote of confidence.

We entered the first room, a giant clock above the door ticking down.

For a split second, Sonny and I looked at each other like deer in headlights. But I threw my bag on the floor, and we both took off around the room, looking for clues and puzzles. A few minutes later, we had solved one puzzle and were working on a second one. There was a third puzzle that would unlock the door to the second room.

Sonny's eyes darted around the room, panicked, raising his eyebrows in a silent question.

I grabbed his hand and said, "We got this one, babe!"

A note written in code on a piece of stationary was next to a black lock box. A couple of minutes later, we solved the code and popped open a secret compartment holding a blank piece of paper and a pencil. We grabbed our prize. I went to a poster, scanning it for hints of a puzzle, and Sonny moved to a desk, finding a padlock on a small container in a drawer with a combination to solve. He'd found part of the third puzzle.

I ran over and looked it over as I huffed out a breath. "Alright, we can figure this out."

We kept searching the desk for something more until we found a riddle tapped underneath.

Seek the clue, don't be shy, the first of each will help you pry.

Parting is such sweet sorrow,
And they will not see each other tomorrow.
For two years, she will be in despair
After these very last words Henry says to Clare.

Standing side by side, I looked up at Sonny. "Do you know the book?"

"I mean... I read it." He rubbed the back of his neck, muttering, "When I found your book."

"Wait, when you found my book? But you asked to borrow it?" I glanced at the clock. "We'll talk about it later. We need to finish this first."

He nodded. My eyes slid to his as he ran his hand through his hair.

I asked, "Do you know this one?"

"Um... I'm not sure."

We both leaned over the desk, reading the clue over and over.

I thought for a moment. "I think I remember this! It's 'Have Mercy, Clare!'"

Once we figured it out, we thought we'd enter the

first letters H-M-C into the lock, but it only had numbers. I wrinkled my brow and started opening the drawers to the desk.

"Is there a cipher somewhere to convert letters to numbers? Where's that pencil and paper?"

Sonny pulled the pencil and paper from his back pocket as I looked through the drawers on the right side of the desk. Finally, the last drawer had several laminated sheets of ciphers. Glancing at the big clock, I tossed them on the desk.

"One of these is the key. We just have to figure out which one." He handed me half of them, and we started creating a list of numbers based on each cipher to see if we could figure out the combination.

Sonny grabbed the lock box and entered the first combination of numbers. It didn't work. He tried two more combinations, and finally, we heard a click. The third one opened the lock, and a small door fell open, revealing a key. He snatched the key and ran to unlock the door for the second half of the game.

Twenty-five minutes later, we solved two of the puzzles in the second room and were down to the last one. Sonny went to look around the walls for clues and asked me to flip through the old leather journal on the table.

As I paged through, it looked like Clare's journal from the book. Certain pages had a random letter written in the corner. At the back was a torn page with a clue:

Read this message loud and clear,
Circle the letters in corners near.
Rearrange them to be found,
And you'll know —you need to __________.

* * *

Sonny was still searching the room, so I unscrambled the letters to find it spelled:

TURNAROUND

What did that have to do with the book?

I turned to ask Sonny if he had any ideas, assuming he was searching the room for a clue to help us. But when I faced him, he was just standing there.

I frowned, puzzled. We only had about ten minutes left to escape the room, and he wasn't even looking for the next clue.

He drew in a shaky breath as he stepped closer, taking my hands in his.

"It's ironic how my greatest joys lie in the simplest things," he murmured.

His voice was steady, but something in his eyes made my stomach flip.

"When we're lying in bed, and you've just washed your hair," he continued, twirling one of my curls between his fingers. "Or even something as ordinary as cream swirling in my coffee or the softness of your skin—those moments awaken my heart."

I tilted my head, a grin forming as recognition dawned. His words sounded so familiar.

I narrowed my eyes playfully. "Are you... are you quoting _The Time Traveler's Wife_?"

He chuckled, shrugging. "Paraphrasing a bit." But there was something beneath his amusement—a flicker of nervousness.

His expression softened, and his grip on my hands tightened ever so slightly. "But there's one thing that touches my soul—a constant that has always shined brighter than anything else. _You._

Always you. You are the center of it all."

Tears pricked my eyes. My breath caught in my throat.

"Sonny..." I whispered, my heart pounding. "What are you doing?"

I glanced at the big clock on the wall, my brain struggling to keep up. "Are we—are we going to finish this? We only have a few minutes left."

He reached into his pocket and pulled something out as he went down on his knee, still holding my other hand.

Oh. My. God. My hand flew up to my mouth as the tears came.

I stared at the beautiful sapphire ring with filigree and diamonds down the sides, not believing what was happening.

"Claire... Poppy, my love, you captured my heart in a way that words cannot describe from the beginning. You are my past, my present, my future, and my forever. Will you marry me?"

I lifted my gaze to his, frozen in utter shock, until he raised his eyebrows in silent anticipation.

Then, a grin broke across my face as I stepped toward him.

"Yes," I breathed, my voice full of certainty. "A thousand times, yes."

Emotion swelled in my chest as I whispered, "I want nothing more."

His eyes shined with emotion as he stood. He slipped the ring on my finger with a trembling hand before sliding his hands around my waist. He leaned in and kissed me. With our foreheads touching, his lips curved against mine as he said, "Claire, you've made me so happy."

I cupped his face in my hands. "I can't wait to marry you." I dropped my voice to a whisper,

"But... we never finished the escape room."

His eyes crinkled as he laughed, "We did." He admitted, "Your answer was the key to the final puzzle."

He brought his hand back to mine, a sudden seriousness flickering in his eyes. "There's something else, Poppy," he confessed. "The inscription..." He trailed off, his gaze dropping to the ring sparkling on my finger.

My breath hitched. "There's an inscription?"

He took a deep breath, his voice husky, and nodded, slipping the ring off my finger to show me the inscription.

He took a deep breath, his voice husky, and nodded, gently slipping the ring from my finger. My heart fluttered as he carefully turned the band, revealing the tiny words engraved inside.

"Always You."

I swallowed hard, emotion tightening my throat as my eyes traced the delicate letters.

"Always you," he murmured, watching my face closely. "Because it's always been you. From the first moment, through everything—it's always been you."

My breath caught as tears pricked my eyes, the simple words resonating deeply inside me. He slowly slid the ring back onto my finger, where it belonged.

A wave of warmth washed over me. "Yeah?"

He leaned in, smiling against my lips just before he kissed me. "We were always meant to be."

Bonus Epilogue - Darci

Seven years later

"Mommy! Can Amelia come over to play?"

I smiled as I turned to watch Lucy clamber over to her booster seat, her purple backpack dropping to the floor of the car. Amelia wasn't far behind as she slid into the other seat, buckling herself in.

"Aunt Darci!" Amelia smiled up at me, both her front teeth missing. "Can you call Mama and ask?"

She tossed her pink sparkle backpack on the seat between them and brushed her carrot top braid behind her. She was a miniature version of her mother down to her curls but with her father's gorgeous eyes, which often twinkled with mischief.

"Actually... we're going on an adventure!"

They both gasped and looked at each other wide-eyed.

Lucy, her dark brown pigtails swinging, asked, "An adventure? Amelia's coming, too? Where are we going?"

One of the teachers was motioning me to drive through the line. I smiled and waved as I muttered, "Geez," and drove away. I looked at both of them in the rearview and said, "It's a surprise. But

369

everyone's coming. Amelia, your dad said he'd meet us there, and your mom's bringing Henry. And Lucy, I think even Daddy might be coming, too."

"Really?" Lucy frowned, "But where are we going?"

"I'll give you both a hint. It's... pink!"

Amelia gasped, "The Barbie Dream House Mama makes us drive by all the time out in the country? Can we finally go inside it?"

"I think we just might go inside today."

I looked back in the rearview to see Lucy wrinkling her little freckled nose as she asked, "Can we get a snack first? I'm starving."

I chuckled. Lucy was always hungry. "How about we stop for ice cream?"

Two little voices yelled, "Yes!"

We stopped at the drive-in for root beer floats and then headed west to Ponder, one of the tiny towns on the outskirts of Denton. This was going to be a big surprise for my best friend. I couldn't wait to see the look on Claire's face.

Years ago, we dubbed it The Barbie Dream House because of its color. It had been Claire's dream house for years, and today, Edison made her dream come true. He had finally sold the film rights to his big fantasy book series, and the first thing that wonderful man did was use some of the money to buy her that house.

I glanced at my watch. I was betting he was at the insurance office in Ponder's tiny downtown, picking up the keys and signing the last of the papers.

We were the first to arrive as I drove through the big imposing iron gate flanked by two giant concrete statues that looked like stacks of books. We rolled the windows down and stayed in the car while the girls slurped up the last dredges of their floats.

I scanned the property, taking in the striking sight before me. It was a breathtaking house—an old Gothic Victorian, towering two stories high, its once-traditional charm transformed by a bold coat of bright pink with black-trimmed spires. Visible for miles, it stood alone beneath the sweeping branches of a grand weeping willow.

Despite sitting empty for years, the gardens were surprisingly well-maintained, a detail that caught me off guard. Someone had been tending to it long after Elodie Blackwood's tragic car accident on the freeway.

Claire had been obsessed with this house for as long as I'd known her. Maybe it was the strange secondhand bookstore, The Enchanted Attic, that once occupied the space, or maybe it just always felt like home to her. There was also that unforgettable run-in with Elodie, the former owner, which I suspected made her feel connected to the place in a way few could understand. Truthfully, I couldn't pinpoint exactly why she loved it so much—only that she did, deeply.

Months ago, Edison called me, his voice edged with excitement. There was a chance the film rights to his book series were going to auction, and if they sold for what his agent anticipated, he was going to try to buy this house for Claire. He told me he could never forget the wistful look on her face every time they drove past it—he just knew it would be a dream come true for her.

A few years after they were married, she called me to tell me about an announcement posted that the house was going up for sale because the owner had died, and there would be an open house. We both wondered if it could be Elodie who had passed away. When Claire found her obituary in the newspaper, it confirmed our suspicions.

The open house was in August during the heat of the summer, and Claire was due with Amelia at any moment. But she insisted they take a look. After she took Edison, she convinced me to see it with her a few days later. Walking into the house, an undercurrent of magic ran through it. I could feel it pulsing through the walls. It made me wonder if making it their home would be a good idea, but there was no discouraging Claire. She swore she belonged there.

The house was huge—three stories if you counted the attic. It had five bedrooms and bathrooms, two kitchens—one on the first floor and another kitchenette on the second floor—and even a finished basement. It was an old home, but it had been well taken care of and seemed perfect for their growing family.

Claire practically floated from room to room, giving me her play-by-play of their lives in the house. Unfortunately, that was as far as it went because they weren't ready to sell Edison's bungalow. But her desire to live here was always a frequent conversation between us.

Months after the open house, Edison called me out of the blue, asked what I thought if he bought that house, and surprised her. I told him to go for it because I knew she'd love it. When his writing career took off under his own name, I knew it was only a matter of time. And today was finally that day.

A few minutes later, Edison's old red truck pulled into the parking lot. I grabbed some baby wipes and helped the girls clean their sticky fingers. He was already walking over as they climbed out of the back seat. I handed him Amelia's backpack and lunch box to toss in his truck.

"Daddy!"

She wrapped her little arms around his legs as he leaned over and kissed the top of her head. "How was school, Mia Bug?"

"Oh, uh, good, I guess, except Jacob will not stop pulling my braid."

He set her bags inside the truck before turning around, wrinkling his eyebrows.

"Well, that's not good. Do I need to talk to him?"

She was distracted, watching Lucy skip over to the koi pond. "I don't know." She craned her neck to look up at him, smiling, "Aunt Darci said we can go inside the pink house today."

He chuckled as he took her hand, and they made their way to the koi pond, "Yep. When your mama gets here with Henry, we'll all go inside. And…" He leaned close, whispering, "You can be the first to pick your room."

She peered up at him, "My own room? I don't have to share with Henry anymore?"

He nodded solemnly as she ran over to Lucy.

"Lucy! I get to pick my room when we go inside!"

Edison walked over as the girls made little splashes with their hands in the water.

"Find the place, okay?" He asked me.

"Are you kidding? I've been here many times." I laughed as we walked to the porch to wait for Claire.

The girls were running and jumping along the koi pond.

A few minutes later, my husband's SUV pulled into the parking lot, his window down, giving me a wave. I felt my cheeks heat as I waved back. We'd been married a few years, and I still got butterflies when he entered a room. I stood up, waiting for him.

"Hey, babe." He said as he walked up the gravel

path, still in scrubs from the hospital, and kissed me.

Edison held out his hand as they shook. "Hey man, glad you could come."

"Claire here?"

Edison pulled out his phone and glanced at it. "Nope, but she's not too far away."

My husband shrugged and sat down on the steps. I sat down next to him.

He leaned to my ear, squeezing my thigh as he whispered, "How did she do on her spelling test?"

In all the excitement, I had totally forgotten after I quizzed Lucy on the way to school this morning.

I slowly turned to him, my hand over my mouth. "Oh… I hadn't looked yet."

He squeezed my thigh again and shrugged, "No worries. I was just curious."

He and Edison were having a boring conversation about yard work. I tuned them out and hopped up to see what the girls were doing at the koi pond, praying they weren't holding fish or mud pies in their hands.

"Mommy, mommy!"

I smiled as I walked up, "What are you two doing over here?"

Lucy smiled proudly, "We're naming the fishies!"

"Oh?"

Amelia piped up, pointing to a big group, "These are all named Goldie. And this one…" She leaned over, trying to point to a fish all by itself on the other side. I grabbed her by the shoulder to prevent her from falling.

"Careful."

Her cheeks turned red as she smiled at me, "Sorry! But… that one, that white one over there with orange spots? That one's name is Arlo."

"Arlo?"

"Yeah..." she breathed out. "We read this book the other day at school about a fish named Arlo. It was so good."

"Hmm, I haven't read that one. I will have to look it up and read it myself."

"Mommy, you could read that one for story time at the library."

I smiled at Lucy, "I sure could."

Just seconds later, a silver minivan pulled into the parking lot.

"Girls, we can't tell Aunt Claire the surprise. Amelia? Let's have Daddy do it, okay?"

"Okay," they said in unison before arguing over more names for the fish.

I went to the parking lot, finding Claire unbuckling Henry's car seat and slipping his shoes on. He was the spitting image of Edison. She brushed his white-blond hair off his face with her fingers as she lifted him. She handed me her diaper bag.

"Hey, Darce, so any idea what we're doing here? Sonny wouldn't say."

I gave her a conspiratorial smile as I swung the bag up on my shoulder. "I think you should let your husband tell you," I said.

She cocked an eyebrow at me as she put Henry on her hip, and we started walking up the pathway. Seeing his sister at the pond, Henry began to wiggle against his mother. At 15 months, he was still a little unsteady on his feet. While he loved being in his mother's arms, he thought his big sister hung the moon and wanted to follow her everywhere. We collected the girls from the pond, and they ran ahead, running up the steps on the porch.

Amelia asked Edison, "Can we go inside now? Please, Daddy?"

Claire looked at Edison expectantly. "Sonny, what's going on?"

A slow grin spread over his entire face. "Well, Poppy... welcome home!" He gestured toward the door, holding up his hand and jiggling a set of keys on his fingers.

Amelia squealed and jumped up and down. She leaned over, cupping Lucy's ear to whisper a secret, and Lucy giggled.

Claire's eyes narrowed. "What did you do?" She gave him a playful smile as she slowly walked up the porch steps, Henry still on her hip.

He ran his hand through his hair. "Well, babe," he huffed out a breath, looking a little nervous. I bought you The Barbie Dreamhouse—Victorian gothic edition, just like your wildest dreams."

She stopped in her tracks, surprise all over her face. "Sonny! Are you serious? You bought this place? But how?"

He nodded. He reached for the baby as he handed her the keys. "The film rights went to auction and went bigger than my agent anticipated."

She looked at the keys dumbfounded and then back up at him. The corners of her mouth inched up. She slowly shook her head. "I can't believe you did this."

She took the keys and unlocked the front door. As soon as she had it open, the girls walked in ahead of everyone.

Standing in the foyer, she grabbed his forearm and whispered, "This is real?"

"It's real, and it's ours." He leaned over to kiss her, Henry wiggling in his arms to be put down.

Amelia ran up the stairs and yelled, "I'm picking my room!" Lucy followed right behind her.

I yelled, "Be careful up there." I'm pretty sure they

ignored me.

We all walked into the living room, and Claire turned towards Edison as he sat Henry down on the wooden floor. She bit the corner of her lip and whispered, "It's really ours?"

Edison ran his hand down her arm, interlacing their fingers. He nodded, "Ours."

I stood to the side, not wanting to intrude, but I found myself smiling as I watched them. My husband quietly came up behind me, sliding his hands around my waist, gently swaying me.

He whispered, "Do I need to get you your very own pink house, Tink?"

I turned in his embrace to face him, but out of the corner of my eye, I noticed Claire and Edison walk hand in hand towards the kitchen, Henry toddling behind them.

"No way, I love our home." I sighed, "I'm not sure I ever want to move. It's where we conceived Lucy and..." I trailed off, not wanting to overshadow Claire's moment.

He narrowed his eyes. He murmured, "And?"

We'd talked about having another baby for a while. We were both on the same page, wanting more, and while we hadn't been actively pursuing it, we hadn't been trying to prevent it either. I leaned forward, giving my husband a lingering kiss. As I pulled back, I smirked, reaching behind me, lacing our fingers together, and bringing them back around to my belly.

"And... this one, too." I chuckled.

My husband's eyebrows shot up, a smile blooming on his face. "What? When? How? You're sure?"

I laughed, "I think you know exactly how, Doctor. As for when... I went to the doctor this morning," I raised my eyebrows, "And she said about 7 weeks."

He let go of my hand and wrapped his arms around my waist a little tighter but gentle as he pulled me against him.

He kissed my forehead, "I love you."

"I love you, too."

THE END

Thank you so much for reading TROUBLE OF THE MOST WONDERFUL KIND, Book 1 in The Enchanted Heart Series, a magical realism romance series.

I hope you enjoyed it! If you did...

1. Help other people find this book by writing a review.
2. Sign up for my email list so you can know when the next book is coming out.
3. Come follow me on Instagram, TikTok, or Facebook.
4. Use the QR code below to visit my website:

Keep reading to get a sneak peek of Darci's story in SOMETIME AROUND MIDNIGHT, coming June 2025!

Sneak Peek
SOMETIME AROUND MIDNIGHT

Darci

Why was I shoving a dozen trash bags full of a dismembered couch into my car at midnight on a Saturday night? Because I thought rescuing curbside furniture was a great idea—until I realized the loveseat I saved smelled like it had spent the last decade chain-smoking in the back of a dive bar.

Lesson learned— never trust curbside furniture. I know, I know—it's tempting. It might seem like a steal, but trust me, there's a reason it's there. You don't want someone else's problems.

I'd been taking care of my best friend, Claire's house while she was visiting her parents down in Galveston with her fiance, Edison. They'd asked me to pick up the mail and water the plants. On my way out of their neighborhood yesterday, I saw a loveseat on the curb and thought I hit the jackpot.

I should have known it was a bad idea when the owner stumbled outside with an unlit cigarette glued to his bottom lip.

"Lemme help you with that," he slurred.

His gravelly rasp should have clued

me in, or maybe the remnants of smoke wafting from his mouth. But none of that tipped me off as he helped me put it in the back of my SUV to take home. Thank god I had the sense to refuse his offer to come inside and "look around."

It wasn't until I dragged it into my apartment and let it sit overnight that I realized my nightmare had just begun. When I walked into the living room in the morning, the overbearing smell of old cigarettes hit me square in the face, so bad my eyes watered.

I scoured the internet for tips on getting rid of the smell and tried every suggestion I could find—baking soda, Febreeze, washing the cushion covers. I left it on the balcony all day, hoping the smell would disappear. As a last resort, I sprayed it with bedbug spray. Why? It was a tip I found on the internet. But that didn't work either.

And that's when the panic set in because the smell! Oh god, the smell was awful, and it was going to seep into everything in my apartment—the walls, the floors, me—everywhere!

My lease had an iron-clad no-smoking policy, and management loved sending threatening letters and voicemails about it regularly. Sure, I seemed like the fun-loving kind of girl, but I'd always been a rule follower through and through, even as a kid.

I needed that loveseat out of here tonight, but it wouldn't be easy. The management also had a hard-on for the dumpsters, posting signs, in Comic Sans no less, about fining anyone who put furniture in the dumpster. So, just chunking it was not an option.

I lay on the floor and muttered to myself, "What am I going to do?"

I was just a hair under five feet tall, so basically fun-size, like a candy bar. How in the hell was I supposed to get rid of it? Simple. Pure spite, sheer desperation, and whatever unholy adrenaline kicks in when you're tiny, desperate, and fueled by iced coffee and zero plan. It was me versus that goddamn couch. And I was not losing.

And that's when I sat up and had a brilliant idea. My one last Hail Mary. I could tear that motherfucker apart and hide all the evidence in trash bags, which could go in the dumpster. It was pure genius!

Minutes later, I found myself down a rabbit hole full of furniture videos. I had no idea deconstructing a couch was even a thing. The only problem was that every single video involved power tools or, at the bare minimum, a saw. My only tools were the screwdriver and hammer from my little pink Do-It-Herself toolkit I bought when I got my first apartment and a serrated bread knife.

It took me all afternoon and most of the night, but I took that loveseat down to the frame with the sweat of my brow and unadulterated hate. Then, I beat the hell out of it until it broke into pieces small enough to fit in trash bags.

Looking at the dismantled remains, I wasn't sure I had ever felt more accomplished. All that was left were the couch cushions, and I sliced those babies into small pieces with the bread knife.

It was after midnight when I finally filled the last of the garbage bags to hide the evidence. By the time I was done, there were at least 10 bags lined up at my front door. Half a dozen were shoved in the backseat and trunk of my SUV, and I put the rest on the roof of the car. Then it was time for a midnight ride to the dumpster.

I was past exhaustion and more than a little pissed off as I tossed trash bags left and right. The sooner I was done, the sooner I'd be standing in a hot shower rinsing the years of cigarette stink off me.

Then, I saw him.

"Oh, for fuck's sake," I muttered.

Sweatpants riding low on his hips, barefoot, and wearing a faded, too-tight A&M T-shirt that hugged every muscle. I spun around quickly, pretending the dumpster was fascinating. As he came closer, I raked a critical glance over him.

He wasn't that tall, maybe a few inches above me. His jaw was sharp enough to cut glass, but the messy red hair and scattering of faded freckles instantly brought to mind a mischievous, carrot-topped little boy. Yet when his eyes locked with mine, even in the darkness, they seemed lit from within—a startling, electric shade of pale blue. Heat rose to my cheeks, and I quickly forced my gaze away, shaking off the unexpected reaction with an annoyed flick of my head.

Definitely not my type, I decided firmly. Maybe I was delirious because I took one more look and thought he looked... well... fucking delicious. Or maybe I was just telling myself that because he looked entirely too good compared to my walking disaster.

SOMETIME AROUND MIDNIGHT

Darci is convinced she's destined to be alone, while Alex is burdened by a tragic past. After an unexpected encounter thrusts them reluctantly into each other's lives, sparks of irritation quickly ignite into undeniable attraction. But can they risk their guarded hearts to rewrite their stories? SOMETIME AROUND MIDNIGHT is a steamy, heartfelt enemies-to-lovers romance about daring to love again.

Coming June 2025!

Acknowledgments

Writing a book is never truly a solo endeavor, and I'm grateful for the encouragement and support that helped bring this story to life.

To my readers—your love for these characters and their journeys means everything. Thank you for spending time in this world with me.

To my husband, Nathan, for the inspiration from our own whirlwind courtship. To the quiet moments, the late-night brainstorming sessions, and the endless questions and discussions as we walked the dog—somehow, we made it through.

To my daughter, Emma, for answering even more endless questions and brainstorming with me.

And finally, to those who believe in love, second chances, and the magic of a good story—this one's for you.

With gratitude,
Stephanie

About the Author

Stephanie Pass hails from a tiny Texas town where she lives with her husband, three of her four children, and a Boxer dog who talks more than she does. She writes contemporary romance with magical realism and is dipping her toe into some sci-fi romance, but one day she will write that romantasy she's dreaming about. She loves books about love, magic, and high fae. She had her own real live romance story come true when a chance encounter led her to meet her now husband. When she's not writing romance stories, Stephanie is a mom blogger dancing to Taylor Swift at https://thetiptoefairy.com. But you can often find her at the roller skating rink or dancing at the goth nightclub.

To learn more about new releases, giveaways, behind-the-scenes, and more, join Stephanie's email list - https://thetiptoefairy.myflodesk.com/join-romance-list